T0030607

CONFESSIONS OF A FORTY-SOMETHING F**K UP

Also by Alexandra Potter

CONFESSIONS OF A FORTY-SOMETHING F**K UP

a novel

ALEXANDRA POTTER

HARPER

NEW YORK · LONDON · TORONTO · SYDNEY

HARPER

This is a work of fiction. Names, characters, places, and incidents are products of the author's imagination or are used fictitiously and are not to be construed as real. Any resemblance to actual events, locales, organizations, or persons, living or dead, is entirely coincidental.

Originally published as *Confessions of a Forty-Something F##k Up* in Great Britain in 2020 by Pan Macmillan UK Ltd.

Quotation from Elizabeth Gilbert's Facebook page. Copyright © Elizabeth Gilbert, 2014, used by permission of The Wylie Agency (UK) Limited.

CONFESSIONS OF A FORTY-SOMETHING F**K UP. Copyright © 2020 by Alexandra Potter. All rights reserved. Printed in the United States of America. No part of this book may be used or reproduced in any manner whatsoever without written permission except in the case of brief quotations embodied in critical articles and reviews. For information, address HarperCollins Publishers, 195 Broadway, New York, NY 10007.

HarperCollins books may be purchased for educational, business, or sales promotional use. For information, please email the Special Markets Department at SPsales@harpercollins.com.

FIRST U.S. EDITION

Designed by Jen Overstreet

Library of Congress Cataloging-in-Publication Data has been applied for.

ISBN 978-0-06-334089-3 (pbk.)

23 24 25 26 27 LBC 5 4 3 2 1

For anyone who's ever laughed in the face of it all.

———

The women whom I love and admire for their strength and grace did not get that way because shit worked out. They got that way because shit went wrong and they handled it. They handled it in a thousand different ways on a thousand different days, but they handled it. Those women are my superheroes.

—Elizabeth Gilbert

Prologue

Hi and welcome to Confessions of a Forty-Something F**k Up, *the podcast for any woman who wonders how the hell she got here, and why life isn't* quite *how she imagined it was going to be.*

It's for anyone who has ever looked around at their life and thought this was never part of The Plan. Who has ever felt like they dropped a ball, or missed a boat, and is still desperately trying to figure it all out while everyone around them is making gluten-free brownies.

But first a disclaimer: I don't pretend to be an expert in anything. I'm not a lifestyle guru, or an influencer, whatever that is, and I'm not here to sell a brand. Or flog a product. Or tell you what you should be doing, because frankly, I haven't a clue either. I'm just someone struggling to recognize their messy life in a world of perfect Instagram ones and feeling like a bit of a fuck up. Even worse, a forty-something fuck up. Someone who reads a life-affirming quote and feels exhausted, not inspired. Who isn't trying to achieve new goals, or set more challenges, because life is enough of a challenge as it is. And who does not feel #blessed and #winningatlife but mostly #noideawhatthefuckIamdoing and #canIgoogleit?

Which is why I started this podcast . . . to tell it like it is, for me anyway. Because Confessions *is a show about the daily trials and tribulations of what it feels like to find yourself on the wrong side of forty, only to discover things haven't worked out how you expected. It's about what happens when shit happens and still being able to laugh in the face of it all. It's about being honest and telling the truth. About friendship and love and disappointment. About asking the big questions and not getting any of the answers. About starting over, when you thought you would be finished already.*

In these episodes, which will take the form of confessions, I'll be sharing with you all the sad bits and the funny bits. I'll be talking about feeling flawed and confused and lonely and scared, about finding hope and joy in the unlikeliest of places, and how no amount of celebrity cookbooks and smashed avocados are going to save you.

Because feeling like a fuck up isn't about being *a failure, it's about* being made to feel like one. *It's the pressure and the panic to tick all the boxes and reach all the goals . . . and what happens when you don't. When you find yourself on the outside. Because on some level, in some aspect of your life, it's so easy to feel like you're failing when everyone around you appears to be succeeding.*

So if there's anyone out there that feels any of this too, this podcast will hopefully make you feel less alone.

Because now there's two of us. And two of us makes a tribe.

JANUARY
#whatthefuckamIdoingwithmylife

New Year's Day

How the hell did I get here?

Not *here* here, as in January, never-ending month of gray and gloom that seems to go on forever, filled with depressing Blue Mondays, failed attempts at resolutions, and an Instagram feed overflowing with celebs boasting about "New Year! New Exciting Projects!"—which does not make me feel #inspired and want to reach for their exercise video or Book of Brag (sorry, I mean Blessed), but has the opposite effect of making me collapse back down on the sofa, feeling #overwhelmed with a family-size packet of cheese puffs.

No, I mean here as in it's my birthday soon, I'm about to turn forty-*something*, and it's just not how I'd imagined. I mean, how did this happen? It's like I missed a turning somewhere. Like there was a destination marked "Forty-Something" and my friends and I were all heading that way, youth in one hand, dreams in the other, excited and full of possibilities. A bit like when you step off the plane on holiday and you go down those moving walkways that swoosh you along with everyone else, following the signs to baggage reclaim, eager to see what's on the other side of those sliding doors.

Except it's not the Bahamas and tropical palm trees; it's Destination Forty-Something and comprises a loving husband, adorable children, and a beautiful home. *Swoosh.* It's a successful career and bifold kitchen doors and clothes from Net-a-Porter. *Swoosh.* It's feeling happy and content, because life is a success and all sorted out and you're exactly where you always imagined you'd be, complete with an Instagram account filled with #Imsoblessed and #livingmybestlife.

It is not, I repeat not, #wheredidIgowrong and #whatthefuck amIdoingwithmylife?

Sitting cross-legged on my bed, I glance around the room, noting the cardboard boxes in the corner and two large unopened suitcases. I still haven't finished unpacking. I stare at them, trying to summon up the enthusiasm, then sink back against the pillows. It can wait.

Instead my eyes fall upon the new notebook on my bedside table. I just bought it today. According to this article I'm reading, the secret to happiness is writing a daily gratitude list.

By writing down all the things you're grateful for, you will feel more positive, stop negative thought patterns, and transform your life.

Reaching for the notebook, I pick up a pen and turn to the first page. I stare at the empty sheet of paper, my mind blank.

If you need some inspiration, here are a few things to get you going:

I am breathing.

Are you kidding me? Breathing? There's grateful and there's pretty much dead if that's not on my list.

I do not feel inspired.

Don't worry if you don't know what to write. Just start with one thing and work up to your five-a-day.

Right, OK. I'm just going to write the first thing that pops into my head.

1. *My air miles*

OK, so perhaps not *exactly* the kind of blessed and spiritual thing the author of the article had in mind, but trust me, I was feeling very bloody blessed to have all those air miles when I flew back to London last week.

I've been living in America for the past ten years, five of them in California with my American fiancé. I loved California. The never-ending sunshine. Wearing flip-flops in January. Our little cafe-cum-bookshop that we sank all our savings into, with its delicious brunches and walls lined with books. I was happy and in love and engaged to be married. The future stretched ahead like candy-colored bunting. Everything was going to work out just like I'd always hoped.

But then our business went bust and our relationship along with it and—*poof*—it all turned back into a pumpkin. I was not going to marry the prince and live happily ever after with our cute kids and adorable rescue dog. Instead I was going to pack up what was left of my life, cash in all my air miles for an upgrade, and sob my way across the Atlantic. Hell, if I was going to be broke and heartbroken, it was going to be on a flat bed with a cheese plate and a free bar, thank you very much.

In my gin-soaked, cheese-and-crackered brain, I was planning to come back to London, rent my own apartment, fill it with scented candles, and get my life back together again. My immigration visa was about to run out and I needed a fresh start, one that didn't constantly remind me of what I no longer had. Plus, Dad had generously offered me a loan to help me get myself back on my feet. My American dream was over: it was time to come home.

But things had changed since I'd left, and I quickly discovered rents had doubled, nay, quadrupled. And gone was my tribe of single friends with their spare rooms and cheap bottles of wine, which we would drink until the early hours telling each other very loudly that he was a total bastard, you're better off without him, and Do Not Panic! There's still plenty of time! All while reeling off a long list of celebrities who were much older than you and had managed to meet the man, push out a baby, and be in *OK!* magazine talking about their miracle birth Before It's Too Late.*

Now all my girlfriends are married, and their spare rooms are filled with babies and bunk beds and nursery-rhyme stickers, and it's cups of herbal tea and bed by 9:30 p.m. Which meant I had two

---

* Otherwise known as BITL. It used to be thirty-nine. Then it crept up to forty-two. Now it's whatever age you can get away with in good lighting.

choices: couch-surf with a cup of chamomile, or move back in with The Parents.

Now, don't get me wrong. I love my parents. But this was never part of The Plan. Nowhere in my twenties and thirties did my vision for the future involve being single, over forty, and sleeping in my old bedroom. Even if Mum had swapped the single bed for a double and redecorated with matching Laura Ashley lamps.

My old bedroom was for visits home with The American Fiancé, soon to be The Handsome Husband. For reliving childhood Christmases in the countryside with our growing rosy-cheeked brood. For weekends when The Parents looked after their beloved grandchildren while we hotfooted it to one of those fancy, over-priced boutique hotels with filament light bulbs draped over a bar, an organic menu filled with grass-fed this, that, and the other, and massages that are never quite hard enough.

2. Spareroomforrent.com

It was actually my best friend Fiona who told me about it, her nanny having told *her* about it.

"You should do it, Nell! It sounds like a lot of fun!" she said brightly across the Carrara marble worktops of her newly renovated open-plan kitchen, where I was slumped, depressed and jet-lagged with a weak cup of some foul-tasting herbal tea, after she'd very kindly offered to put me up for a few days on flying back to London.

Fiona always thinks my life sounds fun. And it probably appears that way when viewed from the security of her happy family life. A bit like how bungee jumping or living in a two hundred square foot tiny house or dyeing your hair purple always looks like fun, when you're not the one doing it.

I mean, don't get me wrong. Bits of it have been a lot of fun. Just not the current bits.

"That's one way of putting it," I quipped, shooting Izzy, my five-year-old goddaughter, a smile as she tucked into her organic porridge. Personally, I had several other words in mind, but Auntie Nell must not say the naughty F word.

"Your goddaughter thinks it sounds like fun, don't you, darling?" enthused Fiona, grabbing herself a bowl and sprinkling in a few fresh blueberries, some chia seeds and a dollop of manuka honey.

I love Fiona—we've been friends since university—but she's living in a completely different universe to me. Happily married to David, a successful lawyer, she's now settled into a comfortable middle-class life in southwest London with their two lovely, privately educated children, a tasteful designer home, and the kind of swingy blonde hair that comes from a professional blow-dry and a great colorist.

Before having children, her job as a museum curator took her around the world, but she gave all that up when Lucas, her eldest, was born, and now her days are filled with myriad school events, remodeling the house, booking lovely family holidays in five-star resorts, and doing Pilates.

Meanwhile, over on Planet What The Fuck Am I Going To Do With My Life:

"You might meet some really interesting people."

She was being so sweet and positive I didn't have the heart to tell her that the thought of meeting interesting people in my pajamas broke me out in hives. I didn't want to share a fridge with strangers. Or, God forbid, a bathroom. It was fun when we were young, but not now. Now it was depressing and soul-destroying and just a little bit terrifying. I mean, I could be murdered in my bed by some weirdo roommate, and end up chopped into little bits and sprinkled on the geraniums.

FORTY-SOMETHING MEETS GRISLY END AT THE HANDS OF ROOMMATE
Her life used to seem so promising, say shocked parents, who were hoping for at least one grandchild.

I voiced my fears but Fiona pooh-poohed me briskly. Her nanny said it was brilliant and that through it she'd met lots of new friends. I didn't point out that her nanny was a twenty-something from Brazil, so of course it was brilliant. Everything was brilliant at that age. Especially if you looked like Fiona's nanny.

"Come on, I'll help you search," she announced, whipping out her iPad. Within seconds she was enthusiastically swiping through photos, as if she was online shopping. Which technically she was. Only it wasn't for a nice table lamp and a cashmere throw, it was for a home for her poor feckless friend.

"Ooh, look! I've found it! This place is perfect!"

3. Arthur

The spare room was in an Edwardian maisonette in Richmond, a leafy suburb of London known for its village atmosphere and family life. I'd been hoping for something more in town and less married with children, but it was available and I could afford it. Plus, when I went round to see it the room looked even larger than in the photos, and it had a little balcony. There was just one catch.

"And so this is the shared bathroom."

Having finished showing me the bedroom, Edward, the owner of the apartment and my prospective landlord, paused by the bathroom door.

"*Shared?*"

"Don't worry, I put the seat down—that's one of the house rules," he joked, opening the door and pulling the light cord.

At least, I thought he was joking. Until I spied his toothbrush in the cup by the sink and my heart sank.

"OK, great." I tried not to think of my en suite back in California. This was going to be fun, remember. It was going to be like *Friends*, only we were in our forties and I looked nothing like Jennifer Aniston. I forced a bright smile. I could do this.

"So, do you have any questions?"

Edward looked older than me, with dark wavy hair that was graying at his temples and square-framed glasses, but I had a sneaking suspicion he was about my age. This keeps happening to me now. It's the weirdest thing. I read articles about middle-aged people as if they're my parents or something, and then I suddenly realize—hang on, we're the same age! But how can this be? I don't look anything like that. At least, I don't think I do.

Do I?

"Um . . . any other rules?" I joked weakly as I followed him back through to the kitchen.

"Yes, I've printed them out for you to have a look through . . ." Reaching into a drawer, he pulled out a ring binder and passed it to me.

"Oh." There were about twenty pages, with lots of highlighted sections. "Gosh, that's a lot of rules."

"I find it better to be clear about everything, don't you? Then there's no room for miscommunication."

My eyes scanned over a few. It was just the usual stuff about loud music, being tidy and respectful, making sure to lock doors.

"There's also a section about being environmentally conscious and conserving energy."

"Right, yes, of course." Now this bit we were in agreement about. I'd spent the last five years living in California. I drove a Prius. I bought organic (when I could afford it). I had a nice selection of reusable bags made from bamboo for my groceries. "I'm all about saving the environment," I told him.

"So, turn the lights off when you leave a room, take showers instead of baths—"

"No baths?" My chest tightened.

"A five-minute shower uses about a third of the water of a bath, so it's much more eco-friendly."

"Yes, of course." I nodded, and he was right, of course he was, but we weren't in California anymore, where there was a drought. We were in England, where it never stops raining. Last year my parents' house flooded twice.

"And I'd prefer it if you didn't touch the thermostat for the central heating."

Instinctively I pulled my coat tighter around me. It was freezing, even inside. I touched a radiator. It was stone cold.

"Even in January?"

I mean, FFS. Who doesn't have the heating on in January?

"It's set to 54 degrees, which is the most efficient setting."

It was at that point I thought, *Sod This*. Since breaking up with The American Fiancé, *Sod This* has become my new approach to life. It's actually better than Fuck It. It requires less effort.

"Well, thanks very much. I've got a few more rooms I'm going to look at . . ."

Enough was enough. OK, so my life was a mess. Nothing had worked out. Time was running out, and it just hadn't happened for me. I was still on the outside, waiting for my happy ever after, whatever that may be. I wasn't a wife or a mummy. Neither was I some high-flying *career woman*, which, according to a newspaper Whose Name I Refuse To Mention, is the reason all women *of a certain age* have got themselves into this position. I was an out-of-work book editor who sank all her savings into a business that went bust, along with her relationship. (On that topic, can someone please tell me why there is no such thing as a *career man*?)

I didn't juice, or bake, or cook healthy nutritious meals in my lovely kitchen, most probably because I currently didn't *have* a kitchen or my own home and, frankly, I'm useless anyway. I hadn't a fucking clue what was going on with Brexit and, more so, I didn't care. I didn't practice mindfulness. Or do yoga. Hell, I couldn't even touch my toes. And I did not have any social media accounts filled with thousands of liked photos documenting my perfect life.

"It was nice meeting you." I made a move for the door.

"Actually, there was one more thing . . ."

I braced myself.

"I'm not here on the weekends."

I paused. "Excuse me?"

At which point Edward proceeded to tell me that he was married with twin boys. Married? He must have noticed my eyes shoot to his bare ring finger as he said something about having left it on the bathroom sink at home. Home being the countryside, where they'd moved "for the schools," but during the week he stayed in London to save on commuting. "I leave on Friday morning and am not back until Monday evening, so you'd have the place to yourself."

Hang on—I quickly did the math. That meant I only had to share with him for three days? For four whole days I had the apartment to myself?

"Except for Arthur."

"*Arthur?*"

At the sound of his name a huge, hairy animal barreled into the kitchen, nearly knocking me sideways with his enormous wagging tail.

"Arthur, sit. *Sit!*"

Arthur took absolutely no notice and continued excitedly jumping up and slobbering all over me, while his owner tried to wrestle him into some kind of sitting position.

"My wife Sophie has allergies, so he stays here with me," he panted. "But on weekends he would stay here with you . . . hence the rent has been adjusted accordingly."

I looked at Edward. His glasses were askew and his sweatshirt was covered in a fine smattering of white fuzz, which was flying around the room, transforming the kitchen into a giant dog-hair snow globe, while his sleeve was fast disappearing into Arthur's jaws.

"OK, great. When can I move in?"

4. *I am not dead of hypothermia.*

Small mercies and all that, but my landlord has gone skiing. He drove up from Kent to meet me on the weekend with the keys and

Arthur, then hotfooted it to Heathrow to celebrate New Year's in Verbier with his family. As soon as he left I cranked up the thermostat to 75 degrees. So now it's lovely and toasty and I'm lying on my bed in just my underwear. I can almost pretend I'm back in California.

On cue my eyes well up. No, I don't want to think about it. I haven't cried for a few days and I don't want to start.

I sniff hard and look at Arthur, who's asleep on the rug by the window, then back at my notebook. I've still got one more thing to write on my gratitude list to make it to my five-a-day, but I'm tired. I'm still battling jet lag. Nothing's springing to mind. I put it back on my bedside table. That's why they call it a daily practice. Tomorrow I'm sure I'll feel much more positive and inspired.

Yes, this year I'm going to completely turn my life around. New Year, fresh start and all that. In fact, by this time *next* year my gratitude list is going to go something like this:

I'm grateful for:
1. *My loving husband, who tells me every day how much he loves me with fresh flowers and mind-blowing sex.*
2. *Snuggles with our own little miracle, who showed her proud grandparents that Mummy was not a forty-something fuck up for whom time finally ran out.*
3. *A successful, high-flying career that provides both satisfaction and a six-figure salary, which I will spend on lovely clothes I see in magazines, and not spend hours trying to find a cheaper version on eBay.*
4. *A Pinterest-worthy home in which to host lots of lovely grown-up dinner parties for all my friends, who are amazed by my flair for interior design and conjuring up delicious, nutritious meals, and teasingly call me the Domestic Goddess.*
5. *This feeling of strength and calm that comes from doing yoga in my new Lululemon outfits, and knowing I am finally where I want to be and am not going to die alone in newspaper shoes.*

The Following Friday

Oh God, it's my birthday.

Remember when you used to actually *look forward* to your birthday? When you'd wake up feeling all happy and excited and planning your barely there outfit? And the celebrations ended at 2 a.m. in a club somewhere, drinking vodka with all your mates and drunkenly yelling in some random guy's ear, "Fuck me, I'm twenty-six! I'm so old!"

Now I really *am* old.

Today when I wake up I feel like I already drank all the vodka. And as I reach for my ringing phone, I catch sight of my arm in the full-length mirror next to my bed and it hits me: This Is It. It's happened. It's time for a bit of a sleeve.

Everyone goes on about the big Four-O, but in reality turning forty is no big deal. Forty is easy. Forty is a big party and a new dress. Forty, you're still in finger-reaching distance of your thirties and nothing feels or looks any different. But then something happens overnight and suddenly you're *forty-something* and things have started to . . . how shall I put it?

Sag would be one word. *Crinkle* would be another. *Crinkle and Sag.* It sounds like a new flavor of chips or a favorite pub, except it's neither. It's this strange thing that's happening to your body and you don't like it. You pull out your trusty bikini for the summer holidays and start seriously wondering about a one-piece. You find a gray hair and *it's not up there*. It's the weirdest thing.

Time feels like it's speeding up. And running out. You start looking back, trying to figure out how on earth you got here, instead of forward, as frankly it frightens the living daylights out of you. You're hurtling past the halfway mark *if you're lucky*, and nothing is how you thought it would be when you were yelling in strangers' ears in dodgy nightclubs.

But then maybe that's how everyone feels about their birthdays at this age. Though, judging by everyone's photos on Facebook, of weekends spent celebrating in cozy cottages in the Cotswolds and family selfies where everyone's wearing matching smiles and wellies—even the Labrador—I'm not convinced. They do not look shocked and bewildered at how this can be happening to them. They look like something from a J.Crew catalog.

Mum and Dad are the first to call and wish me a happy birthday.

"So have you heard from anyone else?" asks Mum, after Dad has finished singing and gone to his plot in the community garden.

Mum is fishing. I still haven't gone into the details about what happened with The American Fiancé, only that the wedding was off and I was moving back to London.

"Um . . . it's seven thirty in the morning, it's still a bit early."

"What time is it in California?"

I knew it.

"Half past eleven the night before."

"Is it really?"

In all the years I lived in America, Mum and Dad never got the hang of the time difference. Conversations always started with, "What time is it there?" complete with flabbergasted reactions when I told them, and I was forever getting woken up by FaceTime calls in the middle of the night. Because of course I couldn't turn my phone off, *in case something happens.* Which is another thing that happens when you reach a certain age. It's like the magnetic poles switch, and after years of your parents worrying about you, you start worrying about them. It's like having children, only I skipped the cute baby stage and mine are seventy and seventy-two.

"So it's not your birthday yet there, then?"

Poor Mum. I think she's clinging on to the hope that this breakup isn't permanent and the wedding will soon be back on.

"No, not yet."

"Oh good." She sounds relieved. "So what are you going to do to celebrate?"

"I'm meeting friends for a drink."

"Well, that sounds nice."

"Yes, it'll be good to see everyone and catch up."

"Because you know, your father and I are a bit worried about you—"

"Mum, I'm fine—honestly, you don't need to worry. As soon as I've sorted out a few things here, I'll come home for a couple of days."

"That would be lovely."

"OK Mum, bye—"

"I know what I wanted to tell you!"

You know how some words mean different things to different people? Well, the word *bye* to my mum does not mean the end of the conversation. On the contrary, it means starting a whole new topic, usually involving telling me about someone I don't know, who is related to someone else I don't know, who lives next door to someone I truly have never heard of, who has died.

I brace myself.

"If you do want to come and visit, we just need a little bit of notice now that we're doing Airbnb."

I stare at my phone, as if I've misheard.

"Airbnb?"

"Yes, didn't I mention it? Your father and I watched a program about it and decided to give it a go. We've been Airbnbing your old bedroom and we've been inundated with bookings."

So that's what the new matching Laura Ashley lamps were about.

"We've got a lovely young couple staying this week, on honeymoon no less!"

And there you have it. Just when you think your life can't get any worse, there's always the discovery that a couple of newlyweds are shagging in your old bedroom to plunge you to new depths.

"What about Richard's old bedroom?"

"Well, he comes home more often to visit."

I grit my teeth as the knife turns. Richard is my little brother and he can do no wrong. He lives in Manchester and has a craft beer start-up with some friends. Every couple of weeks he visits my parents with bags of dirty laundry and a different girlfriend. Rich is thirty-nine and says he's not ready to settle down yet, but no one is worried, least of all Rich. He's a man. It's different. There is no BITL.

"OK, well I really have to go."

"Of course, you must be busy. Speak later. Have a lovely day!"

After I put the phone down I feel a bit guilty. I didn't really have to go. It's not as if I had a pressing engagement; like children to get ready for school or a job to go to. I think about my career, then try not to. It's ten years since I moved from London with my full-time job as a book editor to my publishing company's New York office. It was a great opportunity and the timing was perfect—a relationship had just ended and I was eager for a change of scene—and I threw myself into my new job, along with the New York dating scene.

But five years later I was still single and fast losing hope of ever meeting anyone. So when I met a handsome, dark-eyed chef in a bar, I followed both him and my heart to the West Coast, where we got engaged, quit both our jobs, and moved to Ojai, a small town northwest of Los Angeles, to open our little cafe-cum-bookshop. My parents were delighted but worried. I was gaining a fiancé but giving up a good job, and my dad urged caution.

But I was not in the mood for caution. I was in my late thirties. I had met The One. We were going to get married, have babies, and spend the rest of our lives together. Setting up our own business was the icing on the cake. It combined my love of books and his love of food, and we worked day and night to make it a success. So what if half of businesses failed in the first year? We would be in the other 50 percent.

And for a few years we were—but eventually rising rents, long hours, fast-disappearing savings, and a whole bunch of other stuff finally took its toll, on both the business and our relationship. So, here I am.

#singleunemployedandfortysomething

My phone beeps. It's my friend Holly. Holly is married to Adam and they have Olivia, who's three.

> We can't make it tonight. The babysitter's sick! ☹ ☹ Sorry!! I'll call you later. Happy birthday and have fun tonight! Xxxx

My phone beeps again. This time it's Max, who I met in a youth hostel in Rome when I was eighteen; we spent the summer back-packing around Europe together. He's married to Michelle now, and has three children and another on the way, but we've remained good friends. I'm even godmother to his eldest, Freddy.

> Happy birthday Stevens! Totally forgot about this parent–teacher tonight. If I don't go Michelle will chop my balls off. Come over for dinner next week instead. M

Two down. One to go.

Fiona calls an hour later. "You're going to kill me—"

In the end everyone canceled. Which was fine. I totally understood. These things happen. Busy family lives and all that. It's just, well, I'd be lying if I said I wasn't a bit disappointed.

Oh, who am I kidding? I was totally bummed out. But not with my friends; with my situation. So I went to therapy.

Of the retail kind.

As I hit the main street I feel immediately cheered up. Who needs a loving partner to take them for a romantic dinner in a lovely restaurant when there's a hot pink jumpsuit with cute little cap sleeves? Or children to make me birthday cards that I'll keep forever on the fridge, when I can actually find a pair of skinny white jeans that don't make me look huge? And so what if I don't have a job or my own home when there's a gorgeous pair of candy-striped straw stilettos I can afford with the birthday money Mum and Dad sent me?

Where exactly I'm going to wear skinny white jeans, hot pink jumpsuits, and straw stilettos in the freezing cold weather that is January in London, I have no idea. Plus, I didn't actually try any of it on as the lines were so long. But who cares about such niggling details, I decide later, as I head home on the bus, looking out the window and merrily sipping one of those cans of premixed gin and tonic. Birthday treat and all that.

It does briefly cross my mind that maybe this is how it starts. One minute it's your forty-something birthday, and you're shopping at Zara for a bit of a sleeve and enjoying a celebratory little cocktail on public transport. Then, before you know it, you're glugging whiskey from a paper bag and it's all over. I suddenly feel like the girl on the train, only on a bus.

Oh God. Still, at least I'm not about to start murdering my exes.

I think about The American Fiancé and dig out my phone. *Nothing.*

And just like that my cheerful mood crumbles. Tears prickle my eyelashes and, blinking furiously, I stick my phone back in my pocket and reach into my shopping bag.

Sod This. I pull out another can.

I'm grateful for:
1. *My mum and everything she does for me, and I look forward to finding availability to stay in my old bedroom.*
2. *Zara, even though I can't get the jeans past my knees and the hot pink jumpsuit looks hideous on me.*
3. *Whoever had the genius idea to premix gin and tonic and put them in a nifty little can.*
4. *The stranger, whose shoulder I fell asleep and drooled on, who woke me up before I missed my stop.*
5. *That I don't have a corkscrew, and that my ex lives five thousand miles away.*

The Next Day

My head feels like it's about to explode.

That's it: I am never drinking again. I'm going to do dry January. OK, so it's a bit late considering we're a week in, but better late than never, right?

Right?

So, last night the plan was to stay in and attempt to cook my own fancy birthday dinner, only by the time I got home my desire to be a domestic goddess had deserted me. It was all too much effort for one person. Plus, once the buzz of the G&Ts started wearing off, it all felt a bit sad.

So instead I took Arthur out for a walk. I hadn't yet had a chance to explore my new neighborhood, and we zigzagged through unfamiliar lamp-lit streets. It felt strange to be back in London, though this was nothing like the London I remembered. Before I left for New York I rented an apartment above a shop, slap bang in the middle of the city, with traffic, noise, and pollution on all sides—but this was a much quieter suburb, with neat rows of cottages and smart Victorian townhouses with checkerboard paths.

As I walked past, my gaze brushed over all the different windows, like flicking through a picture book. Inside all the homes I caught snapshots of family life. A mum in an upstairs window brushing her little girl's hair after her bath; a couple snuggled up together on the sofa watching TV, the screen reflected on their faces; a man with a backpack closing the front door behind him to squeals of "Daddy's home!"

I paused. If ever there was a metaphor for my life, this was it. Me on the outside, looking in on everyone on the inside. All these cozy scenes of domestic bliss. I gave a little shiver and pulled my woolly hat down over my ears. I was, quite literally, out in the cold.

And yet . . .

OK, so in the spirit of full disclosure, I have a confession.

As much as part of me craves all of this, there's another part of me that fears it. The part of me that swore in her diary she'd never end up like her parents. That read books by flashlight under the bedcovers and dreamed of passionate romances and travel to far-off lands. That was determined to lead a life less ordinary, filled with freedom and excitement and adventure, *with something different*—

Yanked backward by Arthur's retractable lead, I turned to see him squatting on the driveway of a large house, doing a huge dump.

Meanwhile, here I was picking up dog shit.

I tried not to think about any more metaphors, but stuck my gloved hand in the poo bag and started scooping it up. I use the word *scoop* as Arthur's stomach is always off and it's never a case of simply picking it up, but having to literally scrape it from the asphalt. I forced myself not to gag as the homeowner appeared in the window and both he and Arthur stood and watched me. I swear there's something very wrong with this aspect of the man–dog relationship. If aliens ever did land on earth, who would they think was in charge? Not the humans, that's for sure.

I carried on scraping . . . there, I thought I'd got it all . . . I shone my iPhone flashlight on the drive to check. See, Mr. Owner of the Big Grown-Up House. I might feel like a fuck up, but I am a very responsible person! I felt a slight sense of triumph.

Followed by a sickening horror as the beam of light swung from the asphalt onto the poo bag.

Oh my God. It had ripped! My fingers had gone through it! It was all over one of the glittery cashmere gloves that I'd got for Christmas! I yanked it off. Fuck! *Fuck!* FUCK!

I could have cried. Literally lain down and wept. It did actually cross my mind. I could imagine the owner calling through to his wife in the kitchen, "Darling, there's a strange woman lying on our driveway covered in dog poo and weeping hysterically. I can't quite hear through the double glazing but I think she's saying something about how it's her birthday. Perhaps we should call the police. She's going to scare the children."

Only, Arthur had other ideas. Spotting a squirrel, he let out a howl and took off, taking me with him as he charged down the sidewalk while I hung on for dear life. He didn't catch it, of course. It disappeared up a tree and Arthur stood at the bottom, barking his head off. Poor Arthur, I did feel a bit sorry for him. You'd think he would have learned by now. Then again, how many years did it take for me to learn that when a man disappears by not returning your call, barking my head off by sending him endless texts wasn't going to work either.

Which is kind of the same thing. Sort of.

We turned to head home, and I was already mentally running the bath and getting into bed with my iPhone to scroll through photos of sunsets and what everyone had eaten for dinner, when I caught a waft of fish and chips coming from a pub on the corner. Well, it was my birthday.

Inside there looked to be a few locals enjoying a quiet drink. I tied Arthur to a table leg in the corner while I went to wash my hands and order a glass of wine and fish and chips at the bar. When I reappeared five minutes later, I half expected him to have dragged the table across the pub. Instead he was sitting there obediently, having his ears scratched by a small boy in a beanie.

"He likes that." I smiled.

The boy looked up, as if he'd been caught doing something he shouldn't. "Oh, is he your dog?"

I was about to say no, that he belonged to my landlord, when something changed my mind. "Yes, he's my dog."

"What's his name?"

"Arthur."

The little boy grinned wider, revealing a missing tooth. "Like King Arthur?"

"Exactly." I nodded, glancing at Arthur, who was sitting there looking quite regal while having his head stroked. It wasn't a bad prefix considering who seemed to be in charge around here; it certainly wasn't me. "King Arthur."

The little boy's eyes lit up and he buried his hands deep into Arthur's fur. "I want a dog but Mummy won't let me. She says I can only have a hamster."

"Well, hamsters can be fun."

He looked unconvinced. "But it's not like King Arthur," he replied.

"No, it's not," I admitted.

"Oliver, there you are!"

A male voice caused us both to look up.

"I wondered where you'd got to—"

A man appeared from the other side of the pub, looking like he'd just come in from outside. Wearing a down jacket, a thick scarf, and gloves, he had short dark hair and was the spitting image of Oliver. So this must be his dad.

Oliver reached for his sleeve excitedly. "Guess what his name is! It's King Arthur. Like in the movie we saw!"

"He's not bothering you, is he?"

"No, no . . . not at all."

He had really nice eyes. Pale blue, the color of faded denim.

"That's good." He smiled, then winked at his son. "Come on, we're late."

He was attractive, in a dad kind of way.

"Scratch his ears! He loves it!"

He dutifully squatted down, took off one of his gloves and scratched Arthur's ears. Arthur was loving the attention. "Now, do you think he'll scratch mine," he said with a straight face, tilting his head sideways and sending Oliver into fits of giggles.

"OK, come on you, we really must go or your mum will kill me. She's waiting for us at the cinema."

"Bye, King Arthur . . . bye." Oliver waved to us both.

"Bye." I waved back. "Enjoy the movie."

"Thanks." His dad smiled and took his son's hand.

I watched them walk out of the pub together, and for a moment I couldn't help wishing I was the lucky woman waiting at the cinema. Not just because they looked so cute, father and son, hand in hand. But because I couldn't help noticing how he filled out those jeans—

Whoa, Nell!

It took me by surprise. This was the first man I'd noticed since The American Fiancé, never mind found attractive. Followed by resignation that he was someone's husband, which sadly did *not* take me by surprise because at my age all the good ones are taken.

But somewhere, deep inside this wounded soul of mine, it also ignited a little flicker of hope that maybe, just maybe, it wasn't over for me yet.

I'm grateful for:
1. *My wine, which was so delicious I had to order two more glasses.*
2. *Arthur knowing his way home.*
3. *Ibuprofen.*
4. *The flashback from last night, otherwise I would not have just remembered that in all the mayhem of shit-gate I left behind the offending poo bag and glove, and will have to go back and retrieve them while leaving a groveling apology.*
5. *The fact there are not "Wanted" posters of me up in the village already.**

Sunday Lunch

This morning I wake to a group WhatsApp from my friends, inviting me to lunch at an Italian place in town. Belated birthday and all that.

Fab! What time?

---

* But just in case, I will wear a hat.

Holly
Can we do 11:30? Olivia naps at 2.

Max
Freddy's got soccer first. We can't make it till one.

Fiona
Swim club is 12–2, but any time after is good.

I'm tempted to say I'm napping at three, which isn't a lie, considering I still haven't fully shaken my godawful jet lag, but instead I stay silent and let them fight it out between naps and swimming classes and soccer. Which, judging by the number of WhatsApps that ping in, makes negotiating Brexit look easy.

Finally we reach a solution and, pleased, I jump in the shower. I'm really looking forward to seeing everyone, but as Arthur watches me getting ready I feel suddenly guilty about leaving him.

"Don't worry, I won't be long," I promise, giving his ears a tickle as he looks at me with his big brown eyes.

I head into town. I haven't been out properly since I got back to London, so I've dressed up. I'm even wearing a bit of a heel. Well, it is my birthday, even if it's belated. So my heart sinks a little when I arrive at the Italian restaurant to see a pile of double strollers by the door and a sign saying there's a children's play area downstairs. Don't get me wrong, I love kids, but I was hoping for something a little more . . .

I open the door to a crescendo of noise . . . *quiet?*

A waiter rescues me, and I'm shown to our table where I order a carafe of wine and pour myself a large glass.

"Gorgeous birthday girl!"

I look up to see Fiona charging across the restaurant, her children in tow. She swoops upon me, giving me a big bear hug. "I'm so sorry about canceling on Friday, I felt terrible—"

"Don't worry, it's fine, I know you're busy," I say, hugging her back.

"I just completely forgot I'd promised Annabel I'd help with her invitations—"

"Annabel?"

"She's a mum at Izzy's new school. She's organizing this big charity fundraiser."

"That sounds a lot more important than my birthday." I laugh. "Anyway, I'm just happy you could all make it today."

"Me too. So, how are you?"

"Old." I smile.

She swats me. "Nonsense! You look the same as you did at twenty-five."

Fiona's a sweetheart, but she's also started holding things at arm's length and squinting at them. I probably look a little fuzzy too. Which is no bad thing. My theory is that's why our eyesight goes as we get older: to protect us from seeing ourselves in sharp focus.

"Izzy, give Auntie Nell our card."

Izzy is wearing a pair of fairy wings and she jumps into my lap, thrusting a card at me with her chubby fingers.

"Thanks, fairy." I grin, tearing it open. "Wow, neat hand-writing."

"Can I see?" She pushes her blonde curls out of her eyes, which are big and blue and framed with the longest of lashes, which sweep over her cheeks. Izzy has skin like a peach and has nothing to fear from being in sharp focus. But then she is only five.

"Thank you, Izzy."

"And Lucas, have you got the present?"

Lucas is seven and is clutching his Matchbox cars as if every-one in the restaurant might want to steal them. He shakes his head.

"Oh no, it must still be on the kitchen table," groans Fiona. She looks at Lucas. "Did you forget to bring it, darling?" He nods. Lucas is a man of few words, like his father.

Fortunately, at that moment David appears from parking the car, brandishing a beautifully wrapped box that he found in the back seat. Fiona always does really lovely presents. When we first met, we were both as broke as each other and our go-to gift was a scented candle, but then she married David and things changed. She's still the same girl in so many ways, but now her gifts come from those expensive boutiques that I daren't even go into as everything spontaneously falls off the hangers when I go near, and the assistants give me the stink eye as it's quite obvious I can't afford anything anyway.

"Oh wow, it's gorgeous," I gasp, as I unwrap a butter-soft cashmere scarf. "You shouldn't have—"

"Do you like it?"

"Like it? I *love* it!" I shriek, giving her and the children big hugs.

Fiona looks pleased. "It's from Annabel's shop; she helped me pick it out. She's got the most amazing taste. I can't wait for you to meet her. You're going to love her!"

"I can't wait either." I smile, but at the mention of her name again I feel a slight niggle. I catch myself. The scarf's beautiful. I'm being ridiculous.

"Oh look, everyone's here!"

I forget all about it as the door swings open, and Holly and Adam arrive with Olivia at the same time as Max and Michelle with their three, and we spend the next five minutes kissing cheeks and giving hugs and remarking on how tall everyone's children have grown and how wonderful it is to see each other again.

Because it is wonderful. Truly, there's nothing better than being with old friends. You just pick up where you left off, as if you were in the middle of a conversation. Except we've not seen each other since last summer and there's lots to catch up on. New houses, new promotions, new babies.

"Number four, we must be mad!" laugh Max and Michelle, grinning at each other over plates of penne arrabbiata, while Adam tries to wangle free legal advice from David about the holiday home in France they're considering buying by offering him the salami from his pizza, and Fiona and Holly unpack towers of Tupperware boxes filled with rice cakes and blueberries that go flying everywhere.

I order another carafe of wine.

"So what about you, Nell?"

After the waiters have cleared away our plates, the children go downstairs to the play area, supervised by Freddy who's been bribed with his dad's new iPhone, and the table falls quiet.

"What's new?" asks Holly, who I met when we were first temping in London. We bonded immediately over microwaved baked potatoes and Excel spreadsheets. Tucking her dark, neat bob behind her ears, she looks at me expectantly across the table.

I hesitate. The only new things I have to report are a broken engagement, a rented room, and my recent unemployment. Not quite the same as new promotions and babies.

"I want to hear all about the cafe—"

"How are the wedding plans coming on?"

"When are you flying back?"

As my friends fire me with questions, I brace myself to tell them my news. When I told Fiona, I swore her to secrecy. I felt like such a failure. But they're my oldest friends. They won't judge me.

That's my job.

"Well, you see, that's the thing. When I made that joke about forgetting to pack my ring, it wasn't actually a joke . . ." I hesitate, wondering how to put it, then blurt it out. "We've broken up and I've moved back to London."

There are a few shocked expressions around the table.

"Did you know about this?" accuses Holly, glancing at Fiona, who reddens and buries her face into her wineglass. "Nell, why didn't you tell me?"

"I'm telling you now, aren't I?"

I don't want to remind Holly that whenever I've tried calling her she's always busy. Holly is something of a wonder woman. When she's not taking Olivia to something, she's training for another triathlon, or rushing into an important meeting at the hospital where she works as a manager, dealing with life-and-death stuff on a daily basis. She's so successful and sorted out and *capable*, I didn't want to bother her with my pathetic tales of relationship woe.

"Don't tell me, another woman," says Max.

"Max!" gasps Michelle, swatting him on his shoulder.

"How do you know it's not another man?" I counter.

"Fuck. He's got another man?"

"MAX!" the whole table yells, and David throws a napkin at him. Trust Max. Always the joker.

"Nell doesn't have to tell us the reasons why," says Michelle, scowling at her husband. Michelle might only be five foot, but she inherited a fiery Latin temper from her tiny Sicilian grandmother, and it can be terrifying. Max looks suitably chastened.

"It's OK, it's no big deal," I fib, trying to shrug it off. "Just a case of cold feet."

"In California?" demands Holly.

That makes me smile, even though inside I feel wretched.

"Well, he's a bloody idiot to let you go," says Max, loyally.

"His loss is our gain," adds Fiona, giving my hand a little squeeze. "I know Izzy will certainly be thrilled to see more of her godmum."

"Freddy too," says Michelle, "as long as you don't mind freezing on the edge of a soccer field. He's obsessed."

"I can't wait." I smile.

"He's not *obsessed*, he's talented," corrects Max, "like his father. You know I could have turned professional if it wasn't for my knee injury—"

"Argh, Max, no! Not the knee story again!" The whole table erupts rowdily, and the conversation moves swiftly on to making fun of Max for his insistence that he could have been better than Beckham if it hadn't been for his dodgy knees. Which is way more interesting than my disastrous love life, frankly.

Then the kids come back and a chocolate cake appears with a candle in it, and everyone sings "Happy Birthday" and tucks into the cake, which is truly delicious. After which David very generously pays the bill before any of us see it, and we all say our goodbyes as they bundle themselves into their cars, Fiona and Max apologizing that they can't give me a lift because of all the car seats.

"We're going the other direction, but we can drop you at the tube?" offers Holly.

"It's fine, don't worry—I need to walk off this pizza." I smile, waving as they drive off with the heaters blasting.

Left alone on the sidewalk, suddenly it all seems so very quiet. That's another thing about being on your own: you've got no one to gossip with on the way home. To laugh with about Adam's new goatee, or to recount the funny thing Izzy said to the waiter, or to wonder exactly just how big David's bonus was last year.

Or to glance across at you when you're laughing, with a look in their eyes that says "I love you" for no reason other than you're theirs.

Automatically I check my phone. No messages.

Right, well, no point standing here freezing to death.

I put on my lovely new scarf and one glove, and set off walking to the tube.

I'm grateful for:
1. *My lovely friends.*
2. *The choice of restaurant as I got to celebrate my birthday with all their kids too, two of whom are my godchildren and I never see nearly enough, which was really good fun.*
3. *The downstairs play area (for when it got a bit TOO much fun).*
4. *Ricolas, as I have a sore throat from all that yelling.*
5. *Arthur, who was waiting by the door to welcome me home.*

The Battle of the Thermostat

Oh my God, he's back. My landlord. Keeper of the thermostat.

The apartment is FREEZING.

It's been this way since his return on Monday. No doubt this is Edward's way of offsetting his carbon footprint caused by flying a family of four to Verbier. He arrived back late on Monday night, but I didn't see him as I was already tucked up in bed watching *The Crown* on Netflix on my laptop.

I am in love with that show. As a little girl I was obsessed with Princess Diana and her pie-crust blouses, but now I'm all over Princess Margaret. All that flouncing around, drinking and smoking and dating unsuitable men. That was me when I was younger. Though now I fear I'm more like the Queen was. Standing around with my arms folded, looking disapproving in a cardie and a pair of comfy shoes.

Braving the icy temperatures, I venture into the kitchen to make something to eat. Aside from watching *The Crown*, I've spent the last couple of weeks firing off emails to various old contacts inquiring after (pleading for) work. I can't believe it's already the middle of January and I still haven't finished unpacking, or got myself a job, or managed to turn my life around from Fuck Up to Total Success. I'm going to have to really get a move on.

I'm just putting some bread in the toaster when I hear my landlord's key in the latch. Arthur hears it too and races to the front door. We haven't really seen each other since he got back, except for exchanging a few pleasantries as he rushes out the door in the morning. Every day this week he's arrived home late, by which time I've been in bed, but this evening he's home early.

"Penelope, hello." He beams, appearing in the kitchen carrying his fold-up Brompton bicycle, Arthur in his wake. Edward always insists on calling me by my full name.

"Hi Edward." I smile. I tried Eddie, but he wasn't having any of it.

"How are you settling in?"

"Good," I reply politely. "Still got some unpacking to do, but getting there . . . How was your trip?"

"Excellent. Perfect conditions."

His face is tanned beneath his helmet, apart from two big white circles around his eyes from where his ski goggles must have been. If he was a friend I'd tease him about them. But he's not. So I don't.

"Great." I shift awkwardly on the other side of the kitchen island. "Do you ski?"

"No, not really. Once. On a school trip."

"Oh. Shame."

The conversation stalls and I turn back to the toaster. It's really very odd, this sharing a house thing, in your forties. Here we are, two complete strangers with our own lives and nothing in common, except the fact that we're both now living under the same roof. Which, now I think about it, is how my relationship felt toward the end.

"It's like a sauna in here, have you turned up the heating?"

I look up to see Edward taking off his bicycle helmet and reflective jacket. His eyes dart to the thermostat.

"I haven't touched it," I protest, suddenly back in teenager mode and living with my parents. My face floods. I am a horrible liar.

His face seems to relax as it's confirmed that the thermostat is still set to Arctic, and he continues removing layers until he's down to a T-shirt. Meanwhile I'm standing here looking like I'm trying to avoid paying for checked baggage at the easyJet counter by wearing the entire contents of my suitcase.

What is it with men and women and the constant battle over the central heating? Growing up, I can remember how every winter my dad turned into Chief Inspector Stevens of the Heating Police, constantly policing the thermostat and turning down the dial a click. Only for him to go to work and Mum to turn it back up two notches. Back and forth it went for my entire childhood.

"I think your toast is burning . . ."

Edward's voice interrupts my thoughts and I snap back to see a plume of smoke. "Oh shit!" I quickly press cancel at the same time as the smoke alarm starts wailing.

"Don't worry, I've got it."

I finish jabbing the charred remains from the toaster to see my landlord fanning the alarm with a dish towel and opening a window.

"Thanks." I smile apologetically and go to throw them away and start again, when Edward stops me.

"I'll eat it, I love burnt toast."

"You do?"

"Sophie was addicted to it when we lived in France and she was pregnant with the twins; I was forever making it for her."

I feel myself soften. See. He's a nice man really. He doesn't mean to freeze his tenant to death.

"You lived in France?"

"Yes. Sophie's French; that's where we met. We moved back when the boys started school."

"How old are the twins now?"

"Fifteen . . . going on twenty-five." He smiles through a mouthful of blackened teeth from the charred toast. "Not my little boys anymore."

"You must miss them during the week."

"Yes." He nods, then shrugs. "Though I'm not sure they miss me. Too busy with their heads buried in their phones to notice I'm gone, most likely."

For a moment I feel a bit sorry for him. Perched on his barstool, eating my burnt toast. It can't be any fun for him either. Cycling home from a long day spent in the office to find some stranger in your kitchen, setting off fire alarms.

An icy blast blows in from the open window and I shiver. Actually, forget the toast, I'm too cold.

"Well, have a good evening . . ." Flinging the bread back in the fridge, I grab a couple of cans of premixed G&Ts—I've bought a whole stash—then quickly head back upstairs. I'm going to spend the rest of the evening keeping warm under my duvet, swigging gin and imagining I'm Princess Margaret.

I'm grateful for:
1. *Amazon's one-click ordering, as my fingers are frozen solid.*
2. *My new electric blanket.*
3. *Gin and Princess Margaret (in no particular order).*

To: Caroline Robinson—Shawpoint Publications
Subject: Editing projects

Dear Caroline,

Hope this email finds you well! It's been a while since we last spoke as I have been living and working in America, but I'm now back in London and looking for new and exciting projects. As you know from when we worked together, I have a wealth of skills and experience from my role as an editor and would relish the opportunity to bring these to your publications. I also have some exciting ideas I'd love to talk to you about. Let me know when is a convenient time to call, or maybe we can catch up over coffee?

Look forward to hearing from you.

Best wishes,

Penelope Stevens

To: Penelope Stevens
Automated Reply: Editing projects

Caroline Robinson-Fletcher is currently on maternity leave.

Sod This Sunday

Since breaking up with The American Fiancé I've begun to dread the weekends.

It was different when I was part of a couple; I used to look forward to Friday nights curled up together on the sofa with a movie and a bottle of wine; Saturdays spent catching up with friends after we'd closed the cafe; and Sundays—well, Sundays were always my favorite. We would get up early and cycle to the local farmers' market, returning with bags filled with fresh ingredients from which he'd create new recipes in the kitchen, while I lazed in the garden reading a book and performing my role as official taste tester.

Now when Friday night rolls around, I'm left facing another weekend on my own. Funny, I used to think loneliness was just something that affects elderly people. A frail old lady sitting in an armchair. Not someone in their forties with 147 Facebook friends.

I tried rallying the troops, but as usual everyone had plans. Max and Michelle were visiting his parents, while Holly and Adam were cozying up to the vicar at a local church event. Since discovering the price of private school fees, atheist Adam has suddenly "got" religion. Nothing at all to do with the fact that their local church primary was rated "outstanding by Ofsted (Office for Standards in Education, Children's Services and Skills)." A phrase I now hear bandied about by all my girlfriends with the same breathless urgency that used to be reserved for "he drives a convertible."

As for Fiona, she and David had been invited to a dinner party at Annabel and her husband Clive's new house. Not only does Annabel organize charity fundraisers and have amazing taste in cashmere scarves; apparently she's also the most amazing hostess. Not that I'm jealous. Well, maybe a little bit, but only because she appears to have added stealing my best friend to her long list of achievements.

"You need to meet some new people."

I'm FaceTiming my friend Liza in LA. It's 8 p.m. and I'm already in my pajamas. Sitting in bed, I stare at my phone screen. Her face looms large against a backdrop of bright blue sky and sunshine. Rain drums against my windowpane and I feel suddenly homesick for my old life.

"Make some new friends," she continues.

"I have plenty of friends."

I quickly pull myself together. Who needs life-affirming sunshine and tanned feet in flip-flops when you can have an electric blanket?

Determinedly I turn up the dial from one to three.

"They're all married with children. You need single friends. An activity—"

"You mean, like a job?"

Liza waves that statement away like an annoying fly. "You're just having some downtime. You need to practice patience."

I know she's right, but moving back to London has been expensive and, although the loan from my father was very generous, it won't last forever: I'm practicing panic, not patience.

"No, what you need is to meet some like-minded people—"

"I am not doing yoga," I cut her off.

Liza is a kickass yoga instructor and has just got back from teaching a retreat in Costa Rica. We met when I first moved to LA and, keen to adopt the lifestyle, I signed up for one of her classes. Luckily she didn't hold it against me, and we've been friends ever since. Tonight's the first time we've had a chance to catch up since I got back to London.

She lets out a loud cackle of laughter. "No one is going to be your friend if they see you doing yoga, sweetie."

"*Namaste* to you too."

"What about a book club?" she suggests brightly.

My heart sinks. There's something about a book club that screams middle-aged women. A thought strikes. *I am a middle-aged woman.*

"How's things with you and Brad?" I change the subject.

Brad is her fellow yoga teacher and on-off boyfriend. Though recently it's more off than on.

She shrugs. "He says he's confused."

"About what?"

"Whether he wants a serious relationship."

I really don't get what Liza sees in Brad. She's funny and kind and smart. She has the kind of yoga body that makes you want to weep. Plus she's a millennial. She only just turned thirty! Which means there are still plenty of empty seats in the musical chairs of romance, and there is absolutely no need to date an insecure little twerp, who tries to bully and control her while wearing beads and pretending to be Mr. Spiritual.

Namaste.

"Our couples therapist says he's got intimacy issues." Liza looks embarrassed. "I know what you're thinking."

"What am I thinking?"

"That I'm an idiot and I should leave him."

"You're not an idiot. He's the idiot."

She smiles gratefully. "Hey, I've got an idea! What about a sound gong bath? You'll meet all kinds of awesome people."

"I will?" I ask dubiously.

"They must have one in London—"

But before she can google it, a text beeps on my phone. It's from Sadiq, an old journalist friend of mine. I open it.

Stevens, your email went into my junk folder!
Call me. I have a job for you.

Life and Death

"You want me to write about dead people?"

We met this morning near his office, in one of those artisan-style cafes. All scrubbed wooden tables and chalkboards and freshly baked brownies left out on the side where everyone can cough and sneeze on them.

Sadiq paused from eating his grilled Halloumi flatbread. "Well, that's kind of the rule with obituaries, Nell. The people have to be dead."

I've known Sadiq for nearly twenty years. He was one of my roommates when I first moved to London, and back then he was a junior reporter at one of the tabloids. Now he's lifestyle editor at one of the big Sunday papers.

"Our regular freelancer just moved on to the travel section, so I immediately thought of you."

I smiled. Though I wasn't sure if I should take that as a compliment.

The waitress put down two more flat whites between us. Sadiq's had a little love heart in the foam. Mine didn't.

"I didn't get a heart."

"Huh?" Sadiq finished his flatbread and took a sip of his coffee.

I felt a clang of doom. It was a sign. That was it for me. No more love. Just death to look forward to.

I watched as he swallowed the little heart without even noticing. Well, why would he? Sadiq isn't looking out for signs from the universe. He's happily married, with two gorgeous children and an impressive career. His life is a success by anyone's standards. I bet he doesn't even read his horoscope.

"Oh, nothing," I said quickly, shaking my head with an embarrassed smile. "I really appreciate you thinking of me."

"So, are you interested or not?"

"Absolutely." I nodded. "But are you sure I have the right experience? I'm a book editor, not a journalist."

Sadiq batted away my concerns. "It's basically editing down someone's life into a thousand words. You'll be perfect. Plus, the good thing about obituaries is the work's never going to dry up," he added cheerfully.

"Now I remember why we are such good friends." I smiled.

"And anyway, I owe you a favor."

"You do?"

"If it wasn't for you, I wouldn't be with Patrick. Remember how you told me he was the best thing to happen to me when I couldn't see it?"

My mind flicked back twenty years: Sadiq and me sitting on my futon night after night, talking into the early hours with a cheap bottle of wine and a packet of Marlboro Lights. It was during one of those conversations that Sadiq came out to me, even though of course I already knew. Just as I knew he was in love with the shy, blue-eyed Irishman who worked behind the bar at our local pub.

I smiled. "You just needed a nudge."

He passed his credit card to the waitress to pay the bill, then grabbed his jacket from the back of his chair. "Well, now I'm giving you one."

We agree on the fee, which isn't much, but together with Dad's loan and my cheap rent is enough to live on. So now I'm on the tube heading to my first interview with the widow of an esteemed playwright. His obituary was originally scheduled to be published next week but the newspaper has decided to make it into a full-length feature for February, so I'm hoping to get a little bit of what Sadiq described as "life." An ironic choice of words, considering the subject matter, but apparently the risk with obituaries is they can easily turn into a dull shopping list of achievements.

At least that's one thing I don't have to worry about. At this rate my obituary could be written on a Post-it note.

The address is just off Portobello: a tall, skinny house painted lilac. Climbing the front steps, I rehearse my introduction. "I'm so sorry for your loss . . . I'm so grateful for you taking the time to speak to me . . ." I spent the tube journey quickly reading through some research that Sadiq had provided and, by all accounts, Monty Williamson was quite a character. Together with his wife, he led a fascinating life, traveling all over the world and meeting lots of famous people. I feel a beat of nervous excitement. I'm sure she's going to have lots of amazing stories. Still, I have to be mindful. The woman is in her eighties and has just lost her husband. She's probably very fragile.

And hard of hearing, the poor thing, I decide after ringing the bell for several minutes and not getting any answer. I knock loudly on the door. There's the sound of footsteps and abruptly it's flung open.

"Hello, I'm Nell Stevens, here to do the interview—"

"Sorry, have you been knocking long? I was painting and listening to my podcast."

If I was imagining a frail, hand-wringing widow shuffling to greet me, I was sorely mistaken. Standing before me is a tall, vibrant woman with thick gray hair cut attractively into a bob. She's wearing red lipstick, paint-splattered overalls, and sequined lace-up tennis shoes.

"Don't tell me—you were imagining someone in mourning dress with a blue rinse." She laughs at my expression. "I much prefer a bit of sparkle, don't you?"

Standing in front of her on the doorstep, I think I love her already.

"Sorry, I'm forgetting my manners. Please, do come in . . ." Opening the door wider to let me enter, she extends a bony hand with fingers full of rings and gives me a firm handshake. "Pleasure to meet you."

I break into a smile. "Likewise."

I'm grateful for:
1. *Sadiq, for not only offering me a job but simultaneously saving me from the hell that is having a gong bashed in my ear for an hour whilst lying under a blanket.*
2. *Monty Williamson's widow, for being so fabulous.*
3. *The barista at Starbucks, for making me the latte I drank on the way home. Who needs a love heart when you can have a smiling panda face?*

FEBRUARY
#socialmediablackout

Death by Blue Rinse

OK, so it's not exactly what I'd call my *dream* job. No one says "when I grow up I want to write about dead people," but let's face it, some of the most fascinating people that ever lived are now dead, and some of the most boring are still alive, and I know which I'd rather write about.

It's Friday night and in lieu of going out, I'm at my desk putting the finishing touches to my first obituary. It's taken a bit longer than I thought, as I got sucked into the vortex that is Google. One minute I was researching Monty Williamson's plays and the next I was googling "signs of sepsis" because I had an itchy rash on my elbow, or "can dogs eat apples" because Arthur stole the apple core out of my trash can when I wasn't looking.

Anyway, it's almost finished. I press the recording on my iPhone from our interview a few days ago and his widow's voice fills my bedroom . . .

"Please, call me Cricket."

"Like the sport?"

"Like the insect." She laughs. "It's Catherine really, but it was my nickname as a child and it's stuck. My husband always said I was chirpy."

Cricket lives in the kind of house you imagine to be the home of a playwright. Floor-to-ceiling bookcases bursting with so many books they're wedged into every available nook and cranny, walls lined with photographs and framed theater posters, ornaments and artifacts from far-flung travels: a tribal mask, painted wall plates, exotic-looking rugs. It has that slightly chaotic feel of someone who lived an unscripted life.

Our interview was along similar lines.

"Please—sit down, make yourself comfortable," she said, after I followed her through into the living room where we were to conduct our interview.

I looked around for a chair, but all the furniture appeared to be draped in paint-splattered sheets.

"There's a sofa underneath that one."

"You're decorating?" It suddenly dawned on me as I noticed the set of ladders and various pots of paint dotted around. "I thought when you said painting, you were doing oil or watercolors."

"Heavens, no." She laughed cheerfully. "The house needed a good lick of paint, so I thought no time like the present."

I don't know what I was more surprised by. The fact that a woman in her eighties was up a ladder with a roller, or that she was in such remarkably good spirits considering her husband had just died.

"I always wanted this room to be yellow, but Monty would never hear of it—which do you prefer?" She gestured to two paint samples on the wall. "The one on the left is Bumblebee and to the right is Tuscan Sun."

"Hmm . . . I think I prefer Bumblebee."

She looked pleased. "Great minds think alike. Who wouldn't want to sit in a room painted such a fabulous name?" She grinned, before disappearing into the kitchen to make tea and bring cookies: "Delicious chocolaty ones that are terribly bad for us."

I liked Cricket from the get-go. She was sharp and irreverent, and as our interview got underway she brought out old photograph albums and regaled me with stories of scandal and intrigue from the fascinating career of her husband, sprinkling the names of stars of the stage and screen like fairy dust through our conversation. But she was also incredibly honest. Once the curtain came down, life wasn't all glitz and glamour. Critical reviews. Financial hardships. Cancer. His suffering toward the end, and her relief and guilt at his death. The stuff real life was made of. The stuff that doesn't make the photo album.

"I met Monty when I'd given up on the notion of falling in love again. It was quite unexpected. I was about to turn fifty and assumed any recklessness was behind me. Marriage and children had evaded me . . . or had I, in fact, evaded them?" She smiled, a flicker of mischief in her eyes, and it struck me that I was far more interested in Cricket than I was her famous late husband.

"How did you both meet?"

"I was an actress in those days—not a very good one, I might add—and I'd had my fill of passionate love affairs and doomed romances. I'd been engaged several times; once I even bought the wedding dress, a hideous netted thing I seem to remember . . ." She shuddered, her mind casting back. "Fortunately the groom saved me from having to wear the damned thing by confessing he was already married a few days before the ceremony. And to think it caused such a ruckus at the time."

She laughed heartily.

"But that's one of the good things about getting older: often the most terrible of things turn into the most amusing through the lens of time."

My mind flicked to my own broken engagement. Would I really be laughing at that in decades to come?

"After that I decided I was done. Love didn't suit me. I would get myself a cat and take up the viola—"

"Why the viola?"

"Why not?"

I smiled. "Why not" seemed like a good philosophy for life.

"I was quite happy. But then some months later I auditioned for a play and met Monty and everything fell away. Which was lucky in some ways, as I later discovered I was terribly allergic to cats and couldn't hold a note. More tea?"

So we drank more tea and, as the weak February sunshine gave way to dusk, Cricket told me that although they were together for over thirty years, they didn't get married until they were in their seventies. "And only then because his health was failing and Monty wanted to avoid all that tax nonsense. We married in New York. No fuss. Just the two of us. I remember thinking, to anyone watching us on the steps of City Hall, we must look like a couple of old dears, me with my gray hair and Monty with his walker, but I felt eighteen again. You know, despite everything I was dippy about him . . ."

She trailed off, transported back to the steps of City Hall.

"Have you ever felt dippy about someone, Nell?"

I faltered for a moment as the spotlight turned to me.

"Yes." I nodded.

"And?"

"And he wasn't dippy about me."

Her eyes met mine. "My dear girl."

She said it with such kindness it almost made me cry. I'd been bottling it up and putting on a brave face, being flippant and trying to make light of things, because it was the only way I could cope with what happened. Because I feared that if I started talking about it, I might just fall apart. But thankfully she didn't ask for details, and I didn't have to give any, except to say I'd recently broken up with my fiancé in America and moved back to London to start over.

"And I'm forty-something."

"So? I'm eighty-something."

I smiled, despite myself.

"Don't worry about getting older, worry about becoming dull."

Somehow I couldn't imagine Cricket ever being dull.

"The only problem with getting older is you lose your friends and loved ones," she continued. "They die off all around you, one by one. Losing Monty has been very hard, but I lived a large part of my life before we met. When we did get together he was a workaholic and often away. I grew used to him not being here . . . But losing my girlfriends has in many ways been much harder . . ."

She stood up and plucked a photograph from a collection on a side table. It was of four women, all sitting in deck chairs and smiling. The one with dark hair was obviously Cricket when she was much younger.

"They were my sisterhood." She gazed upon them for a moment, then pointed each of them out. "This is Una. She was my best friend. We used to share digs together in London and would speak every day, sometimes several times a day. Veronica I met when we were in a play together . . . we used to go to a matinee every Wednesday. And Cissy worked at the local library where Monty often liked to go and write. At first I was horribly jealous, you know. I thought he might take a shine to her. She was ever so pretty." She smiled. "But then we became the best of friends. She was forever giving me books she'd read and loved . . ." She trailed off, remembering. "They were always here for me. I miss them all terribly."

Listening to her talking, I realized that in a funny kind of way we had something in common. I knew how she felt. My friends hadn't died, they'd just got married and had babies, but I missed them too.

"But let's not be gloomy." She shook herself, and replaced the photograph. "I'm sure I've taken up quite enough of your time."

"Not at all," I protested, but it was late. I thanked Cricket for the interview and as we said goodbye, she called after me.

"By the way, it was my friend Una who told me never to join the Blue Rinse Brigade." She waved cheerfully. "She said they might kill you."

I'm grateful for:
1. *Google's 52.5 million results for "What questions do you ask a widow?"*
2. *Knowing that although death, like taxes, can't be avoided, it's not going to be by Blue Rinse.*
3. *It's not sepsis.*

An Unexpected Guest

After talking to Cricket, I'm more determined than ever to see my friends, so I arrange to meet Fiona at the playground. David's taken Lucas to judo, so it's a good chance to catch up and try to snatch a few bits of conversation in between throwing myself down slides and getting buried in the sandbox, as all good godmothers do.

The weather is cold and it's raining, so I bundle up in several sweaters and a cheap waterproof jacket I recently bought in an act of desperation, after yet another umbrella blew inside out. It's green and made of plastic and makes me look like I'm wearing one of those green trash bags that you put the gardening cuttings in.

I also find a pair of Edward's old green wellies in the cloakroom under the stairs. They're a little on the big side and splattered with creosote from when he once painted the fence, but they're much better than my sneakers. Or flip-flops, which seem to be the extent of the summer footwear I brought back from California.

As I dash out of the house, coat and wellies flapping, I catch my reflection in the mirror and look askance. I quickly console myself. Who cares about fashion? I'm going to a playground to see my best friend and play in the sandbox with my lovely goddaughter. Who's going to see me?

Shoving on a woolly hat, I hurry to the tube. As long as I'm dry, that's all that matters.

"Oh look, it's Annabel!"

WTF?

She appears like a goddess through the foggy mists of the local playground. A tanned vision of perfection in her Moncler jacket, skinny jeans, and Le Chameau wellington boots. I watch as she glides toward us in slo-mo, children parting like the Red Sea, accompanied by a mini-me version who is clearly her daughter, and a French bulldog dressed in a quilted Barbour jacket that trots obediently beside her.

She warmly kisses Fiona on both cheeks, then turns to look over at me with the kind of fearful curiosity usually reserved for when you find something unsavory in a salad.

Somewhere, silently, I feel the battle lines drawn.

"This is my friend Nell," says Fiona, eagerly introducing me.

"Hi." I look up from where I'm being buried in the sandbox by Izzy, and give a little wave.

"I've heard so much about you." She smiles.

It's perfect, like everything about her.

"Likewise." I smile back, standing up and brushing off the clumps of wet sand as her daughter races over to say hi to Izzy.

"Clementine, darling, not in the sandbox," instructs Annabel sharply, before adding sweetly, "Mummy doesn't want you to get dirty. What about hopscotch? That looks like fun."

Izzy glances up at me warily. I know what she's thinking. Hopscotch does not look like fun. Burying Auntie Nell in the wet sandbox looks fun. "Go on, you can bury me later," I whisper, giving her a wink.

"Even your head?"

"Even my head," I promise.

Izzy grins happily and together the two girls race dutifully across the playground.

"I'm so excited for you to finally meet," enthuses Fiona as I join them. "I've been telling Annabel all about how you used to run this amazing cafe in America."

"Well, I wouldn't call it amazing." I pull a face, feeling a bit embarrassed as Fiona beams proudly.

"Oh, is that the one you had to close down?" Annabel shoots me a look of sympathy. "Such a shame."

"Yes, it was." I bristle.

"I know how tough it can be running a business. So many fail."

OK, I'm just being sensitive. She's being nice.

"Annabel used to run a really successful interior design business before she opened her shop," continues Fiona eagerly. "Maybe she can help give you some advice. Get you going again."

"Thanks, but . . . no, I don't think so." I smile politely.

"Very wise." Annabel nods. "Like I always say to my husband Clive, success really separates the wheat from the chaff."

I'm still smiling as it takes a moment to register. Hang on a minute. Who's the chaff?

Am I the chaff?

"But if you need any style advice, I'd be more than happy to help," she continues, her gaze sweeping over my outfit as she takes a sip of her soy latte.

"Annabel has incredible taste," continues Fiona obliviously.

"You mean, you don't think I'm stylish enough?" I retort, ignoring Annabel's disdain and pulling a face that makes Fiona laugh. "What about the trash bag I wore at Glastonbury that time?"

"Oh God, how could I forget? I wore one too." She giggles.

"We went through a whole roll of them!"

"I was completely covered in mud the whole weekend. When I took my washing home to Mum, she put it through about ten cycles—"

"Mine just threw all my stuff away!"

We both burst out laughing, remembering.

"So Fiona, you must come over and swim in the new pool," interrupts Annabel. "Izzy will love it."

Fiona stops laughing and turns back to her friend.

"Annabel's just moved into a house with an outdoor swimming pool," she explains for my benefit.

"Won't it be a little chilly?"

Annabel looks at me like I'm a total moron. "It's heated."

"Right, yes, of course." I nod.

Like my electric blanket.

"Gosh yes, Izzy would love that," says Fiona. "She's getting quite good at swimming."

"Bring your bikini too. We'll make a girly day of it."

"Ooh, yes!" Fiona beams across at me. "Doesn't that sound fun, Nell?"

I glance at Annabel, who shifts uncomfortably. It might not be apparent to Fiona, but it's obvious to both of us that the invitation didn't include a plus-one.

"And of course you too, Nell," she adds with a rictus smile.

"Sounds great!" I say.

Of course I'm lying. There is nothing remotely great or fun about being in a bikini next to perfect Annabel, but I know how much it means to Fiona for us to get along.

"See! I knew you two were going to be the best of friends!" says Fiona, as Annabel and I exchange withering looks. And, throwing her arms around us, she pulls us into a group hug.

I'm grateful for:

1. *Being of an age where I don't care about looking like something the sanitation workers collect on a Tuesday.*
2. *Keeping my composure and not telling Annabel to stuff her swimming pool where the sun don't shine.*
3. *My goddaughter, for:*
   a. *making me smile as I push her "higher, Auntie Nell, no HIGHER" on the swings, which totally freaks me out, but makes her laugh like a hyena as she plunges toward the asphalt at a hundred miles an hour.*
   b. *teaching me that this is probably how I should be approaching this scary mid-life business. Laughing like a hyena as I hurtle single, broke and childless toward one-piece bathing suits and hot flashes, the wind in my soon-to-turn-gray hair, and time running out fast before I go splat on the asphalt that is Too Late.**

---

* Otherwise known as TL. This is the terrifying fate that awaits you if you don't get your shit together BITL. It's the scary monster that keeps you awake at night. Like the bogeyman, only with bad fillers and Botox.

Battle of the Dishwasher

Since when did it get to be so complicated?

Finishing rinsing the plates, I carefully slot them into the racks in the dishwasher, then make a start on the cutlery. Knives at the front, blades down, forks to the back, prongs up, teaspoons to the right . . . or, hang on, do those go at the front? I hesitate, trying to remember, then switch them around. I used to just bung everything in as it came. Higgledy-piggledy. Wedging bowls against plates, chucking in fistfuls of cutlery.

But not anymore.

I grab a large chef's knife and looked for somewhere to stuff it. That was in my old life. When I *had* a life. One that included a house and a fiancé and my own dishwasher that I could load any damn way I liked.

"Those knives don't go in the dishwasher, Penelope."

I look up to see Edward standing in the doorway. Back from the early morning yoga class that he takes before leaving for the office, he's wearing his workout gear and a disapproving expression. Still in my robe, I feel like a slattern.

"It dulls the blades. You need to hand wash them separately."

He walks over to me and starts inspecting the contents of the dishwasher. "No, the wineglasses go on this side." He begins dismantling my stacking and rearranging things to his own strict rules, tutting all the while. "The smaller tumblers go here, see?"

I glance at the chopping knife still in my hand with its six-inch blade. Trust me, I'm tempted. In fact, there have been many times this past month that I've come close to murdering my new landlord.

"And don't forget to put it on the economy setting to conserve energy," he instructs, before going upstairs to take a lukewarm twenty-second shower.

"Gotcha." I smile tightly.

Though quite frankly, considering the endless provocation, I'd call it manslaughter.

An Obituary

*Monty Williamson, London's legendary playwright,
who inspired a generation and the love of his wife.*

My first obituary is in the newspaper! I ring Mum excitedly.

"Do you remember Monty Williamson, the famous playwright and theater director?"

"Hmm, the name doesn't ring a bell."

"He wrote *No One Is Listening*?"

"To be honest, your father and I don't go in for the theater much. Not since he fell asleep that time at *The Lion King* and started snoring—"

I persevere. "You must know him. He was a bit of a playboy, and went out with all those famous models in the Swinging Sixties before he got married to an actress called Catherine Farrah."

"Did he? Honestly, my memory's like a sieve these days. Hang on, let me ask your father . . . Philip! Phi-LIP!" After much calling in the background, I hear her explaining to Dad, then: "No, he doesn't know either. Why?"

Only at this point do I realize I have spent the last five minutes telling her about someone she doesn't know, has never met, who went out with someone she doesn't know either and wrote a play she has truly never heard of, who has died. It's true what they say. I have actually turned into my mother.

Luckily Mum doesn't hold it against me, but instead rushes out and buys several copies and proudly shows all the neighbors. Meanwhile I suddenly get an attack of the guilts. Is it wrong to be excited about writing an article which effectively is about someone dying? Making money from someone else's sorrow. I mean, it's a bit messed up when you think about it.

But then I get an email from Cricket telling me how much she loves it, how I've captured the essence of him wonderfully, and what a lovely tribute it is to her beloved Monty. So I feel much better. Dare I say it, I even feel a glow of pride.

Unconsciously Uncoupling

Initially when I decided to leave LA and move back to London, I was worried I'd regret my decision. I had images of me crying a lot and stalking my ex on Facebook. Well, bollocks to that. I haven't cried once and I rarely use Facebook.

OK, so that's not *exactly* true. I've welled up a few times and glanced at his page, but he never updates it anyway, so there really is nothing to be gained by looking at an old photo of him scuba diving in Thailand in 2009. Apart from cheering me up by reminding me just how ridiculous he looks in a wet suit and how much hair he's lost since then.

As one can see, I'm not of the consciously uncoupled mindset just yet. I don't know how all the Hollywood celebs do it. But then, does anyone really believe those press statements? All that stuff about still being besties and very much in love and excited to continue cherishing and adoring each other, only this time from afar. When everyone knows they should really read: *he shagged the nanny* or *she's addicted to plastic surgery* or *when we finally stopped taking selfies we realized we can't stand each other and no filter could save us.*

Or what about: *he stopped loving me so I left.* That would have been our press statement. Only in our case, it was true. And completely depressing. Now I see why they talk about sharing wonderful adventures, just not with each other. It's because everyone wants a happy ending, even if you're splitting up. No one can admit they're sad and angry and heartbroken. That life is complicated.

It's late. Lying in bed, I log on to Facebook and stare at his photo.

That even in that ridiculous wet suit that makes him look like a pregnant seal, part of me still loves him.

Shit.

Death by Pancake

February is a bit of a dismal month. What with the constant drizzle, wind, and never-ending gray. My sweaters pilling as I never take the bloody things off. Scrolling through a certain supermodel's bikini selfies on white sandy beaches as I try to shelter at the bus stop.

"The woman's over fifty! How does she do it?" I demand of Michelle, when she calls me later to ask if I'll babysit next month as it's Max's birthday.

"I don't know, but she's an inspiration. Maybe she's eating lots of salad?"

"Who wants to eat a lettuce leaf when it's freezing cold? I'm craving comfort food!"

Which explains right there why I am not, and never will be, taking a bikini selfie.

"Me too! I'm going to be eating my fair share of pancakes tonight."

"Pancakes?"

"It's Pancake Day today. Had you forgotten?"

Yes I had, completely, but now I feel a surge of hot-battered, lemon-sugared joy. This is one of the things I *do* love about being in the UK in February.

"Thanks for reminding me. I wonder if my landlord has a frying pan?"

"How is your new landlord? Is he nice?"

"We're currently battling over the thermostat and the dishwasher."

"It sounds like being married." She laughs, then catches herself. "Sorry, I didn't mean to be tactless—"

"You're not, it's OK." I reassure her as much as myself.

I hear children's voices in the background. "They're so excited about getting to flip the pancakes," confides Michelle. "They're drawing straws to see whose turn is first. Freddy is having none of it, of course. I just hope I've made enough batter. Last year he ate five pancakes—"

She's interrupted as Freddy yells, "SIX!"

"I reckon I'm going to beat him this year. That's one of the best bits about being pregnant. Being able to eat as many pancakes as you want." She laughs.

"So what's my excuse?" I joke, but inside I feel a sudden ache. Our lives couldn't be more different. There's Michelle, with her scene of domestic bliss. Happily married and heavily pregnant in her lovely home. Abruptly I feel more alone than ever.

"So you're sure you're OK to babysit?"

"Yes, of course. Get to spend time with my godson—"

"Thanks again, Nell, speak soon."

After we hang up I go on the hunt for a frying pan. So what if it's just me. More pancakes for yours truly. I find it in the back of the cupboard, then nip out to the corner shop for ingredients and start making the batter.

As a child, Pancake Day was one of my favorite times of year. Mum used to fire up the frying pan and we'd take turns trying to toss them. My brother Rich would do these perfect pancake double backflips. Mine would end up everywhere but back in the frying pan. It was a running family joke.

"Where will Nell's end up this year?" Dad used to laugh, as they went splat all over the kitchen. I think the all-time winner was the one that got stuck on the ceiling and fried by the overhead lights, to much shrieking from Mum who thought it would set the house on fire. Just imagine. Death by Pancake.

But it turns out Pancake Day isn't that much fun when it's just me and Arthur, who watches my every move, willing me to fail so he can gobble them off the kitchen floor. Still, I persevere, and am just undoing the top button of my jeans and wondering whether or not to go for a fourth, when I hear the key in the latch and Edward arrives home from work.

I feel a sudden panic. The kitchen is a bomb site. I brace myself as he appears in the kitchen in his hi-vis cycling jacket, carrying his fold-up bicycle and sniffing like a bloodhound. "What are you cooking?"

"Pancakes . . ." I gesture to the frying pan.

"Of course. Shrove Tuesday." He puts down his bicycle and takes off his helmet. "Mmm, I haven't had those for years."

Expecting to be reprimanded about the state of the kitchen, I'm slightly thrown.

"Don't the French have Pancake Day?" I think about his wife, Sophie.

He nods. "*La Chandeleur*. Only it's crêpes, of course."

So that's how French women don't get fat. They even eat skinny pancakes.

"But Sophie doesn't eat them. She prefers to watch her figure."

I decide against pancake number four.

"Would you mind if I—?" He gestures to the large bowl of batter. "They smell delicious."

"Oh . . . no, no of course, go ahead. I'd offer to make one for you, but I'm afraid I'm hopeless at flipping them."

"Ah well, that was always my strong point. All my years of tennis. Good reflexes." Rolling up his sleeves, he ladles in the batter, carefully rolls it around the edges until it's covering the bottom and has turned golden brown, then with an expert flick of his wrist tosses it in the air. It lands perfectly. "Ta-dah!" He flashes a broad grin, his face lit up. I'm taken aback. I've never seen this side to him.

"Wow, amazing." I give a little round of applause, and he takes a bow.

"Here, why not have a go—"

"No, honestly. I don't think you want pancakes on your ceiling."

"I used to coach tennis. Look, I'll show you . . ." He pours in another ladleful, and then before I know it he's giving me a lesson in pancake-flipping, and after a few false starts—one somehow manages to *wrap* itself around the kettle—lo and behold, I actually get one to land in the pan. First time ever! Who would've thought?

I'm grateful for:
1. *Jesus, for giving me pancakes.*
2. *My landlord Edward, for not only being my Pancake Day plus-one but also suggesting Nutella and marshmallows as a topping; SO much more delicious than all those gluten-free versions with blueberries, low-fat yogurt, and chia seeds clogging up my feeds.*
3. *Not having to clear up Michelle's kitchen, which, in the photo she texted me later, looked less like a scene of domestic bliss and more like a scene from the horror movie Putney Pancake Massacre.*
4. *Never having to take a bikini selfie—in the end I ate seven and am officially a pig.*
5. *Elasticated pajama bottoms.*

Valentine's Day

I think under the circumstances, this year I'm going to ignore it. Pretend it's not even happening. Which can only mean one thing:

TOTAL SOCIAL MEDIA BLACKOUT.

Thankfully, I've never been that into Valentine's Day. At school I was a bit of a late developer so I didn't have too many admirers, secret or otherwise. But what I did have was my dad, who every year would send me a card signed S.W.A.L.K. in his handwriting, and every year I would pretend not to know who it was from.

As I've gotten older, I've had my fair share of cards and bouquets but I've always felt it's all too contrived. Surely romance isn't about overpriced flowers and an expensive restaurant?

Luckily The American Fiancé was of the same mindset, so one year we made a pact to ignore it. We loved each other. We didn't need to prove it on a specific day. But then he really did ignore it.

"Why are you upset? You said it was commercial nonsense."

"It is, but I can't believe you didn't even get me a card."

"But you told me to ignore it."

"Yes, but you weren't *really* supposed to ignore it."

"So why didn't you tell me that?"

"Because I thought you knew!"

"Knew what? That my girlfriend talks in riddles!"

"Stop shouting!"

"I'm not shouting. You're the one that's shouting!"

Honestly, no wonder men and women have difficulty communicating. Just because a woman *says* something, it doesn't mean she actually *means* it. If that were the case, when a man asks a woman what's wrong and she says "nothing," she would actually mean nothing, and not, in fact, that she is furious with him for a variety of reasons and he'd better work out quickly what they are, otherwise there's going to be trouble and lots of banging of pots in the kitchen.

Anyway, like I said, this year I'm on Valentine's Day lockdown. Which is relatively easy, considering I work from home and not in an office. But it's lining up at the bank that proves to be my downfall. Have you ever *tried* to do a Total Social Media Blackout while waiting in line? I try practicing mindfulness for, like, two minutes, then cave in and scroll through endless photos of gorgeous bouquets, "cryptic" celeb tweets, and love messages scrawled in the sand.

In the end I feel thoroughly depressed. But I'm being silly. So what if I have no one to send me flowers; I am a strong independent woman! So in the spirit of *Sod This* I decide to go to the pub. No doubt it will be full of romantic couples and I will be on my own, but I refuse to hide away like some character in a Victorian novel. I'll take Arthur with me.

And a book. Things are always better with a book.

The pub is relatively quiet. It turns out most couples have gone to the overpriced restaurants, and there are just a few scattered here and there. Apart from a couple of heart-shaped balloons behind the bar and a special Valentine's Day champagne cocktail, I'm in pretty safe territory. Emboldened, I even order the cocktail in a defiant spirit, then go to find a seat.

I'm just sitting down when I spot a familiar face in the corner. It's the Hot Dad I saw here before. I feel both a frisson of excitement and relief that I've actually put on some makeup and dragged a comb through my hair for once. Obviously he's taken, but I still have a certain pride. Old feelings of embarrassment that I'm on my own on Valentine's Day surface, but I push them down determinedly. There is nothing to be ashamed of.

I focus on my book and start reading, but it's hard to concentrate when Hot Dad is only feet away. He's sitting at a table, but his companion is hidden. It must be his wife. I try surreptitiously to crane my neck to get a look. I'm curious to see what she looks like. I'm sure she's completely lovely. He looks like he'd have a lovely wife, and their little boy is gorgeous. He glances over—oh shit— and I turn quickly away.

"Here's your Valentine's Day cocktail," says the barman, bringing it over.

"Thanks." I smile. It has a cocktail stick with a big strawberry cut into the shape of a love heart.

Only now I feel like a total loon and not a single, empowered woman. I quickly eat the strawberry and lean forward to try and move out of view. A text beeps: **S.W.A.L.K.** I smile. It's my dad wishing me a happy Valentine's Day like always.

I think about last year's Valentine's Day. After the ignoring debacle, The American Fiancé made me a puttanesca. Which might not sound like much, unless you've tasted a really good puttanesca, and his was the best. His Italian grandmother gave him the recipe and it was as salty as it was sweet, with the kind of al dente pasta that walls are made for. I smile at the memory.

God, I miss him. It hits me, hard and fast in the pit of my stomach. I wonder if he's thinking about me. If I come into his head randomly throughout the day, like he does in mine. Or has he moved on already, and I'm just a distant memory?

But let's not be gloomy.

Cricket's voice sounds in my ear and I wonder if she's finding today difficult too. Since the interview we've begun emailing, and I resolve to send her a quick note when I get home. Speaking of. I quickly glug back my Valentine's Day cocktail. Time to go. I don't need to prove anything to anyone. Least of all to myself. I get up and tug on Arthur's lead, then turn toward the door—

"Excuse me—"

And bump straight into the Hot Dad.

"Oh, sorry."

Or did he bump into me?

"Sorry, did I get you?"

He's carrying a pint and a glass of wine. I notice he's spilled some.

"No, not at all, it's fine, totally, it's just this old thing . . ." I'm gabbling. I'm actually gabbling.

"It's King Arthur, right?"

"No, Nell."

Oh crap, that cocktail was really strong. It's gone straight to my head. "Sorry, I thought you meant—" I stop talking. It's safest.

"Well, pleased to meet you, Nell. I'd better go . . ." He gestures toward his table in the corner.

"Yes, me too."

"Maybe see you around."

"Yes, maybe."

"Bye, King Arthur." He smiles, and the corners of his eyes crinkle up. He really does have the most gorgeous eyes.

60

I smile back, and it's as I turn to leave that I notice his hand around the pint glass. He's not wearing gloves.

He's also not wearing a wedding ring.

I'm grateful for:
1. *Do I really need to spell it out??? Hot Dad must be single!*

The Day After

Or B) Having an affair.

Shit. I wonder if he is? I wonder if that's why he was tucked around the corner where no one could see him. No, he can't be. Not with those eyes.

Or C) Maybe he's like the royal family and doesn't wear a wedding ring (unless of course you're Harry).

Or D) I looked at the wrong hand entirely as I was actually quite drunk.

A Moment of Truth

"He could be divorced and having dinner with his ex-wife." Liza calls me a couple of days later, when I'm out walking Arthur.

"It was Valentine's Day."

"Maybe the divorce was really amicable?"

Liza is not one to be deterred by such a minor detail.

"There's amicable and there's weird."

"You need to be more open."

I'm lurking underneath a tree in the park, trying to get a better signal.

"This isn't California."

She ignores me. "So you like him?"

"I don't know him, but . . . well, he's the first man I've noticed since—" I don't finish the sentence. I don't have to. Liza knows all the details.

"You need to start dating."

I can't believe I'm having this conversation. A few months ago my life was all mapped out. Now everything's turned upside down and I'm back here again. I feel a raindrop on my face and look up at the sky. Dark clouds have started to form.

"It's too soon."

She doesn't miss a beat.

"Better that than it's too late."

Plus-One

I've decided Liza is right—I need to make more of an effort to get out—so a few days ago I took matters in hand.

"A concert?" Fiona balked at me across her kitchen island, after I rushed around to hers with a surprise.

"It's an eighties reunion concert!"

As teenagers, Fiona and I were huge fans of all the big eighties bands. But we only discovered our shared love when we both turned up to a costume party at orientation week, sporting backcombed hair, neckerchiefs, and overalls. She was Siobhan from Bananarama; I was Kevin from Dexys Midnight Runners. When I discovered lots of our favorite artists had reunited for a tour, I was so excited.

"When is it?"

"This Saturday. And guess what? I managed to get us two tickets!"

This would make it up to her for all those gifts of books and candles over the years. Fiona *loves* these bands. Some of the biggest stars of the eighties are performing. She's going to be over the moon.

There was a pause. I suddenly doubted my impulsiveness. I should have checked first.

"Oh Nell, I'd love to, but I'm busy that night."

"Even if Robert De Niro's waiting?" I joked, trying to conceal my disappointment.

"Sorry, it's just that I'm going to the Savoy."

"Oh, wow. Fancy!"

"I know, right?" she agreed. "It's the charity fundraiser I was telling you about that Annabel's organized."

Suddenly my enthusiasm popped, like a balloon.

"Annabel?"

"Yes, her husband's company bought a table, but he's had to go away on business so she asked me as her plus-one—"

"Right, yes. Of course."

"Sorry."

"Oh, don't worry, it's fine. I know it's last-minute. I just thought . . ." I trailed off. I felt foolish. What was I thinking? That we were going to dress up in dungarees and backcomb our hair like we did when we were eighteen? Fiona couldn't go gallivanting off at the drop of a hat to a concert with her desperate old fart of a friend. She had some swanky fundraiser at the Savoy to go to. *With Annabel.*

"What about Holly?" she suggested.

"Does she like eighties music?"

"Doesn't everyone?"

"Don't worry. I'm sure I'll find someone who wants a free ticket."

Except I couldn't. All my friends already had plans or couldn't get a babysitter. I did think about going by myself. I used to love taking myself off to movie matinees when I lived in New York. But showing up alone to a concert and singing along to some of the greatest hits of my youth felt different, so I decided to resell the tickets and accept I'd lose about a hundred quid.

Then I had an idea.

"I haven't been to a pop concert for years!"

Cricket looks across at me excitedly as we make our way into the arena.

"I hope you like the music."

"I do already! I downloaded *Now That's What I Call the 80s* in the Uber and listened to a few songs on the way here, instead of my podcast."

"That's great," I say, impressed.

I invited Cricket at the last minute. With only a few hours to go, I was about to sell my tickets on eBay when I remembered her telling me how she had no one to do things with now that her friends had all died, and on impulse sent her an email. She emailed me immediately saying she'd be delighted, and got straight in a cab to meet me.

"The one about Vienna was my favorite. Monty and I used to love going there to the opera—"

And now I want to ask her a million questions, but she's already at the bar ordering a couple of drinks, after which we head to our seats. If I was worried about Cricket managing the stairs, I needn't be. She bounds up them in giant strides. Best of all, she's still wearing her paint-splattered overalls, as she'd been in the middle of decorating when she'd received my email and hadn't had time to change. She couldn't look more the part.

"My, isn't this fun?"

"Yes," I reply, hurrying to keep up with her. It's more fun than I've had in ages. I look around at the audience, which is buzzing with anticipation. It's a mix of young and old, but none as old as Cricket, though she seems completely unfazed. In fact, I'm not sure she's even noticed.

"Did you and your fellow go to concerts?"

"No, Ethan didn't like live music," I say, and realize it's the first time I've been able to bring myself to say his name. "He always complained they never sounded as good, and it was better to listen to their albums at home."

"And that, my dear, is reason enough not to marry him." She smiles, and despite the ache I feel inside, I smile too.

"We had a lot of differences," I acknowledge.

"Differences can make or break a marriage. Often the differences you love in the beginning can be the reasons you want to murder them five years later."

I laugh. For the first time, I can actually laugh about it.

She drums her fingers on her knees impatiently. "So when are they coming on?"

"I'm not sure. Soon, I think."

"Oh how marvelous . . ." Her eyes grow wide and, taking out her phone, she begins snapping photographs, then leans in toward me. "Shall we do a quick selfie?"

"A *selfie*?"

"It's when you take a picture of yourself like this," she explains innocently, angling her phone out in front of us. "Smile!"

We end up taking quite a few selfies as we wait for the concert to start, while chatting about all kinds of things. From tales about Monty and the time they were offered tickets to see a new band, but they'd never heard of them so went to the pictures instead—"and it turned out to be the Beatles, would you believe!"—to the new podcast she's listening to—"my favorites are true crime"—to an exhibition she wants to see at the Victoria and Albert Museum—"I don't know if you're interested, but I'm a member so I can take in a free guest . . ."

It's really quite refreshing. As much as I love my friends, I can't quite join in their conversations about children and husbands and home improvements. At my birthday lunch, school catchment areas were mentioned and it was like a black hole everyone disappeared into, until the waiter rescued us with grated Parmesan and the large pepper grinder.

Then the houselights go down and the strobe lights go up, and suddenly one of my all-time favorite bands is onstage, singing and dancing, and Cricket is straight up on her feet. A few people behind tell her to sit down, but she just says politely, "If I sit down, my dear, I may never get up again," and carries on jigging around delightedly.

Good for her; at eighty-something she's earned the right to dance at a concert.

Meanwhile, I'm not so brave and remain pinned to my chair by the laser-like glares in my back from the people in the row behind us. Honestly, how can people come to concerts and *not want to dance*? I think about my teenage fan-self who had posters on her bedroom wall and backcombed her hair. What would she think if she saw me sitting here?

That does it. *Sod This.*

As they launch into one of their biggest hits, I take my cue from Cricket and jump up. At forty-something I've earned the right to dance too.

I'm grateful for:
1. *A brilliant evening.*
2. *Cricket being OK after she lost her footing when she was dancing and spilled her red wine all over the grumpy woman behind us, which of course was just an accident and not at all done on purpose—I don't know what the woman was talking about.*
3. *Kevin, the Uber driver, for taking me home, as, although I felt eighteen again, I am not in fact eighteen, and all that dancing did my back in.*
4. *The eighties.*

Delete Contact

I deleted Ethan from my phone today. I was scrolling through my contacts to call someone about work and then suddenly there he was: *Ethan DeLuca*. The American Fiancé. The Ex. The Man Who Broke My Heart.

Except, of course, it didn't say any of those things. Just his name and his number. I remember him putting his details into my phone. I was in a bar, celebrating a colleague's birthday but planning to leave early—I was tired and wanted to go home—until I was persuaded to stay for another drink.

Sliding doors. Isn't that what they call it? When a split-second decision changes the course of your life.

If I hadn't stayed longer, I wouldn't have been introduced to my colleague's dark-haired friend, who arrived late as he'd just flown in from California. That one drink wouldn't have turned into several and he wouldn't have asked for my number. I wouldn't have refused because I'd just come out of another short-lived relationship and sworn off men. He wouldn't have punched his number into my phone, and I wouldn't have laughed and thought, "I like this man."

Instead I would have left the bar and gone home to bed, and life would have gone on as before.

But it did happen. And the next day I did something very unlike me.

I called him.

In the beginning Ethan made me laugh a lot. He wrote funny emails and told me quirky, self-deprecating stories about life as a chef when we would FaceTime. He had an odd way of looking at life, like he was seeing it through a completely different lens to everyone else. Yet he was uniquely observant. He saw things in people they didn't see themselves. He saw things in me.

It's a powerful thing, feeling like you're understood without ever having to explain. To have that connection. I once read some-where that the reason two people come together is to feel like they're not alone. Not physically, but emotionally. That's how I felt when I fell in love with Ethan. Like a part of me that I'd kept hidden from everyone else was being reflected back at me. That finally, after all those bad dates and wrong men and relationships that didn't work out, I'd found someone who *got* me.

But a lot can happen in five years. You can go from feeling glo-riously happy to feeling like you're never going to be happy again. From believing you're in this together to discovering that you're in this alone. From that delicious tingle of anticipation as the hand-some stranger in the bar types his details into your phone to a cafe on a random rainy day, as you press edit and scroll down the screen until there it is, at the bottom, in red: *Delete Contact.*

Five years of moments shared and memories made, of a lifetime you thought you were going to spend together, and with one press of your thumb—click—they're gone.

I'm grateful for:
1. *Wonderful memories, even though I can't help wishing it was just as easy to delete them from my heart.*
2. *Arthur's fur to bury my face into, as it soaks up all my tears.*
3. *No longer getting that annoying "storage almost full" mes-sage, as a result of deleting all the photos of Ethan on my phone. Proof that there is always a silver lining, no matter how shitty things may seem.*

MARCH
#easterbunnybombshell

Question and Answer

I wake up to three missed calls and a new voicemail from Michelle about babysitting. Blearily, I squint at the time. It's not even 8 a.m.

"Nell! Where are you? I've been trying to get hold of you for hours!"

I'm still in bed, I'm about to say, when I call her back to re-assure her that no, I haven't forgotten about babysitting, and yes, I'll be there at six forty-five on the dot. But after listening to the long list of all the tasks she's already completed before breakfast, I decide against it.

It's not just Michelle who's keen to tell me how busy she is; we're all at it. It's like there's this new competition to see who can be the busiest. "How are you?" "Crazy busy!" "Me too! Absolutely manic!" Conversations are spent comparing hectic schedules and reeling off endless to-do lists, but mostly we just text because, seriously, who has time for an actual conversation?

What I want to know is, when did busy become better? When did a jam-packed diary become a measure of success? And does that mean I'm failing because, since losing everything, I'm currently *not* that rushed off my feet, but lying in bed thinking about Max's birthday and wondering how on earth one of my friends can be turning fifty? *Fifty.* How is this even *possible*? Fifty is your dad's age. It's the age of the politician on the news with the terrible comb-over and bad taste in ties.

It's MIDDLE-AGED! (And I mean *really* middle-aged, not just *feeling* middle-aged.)

It is not, I repeat, not someone you went inter-railing around Europe with the summer you were eighteen, sleeping on beaches because you spent all your youth-hostel money on straw-bottomed bottles of Chianti that you swigged on the Spanish Steps at midnight, thinking "life doesn't get better than this."

Actually, I'm not sure life does get better than that. I can afford nicer wine now, but nothing tastes as good as that cheap Chianti did. And, despite spending a fortune on a Tempur-Pedic mattress and Hungarian goose-down duvet when I lived in California, the best sleep I've ever had was in my moth-eaten sleeping bag on the sand.

So what's the answer?

I have no idea. Truly, I really do not know what the answer is, to this and many of the other big questions life seems to be throwing at me right now. But I do know I need to get up, make some coffee, and do some work on this week's obituary—life of a freelancer and all that—then walk Arthur. I'll think about it tonight when I'm babysitting and all the children are tucked up in bed. I'll have plenty of time then to sit on the sofa watching TV and thinking about life. When I'm not so busy. Ha.

The Surprise

What on earth was I thinking? It's after midnight and they're STILL refusing to go to bed! This is a nightmare. I can barely hear myself think over the screaming and yelling. As for sitting on the sofa, er, hello. I've just spent the last five hours running up and down the stairs after children.

I'm exhausted. Broken, in fact. Not only that, but they've turned from being adorable five- and six-year-olds, with cute, old-fashioned flowery names like Rosie and Lily, into monsters who demand Disney movies and throw slime everywhere. Even sweet, darling

Freddy, who, last year when I babysat, curled up in the crook of my arm and told me he wanted to marry me, has turned gangsta and is insisting he's allowed to stay up and watch *Peaky Blinders* until "the olds" come home.

Freddy is ten.

Meanwhile, I feel about a hundred. I haven't eaten. I have slime in my hair. My ears are ringing. The takeaway I ordered has gone cold as I was too busy—God, that word again—corralling three children into the bathroom. Little did I know then of the horror that an innocent phrase like "clean your teeth" could create. I turned my back for two minutes and there was toothpaste everywhere. The bathroom mirror looks like a Jackson Pollock.

I call Mum in desperation. "Just be firm," she advises, after I wake her up. "Don't take no for an answer. Children need to know who's boss."

Right. OK. This is ridiculous. I've hiked down the Grand Canyon. I've negotiated the freeways in Los Angeles. I've given a speech at my granddad's funeral in front of a packed congregation. Surely I can get three small children into their bunk beds?

So I get tough and march them upstairs to bed, despite the wails and howls of protestation. No longer am I fun godmother. I'm horrid godmother. They hate me. Lily even kicks me. As soon as I get them into bed and go downstairs, they get out again and I have to march them back upstairs. Up, down. Up, down. I don't feel like the boss. I feel like the frigging Grand Old Duke of York.

In the middle of it all, my phone beeps. It's Michelle, texting to make sure everything's OK.

Absolutely fine! Children fast asleep and I'm watching TV ☺

Of course, it is all a complete lie. It's chaos over here. Total anarchy. But I don't want to spoil Max's birthday. Or admit I've completely failed at my bedtime duties. Maybe there's a reason I'm not a mum: I'd be rubbish at it.

Finally, after resorting to bribery (Lily and Rosie get five each, Freddy gets ten, and there was me remembering when I used to be the one getting paid for babysitting, not the other way around), I get them all into bed, and by the time I've cleaned up the bathroom they've fallen asleep and I flop face down on the sofa.

Just in time to hear the key in the door.

I sit bolt upright and pretend to be idly flicking through an interiors magazine featuring gorgeous homes (to rub salt in the wounds) as Max and Michelle appear, laughing and giddy after their night out. Max is drunk and collapses on the sofa next to me, while Michelle announces, "This baby is pressing on my bladder!" and nips upstairs to the bathroom.

"So, I guess you were in on the secret?" Max grins drunkenly as she disappears.

Already jabbing with relief at my Uber app, I'm not really listening. "What secret?"

"The surprise party."

I look up from my iPhone. *A surprise party?*

"But I thought you were having dinner? Just the two of you." My voice sounds a bit strangled.

"Me too. Nudge nudge, wink wink, eh?" He laughs, tapping his nose and trying to wink, but closing both eyes instead. "Thanks for babysitting for us, Nell . . . really appreciate it . . . such a good friend . . ."

Then his head rolls, and he's fast asleep.

I'm grateful for:
1. *A slime-free bedroom, in which to collapse exhausted, bruised and starving, and covered in stickers.*
2. *Being child-free, so I can spend tomorrow busy sleeping until noon.*
3. *Having the maturity and wisdom not to feel hurt or annoyed that I wasn't invited to the party, but to accept it with good grace and understanding.*

WhatsApp Chat with Fiona

I can't believe what happened at the weekend!

Who is this?

Nell!

Is that not Fiona???

Sorry yes, haven't got my glasses

Hang on, reading

Ooh! Did you meet someone?!

No! ☹

Michelle asked me to babysit as it was
Max's birthday and guess what?

What?

Afterward I found out she'd thrown a
surprise birthday party for him!

Yes, I know

And I wasn't invited!!

Wait

How do you know?

Fiona is typing

Are you still there?

Fiona is typing

Fiona???

We went on Saturday.

What?? I'm calling you right now

Missed voice call at 09:28

You're not answering!

I'm in Pies and Lattes

Where??

PILATES
Sorry. Autocorrect

Who else was there?

Just a few friends . . .

Did Holly and Adam go?

Yes.

I can't ducking believe it
DUCKING
Argh.
Why didn't Michelle invite me??!!

It wasn't Michelle who arranged it.

What?

It was Annabel.

Annabel!

Fiona is typing

Michelle asked me for a restaurant recommendation,
so I asked Annabel as she knows all the trendy places.
She suggested this great new Mexican place and
knew the owners, so she made the reservation . . .

Fiona is typing

It was her idea to invite a few of their friends along
as a surprise. I thought it was a great idea! You
know how Max loves a party. And he was fifty!

I can't believe I missed it. ☹

She said she invited you, but you never replied to her email.

What email?

I gave her everyone's email address.
Maybe yours went to your junk?

Hang on, I'll look.
No.

How strange!

                                 Yes, very.

I should have mentioned it, but when you said
you were babysitting for Max and Michelle,
I just assumed you knew all about it.
What a shame.

                                        Yes

Annabel will be really upset when I tell
her you never got the invitation

                                        I bet

She's so sweet and generous, she even picked up the
entire bill as her birthday present! Max couldn't believe it.

                              That's so nice of her.

Look, better go. The teacher is giving me
the dead eye. Let's speak later.
xxx

                                        XX

I'm grateful for:
1. *Keeping my cool.*
2. *Not calling Annabel a total cow.*
3. *Pies and lattes. No, really. That is not autocorrect.*

The Fear

It's waiting for me when I wake up. Like a school bully, lurking in the corridor, ready to pounce. I can sense it before I even open my eyes, its tight fists tying up my stomach in knots and heavy boots pressing down on my chest.

It's been a while since it last paid me a visit. I was at home, in bed, next to Ethan. He was sleeping soundly, but I'd never been more wide awake. California was in the grip of a heat wave, and despite a fan, the room was hot and claustrophobic. I lay naked in the darkness listening to him breathing. Trying, but failing, to find comfort in its steady rhythm. It was a year ago today. I remember, as it was the day we'd been to the hospital.

That time it beat me up pretty badly, leaving me feeling bruised and battered for weeks. I didn't tell anyone, least of all Ethan. It was hard to describe my attacker when I didn't know what it was. Worse, I felt ashamed I couldn't fight it off. I blamed myself for being weak and pathetic. It was all my fault.

Some people might name this bully Anxiety or Depression. Others label it a Panic Attack. While many describe it as the famous Black Dog that you can't chase away. But I simply call it The Fear. A nameless terror that scares the living daylights out of me. Because it's not like feeling a bit down because you're broke, or fed up because it's March and still constant gray skies.

The Fear paralyzes you. It grips you by the throat so you can't breathe and makes your heart thump loud and fast in your ears. It makes you feel like you're going to die and part of you wants to. That's why it's so horrible. Because after it's finished beating you up, you beat yourself up even more. It's your dirty little secret, and I've kept mine for years.

I was a freshman at university when I first met The Fear. I remember being on a high, excited about leaving home for the first time, so it came as a shock to find a terrifying monster waiting for me when I arrived. Lurking in the shadows after lectures. Preparing to pounce late at night in the halls of residence.

I was too scared to tell my parents. I didn't want to worry them or admit what was happening. Instead I tried to ignore it, and after a while it must have got bored and gone to pick on some other poor soul. I didn't see it again until years afterward, when it paid me a surprise visit at work and I tried to hide from it in the ladies', crying. Now, most of the time it leaves me alone.

Until today.

I lie here for a few moments, willing it to go away. I'd hoped that by moving back to London I could leave it behind, with no forwarding address. But now it's found me and it's not giving up without a fight. *But neither am I.* Summoning my courage, I throw back my duvet. Because if there's one thing I do know, it's that you must never give in to a bully. And The Fear is the very worst kind.

I'm grateful for:
1. *Strong coffee, the love of a dog, and a sense of humor that never abandons me, even on the scariest of days.*
2. *Knowing that tomorrow's another day.*

Big Little Brother

It's Mother's Day tomorrow—in the UK it's earlier than in the US—so I text my little brother Rich to remind him to call Mum. Instead he calls me.

"Oh shit, I forgot."

"I know."

"How did you know?" he accuses.

"Because you forget every year."

"Did you send her a card?"

"Yes."

He groans.

"And some flowers," I can't help adding.

I hold the phone away from my ear as he groans even louder. He does this every year. Even when I lived in America and had to deal with the godawful post and trying to ring the local florist at the crack of dawn because of the time difference, every year I send a card and flowers. And every year he conveniently "forgets."

"Did you say they were from me too?" he whimpers, despite knowing full well that I always put his name on the note that accompanies the flowers. For Mum's sake, not his.

"Sis?" he says doubtfully when I don't reply.

I toy with the idea of letting him suffer this time, then give in. "Of course."

"I knew you would have done," he says cheerfully, and I can hear him grinning down the phone. "So are you coming up for Easter?"

My heart sinks a little. Easter. Another family holiday when everyone gets together with their other half and children, whereas I get to go home to my parents' to sleep in my old bedroom by myself.

"I don't know yet. Are you?"

"Yes. I'm bringing Nathalie."

"Who's Nathalie?"

"My girlfriend!" He sounds hurt.

"I thought she was called Rachel."

"We broke up. She was crazy."

"Why do men always say their ex-girlfriends are crazy?"

"Maybe because they are—"

"So does that mean Ethan's going to say I'm crazy?"

"Total nut job," he quips, before realizing that I might not actually find that as funny as he does. "Nell, I'm sorry . . . about what happened with Ethan. Mum's told me the wedding's off."

"She's dying to find out all the details."

"I know, it's killing her," he replies, and I can tell he's smiling on the other end of the phone. At least our parents are something we always agree on.

"But he was a bit of a dickhead, let's be honest."

"I thought you liked him?" I say, shocked.

"Well, I had to say that, you were marrying the guy."

"You said he was fun."

"He was. But fun's not the same as nice, is it?"

I fall quiet, thinking about Ethan, how he was always so charming and funny on the outside, but only I got to see the person behind the jokes.

"Maybe you're right," I admit, probably for the first time in my life.

"Crikey, you feeling all right?" He laughs, and I laugh too, but to be honest, I'm not entirely sure anymore.

Mother's Day

I always think life's a bit like an obstacle course. As soon as you've gotten through one, there's always another waiting, and recently it seems to be in the shape of yet another Hallmark holiday to remind me of what I don't have.

Last month it was Valentine's Day; this month it's the turn of Mother's Day, and I wake up to find my socials awash with bouquets of flowers, breakfast-in-bed trays, and cute handmade glitter-glue cards, all of which are lovely but make me feel a bit left out and less than.

Even if I have a sneaking suspicion there's glitter glue all over the sofas, and a lot of panicked dads wondering how to entertain the kids while grateful Mummy gets a well-deserved lie-in.

To cheer myself up, I call my own mum, who's thrilled with her flowers. "Like I said to Richard, you really shouldn't have," she chirps happily down the phone, and I try not to feel a familiar annoying niggle that my brother has been on the phone already, taking all the credit. It's not a competition, I have to remind myself.

"Did you get my card?"

"No, when did you send it?"

"Last week. Damn. It must have got lost in the mail."

"Oh, well never mind," she soothes, before adding, "I got Richard's."

"You *did*?"

"Yes, he sent me one of those animated ones online. It was really clever and, like he said, so much better for the environment. Less waste."

I am going to kill my baby brother.

"So are you coming up for Easter, or are you too busy with work?"

I feel a stab of guilt. I still haven't been to visit my parents. I've been finding excuses not to go. Not because I don't want to see them, but because I haven't wanted to face the barrage of questions from Mum, and Dad's kind concern, which will annoy me and make me cry in equal measure.

"Well, that's the thing . . ." I begin.

"Because I just wanted to check as we've had lots of inquiries on Airbnb."

My guilt swiftly evaporates. "You want to rent out my room?" And there was me thinking this was about wanting to see her daughter.

"Well, Easter is one of our busiest times," she replies, then proceeds to tell me about the elderly couple from Zurich that she's struck up quite a friendship with on email: ". . . and when I told her I was a fan of Andrea Bocelli, she said he's performing there in September and they have two spare tickets!"

Mum's voice is breathless with excitement.

"So I thought, if you're not coming—"

"Of course I'm coming," I interrupt, before my room is booked.

"Oh, great!" she enthuses, but I swear I can detect a flicker of disappointment. Mum's had a crush on Andrea Bocelli for years. "It'll be lovely to have all the family together again. It's been forever."

It was last summer. Ethan and I flew over to celebrate Mum's seventieth. Richard and I threw her a surprise party. Well, I organized the party; Richard supplied the craft beer. All our friends and family came, and I wore a new dress and spent the evening proudly showing off Ethan and my ring, putting paid to a few of my older relatives' whispers about my sexuality ("well, she does live in America, you know . . .").

We hired a DJ to play all Mum's favorites, and I remember leaving Ethan to go to the bathroom and coming back to my parents dancing to Frankie Valli and the Four Seasons. Dad knew all the words to "Can't Take My Eyes Off You," and Mum was laughing and blushing. I remember watching them and feeling proud at everything they had created together—even my gormless brother who'd drunk too much of his own beer and passed out in the rosebushes—and wanting that too.

But when I glanced across the room at Ethan, something inside me just knew we'd never get there.

Six months later I moved out.

I chat to Mum a bit longer, before we say goodbye. Afterward she sends me a photo of her bouquet. It's beautiful. As are all the Mother's Day flowers and cards and presents my friends post pictures of. But it does make me wonder a bit, about where I fit in.

I mean, if I'm not a member of the Mummy Club, what club am I in?

"You need to start your own club," suggests Cricket cheerfully, clutching the brim of her purple fedora as we turn a corner and it's nearly whipped away by a sharp blast of easterly wind. "I'll be your first member."

It's later that afternoon and we're heading down the main street, carrying a blue IKEA bag brimming with books between us. I'd called her after getting off the phone with Mum. I knew she, unlike the rest of my friends, wouldn't be busy celebrating the day with her husband and children and, with her own mother having died some years ago, I thought today might be hard for her.

She was delighted to hear from me, not because of the day's significance, but because she had discovered "a few" library books

Monty never returned, and needed a hand taking them back. Most libraries were closed on a Sunday, but this one was open.

"Are we nearly there yet?" I adjust my grip on the handle, which is cutting into the palm of my hand. Unlike Cricket, I am not wearing lined leather gloves—"a present from Harrods."

"Not much further."

"This thing weighs a ton!" I glance across at Cricket. She might be twice my age, yet she's got the kind of old-fashioned stamina that doesn't come from any kind of gym, but rather from the school of not complaining and just getting on with it.

"Here we are!" She comes to a halt outside a Victorian red-brick building. Steps lead up to the entrance and we put the bag down on the sidewalk to catch our breath.

"I thought you said it was just a few books?" Heaving a sigh of relief, I flex my fingers gratefully.

"Well, that's the thing, you see. Monty never fully understood the basic principle that when you borrow a book from the library, you are supposed to return it."

"You don't say." I look down at the bag, which holds enough volumes to stack a reasonably sized bookcase. "Most of them are hardbacks," I note.

"He didn't like paperbacks. He always said he liked the feel of a hardback book in his hands."

"Well, he does have a point," I agree, bending down and picking one up. It feels valuable, and not in the monetary sense. "I've got a Kindle, but it's just not the same. I miss my books. I left most of them behind in America . . . it was just too expensive to ship them over." I run my thumb over the edges of the pages. "I left a lot behind in America," I add as an afterthought.

Cricket gives me a sympathetic look and I force a smile. Cricket has a lot more to feel sad about than I do. If she can remain cheerful through all of this, then so can I.

"You know, Monty brought me here on our first date," she says, looking up at the building.

"What? To the library?"

"He said I should meet his first love; he thought I should know what I was up against."

I stand up, listening. "Surely you don't mean your friend Cissy?"

Cricket looks amused. "Trust me, I did wonder. I remember him taking me by the hand as we climbed the staircase and me thinking what on earth . . . ? When we finally reached the second floor, he took me into the far corner, by a row of arched windows, and introduced me to his beloved Shakespeare. A whole bookcase, filled with his work—"

She breaks off, remembering.

"He came here since he was a small boy, when his parents were too poor to afford books. This is where his dream began, to one day grow up and be a famous playwright."

Together, we both stare up at the grand facade. I wonder how many other people have walked through its doors over the years. How many other stories it has inspired.

As my eyes fall, my attention is caught by a notice erected outside. I step forward, then frown. "Have you read this?"

She squints and shakes her head. "I haven't got my reading glasses. What does it say?"

"That the library's closing . . . Something about redevelopment."

Cricket's face drops. "So it's finally happening . . . there was talk of it being turned into luxury apartments. I know Monty was very upset. He said the community needs a library, it doesn't need apartments no one can afford."

"Is there nothing anyone can do?"

"There was a local petition to try and save it, but the council said it had to make cuts."

I give her arm a squeeze through her thick winter coat, and for a moment we both fall silent.

"OK, so shall we go and return these?" I say after a beat.

"I've got my checkbook at the ready." She pats her handbag with a rueful smile.

We reach for a handle each, and hoist the bag up between us. "Oof! It's like carrying a dead body," I exclaim loudly.

Oh no—did I just say—

I look at Cricket, horrified. And she looks at me. Then together we burst out laughing.

The librarian lets Cricket off with a slap on the wrist and her heart-felt sympathies: everyone loved Monty and he's sadly missed. She points to where he used to sit, tucked away at the desk in the corner.

It's not the same without him, she says.

No, it's not, says Cricket.

I hang back, not wanting to intrude, pretending to be interested in a book about engineering. A young guy with headphones and a laptop sits down at Monty's desk, oblivious to the widow watching him from across the room. Life moves on. It has to. And yet . . .

And yet how can the world keep on turning, business as usual, without them in it? As time moves on, the further away you become from the last moment you saw them. They retreat into your past as you travel into the future. The distance between you growing as their voice fades and the memories blur.

"I've joined an art class. Do you want to come along?"

I snap back. Am I thinking about Monty, or Ethan?

"Thanks, but I can't draw."

"Nonsense. Everyone can draw."

We turn to leave and begin descending the staircase toward the exit.

"No, seriously, I really can't."

"Didn't you ever learn there's no such word as can't?"

I used to hate it when teachers would say that and I open my mouth to protest—then I pause. After all, I've got nothing else to do.

Reaching the ground floor, I push open the door and we walk out onto the street. "OK, but I can't be long. I need to get home to feed Arthur."

Rule number one: Always have a get-out clause.

Cricket pauses and turns to me. "Thank you."

"You haven't seen me draw yet." I smile.

"I'm not talking about the class. I mean, up there. In the library." She looks back at the building. "It was harder than I thought. You being there meant I wasn't alone."

"Oh, it was nothing."

"No, it was everything."

Turning to me again, her eyes meet mine. "I was joking when I said start your own club, but there's a lot of truth in that . . . You know, I was always something of an outsider growing up. I had a very conservative upbringing, but I was allergic to conformity. My parents sent me to Catholic school but I never felt like I belonged. I didn't believe in God, not their God anyway. I had friends, but I didn't fit in . . ."

She pauses, remembering.

"Then by chance I discovered the theater and found I wasn't alone. That there were people in the world who were just like me. Strange, weird, wonderful people. People who inspired and challenged me. People who understood me . . . And do you want to know the best part?"

I nod, listening.

"I finally found myself . . . and in doing so, I found a different kind of faith . . . Does that make sense?"

I look across at Cricket, a woman twice my age, and feel a sudden sense of connection. "Yes. It makes perfect sense."

She smiles, the well-worn creases around her eyes making her face come alive.

"What I'm trying to say is, you need to find your own people, Nell."

I'm grateful for:
1. *All the amazing mums out there doing an incredible job, including my own wonderful mum, who has sacrificed so much for me; not just free Andrea Bocelli tickets.*

2. *All those mothering in other ways, by caring, supporting, and loving.*
3. *A widow in her eighties, for showing me that you can find your tribe in the most unexpected of places.*
4. *Getting through today.*

The Naked Truth

When you get to my age, you start to think that there's nothing left in life that can surprise you. I mean, you've seen it all, right?

Wrong. I was so very, *very* wrong.

Yesterday, after the library, Cricket and I got an Uber to her art class. The art school was inside an old warehouse with large arched windows and a black metal fire escape that spidered its way down the side of the building. It smelled of turpentine and paint. Overhead, fluorescent strip lighting led the way. I had no idea what to expect.

"Why, hello again."

But it certainly wasn't bumping into Hot Dad.

"Oh . . . hi!" It took me a moment to place him.

"Aren't you going to introduce me?" chimed Cricket.

"Sorry, yes, this is Cricket," I said, before realizing that I had no idea of his real name.

"Johnny." He smiled, saving my embarrassment.

"A pleasure," she said, extending a hand, and I could have sworn she was flirting. "Are you here for the class?"

"Yes, I'll see you in there. I've just got a few things to do first." He motioned to the bathroom.

"OK, great," I said, for want of something better to say. "See you in there."

Of course, Cricket wanted to know all about him. So, after speaking to the teacher about joining the class and finding a spare seat behind the easels, I told her everything I knew. Which wasn't very much, but it was enough to distract me from the chaise longue in the middle of the room, until it suddenly dawned on me.

"You didn't tell me it's a life drawing class," I hissed.

"You didn't ask." She shrugged.

I looked around for Johnny, but he must have still been in the bathroom. I searched a few faces, looking for a conspirator, but everyone was being very serious and earnest behind their easels. Teenage giggles threatened to surface.

No one ever tells you that when you're younger, do they? That inside all those boring-looking old people there still beats a teenage heart that finds the same things funny.

I picked up a pencil and tried to compose myself; I was being immature. It was only a naked body. Then the model walked in and I couldn't believe it.

Oh my God, it was Johnny. It was the Hot Dad!

We locked eyes, then he dropped his robe.

"*And?*" Liza stares at me, goggle-eyed, from my laptop screen.

"Well, I didn't know where to look."

"Are you kidding me? I'd know where to look!"

It's 2 a.m. and, unable to sleep, I'm FaceTiming Liza. Sometimes there are advantages to an eight-hour time difference.

I laugh, reliving the moment he removed his robe and reclined, naked, on the chaise longue. Talk about avoiding eye contact.

"So, he's a life model?"

"Apparently he does it part-time."

Afterward, I tried to hurry Cricket out of the building, as I was too embarrassed to know what to say if I bumped into him *with his clothes on*, but she'd already got the information from the art teacher.

"So what does he do the rest of the time?"

"I don't know. I wasn't asking questions. I was too busy sketching his penis."

Liza snorts with laughter. It's like we're back in LA, catching up over coffee. Only the blue sky and sunshine in the background of her window reminds me there's five thousand miles between us.

"Well, all I can say is lucky you. I haven't seen a naked body in a while."

"What about Brad?"

"We broke up."

"*Again?*"

"It's for good this time."

She's said it before, but something makes me believe her now.

"I'm sorry."

"No, you're not."

"OK, you're right, I'm not," I admit. "Still. Are you OK?"

"At this moment, yeah." She nods. "It's all good." Then she smiles. "What about you?"

I pause and think about it, and for once my mind doesn't flick sadly into the past or race fearfully into the future. It stays right where it is.

"Yeah." I nod. "At this moment, it's all good."

I'm grateful for:
1. *Getting a lot more than a handmade glitter-glue card and breakfast in bed. #nakedhotdad*
2. *Friends like Liza, for reminding me to stay in the moment, because the moment is all we ever really have.*

Let There Be Light

Edward is still going on about the dishwasher and the heating. But now he's added a third complaint: leaving the lights on.

"I don't understand why you can't turn the light off when you leave the room," he complains, switching the light off in the hallway as he follows me into the kitchen.

"Because I might go back in it."

Edward frowns at this piece of logic.

"What do you think the on/off switch is for?"

I ignore him. "I like leaving lamps on."

"I've noticed. So must have all the neighbors. As I cycled home down the street the house was lit up like a Christmas tree."

My jaw sets as I grab the kettle to make a cup of tea. "I don't like being in a dark house." Turning on the tap, I fill it up noisily.

"But you can only be in one room at once," he argues exasperatedly.

"Tea?"

"Yes, please."

I switch on the kettle, then grab two mugs from the shelf and throw in two tea bags. I dare him to say anything about using a teapot and only one bag.

"It's spooky."

"*Spooky?*" He looks at me like I'm bananas. "How on earth can a living room be spooky?"

"Haven't you seen all those true-life murders on TV? They always seem to happen in your own home."

"And leaving a lamp on is going to save you?"

He stares at me across the countertop, scraping his hair back to stop it falling in his eyes. I notice it's grown quite long.

"I'd see the intruder."

"Then what? You'd hit him over the head with it?"

"Well, it worked for Colonel Mustard with the candlestick."

He cracks a smile. Finally.

"Are you really telling me you're scared in the house alone?" he says, softening.

"No, not really," I admit, getting the milk from the fridge. "Especially not with Arthur. I just like the lights on, that's all.

I mean, there's not always a logical reason for everything, is there?"

I glance at Edward but, judging by his puzzled expression, it's obvious the concept is new to him. The kettle boils and clicks off and I fill up the mugs, before putting it back on its stand.

"And that's another thing."

Oh no, what now? I mash the tea bags against the sides of the mugs.

"Can you please switch off the kettle after use."

"It is switched off."

"No, at the wall. It consumes energy and wastes money. And it's better for the environment."

"Edward, it's a kettle." I put milk in the tea and pass him a mug.

"Every little bit counts. It's the same with all the kitchen appliances," he continues, going around the kitchen with his tea, flicking switches.

"Because the digital clock must be really adding to our carbon footprint," I say as he turns off the microwave.

He shoots me a look, but I swear I saw a flash of amusement in his eyes.

"Anyway, about Easter."

Not him as well. Everyone is going on about Easter.

"What are we going to do about Arthur?"

"I'm going to my parents'."

"Can you take him with you?"

I'm about to say yes, then think about his constant complaints about the heating and the dishwasher and the lighting, and feel a twinge of stubbornness.

"Actually no, I can't. You'll have to take him."

"But you said you would look after him on the weekends."

"It's a bank holiday. It's different."

Edward and I appear to have gotten ourselves embroiled in a dog custody battle. We face each other across the kitchen counter, mugs in hand.

"Don't your sons want to see Arthur? Surely they must miss him."

Edward looks suddenly uncomfortable. "They do, but it's just very difficult."

And now I feel bad. It must be really hard for Edward, with Arthur and his wife's allergies and everything. "OK, Arthur can come with me."

He smiles then. "Thank you."

"No problem."

Taking my tea, I walk out of the room, remembering to switch the light off as I leave.

"Hey!"

As he calls after me in the darkness, I smile to myself.

Feeling Inspired

Embrace your new life! Don't look back! Every day is another chance to change your life! When nothing is certain everything is possible!

Who doesn't love a daily affirmation? Especially when it's written in vintage typewriter font and given a filter. Though to be honest, the more people post inspirational quotes, the more I worry about them.

Here are a few of mine today:

```
Embrace a freezing cold house!
Don't kill your landlord!
Every day is another chance to watch
Grand Designs and realize that the couple
building their amazing architect-designed
eco house on the side of a mountain are al-
most half your age!
```

```
When nothing is certain, everything can go
tits up!
```

But my favorite has to be:

```
Embrace your sense of humor, don't ever take
yourself too seriously, every day is another
chance to laugh instead of cry, and when
nothing is certain, everything is a hell of
a lot less scary when you make fun of it.
Amen.
```

Good Friday

As I walk into Euston station to catch the train to my parents', I'm determined that today is indeed going to be a good day. I'm going to have a lovely Easter with my family. Mum and I are going to have lots of mother–daughter bonding conversations that don't involve my breakup or other people's grandchildren. My brother is not going to annoy me. Dad will buy me an Easter egg. It's going to be fab.

In theory.

Greeted by the bank holiday chaos, Arthur and I have to push our way through the crowds and onto the train to Carlisle. Luckily we get our seats, but my heart sinks when I realize I've accidentally booked us a table. Whoever designed those tables obviously envisaged a utopian scene of strangers sharing their space with their neighbors. Not being pinned to the window by a businessman's elbow, huge laptop, and charger that stretches its tangled wires all over me, and opposite a young couple who like gazing into each other's eyes while he brushes invisible hairs from her face.

Meanwhile, I'm getting texts from Fiona who's having a lovely time in the Cotswolds. She and David have taken the children on their first camping trip, though judging by the photos of the rain-forest shower, white feather beds, and hay bales round a firepit, it's a slightly different experience to the soggy anoraks and baked beans welded to the frying pan that were my childhood camping trips.

I glance out of the window. Outside, the city has given way to countryside. I look at my watch—still hours to go—and stick in my headphones. I've downloaded a new podcast Cricket has been raving about and, resting my head against the window, I press play.

After a couple of train changes, we pull into the station. It's raining and there's a mist rolling in from the fells. I rub a hole in the condensation on the window and peer out. California suddenly seems so far, far away. It's hard to believe it even exists. That somewhere, on the other side of the planet, Ethan is waking up and pulling up the shades on our bedroom window, looking out at blue skies and desert sunshine. It feels like one of those old movies where the screen splits. Him on one side, me on the other.

Oh, *Sod This*.

As my mind starts wandering down a very dangerous path, I snatch up my wheelie bag and Arthur's lead and clamber out onto the platform. Constant blue skies and sunshine are totally over-rated. And as for all that desert heat, it's horribly aging.

As the horizontal rain hits me full blast, I march determinedly to the exit. Give me fresh air and the English countryside any day. So what if I'm soaked to the skin already? Or that poor Arthur just nearly got blown onto the train tracks? This is wonderful. I am so blessed. There are not enough hashtags in the world to say how much I am embracing my new and fabulous life.

Dad's waiting for me outside in his old Land Rover, engine running.

"Hello, love."

"Hi Dad."

We greet each other as if we only saw each other yesterday, as is the northern way. A quick hug. Not too much fuss. But my heart swells to see him.

"You didn't mention you were bringing this one," he says, motioning to Arthur who's already jumped in the back. "Your mother will have a fit about her carpets."

"I know."

We both look at each other and break into a grin.

"Well, at least it stops me being in the doghouse." He laughs, holding the door open for me as I climb inside. The seats are all split and it smells of muddy boots, rolling tobacco, and topping soil. I fill my lungs with it.

Then we're rattling and jolting our way home along winding lanes. Past scenery that is as magnificent as it is familiar. The Lake District is just as I left it. Not much changes here, except the seasons. Funny, I used to hate that when I was younger; now it comforts me.

"So—how've you been?"

Terrible. Awful. Heartbroken. Terrified.

"All right." I shrug.

The windshield wipers creak backward and forward, clearing just one small triangle for Dad to peer through. My side isn't working. I can't remember it ever working. I glance across at Dad. At his strong hands on the steering wheel. Dad has big, capable hands. I remember now that I never liked Ethan's small, slim fingers.

"How are you for money?"

"Fine, thanks," I fib. I'm just about managing to get by. The obituaries aren't paying a huge amount, and Dad's loan won't last forever. Still, it's only March. It's early days.

"It's good to see you, Dad."

"You too, love." Glancing across at me, he takes one hand off the steering wheel and gives my knee a gentle squeeze. "It's good to have my little girl home again."

*

As soon as I walk into the kitchen, Mum promptly tells me I've lost weight, puts the kettle on, and shoves the biscuit tin under my nose.

"Take two," she instructs. "There's nothing of you."

"Mum, there's plenty of me," I protest, but she ignores me and pushes a packet of digestives at me.

Then she shrieks at the sight of Arthur, who's been sniffing outside in the garden and makes his entrance, bounding into the kitchen, muddy paws and all.

"This is Arthur," I say, grabbing him by his collar before he goes for the biscuit tin.

"You've got a dog?"

"He's my landlord's. It's a long story."

Hair is flying everywhere. I can already see muddy footprints on Mum's newly washed kitchen floor. I quickly herd Arthur into the hallway, from where I can hear loud whispers in the kitchen—"I mean, I ask you, Philip. A dog! And a great big dirty hairy one too!"—while Dad tries to placate her. A few moments later, he appears in the hallway.

"Just keep him away from the lemon meringue," he warns. "It's your brother's favorite, she made it specially."

"Is Rich here?"

"Not yet. Some last-minute business cropped up."

I feel a niggle. Code for he's slept in late, no doubt.

"I'm going to the community garden. Why don't you and your mum have a chat? I know she's dying for a proper catch-up."

"In other words, she wants to ask me a million questions," I grumble.

"Now then, go easy on her, she means no harm. She's concerned, that's all. It was a bit of a shock."

"I didn't want to worry you."

"We're your parents. That's our job."

"I'm sorry."

And now I feel bad. I'm taking it out on Mum. It's not her fault.

"What're you sorry for?"

"Everything. I know Mum was really looking forward to the wedding."

"Don't be daft." He smiles, ruffling my hair. "It doesn't matter. We just want you to be happy."

"Nell?" Mum pops her head out of the kitchen. "The kettle's boiled."

I hesitate. I'm trying not to dwell upon the fact that my next visit home was supposed to be as a newlywed with Ethan in the summer. We were planning to have a small ceremony in California, just family and friends, then tour the British Isles as part of our honeymoon. My insides twist.

"Actually, I think I'm going to take Arthur out for a walk." Mum's face falls, but I can't help it. I'm just not ready yet.

"OK, well don't be late. Dinner's ready soon."

Luckily the rain has stopped and I walk along the river, throwing sticks for Arthur, who plunges into the icy water as if it's a warm bath, then loop back through the village. On returning to the house I find a shiny new car in the drive and my little brother, feet up on the coffee table, eating a large slice of lemon meringue pie while Mum fusses around him.

"Hello, Rich."

"Nell." He grins, but doesn't get up.

"Is that your new car in the drive?"

"Yes, I just got it. Do you like it? I couldn't decide between an Audi or BMW, so I went for a Range Rover."

"Wow, you must be selling a lot of beer."

"We're inundated with orders, we can't keep up with demand." He smiles.

"Now don't you go working too hard," warns Mum, smoothing down his hair. "You need to keep your strength up."

He nods dutifully. "Mmm, delicious pie, Mum . . . any more?"

She beams proudly as he eats the last mouthful. "Well, dinner's nearly ready," she protests weakly, before taking his plate from him and disappearing into the kitchen.

"Only a little one," he calls after her, from the comfort of the sofa. "Don't want to spoil my appetite."

He catches my look.

"What?" he protests as I jab him with my foot. He yelps loudly. Way too loudly.

Mum quickly reappears with another giant slice of lemon meringue. "Now, you two, stop it."

"She started it," he whines, and I glare at him.

This is going to be one very long weekend.

We're interrupted by the sound of footsteps on the ceiling and a bedroom door opening.

"I thought Dad was at his garden—" I stop midsentence as a pretty brunette appears in the doorway of the living room.

"Everything fine for you, love?" Mum asks her.

"Yes, thank you." She smiles. "Just freshening up."

So this must be Nathalie, my brother's new girlfriend. "Hi." I smile. "I'm Nell, Richard's sister."

"Rich has told me all about you." She smiles nervously.

"I'm not sure I like the sound of that." I grin, catching my brother's eye. "Still, in that case it's my turn to tell you all about him—" I begin, but he hits me with a cushion.

The front door slams. Dad's back. It's Mum's cue. As he washes his hands, she ushers us into the tiny dining room that's laid for dinner. I notice she's used her best silverware, and instead of the usual kitchen roll plonked in the middle of the table, there are napkins.

A large fish pie, browned on top, is placed on the table together with bowls of steaming vegetables. Mum does not do small portions. Meanwhile, Dad gets the wine out of the fridge and begins filling everyone's glasses.

"What shall we raise a toast to?" he asks, when he's finished pouring.

"To the family being all back together," says Mum.

"And to your mother's fish pie," he adds, as we all raise our glasses.

"Oh Philip, honestly," she tuts, but I can tell she's pleased really.

The toasts over, I go to take a large gulp of wine, but my brother gets up from his chair and starts tapping his knife against the rim of his glass.

"Actually, there's something else."

I glance up at him, expecting some kind of joke, but his expression is deadly serious. He clears his throat. I suddenly realize my brother is nervous.

"Nathalie and I have a bit of an announcement."

Mum visibly vibrates.

You *are* kidding. It's been, what? Three months?

But Nathalie, who until now, I realize, has had her cardigan sleeves pulled down over her fingers, suddenly reveals her left hand. A diamond solitaire sparkles.

There's a scream from Mum as she jumps up and begins throwing her arms around Richard and Nathalie. "Oh, is it true? You're getting married! Oh, this is wonderful," and there's a flurry of congratulations and lots of backslapping from Dad.

Slightly stunned, I watch for a moment from the sidelines. And then it's my turn and I'm giving them both hugs and congratulations. OK, so it's a little quick, but they seem very happy, and I'm happy for them, of course I am. I catch Dad's eye. He smiles supportively. I swear I couldn't be more thrilled.

"But there's more news!"

Seriously, I'm doing really well up until he drops The Bombshell.

So my baby brother is going to be a daddy. I still can't quite believe it. I mean, I'm pleased for them, really I am, and Mum and Dad looked so happy. Their first grandchild and all that. It's just—lying in my old bedroom, I feel a stab of such sadness I break down in tears in the darkness.

I let them fall, burying my head into my pillow, until I feel a wet tongue on my hand and turn on the light to see Arthur standing beside the bed, his sad eyes searching out mine.

"Hey boy, I'm OK, really, I'm OK," I soothe, patting his furry head and feeling comforted until finally, satisfied, he returns to his blanket in the corner.

I pick up my book to read, but I feel unsettled. I can't concentrate. My phone beeps. It's a text from Holly and Adam in Spain, wishing me a happy Easter. I text back, then scroll through my feeds as a distraction, but just looking at all those perfect lives makes me feel even more lonely and inadequate. Of course I know it's all heavily filtered and edited, but I'm yet to find the filter that can turn my old bedroom into a four-bedroom house in the country, or Arthur into a loving husband.

Instead I go to grab my headphones to listen to a podcast, and as I do I notice the little sign on the bedside table, telling me the Wi-Fi code and thanking me for not smoking.

And suddenly something snaps. Oh, screw designer picture walls and oufits and gorgeous Pinterest houses. Stuff all those white sandy beaches and yoga poses and sunset strolls with the handsome husband. I'm sorry but I've had enough.

My headphones are all tangled up and I start unpicking them, any sadness I felt giving way to frustration.

Someone needs to do the antidote. Someone needs to tell it how it really is when shit happens and life doesn't work out how you expected. When your life doesn't look anything like any of that. I give up trying to untangle my headphones and just stick in one earpiece. I hit the podcast app on my phone. Seriously, someone should do a podcast about feeling like a forty-something fuck up.

Actually . . .

About to press play, I pause. *That's not a bad idea.*

I'm grateful for:
1. *My lovely dad who gave me my Easter egg, proving that chocolate really is the silver lining at Easter.*

2. *My podcast idea. Tomorrow I'm going to look online and find out what I need to do to get it started. So what if no one listens? I need to get things off my chest.*
3. *The gift that is my new niece or nephew, for whom I'm going to be the coolest auntie.*
4. *The Wi-Fi code and not smoking.*

APRIL

#whosthefool?

April 1

OK, so I have a confession. I'm not really single, broke, and over forty, back at my parents' in my old bedroom with only a flatulent dog for company, eating the stale, broken remnants of my Easter egg for breakfast and feeling like I am really *not* winning at this thing called life.

God, no. I'm actually happily married and living in a lovely big house with my gorgeous husband and two adorable children, excelling in my career, having an amazing sex life, exercising regularly, practicing mindfulness, wearing fashionable outfits of the day, and finding time in my busy schedule to post them on Instagram, while green juicing daily and remembering to breathe.

Because of course, breathing is quite important.

And last, but certainly not least: Being Happy All of the Fucking Time.

April Fool!!!

I'm grateful for:
1. *My sense of humor.*
2. *My brother being too busy getting married and having a baby to want to play a "hilarious" prank on me, which in previous years has invariably led to him accusing me of "not seeing the funny side" and me wanting to kill him.*
3. *Panorama's spaghetti-tree harvest, which has to be the best April Fool ever and brings a whole new meaning to fake news.*
4. *Chocolate. Did I mention chocolate?*

Easter Monday

When my brother and I were children, our favorite game was Rock-Paper-Scissors. We would play it for hours. The rules are very simple, so simple that apparently in Japan scientists have taught chimpanzees to play it (not that I think chimpanzees are stupid—on the contrary, I think they're smarter than a lot of humans, but that's a whole other discussion).

In case you've been living under a rock (no pun intended), this is a game where each player simultaneously makes one of three shapes with an outstretched hand: "rock" (a fist), "paper" (a flat hand), and "scissors" (a fist with two fingers extended). A simple rule determines the winner: "Rock breaks scissors, scissors cut paper, paper covers rock." If both players choose the same sign, it's a tie.

Why am I telling you all this?

Because you can apply the same rules to life; only now it's not rocks, paper, and scissors, it's a wedding and a baby and a broken engagement. And it's no longer a game of chance. On the contrary. In the Rock-Paper-Scissors of life, an impending wedding and new baby trumps a broken engagement every time. It's unbeatable. Which means my brother has emerged as the clear winner.

And I'm the loser.

On the plus side, no one is asking me any questions about my breakup from Ethan. In fact, since Rich's announcement Mum seems to have forgotten about it entirely. Instead she's consumed with excitement about the new baby and the wedding. When she's not fussing around Nathalie or ferrying cups of tea up and down the stairs to my brother, who is holed up in the bedroom "busy working to a deadline" (which apparently involves sharing videos on Facebook), she's proudly telling everyone she's going to be mother of the groom *and* a grandmother.

Including the cold caller who rang asking if she wanted to claim compensation for an injury and was forced to hang up, instead of the other way around. So you see, there are lots of positives.

But seriously, joking aside, the truth is I couldn't be more relieved to have the spotlight taken off me. The last thing I want is to rake over the coals of my failed relationship and do a Q&A with my family on What Went Wrong. That said, I lived in California long enough to know that's *exactly* what I should be doing: opening up and talking about it. Any good therapist will tell you it's the key to recovery, and how only then will you begin the healing process that will allow you to truly move on.

But I just don't want to. For these few days back home, all I want to do is forget about it all and curl up next to Dad on the sofa, my head resting against his scratchy woolly sweatered shoulder. I want to eat too many Easter eggs, drink too many cups of sugary tea, and be too hot for the first time since I left California, as Mum has taken control of the thermostat and the house is like a sauna.

And I want to almost die laughing when we get out the old family albums at breakfast to show Nathalie and uncover photographic evidence of the time I stole Mum's makeup bag and covered my little brother in silver eye shadow and lip gloss.

"No way! Richard, is that you?" shrieks Nathalie, staring goggle-eyed at the photo.

Rich goes bright red. "It wasn't my idea," he grumbles.

"You loved it!" I protest. "You begged for more blusher!"

Nathalie snorts with laughter and pounces delightedly on another photo in the album. "What are you doing here?"

"Oh, that's when our Nell was desperate for a dog but we wouldn't let her have one." Dad grins, appearing fresh from his morning shower and peering over her shoulder.

"She made Rich a pair of ears and a tail, and led him around the living room with the belt from my robe."

"He used to follow Nell around like a puppy dog for hours,"

chimes in Mum, passing Dad a mug of tea as he sits down at the dining room table.

Rich glowers and continues buttering a slice of toast. For someone who prides himself on being a "bit of a joker," he hates it when the joke's on him.

"Oh, c'mon babe, we're only teasing." Nathalie smiles, reaching for his hand and squeezing his fingers. When my brother's not happy, he has a tendency to sulk, and nothing anyone says can snap him out of it.

"My bark was always worse than my bite." He smiles contritely, giving her a kiss.

I watch them across the table. If I wasn't sure about Nathalie before, I am now. It's like she has the key to my brother that none of us could ever find.

As Mum goes into the kitchen to make more tea, Dad reaches for another album. "Look at my moustache." He laughs, pointing at a picture of him and me standing in the driveway next to his old estate car, which is filled to the brim with cardboard boxes.

"Never mind your moustache, look at my big hair!" I gasp, peering at the photograph. I almost don't recognize the skinny girl in black leggings and an oversize sweater, wearing too much makeup and an excited smile to mask her nerves.

"When was that taken?"

"The day I left for university."

I gaze at my eighteen-year-old self and it's like looking at a different person. Staring defiantly into the lens and a future that lies ahead of her, she thinks she knows everything when, in fact, she knows nothing at all. I feel affection and an overwhelming protectiveness toward her.

"Any toast left?"

I snap back to see Dad waving the butter knife around like a conductor.

"Oh sorry, I took the last of it. Mum said you were just having muesli," says Rich, finishing off a large buttery slice.

Mum has recently put herself and Dad on a healthy eating regime, as there was an article about it in "one of her magazines." My mother's magazines are famous in our family, and the reason for our wallpaper borders, macramé plant hangers, and a city break to Amsterdam where my father smoked a "funny cigarette" and fell off his bicycle, narrowly missing a canal.

Which apparently was *not* on the recommended tourist list of "things to do."

Dad's face falls. "How's a man supposed to do a day's work on hamster food?" he grumbles, glaring at the box of muesli sitting on the table as if it's actually attacking him.

"That hamster food is good for your cholesterol!"

My mother's ears are like an elephant's, and she shouts from the kitchen. We do this a lot in our house: shouting at each other from different rooms. It's our family's way of communicating. Why speak to each other when you're in the same room, when you can wait until the person goes into another one then start yelling through the door?

"And you're not doing a day of work, you're retired."

My mother returns brandishing the teapot, resplendent in its new hand-knitted orange mohair cozy. Which had been in July's issue.

"I'll have you know I work harder down in that community garden than I ever did at the council." Draining his mug of tea, Dad gets up from his chair. "Right, well, if anyone wants me that's where I'll be."

"On an empty stomach?" Mum looks flustered as he gives her a quick peck on the cheek. "And what about your packed lunch?"

But he's already halfway out of the door with his coat on.

"Don't worry about me, love. I'll be fine."

At which point the expression on Mum's face changes from worried concern for her husband to a sudden realization. "Philip Stevens! Don't you dare be getting a bacon sandwich from The Walkers Cafe—"

The door slams behind him.

"Honestly, your father!" With an exasperated gasp, she puts the teapot on the table. "He'll be the death of me."

"Not yet, we need you to babysit," quips Richard.

She brightens immediately and once again the conversation turns to the new baby. Now the shock has worn off, I couldn't be happier for Rich. Nathalie is lovely and Mum is just so thrilled. It's still very early days—the baby's not due until November—but they couldn't wait to share their news.

I sit and listen for a few moments, looking at their happy, excited expressions, but there's only so long you can put a brave face on things and I make my excuses and leave. They don't notice me go.

They say America has big skies, but the Lake District's are as vast and spectacular as anything I've seen. Brooding with cloud, they form a dramatic canopy as I head out into the bracing wind blasting down from the fells.

Despite the freezing temperatures, it feels good to be outside. Wrapped up in several layers, I set off walking at a pace, Arthur scampering beside me, excited by the new smells. Along the way I pass several of the locals, many of whom I've known since I was a child, and I smile and nod and wave.

The village prides itself on being a community, but with summer fetes and bunting comes a total lack of anonymity. Everyone knows everyone's business. I'm Carol and Philip's weird daughter, the one who moved to London then to America and still isn't married with children. Rumor has it she's a vegan.

Dad's garden is down by the river, next to the twelfth-century church it officially belongs to. The vicar gave it to my dad years ago, in exchange for tidying it up. It used to be just a patch of land filled with junk, but now Dad grows vegetables and keeps his hives there. He took up beekeeping when he retired, saying he wanted to help with climate change and protect their species, though I have a suspicion it was less to do with climate change and more to do with getting out of Mum's way.

"I brought you your packed lunch from Mum."

I find him sitting in a deck chair next to his potting shed, reading the paper. A bacon sandwich wrapper from the local cafe lies next to him. He looks up when he hears me.

"Mum'd kill you if she knew."

He smiles. "Let that be our little secret." Scrunching it up, he chucks it in the oil drum along with the rest of the garden waste, ready to be burned.

I grin and hand the lunch over. He immediately unscrews the thermos. "Tea?"

"Yes, please."

I sit down next to him on a deck chair as he pours out two steaming mugs and hands me one. Then, for a few minutes, we just sit there, sipping the hot liquid, warming our hands on the mugs, and looking out over his garden as Arthur lies at our feet. Nobody says anything. Nobody has to.

That's one of the things I love most about my dad, the ability to just be in his presence and never feel the pressure to say anything at all. There's never any awkwardness or need to explain, to talk about emotions, or to ask and answer questions. Ours is a comfortable silence and there're so few people you can find that with. In relationships we're taught to be afraid of what happens when there's nothing left to say, like I was with Ethan. But the truth is, if you're with the right person, you don't need to say anything.

Several minutes go by. We drink more tea. Dad scratches Arthur's ears. Several magpies dip and swoop. I try not to count them.

"How are your bees?" I say finally, my eyes falling on his hives at the bottom of the garden.

"Hibernating. They won't be doing much until it gets a bit warmer. Bit like me really." He slips a KitKat out of his pocket and slides his thumbnail down the middle of the silver wrapper. "Though I've got a shed full of bulbs and seeds that need planting. Don't suppose you fancy giving me a hand?" He holds out a chocolate bar.

"Are you trying to bribe me?"

"Never," he says, his face poker straight.

Smiling, I accept his bribe and enjoy the combination of hot tea and melted chocolate as he disappears inside his shed. Several minutes later he reappears with an assortment of bulbs and packets of seeds and sets off across his garden.

"This way," he calls, as Arthur and I follow him, picking our way between the neat rows of canes. "Right, this'll do." He hands me a trowel and a handful of bulbs. "Make sure to place them with their nose facing upward."

"Nose?" I look at him doubtfully, but he's already dropped to his knees.

"You know, their shoots."

Truthfully, no, I don't know anything about their shoots, or noses, or planting bulbs. Dad's gardened his whole life, but when I was in my teens and twenties I never took any interest. I used to think gardening was for old people. Only now I *am* that old person. I look at the damp soil beneath my feet. I'm wearing my only clean pair of trousers. I hesitate, then drop down next to him.

"Plant them about eight inches deep and six inches apart, like this."

"What are they?"

"Gladioli. Your mother's favorite. They bloom just in time for her birthday."

"But that's not until August."

"Everybody wants things to happen yesterday—nature's not like that."

Side by side, we start to plant them. His hands are dirty with the soil, and we work together silently, methodically. When we're finished, we move over to an empty vegetable patch and he hands me various packets of seeds.

"Zucchini, peas, and beetroot . . . sow them in rows. Make sure they're buried nice and deep."

I shake the seeds out into my palm. "It's hard to believe these will go from this—to this," I marvel, looking at the tiny, dried-up specks in my hand and the photo of a large, plump zucchini on the packet. "It seems impossible."

"Nature teaches you to have patience and faith. Life's just a cycle, you know. Things might seem dead, but they always come back to life . . ."

My eyes meet Dad's pale gray ones, half hidden under his shaggy eyebrows. We're not talking about gardening anymore.

"Remember that, love. When life buries us under all its heartache and disappointment, think about a seed. It needs to be buried in order for it to grow. That's how the magic happens. But you have to have faith. Remember that. Patience and faith."

I'm grateful for:
1. *The local vet, for saving Arthur after he went on his own Easter egg hunt this evening and wolfed down all the chocolate that the local kids in the village didn't find.*
2. *Celebrities, for sharing photos of their much-needed Easter breaks in the Maldives and telling us that to be happy we need to #stopscrolling and buy their new products #linkinbio, which reminded me to order the microphone for my new podcast and #tellitlikeitis.*
3. *Dad, for being the one man I can always rely on to be there for me.*
4. *Being a seed.*

My First Confession

Back in London and my microphone arrived today. Feeling very BBC newsreader, I set it up on my desk and do a bit of testing, testing, one-two-three.

So, after doing some research, it turns out starting your own podcast is really simple, even for someone like me who still hasn't figured out how to use Siri, and steadfastly ignores all those software update notifications that nag me even more than my own mother. I just had to download a free app, choose a name, then record my first episode. Easy!

Now I just have to think of a name. I frown at my screen. This is the hardest bit. I've been sitting here for ages trying to think of something really clever and witty, and I can't think of anything. I need to come up with a title that's cool, stylish, confident, hip—

Basically everything that I am completely not.

Oh *Sod This*, I'm just going to call it what it is.

Clearing my throat, I take a swig from my can of G&T to steady my nerves. I suddenly feel absurdly nervous. Which is ridiculous. It's not as if anyone is ever really going to listen to this. It's just me getting things off my chest.

I tap the microphone.

OK, well here goes. I'm not sure where to start so I'm just going to dive straight in . . . I press record.

"*Hi and welcome to* Confessions of a Forty-Something F**k Up, *the podcast for any woman who wonders how the hell she got here, and why life isn't* quite *how she imagined it was going to be.*"

Nervously, I clear my throat.

"*It's for anyone who has ever looked around at their life and thought this was never part of The Plan. Who has ever felt like they dropped a ball, or missed a boat, and is still desperately trying to figure it all out while everyone around them is making gluten-free brownies.*"

Or maybe I'm the only one that feels this way? Maybe this is just my truth? I break off, suddenly plagued by doubts, but carry on.

"*But first a disclaimer: I don't pretend to be an expert in any-*

thing. *I'm not a lifestyle guru, or an influencer, whatever that is, and I'm not here to sell a brand. Or flog a product. Or tell you what you should be doing, because frankly, I haven't a clue either. I'm just someone struggling to recognize their messy life in a world of perfect Instagram ones and feeling like a bit of a fuck up. Even worse, a forty-something fuck up. Someone who reads a life-affirming quote and feels exhausted, not inspired. Who isn't trying to achieve new goals, or set more challenges, because life is enough of a challenge as it is. And who does not feel #blessed and #winningatlife but mostly #noideawhatthefuckIamdoing and #canIgoogleit?"*

I swallow hard, feeling my confidence growing. *Sod This.* If I'm the only one that feels like this, so be it. I'm getting it out there.

"Which is why I started this podcast . . . to tell it like it is, for me anyway. Because Confessions *is a show about the daily trials and tribulations of what it feels like to find yourself on the wrong side of forty, only to discover things haven't worked out how you expected. It's about what happens when shit happens and still being able to laugh in the face of it all. It's about being honest and telling the truth. About friendship and love and disappointment. About asking the big questions and not getting any of the answers. About starting over, when you thought you would be finished already."*

I'm on a bit of a roll now.

"In these episodes, which will take the form of confessions, I'll be sharing with you all the sad bits and the funny bits. I'll be talking about feeling flawed and confused and lonely and scared, about finding hope and joy in the unlikeliest of places, and how no amount of celebrity cookbooks and smashed avocados are going to save you.

Because feeling like a fuck up isn't about being *a failure, it's about* being made to feel like one. *It's the pressure and the panic to tick all the boxes and reach all the goals . . . and what happens when you don't. When you find yourself on the outside. Because on some level, in some aspect of your life, it's so easy to feel like you're failing when everyone around you appears to be succeeding."*

I pause, my heart thumping.

"So if there's anyone out there that feels any of this too, this podcast will hopefully make you feel less alone."

I take a deep breath.

"Because now there's two of us. And two of us makes a tribe."

Let It Snow

Nature is a lot like life. Just when I was thinking we'd finally seen off the worst of winter and I could retire my fuzzy sweaters (which are now more fuzz and less sweater) and we were smooth sailing into spring, it throws you a curveball.

It snows.

I wake up a few days after returning from the Lake District and pull up the blinds to discover that the street is covered in a fluffy blanket of white. Thick, heavy snowflakes are cartwheeling past the windowpane and landing softly on the sidewalk, and for a few moments I stand transfixed at the window, feeling a surge of childish delight.

After shoving in some burnt toast and a few gulps of coffee, I head outside with Arthur, who immediately bounds excitedly into the powder snow. There's something so magical about a city when it first snows. *So romantic*, I reflect wistfully, as a couple stop to take a selfie, like two figures in a snow globe.

As we cross the village green, which has now turned to white, I hear squeals of delight, and see children in snow boots and bobble hats being pulled on sleds and throwing snowballs. School must be canceled. As Arthur stops to sniff, I notice a little girl making a snow angel. She is flapping her arms delightedly while her mum is taking a photo.

I look down at Arthur. "Shall we take a snow selfie?"

Cocking his leg, he turns the snow yellow. On second thought, perhaps not.

We head toward the park, and I stick in my headphones to listen to a podcast—I'm doing research for my own and have discovered some I really enjoy—when suddenly I feel like Arthur when he sees a squirrel. I stop dead in my tracks and my whole body goes tense. HOT DAD ALERT. I spot him across the street. *Johnny.* He's wearing a beanie and drinking a take-out coffee. He looks cute.

Meanwhile I'm wearing Edward's creosote-covered wellies, my garden-trash-bag jacket, and one glove. I do not look cute. OK, just keep walking. Hopefully he won't see me. I put my head down and focus on Arthur, tugging on his lead as he slows down to sniff someone's gatepost. I don't want another episode of shit-gate. Which reminds me, I never went back for my other glove—

"Hello again."

I look up and he's right there, on the sidewalk in front of me.

"Er, hi . . . hello!" I smile cheerfully, yanking out my headphones.

Why is it you always bump into someone when you look terrible *and never* when you've had a blow-dry? It's like some horrible cosmic law.

"I didn't know if you'd recognize me with my clothes on."

I can't think of a single witty thing to say.

"I'm joking." He laughs.

"Oh right, yes, of course."

You'd think by my age I'd be a flirting pro. After all, I've had a lifetime of experience when it comes to men. Good *and* bad. Yet, faced with a man I find very attractive, I don't feel much different to how I did at thirteen when I had a crush on the paperboy.

"Hi, Arthur."

Arthur wags his tail as Hot Dad bends down to pat him. I take the opportunity to glance at his hands and play ring detective, but he's got his gloves on again.

"So how did you enjoy the class?"

In hindsight, I had the perfect opportunity to look at his hands in the art class, but let's just say I was too distracted by other things.

"It was great!"

Was that a bit too enthusiastic? He was naked, remember.

"Really interesting," I try to clarify, "the stuff about perspective . . ."

And now I can feel myself veering off into dangerous territory. There must be some rule for never talking about perspective when it's a man's penis in question.

"That's good. I know some people get really embarrassed."

"Really?" I feign surprise.

"Yeah, you know, *some people*." He pulls a face.

I tut and roll my eyes. "Oh, I know. Honestly, *some people*. They can be so immature."

"And narrow-minded." He nods.

"I know, right?" I say, agreeing. "Not me. I'm so open-minded. When you get to my age you've seen it all."

"So nothing shocks you, huh?" He smiles and does this sort of wink that would have made my younger self think he was flirting, and my forty-something self wonder if it's less of a wink and more of a squint as his eyes "are going." A phrase that my whole life I've never really paid attention to, but in recent years has entered the vocabulary of my girlfriends and is now bandied about with a certain resigned dread.

"Not much." I laugh, though I'm not quite sure how this image of me fits with one of me at home with my electric blanket on a Friday night watching Netflix.

"Anyway, I was hoping I'd see you—"

"You were?" My stomach leaps a little.

"Yeah." He nods. "I've got something for you."

"*You have?*" My mind flashes back and forth. What on earth can it be?

He begins fishing around in the pocket of his jacket. "I've been carrying it around for a while now . . ." He pulls something out. It's black and sparkly.

Abruptly it dawns on me with horror. *Please* don't let him be holding what I think he's holding.

"I noticed the last time I saw you, that you were wearing just one . . . so when I recognized this, I put two and two together . . . and made a pair." He holds it out toward me, smiling.

"My glove," I say weakly.

"Don't worry, it's been washed."

My glittery shittery glove.

"Thanks." Mortified, I take it from him hurriedly. "I wondered where I'd lost it . . ." Forcing a cheerful smile, I put it on and give him a little jazz hands wave. "I can't imagine where it went."

"It was on my sister's driveway."

Kill. Me. Now.

"Wow, that was lucky!"

"I know, right? I was dropping my nephew off and I spotted it behind the recycling bins."

"Your nephew?"

"Oliver. You met him in the pub—he fell in love with King Arthur."

"That's your nephew?" Suddenly, all thoughts of my glove are forgotten. "But I thought—"

"He was my son?" He laughs. "I know. It's the McCreary genes. No, I'm just the fun uncle."

"I see." I smile, but I'm still taking in this new turn of events.

"So, anyway . . ." He trails off and for a moment the conversation stalls. "Glad you got your glove back."

"Oh . . . yes, thanks." I don't even want to *begin* to think who washed it. Or that it must have been his brother-in-law watching me from the window. "Well, I'd better be going."

I tug Arthur who, having grown bored of waiting, is circling ominously around in the snow. He looks up at me with the same disgruntled expression as my father when we knock on the bathroom door, needing to use the toilet. Well, he will go in there with the Sunday papers.

"Maybe see you again at the art class?"

"Yeah, maybe."

And, giving him a wave of my glove, I set off dragging Arthur down the sidewalk.

I'm grateful for:
1. *Hindsight, because it has the ability to transform things that seemed absolutely mortifying at the time into something absolutely hysterical with Liza several hours later.*
2. *The unexpected joy that came from bounding around with Arthur in the snow, though his snow angels are a bit crap as they're basically just him rolling about in fox poo.*
3. *Years of snowball practice with my little brother, so that when I was caught in the cross fire between the local teenagers on my street, I knew how to whack a really hard frozen one back.*
4. *Edward's bicycle helmet, which saved him from concussion as he cycled home; my aim was never my strong point.*
5. *The ability to laugh at myself, which, unlike my eyesight, isn't going anywhere.*
6. *More material for my podcast, which, when I listened back to it the other day, was a bit cringe—it sounds nothing like the real me, but instead like me trying to sound posh on the telephone.*
7. *The revelation that Married Hot Dad is now Single Fun Uncle.*

Going, Going, Gone

Bumping into Johnny yesterday got me thinking. It seems that at this age, lots of things "are going." If it's not eyes, it's upper arms . . . or knees . . . or necks . . . It's like being in an auction, only the lots aren't a nice mahogany dresser or a pair of silver candlesticks; they're parts of my body. Soon everything will be going, going, GONE!

Though to where, I have no idea. But you can guarantee it's sure as hell not to somewhere fun like Ibiza or the South of France, which are the only places I want to be going, frankly.

WhatsApp Group:
Michelle's Baby Shower

Fiona
Just a reminder everyone, it's at 1 p.m. tomorrow, looking forward to seeing you all.

Holly
Me too, see you soon.

Remind me again of the address.

Holly immediately sends a Google Map complete with directions.

Thx. Is that a restaurant?

Annabel
No, it's my house.

She just pops up from out of nowhere. WTF? Annabel is in our WhatsApp group?!

Fiona
Wait till you see her house, ladies, it's amazing!

Annabel
Don't forget to bring your swimsuits, ladies!

Sometimes in life there are no words.

The Baby Shower

To be honest, I wasn't much looking forward to the baby shower in the first place. I went to quite a few when I lived in America, and whenever I found myself in a circle of women playing "Guess the Poo" with melted chocolate bars and diapers, I was forever grateful this was one tradition we hadn't adopted in the UK.

But like I said, a lot's changed since I've been gone.

It's not just the inane games; it's the pressure to buy the best present, even though I can never help feeling a bit superstitious about buying a gift before the baby is born. Then there's the celebrated diaper cake, a tradition I'm hoping has stayed firmly on that side of the Atlantic, and the endless talk about pregnancy and babies. Which is natural, of course—it *is* a baby shower, after all—but if you don't have one or want one, it's hard not to feel a bit alienated.

Discovering yesterday that Perfect Annabel is throwing the shower at her house is the icing on the proverbial diaper cake. Of course I want to celebrate Michelle having a baby and see her looking all happy and excited and being spoiled rotten. I love Michelle. She's one of my best friends. But when you're child-free/-less, and all the other women are either pregnant or mums, it can be agony in more ways than one.*

Thankfully the snow has melted, so I can wear something that doesn't involve wellingtons. I was planning to wear jeans and a jacket, but now I feel extra pressure and put on heels and my one decent dress. I even attempt the curling iron on my hair, which as always ends with

---

* Disclaimer: Not all baby showers are awful. I went to one for a work colleague in upstate New York that was a really lovely celebration; no gifts or games were allowed, but instead we got to make pizzas and wishes for the baby, which we wrote on scraps of paper and threw into the firepit where they were carried as sparks into the future. And yes, I know it all sounds a bit hippy-dippy, but it really was as lovely and hippy-dippy as it sounds.

bangs that flick the wrong way and burned fingers, even with that little glove they give you.

Still, by the end of it all, I look quite presentable. So much so that Arthur barks when I come downstairs. I don't think he quite recognizes me.

I catch the bus, then the tube to the nearest station, then walk the rest of the way, but it's a lot farther than it looked on Google Maps and there's a wind blowing. I can feel my curls rapidly dropping, along with my spirits. And then, suddenly, there's the house. Sitting directly on the river and surrounded by a large walled garden, like something you see in the pages of *House & Garden*.

I press the shiny brass intercom and try not to feel intimidated. Like my mother always says, I wouldn't want to clean all those windows. Plus, so what if she lives in this fancy big house and I'm renting a room? Money doesn't buy you happiness, remember?

It does, however, buy you several fancy cars parked on the gravel forecourt, a heated outdoor swimming pool, and a turret. *An actual turret*, I note, as I'm buzzed in and the electric gate closes behind me. I walk up the driveway, the gravel crunching underfoot. There's something about the sound that just sounds rich. It reminds me of visits to stately homes. That said, it's terrible when you're wearing heels.

Tutting loudly in dismay as I scuff my beloved pair of Gucci stilettos, which I got on eBay after a frantic bidding war, I reach the glossy front door. I'm greeted by pink balloons and a lovely lady called Mila, who ushers me inside the mosaic-tiled hallway and kindly offers to take my coat.

Then she disappears, and for a moment I find myself alone. I'm almost tempted to make a run for it.

"Nell, welcome." Annabel appears, tanned and barefoot, in a frothy pink concoction of a dress that shows off her sensational figure and makes me feel hideously underdressed. "So wonderful you could make it."

I smile tightly. "Well, I actually got this invitation."

"That's so strange, I definitely sent one for Max's birthday."

"Yes, isn't it? Still, I wouldn't have been able to come. I was babysitting."

"Yes, so I heard. What a trooper friend you are. Missing a fabulous party like that."

Now I know who Annabel reminds me of: Villanelle from *Killing Eve*.

After asking me to take off my shoes, so I feel short and dumpy next to her in my stockinged feet, she leads me through the house to join the others. It's everything I expected. Cushions are plumped. Walls are painted in tasteful shades of Farrow & Ball. Expensive pieces of art are dotted about. It's quite evident Annabel is not someone who has ever shopped for bags of tea lights from IKEA.

Until finally I'm ushered into the living room, where there's a mountain of gifts on display and even more pink balloons, and a large circle of women hovering around a table filled with food. Everything is pink-themed. Annabel has really gone to town.

"Here, let me take those for you," she says, reaching out for my gifts.

I hand over both bags. As well as something for the baby, I've brought the special kind of chocolate-covered marshmallow teacakes that Michelle adores. Max told me she used to eat them as a child growing up in Scotland and can never find them here, but I managed to hunt them down. I feel rather pleased with myself.

Annabel lets out a little shriek as she sees them. "Ooh no, I don't think so," she reprimands, wagging her finger. "Far too many additives and processed baddies. Only nutritious wholesome foods welcome here. I'll put them in the kitchen, out of harm's way."

"But they're Michelle's favorite," I try to argue weakly, but I'm quickly shot down.

"It's very important to eat a healthy diet, especially when you're pregnant. Try a quinoa cupcake with cashew coconut cream frosting."

As she offers me a tray from the table, I force a smile. I have to get along with Annabel, not just for Fiona's sake, but now for Michelle's too.

"Mmm, looks delicious," I say politely, taking one.

Wow. That's some cupcake. It weighs a ton.

A couple of waiters are wafting around serving drinks. "Raspberry smoothies or pink champagne," coos Annabel, "for those of us who aren't pregnant or breastfeeding. All organic, of course."

Of course.

I grab a glass of much-needed alcohol and search around for a familiar face. I'm looking forward to seeing everyone. I haven't seen Holly since my birthday and the last time I saw Fiona she was with Annabel, so it was difficult to have a proper catch-up. Obviously Annabel is here again today, but hopefully she'll be so busy being the host I won't have to talk to her too much.

That said, I can't see Holly or Fiona and Michelle is talking to someone, so I make polite conversation about the quinoa cupcakes with a woman called Susan who's having a loft conversion done to make room for her "growing brood," and Lisa, a newlywed who's six months pregnant with her first and taking a hypnobirthing course.

"How about you?" asks Susan brightly. "Do you have kids?"

As the spotlight swings onto me, I feel my heart sink. I hate this bit. It always feels like such a taboo subject if you say no. No one quite knows how to reply. People don't know whether to be sympathetic or make some quip about how lucky you are and complain about their moody teenagers. Conversely, I never know what to say either as I always feel the pressure to explain why I don't have kids, in a way I'm not sure women who have children do. Basically it's awkward for everyone, so I usually end up trying to make a joke about it so everyone feels *less* awkward.

Except today I'm not feeling very funny.

"No." I smile, struggling to think of something suitably positive to add to qualify my answer. I quickly rootle through the contents of my life's handbag, like when I'm searching for my keys. But all that's in there is a broken engagement, a business that went bust, and a recent move back to London to share a bathroom with a complete stranger.

"I write obituaries."

Well, it's the only thing I can find.

Susan and Lisa sort of freeze, before lots of polite murmuring of, "Oh, how lovely," and, "Have you tried one of the zucchini fritters? They're delicious."

"There you are!"

Several fritters later, I feel a hand on my shoulder and turn to see Fiona.

"Sorry, I was in the bathroom." She smiles, giving me a hug and saving me from another zucchini fritter. "How are you?"

"Happy to see you!" Finally I have a comrade in arms to laugh with about the giant scary-looking flesh-colored balloon baby and the lead-weight cupcakes. "I see you've been coerced." I grin, noticing she's holding one.

"Aren't these just delicious? I've had three! Have you tried one of the cute deviled eggs that look like babies? And the fruit bowl, with the carved melon that looks like a buggy. So adorable!"

I stare at her, agog. What's happened to Fiona? Normally she wouldn't be able to keep a straight face.

"And isn't her house just amazing? Do you know that's a real Andy Warhol! And she got her sofas imported from Italy. She's got such amazing taste. Perfect. Don't you think?"

She's actually gushing.

"Umm, yes, it's lovely."

"Everything Annabel does is just effortless. I'm going to get her to look at my house and give me some interior design tips."

"Your house is lovely already. You don't need any tips."

"Oh, you are sweet, Nell, but Annabel says it's important to keep things fresh and on-trend . . ."

I dread to think what Annabel would say if she ever saw my rented room.

Fortunately, at that moment Holly appears, looking like she's come straight from the gym. Holly is one of the few women I know who wears activewear to actually be active and not just to go to the supermarket.

"Sorry I'm late." She smiles, making a beeline for us. "I had to get in 10K this morning. What did I miss?"

"A tour of the house and one of these." I put a cupcake in the palm of her hand, and it visibly drops.

"Wow, that's a lot of fiber."

"Just in time. Ladies! Time for the gift giving!" We're interrupted by Annabel clapping her hands and demanding we all sit around in a circle. Michelle looks overwhelmed and embarrassed by so many presents, and we all drink champagne (or is that just me?) and ooh and aah over tiny onesies.

Then it's my turn. I gave up trying to think of something unique and all the cashmere stuff was so expensive, so instead I've bought her a cute little stuffed rabbit and some of my favorite body cream.

"Oops, you forgot to take off the price sticker." Annabel swoops on it in the guise of being helpful, and peels it off with her perfectly manicured nail. "Gosh, I didn't know TK Maxx do this brand."

My cheeks flame.

Michelle smiles graciously. "They're both lovely, thanks Nell."

I smile. Things have been a bit awkward between us since I found out about Max's birthday, and we haven't had a chance to talk yet.

"And, last but not least . . ." Annabel wheels in a large, elaborately wrapped present.

"Oh, you shouldn't have, this is far too generous—"

"Nonsense!" Annabel beams as Michelle self-consciously unwraps an ornate, hand-carved crib, painted pastel pink and covered in matching pink bows. "Fiona and I saw it at Easter when we were in this gorgeous little boutique in the Cotswolds, and I knew you'd love it."

"I thought you were camping?" I turn to Fiona.

"The crystals on the bows are Swarovski," interrupts Annabel.

"We went with Annabel and Clive to their cottage."

"Oh, OK." I nod, but I feel oddly upset.

I quickly get a hold of myself. Why does it matter if she didn't mention it? It's no big deal. She can spend time with whoever she wants.

"Did you have a nice time at your mum and dad's?"

Normally I would have told Fiona immediately about Rich, but something stops me.

"Yes, great." I nod. "The best."

I make my excuses and disappear to the bathroom. When I come out, I can hear Annabel suggesting everyone take a dip in the heated pool. I make myself scarce and seek sanctuary in the huge empty kitchen, where I discover the chocolate-covered teacakes. Standing in the darkened room, I unwrap one and am just leaning against the oven, dipping my tongue into the sweet jammy center and plotting my escape, when I hear footsteps.

Oh shit. *Annabel.* I stuff the teacakes back behind the kettle and turn around, bracing myself.

"I wondered where you'd run off to."

It's Michelle.

I feel a beat of relief. "Sorry to be a party pooper."

"That makes two of us." She rubs her belly. "I am *not* getting into a swimsuit. I've still got two months to go, but if I jump in there'll be no water left."

I laugh and we both smile.

"I'm sorry about the birthday mix-up," she says after a moment.

"Oh, it's fine." I bat her apology away.

"No, it's not fine. I'd be pretty pissed off if I'd been stuck with my three while everyone was at a party."

"They were great, honestly—"

She raises an eyebrow.

"Just a bit of a handful at bedtime."

"Don't you mean the spawn of the devil?"

I grin. "Well, I wouldn't go that far . . ."

"You know, I had no idea Annabel was going to throw Max a surprise party. I thought it was going to be just the two of us . . . to be honest, I would have preferred it if it was. What with the kids and Max's new promotion, we never get the chance to spend any time alone together."

Listening, I get the feeling Annabel steamrolled Michelle into it.

"I mean, it was really kind of her and everything—it's the same with this baby shower. At Max's birthday I mentioned I'd never had one with my previous three, and she immediately offered to throw one for me. I tried to say no—she's Fiona's friend, not mine really—but she insisted . . ."

Both of us exchange looks, but neither says anything.

"I didn't want to be ungrateful. It's just, you know me, this isn't really my thing."

No, it's Annabel's thing. It's all about Annabel. About her big fancy house. Her big expensive gift. About being the perfect hostess.

Michelle suddenly notices my half-eaten chocolate teacake. "What are you eating?"

I retrieve the packet I've stuffed behind the kettle and her eyes light up. "Ooh! My favorite! Where did you find those?"

"I bought them, but Annabel wouldn't hear of you eating them. She said they weren't good for the baby."

"Bollocks to that. I was brought up on these! They're full of nutrition."

Grabbing one, she peels off the foil and takes a bite, and then for a few moments we both just stand in the darkness, savoring each mouthful and groaning with delight.

"By the way, I didn't know you were having a girl," I say after a moment.

"Well, that's the thing." She grins. "When do you think I should tell her we're having a boy?"

I'm grateful for:
1. *Annabel's house being so big, as it meant Michelle and I were able to hide out in the kitchen and eat the entire box of chocolate teacakes before we were discovered.*
2. *Missing fun games like "Spin the Breast Pump" and forgetting my swimsuit.**
3. *Not breaking down when I was handed that tiny onesie.*
4. *The latest episode of my podcast, where I get to confess all of this, even the bit about hiding in the bathroom so no one could see me cry.*

Pulling the Trigger

On Sunday I get to catch up with Liza. She's in her car, stuck in traffic on the freeway as usual, and calls me on WhatsApp. We chat about random things—I recount the baby shower; she groans in all the right places—but after five minutes I get the sense that she hasn't just called to chat. There's Something Up.

"So, I saw Ethan at the weekend."

My heart leaps at just the mention of his name. So this is what's up. I'm both desperate to know all the details and desperate not to. Don't ask, Nell. Don't ask. No good can come of it.

"How was he?"

There's a pause. I brace for impact.

"He's met someone."

It's a head-on collision. I'm hurled through the air.

---

* I saw Annabel's swimsuit selfies on Instagram later. Forgetting my swimsuit was no accident.

"I didn't want you to find out from someone else."

A million questions whirl around in my head. I grab one. "Who is she?"

"Just some girl he met at a party."

Just some girl. She says it like it's no big deal, but it feels like a grenade.

"Is she pretty?"

Immediately, I hate myself.

"She's not you, Nell, she'll never be you."

A heavy weight is pressing on my chest. I feel like I'm going to suffocate. I want to burst into tears. I do neither.

"It doesn't mean anything."

"How do you know?" A ball of hurt rises up in my throat and I force it down. I should be over it. I should be just fine.

"Because I'm talking about you, not him. It doesn't have to mean anything to *you*." Her voice is determined on the other end of the phone. "You left, remember. You've moved on."

Liza's certainty is like a net appearing beneath me. I feel her words catching me as I fall.

"Have I, though? Have I really?" My voice is almost a whisper.

Like a runner in a relay, she passes me the baton.

"Well, now that's up to you."

I'm grateful for:
1. *Liza, who steers me through the plethora of dating sites and writes my profile, even though it's a little too "yoga" and I'm not sure I'd describe myself as "a spiritual life force."*
2. *Finally deciding to take the plunge and get back out there. Ethan has moved on and so must I.*
3. *There's no one to hear me scream when I discover my matches look the same age as my dad's friends.*
4. *The trifecta that is cheese puffs, a can of gin and tonic, and gallows humor. Hang on, I wonder if I could put that on my profile?*

Friday the 13th

In the true spirit of Friday the 13th, I decide to scare the living daylights out of myself.

Do I . . .
A) Watch a scary horror film?
B) Log on to my online banking and look at the balance of my current account?
C) Attempt to take a photo of myself for my dating profile?

I'll give you a clue. It's not A.

The Bereavement Bunker

It's only been a week, and, whereas I was expecting the only thing in my dating inbox to be tumbleweeds blowing about, I've had quite a few responses. In fact, so far I appear to have gotten myself into three relationships! Well, I say *relationships*, but what I mean is *online relationships*, as they're all with men I haven't yet met in real life and I'm not sure I'm ever going to.

Remember in the old days when someone would ask you for a drink or invite you to the movies? Now they ask to follow you on Instagram and invite you to like their Facebook page, and before you know it you're having long WhatsApp conversations into the night and liking that cute photo of them with their cat. Emojis are flying back and forth. Flirty texts are being exchanged. Email links to funny articles are being shared.

Until by the end of the week you've met all their family on Facebook and seen what they've had for lunch every day, but you've never actually spoken to them and they never want to meet up. It's like none of it is actually real. It only exists on your screen, and if you shut your laptop and turn off your smartphone—*poof*—it all disappears, like some modern-day fairy tale.

But at least Cinderella got left with a pumpkin. These days it's more likely to be a dick pic.

"A what?" Cricket looks at me like she's misheard.

We arranged to meet at a cafe in Sloane Square and are sitting at a table by the window. We've been admiring the view and drinking tea and oohing and aahing over the chocolate cake, which is all terribly pleasant, but now the conversation's moved on to more of *the basics*, so to speak, and I'm telling her about my dating experiences thus far. Well, she did ask. And I figured that with her attitude to the life drawing class, she could take the grim reality.

She leans toward me. "I'm sorry, my hearing isn't what it used to be."

"No, your hearing's just fine," I assure her. "That's what they call them."

"Are you meaning . . . ?"

I pass her my phone. On the screen is the text I've just received. She doesn't bat an eyelid.

"In my day they used to call it flashing. I remember it happening to Cissy and me one evening, on the platform at Baker Street. Quite unsolicited. Cissy told him to put it away at once."

"And did he?"

"We didn't wait to find out. A train arrived so we escaped on to the Bakerloo Line." She gives a little shake of her shoulders. "No one wants to see it."

"What I don't understand is why a man'd think you would?"

Cricket takes a sip of tea. "Well, I suppose it's a bit like when I had my cat. Tibby would bring dead things in for me. He'd proudly leave them on the mat for me to find of a morning. I know the intention was to show off and please me, but it was quite revolting."

I can't help but laugh. "I'm not sure he'd like being compared to a dead mouse."

"No, I expect not." She smiles. "But it does look rather like one, doesn't it?" She peers back at my phone, pinching the screen with her fingers to make it bigger.

We both pull a face.

"Catherine, what a pleasant surprise!"

A voice causes us both to look up, to see a smartly dressed elderly couple standing by our table. He's carrying a tray laden with tea and cakes, while she's holding several shopping bags. A couple of small children are playing around their legs.

"Lionel—Margaret." Cricket nods. I see she's somewhat taken aback, but recovers quickly.

"How are you? We were so sorry to hear the news about Monty . . ." Margaret goes first.

Followed swiftly by Lionel. "We meant to call, but we've just been so busy."

And back to Margaret. "You know how it is."

"Of course," says Cricket, smiling brightly, and I feel my heart break a little. I know just how lonely she has been since Monty died. Don't these people have a clue?

"We saw the obituary in the paper; a wonderful tribute." They both look at Cricket, with varying expressions of sympathy and pity.

"Thank you. This is the writer and my dear friend, Nell."

"Oh, pleased to meet you."

There's a flutter of hellos, how do you dos, and shaking of hands, before our exchange stalls. I can see from Margaret's body language that she's desperate to leave, but Lionel gives the dying embers of the conversation one last stoke.

"Everyone at bridge was asking after you."

"Well, tell everyone I'm still on the phone. And I still play bridge."

Lionel doesn't know if that was meant to be a joke, and looks to Margaret to see whether he should laugh or not. She steps in quickly to rescue him.

"Well, perhaps we should arrange a dinner, shouldn't we, darling?" She looks to her husband, stroking the lapel of his coat to remove some unseen thread, before turning back to Cricket. "I know everyone would love to see you, Catherine."

"That would be lovely." She smiles graciously.

"Well, we must go, we're with our grandchildren—Florence! Theo!"

There's a loud clatter of trays and a piercing shriek.

"Little rascals." Lionel laughs, moving to catch up with Margaret, who's hurrying over to the dessert counter and the unraveling scene of chaos.

"Hurry, death might just be catching," quips Cricket, as we both watch them scuttling away. "Sorry, that was mean of me," she adds, turning back to me.

"They deserved it," I reply. I feel suddenly and furiously protective of her.

But Cricket merely shrugs. "They're not bad people, really. People just don't know what to do about death. It frightens them. They fear they may be next. I remind them of their own mortality, and nobody wants that now, do they?"

"That's ridiculous."

"Maybe, but it's the reality."

"But that's so unfair."

"They don't do it to be cruel. Quite the opposite. I've found friends and acquaintances keep their distance because they don't want to upset you or say the wrong thing. What they don't realize is you're already upset beyond anything they could ever say or do. It's their silence that upsets you. You feel isolated. Abandoned."

Listening to her talking about her feelings of isolation, I remember how I felt when I first moved back to London, when I would spend weekends alone, not seeing a friendly face apart from Arthur's. And then I met Cricket and everything changed.

"They could have invited you to play bridge with them," I reason, annoyed that she's letting them off so lightly.

"It's different now I'm no longer part of a couple. A single person upsets the numbers. We upset theater rows. Hotel rooms. Sunday pub roasts for two."

Instinctively I reach across the table and squeeze her hand. I might not be a widow, but I know what it's like to find yourself single when everyone around you is in couples.

"That's why you've got me." I smile.

"Oh, you are a dear." She places her free hand upon mine and for a moment we just sit there like that, until suddenly I notice.

"My phone. Where is it?"

"Oh—I thought I put it down . . ." Cricket frowns. "Has it fallen on the floor?"

"Nope."

We're both hunting around us when I spot a small boy sitting with Lionel and Margaret a few tables away, engrossed in a phone. He's swiping the screen as though he's scrolling through photos, and now Margaret has noticed—

"Theo, what have you got there?"

Oh no. Please God, no.

I'm grateful for:
1. *Finding friendship in the unlikeliest of places.*
2. *Not being afraid to send Cricket that email inviting her to the concert, even though at the time I was worried it might be the wrong thing to do, as now I realize it's better to do and say something than nothing.*
3. *My screen lock.*

A Slippery Slope

I have a date! An actual date. And not just a hedge-your-bets coffee, but full-on committed make-an-effort drinks and dinner.

"Is this what they mean when they tell you to set yourself a new challenge?" I ask Liza, peering into my FaceTime camera and waving my hairdryer about, a bed strewn with piles of discarded outfits visible behind me. "Getting ready for a date over forty."

I'd already been getting ready for hours when she called. I can remember when all it took was a bit of flicky eyeliner and whatever was on the sale rack and you'd look amazing. Now it takes ages and costs a fortune, and that's just to get you looking half decent.

"You look amazing," encourages Liza.

God, aren't girlfriends great.

"I should have kept on doing yoga," I protest, angling myself in the mirror to show her my outfit. I need to throw away half of my clothes. They're too small, too short, or too revealing. I'm all for ignoring that rubbish about age-appropriate dressing, but I don't want to show off any crinkle and sag. Yet I still want to look nice, and vaguely sexy, and not like I'm only a chin-whisker away from a polo neck and a pair of statement earrings.

"You wouldn't go to yoga," replies Liza.

"You should have made me." I jiggle my arms.

"No one can make another person do something they don't want to. Anyway, I feared for the safety of my other students." She grins.

I smile. Finally.

"Are you done running yourself down? You're just nervous. It's going to be great. I'm proud of you."

"You are?"

"You've inspired me to get out there again. I'm going on a date too."

"What? When? *With who?*"

But Liza just laughs. "I'll tell you all about it later. You need to finish drying your hair. Those bangs are starting to kink."

I look at my bangs. It's starting to curl up at the edges, like stale bread.

Hanging up, I whack the hairdryer on full blast and start attacking it with my bristle brush, when suddenly there's a bloodcur-
dling scream.

WTF?

I flick off the hairdryer. Silence. I feel relieved and slightly foolish. I must be hearing things. Or maybe it was next door's TV.
They always have the volume too high.

There's a loud thud.

That's not next door's TV. I freeze. Is someone in the house?
It's Monday, but Edward texted earlier to say he was away on business and wouldn't be back until tomorrow night. I look for Arthur,
but he must be downstairs. I didn't hear him bark. All kinds of
scary stories begin flashing through my mind like a newsreel. I
unplug my flat iron—these things are lethal—and gingerly open
my bedroom door.

"Hello . . . ?"

No answer. But then burglars don't normally introduce themselves, do they?

"Is there anyone there?" I call out, my voice wavering slightly.

Suddenly there's the rattling of a lock and the bathroom door is
flung open. A figure appears through a cloud of steam, wearing only
a towel.

"No, I'm not OK!"

"Edward!" I gasp.

"Are you trying to kill me?" he demands.

OK, so there have been moments when the thought has crossed
my mind, but . . .

I stare at him in shock. He stands bare-chested in the hallway;
his hair is wet and has gone all curly, and he's dripping all over the
floorboards.

I avert my eyes quickly. "What are you doing here?"

"I happen to live here, remember."

"But you said you were on a business trip—" I begin, but he
interrupts.

"My plans changed. I've scheduled an important meeting first thing tomorrow, so I came back early and decided to take a shower and, in doing so, NEARLY BROKE MY NECK!"

I open and close my mouth like a fish. "Why has that got anything to do with me?" I manage finally.

"So you wouldn't know anything about the bath being so slippery I had to hang on to the shower curtain for dear life?"

Suddenly I remember the long soak in the bath I just took, with the expensive essential oils I bought especially. "Actually, that might be the bath oil—"

"*Bath oil?*" Edward almost chokes. "It was like an oil slick!"

"I'm sorry."

"Why didn't you clean it afterward?"

"I was going to . . . I didn't think you'd be back until tomorrow . . ."

"It's completely irresponsible, not to mention dangerous!"

"I said I'm sorry."

"I mean, who does that?!"

"Will you stop shouting at me."

"I'm not shouting!" he explodes, then, seeming to suddenly notice his temper, he takes a deep breath and clears his throat. "If you could just be a little more careful next time—" He breaks off to stare at me.

"Are you going out?"

"Yes . . . I've got a date," I add in explanation.

"Oh . . . I see." He nods. "You look very nice."

"Thanks." I realize I'm still brandishing my hair tongs. "Are you staying in?" I let them fall to my side.

"Yes, I just got back from a yoga class. Early night."

"In that case, if you could feed Arthur?"

"Of course." There's a long pause. "Well, have a good evening."

"Thanks, Edward. You too."

I smile, but his expression remains impassive as always, and for a moment we both just look at each other across the landing, before we both turn and retreat into our respective bedrooms.

I'm grateful for:

1. *My nice trouser suit, which covers all the bits I need covered, reveals a bit of cleavage, and, with a pair of heels, makes me feel like I'm still in the game.*
2. *The shower curtain that saved Edward's life, otherwise I could have been up for manslaughter.*

MAY
#maydaymaydaymayday

May Day

Remember when you were a child and May Day meant twirling around a maypole? It used to be so much fun. Fast-forward to forty-something and it's turned into *Mayday, Mayday, Mayday.*

Sitting in an Italian restaurant in Soho, I desperately glance at my watch. It's past midnight and the waiters are clearing up around us. One's even mopping the floor. All the other customers have gone home, which is where I'd like to be. However, my date has other ideas.

"Another two limoncellos, please."

"Of course," nods the waiter, putting down his mop.

Forget having fun with colored ribbons; it's now an emergency distress call to rescue me from my online date.

Nick seemed relatively normal in his profile. He works for a sports company and listed travel, red wine, and running as his interests. I like two out of three, which isn't bad. He also looked quite handsome in his photos, none of which were arty black-and-white headshots or involved him leaping out of planes and hiking up Everest. (I had *no* idea how many men who are online dating have climbed Everest. It almost seems a prerequisite to being on a dating app. That summit must be jammed with single men taking selfies for their online profiles.)

Plus, most importantly, he was keen to meet up in real life. Which would seem kind of obvious to me, being from the old-fashioned dating world where you actually got dressed and left the house, and didn't just loll about on your sofa with your phone sending nude selfies and emojis, which I always struggle to decipher, as I'm not fluent in Emoji.

So I was both pleased and nervous when I walked in and recognized him already waiting at the bar. It's been a long time since I've been on a date. Life before Ethan seems fuzzy and hard to imagine: less bruised, more hopeful, with fewer anxieties and more certainty. I was five years younger and ten pounds lighter. Spaghetti straps were still my friend. Ditto low-waisted jeans. Now it's things I can tuck in and sleeves.

We greeted each other with a polite kiss on each cheek. He was a little shorter in real life than he'd looked in his photos, and his aftershave was a bit overpowering, but he gave me a big smile which immediately put me at ease.

It's just—

I knew. I knew it the moment I walked into the bar and laid eyes on him: he wasn't the one.

"Hi—Nell?"

"Hi, yes—nice to meet you."

I pushed the feeling deep down inside me. I was determined to give him a chance. I hadn't spent *this* long getting ready to turn around and go home again. Plus, perhaps I was wrong. I'd been wrong about a lot of things so far in my life. Trust your instincts, they tell you. Listen to your gut, they say. Except I'd listened to both and look where that had gotten me: sobbing my eyes out 30,000 feet above the Atlantic; overdrawn from a failed business venture; sharing a bathroom with a man I'm not sleeping with.

Standing in a bar in Soho on a Monday night, still looking for love in my forties, and wishing this trouser suit wasn't so tight around the waist.

"Drink?"

"Yes, please. Glass of white wine, thanks."

On the tube ride over, I'd decided it was time to finally use my head when it came to men. My whole life I've gotten into relationships for a variety of reasons, none of which has been particularly sensible. In fact, *choice* probably isn't the correct word when it comes to my love life. It gives the impression of rational thought and deliberation, a weighing up of someone's character and shared interests. Not a series of random, impulsive moments, often involving alcohol, where I leapt, and fell, and was swept away.

Nice eyes; a drunken kiss at the office Christmas party; a nose ring that I knew would shock my mother. That's my twenties gone right there. *Poof.* And don't get me started on my thirties. I've spent more time reflecting on which sandwich filling to choose than I have on who I'm going to sign over my precious heart, soul, and years of my life to.

"So, Nell, how are you finding the dating site?"

"You're my first date."

"I am? Wow. I'm honored. An online-dating virgin!"

So what if there are no sparks or butterflies? Sparks and butterflies break your heart and drive you to the edge of insanity. They give you adrenaline-fueled highs and desperate-on-the-kitchen-floor lows. I've never done heroin but often think it must be like that kind of love. It's an addiction. A craving followed by a fix.

But it's never enough. *You're* never enough.

And I can't do it anymore. The highs just aren't worth the lows. This heart of mine is so cracked and broken it's barely holding together, a bit like my iPhone screen. One more blow and it will shatter forever.

"So, Nell, tell me, what are you looking for?"

"What, you mean, like in life, generally?"

"No, as in a partner."

"Erm, I'm not sure . . . someone kind, funny . . . sane." I try to make a bit of a joke. It feels more like an interview than a date.

"The same life goals are important, don't you think?"

"Oh yes, absolutely. Those too."

I need to do away with these romantic teenage notions. Couples who have been together forty years don't talk about passion and racing pulses. They talk about making compromises and common interests and security—I look at Nick and it hits me. Oh God, it's happening. It's time I gave up looking for chemistry and moved on to the next stage: *companionship*.

I used to always read about companionship in the advice columns of the magazines my mum reads. Middle-aged couples talking about how the spark has gone and how they don't have sex anymore, but how at least they've got someone to watch box sets with and flush the central heating system.

It sounded dreadful. I used to gloss over those articles, like you gloss over adverts for stair lifts and natural-looking dentures, with a shudder and a sense of relief. I was far too young and far too busy having great sex to bother my head with boring things like companionship. That stuff happened to old people, even the tanned and silver-haired couple laughing with abandon on the winter cruise ad.

But now here I am, several hours later, in a restaurant, listening to Nick telling me all about his Fitbit, showing me how to measure my resting pulse and how many calories I'm burning; and part of me is thinking that at least he'd be someone to put out the recycling and go on a cruise with.

"I can get you one if you'd like. I've got a fifty percent off voucher code."

"Oh . . . thank you, that's very generous, but I don't think I'd use it."

"We could share our stats, keep track of how many steps we're taking, set daily goals and challenge each other—just think! There's so much we can do!"

I'm grateful for:
1. *The Uber driver who finally came to my rescue.*
2. *WhatsApp, for allowing us to avoid any awkward phone calls and help keep things on good terms, as I'm able to politely message, "Thanks for a lovely evening, Nick. It was great to*

*meet you, but I don't think we're a good match. I wish you
all the best. Nell." Along with a smiley face emoji.*

3. *Nick's reply, which pinged in a few seconds later: "Couldn't
agree more! You beat me to it. Have a nice life." With no
smiley face emoji, just the voucher code.*

4. *My brave and foolish heart, for refusing to settle for anything
less.*

5. *Being able to put out my own recycling.*

Failing

So, I'm listening to this podcast about how it's important to fail.
Every week a well-known personality is interviewed on what
their failures taught them about how to succeed better. I love
this show; failing is something I appear to be very good at. It's
like discovering a talent I never knew I had, like being able to
play the piano or speak fluent Spanish.

Well, sort of.

It's the succeeding part I'm having a little more trouble with.
A job writing obituaries and one online date is not turning my life
around. And it's May already! Still, no point panicking. I once
watched a documentary about ships, and how they can't just change
direction sharply otherwise they'll tip over, but you have to steer
them around gradually. Maybe I should think of my life as a big ship
that needs to turn around slowly. Maybe I'm like a cruise liner.*

I'm grateful for:
1. *Failing at my career, otherwise I wouldn't have met the wonderful Cricket.*

---

* Just to be clear, this is a metaphor and I'm talking speed not size.

2. *Failing at homeownership, otherwise I wouldn't have met my beloved Arthur.*
3. *Failing at my relationship, otherwise I wouldn't be enjoying the fun of online dating.*
4. *My sense of irony.*

The Raincoat

Life is all about timing. Its very creation is dependent on the egg being released at just the right time for it to be fertilized by the sperm. In love, timing is everything. You can meet the right person at the wrong time and the wrong person at the right time. Even in death, timing is of great significance.

So when Cricket calls me up on the weekend and says, "I'm ready to clear out Monty's clothes," I drop everything and go over to her house.

Because it's not just important for those who have died, but for those left behind.

She greets me at the door, but instead of her usual brisk handshake she gives me an uncharacteristic hug, then leads me up the large central staircase, with its brass stair rods and timeworn carpet, to the second floor.

"It's time," she says, pushing open a door and walking into a bedroom. "And I need you to help me."

For months now, she'd left them. Whenever anyone had gently tried to broach the subject, she would cut them off. What was the rush? Privately to me, she'd admitted to finding great comfort in seeing his shirts hanging in the wardrobe, his coat on the rack in the hall. "I'm not ready yet" was always her response whenever I offered to help. "I like having him around."

"Are you sure?" I pause in the doorway.

"Absolutely." She nods. "I woke up this morning and I just knew. I miss Monty terribly, but keeping his clothes isn't going to bring him back."

She opens the large wardrobe in the corner of the room. It's stuffed to the gills with a rainbow array of shirts and jackets, all jostling for space.

"Monty wasn't organized; he never liked to throw anything away."

I join her in the bedroom and we look at its contents, both slightly paralyzed by the task ahead. Shirts, three to each mahogany hanger, bump shoulders with empty wire hangers, still with their dry-cleaning plastic attached.

"What do you want me to do?"

"Listen to me," she says simply. "No one listens to me anymore. Everyone likes to tell me what to do. They think they're looking after me but I feel like they're suffocating me."

So that's what I do. I go and sit on the edge of the bed. And I listen.

"I kept all his things on hangers because it made me feel like he was coming back. Opening his wardrobe door and seeing them hanging there, being able to touch them and smell them, it's like he was here, it's like he was going to come in at any minute and ask 'What shirt should I wear?' or 'What tie goes with the blue suit, Cricket?'"

She pauses.

"Does that make me sound ridiculous?"

I shake my head. "When my first boyfriend went away to university, I kept his sweaty T-shirt. I didn't wash it and every night I would sleep with it on my pillow."

"Now that *is* ridiculous," she says, and we both smile. "You know, Monty was always going away with his work. He would often tour with the play and he would be gone for weeks . . . months. Sometimes I would go with him. In the early days we were hardly ever at home. We were always on the road, touring different theaters and playhouses around the country—"

She breaks off, her attention caught by a framed theater poster from thirty years ago, hanging on the wall above the chest of drawers.

"I used to think it all sounded very glamorous, but the reality was quite different. That's the magic of theater: you don't see what's going on behind the scenes; the drafty dressing rooms and highway service stations, the bed-and-breakfasts with no hot water." She gives a little shake of her head. "Of course, in his later years it was all very different. Monty always said his success and awards didn't change anything, apart from not having to travel farther than the West End for opening night."

"I wish I could have met Monty."

"Oh, you would have loved him. And he would have *loved* you."

Turning back to the wardrobe, she runs her fingertips along the sleeves of the jackets, like fingers on the keyboard of a piano, but it's a tune that only she can hear.

"When he first died, it was almost like the early days all over again. As if he was just away touring with a play and he'd be coming back . . . I almost convinced myself . . . But he's not coming back, is he?"

She turns to me now, full-on, and I see her expression. She's so sad and trying to be so brave.

"No. He's not," I say softly.

She nods, her body stiffening, and for the first time since I've met Cricket, I see her eyes well with tears.

"One thing I've learned through this bloody awful time is that grief isn't linear. You can be doing all right, then it will suddenly come out of nowhere. It's the silly little things that remind you . . . Only yesterday I was at the supermarket and found myself in the cookie aisle, standing in front of his favorites. Monty used to love these toffee wafers. I never cared for them, but he could eat them by the packet . . . and I burst into tears. It just hit me. I was never going to buy those cookies for him again."

Listening to Cricket, I feel a sudden sense of shame. All this time I've been mistaking her strength and composure for a lack of sentiment and vulnerability. She's been so busy and industrious I've assumed she was coping just fine. She seemed so strong, I thought she was made of sterner stuff than the rest of us, and that somehow she was unaffected by his loss.

I had no idea that behind the brave face and stiff upper lip she was suffering this much inside. Her stoicism seemed to belong to another era, of picking yourself up, dusting yourself off, and just getting on with it, but now I realize it doesn't mean she's any less heartbroken. She just hides it better.

"Fancy crying over a packet of biscuits. Goodness knows what the other shoppers must have thought of me." She sniffs sharply and throws back her shoulders. "Right then. Best crack on." And, pulling out a fistful of hangers, she begins laying them on the bed.

Clearing out someone's possessions is like going through a scrapbook of their life. Everything has a story or a memory attached.

Red silk tie: "He wore this one year to his club's Christmas ball. It was black tie, so of course Monty wore a red one. That was Monty. If you told him to turn left, he would turn right."

Pistachio linen suit: "We were in Venice, for the film festival. On the way to our hotel we got lost down a side street, and he happened to see this in a shopwindow and thought it was marvelous. So very Italian. He bought it to wear at the festival, but it wasn't hemmed in time. Afterward we went to Forte dei Marmi, and he insisted on wearing it to the beach, rolling up the trousers so he could paddle. Monty never learned to swim, you know. He used to say drowning in his emotions was quite enough."

Pair of hand-stitched leather brogues: "He had a shoemaker in the East End. Monty had polio as a child and suffered terribly with his feet, but he swore they could make 'a silk purse out of a pig's ear.' He went there for over fifty years. They even have his shoe last."

Raincoat: "He found it in a cafe in Paris. He was in his early twenties, long before we ever met, but I remember him telling me the story. Apparently someone had left it on the back of a chair and he asked the waiters if they would keep it, in case its owner returned, but they never did, so he claimed it instead. It was a little too big for him in those days, but being a poor playwright, he was thrilled. In later years it became much too small for him, but he could never bring himself to give it away. I think it reminded him of his youth. Of those rainy days in Paris in the 1950s, when he would smoke Gauloises, and sit in cafes scribbling in his notebooks and pretending he was Hemingway."

Several hours later the wardrobe is empty.

"Do you have trash bags? I'll take all these clothes to the charity shop."

"Not trash bags." Cricket shakes her head firmly. "That herringbone suit was cut by one of the finest tailors on Savile Row and worn to the Viennese Opera. It can't ever see the inside of a trash bag, even if it's only temporary. Monty would never forgive me."

So in the end we pack everything neatly away in suitcases—four large ones, the old-fashioned type with leather handles and no wheels—plus two large trunks from his army days. Afterward we call a minicab, but instead of the usual Ford Galaxy, a large, shiny black Mercedes arrives. "Don't worry, it's the same price, I was the first car free," says the driver, helping me load everything into the giant trunk and onto the back seat.

I go to say goodbye to Cricket. It's been a long, emotional day.

"Just one more thing," she says after we hug. "Will you take them to a charity shop in a different neighborhood? I know it sounds silly, but I don't think I could bear bumping into strangers wearing his clothes."

"Of course, there's lots near my house. I'll bring the luggage back later."

"There's no rush."

The driver opens the car door for me, and I climb into the passenger seat.

"You know, it was a big thing you did today," I say to her. "You were very brave. Monty would be proud."

Cricket smiles. "Well, he'd certainly be pleased." She hands me the final piece of luggage, which I balance on my knees, then steps back on the sidewalk as the driver indicates to pull out. "Even in death, he gets to travel in style with an attractive woman half his age."

I'm grateful for:
1. *Learning that listening can be more powerful than talking.*
2. *The privilege of spending the afternoon with Monty.*
3. *Timing, which has brought Cricket and me together when we need each other the most.*

It's Complicated

Tonight I watched the *News at Ten*. It should be renamed the *Bad News at Ten*. It was one horrible headline after another. All around, the world is in chaos. There is so much suffering. So much terror and injustice. The refugee crisis, our oceans filled with plastic, climate change, animal cruelty, gun and knife crime . . . the list is endless. But it's not just the news headlines. I watched David Attenborough's new documentary the other night and it's hard not to despair.

As a human being, when I see these things I suffer the expected emotions—horror, fear, sadness—but also a sense of shame. And not just shame at how we are treating the inhabitants of our planet, but shame that my own problems are completely insignificant when held in context.

How can I wake up with The Fear when I'm lying in bed, safe

and warm, and there are people out there without food or shelter? How can I look in the mirror and feel gloomy about my saggy knees when women younger than me are dying of cancer and it's a *privilege* to age? How can I feel sad about not finding my happy ever after when so much of our planet is being destroyed? And how can I even *concern* myself with my faltering career and failed love life when we have Brexit and Trump?

In short, how dare I complain about my life, when I have so much compared to so many?

The answer is I don't know.

Truly.

I know all these things to be true, and yet I still feel all of these other things. They jostle alongside each other, like the paradox that life so often is. For so much of the day, I forget about the big stuff. Like most people, I'm just focused on getting through each day and the small stuff that affects my life and those closest around me. But then I'll hear about some tragedy or watch the news and suddenly I'm reminded again.

I watch a father sobbing at a news conference because the police have found the body of his missing daughter, or hear about a friend of a friend who has just been diagnosed with something awful, and I swear to myself I'll never complain about anything ever again.

But of course I do. We all do.

Before you know it, you're annoyed with the person who pushed in front of you in the line and that your train is late. Or gutted because he didn't text back or someone else at work got that promotion. Does that make you selfish? I think it just makes you human.

If getting older has taught me one thing, it's that I *feel* so many conflicting things *about* so many different things, and to negate or stifle any of them doesn't make them go away. Emotions don't necessarily have a moral compass. Feelings can't be shamed into disappearing. Suppressing and ignoring them will only make them come back to bite you in the therapist's chair.

Because this is what I've learned:

I can feel like I don't know what the hell I'm doing, and refuse to look in mirrors with overhead lighting, and still go on the Women's March and roar like a motherfucker. I can weep for that father who lost his daughter and pray for the friend I don't know, and a few days later be scrolling and despairing that I am not taking beach selfies with my handsome husband. And I can marvel at a sunset and think how lucky I am, and wake up in the night with The Fear.

Because life is complicated. And so are we.

I'm grateful for:
1. *Everything I have and always counting my blessings,* even when things aren't going so great.*
2. *The latest episode of my podcast, in which I get to confess all this stuff, though I doubt anyone is even listening, and I'm just talking to myself and getting everything off my chest. Still, look at it this way: at least it's cheaper than therapy.*
3. *The funny cat videos, which always make me smile, even when the world is collapsing around my ears.*

Facebook Is Not My Friend

Since moving back to London I've started sleeping with my iPhone. I know. It's bad. All that blue light and electromagnetic stuff disrupting brain patterns and God knows what. When I lived with Ethan, we were very strict about following the No Electronics in the Bedroom rule, but it's a little trickier when you're renting a room and everything you own is crammed into it.

Plus, it beats sleeping alone. My phone and I get to fool around

---

* Which is very different from the humblebrag of feeling #blessed.

on our apps together. And Google is always up for it. But tonight when I look on Facebook, I see that Ethan has been tagged in a photo with a girl at a party.

Just some girl.

I'm not expecting it. He never uses social media. I was expecting to scroll through a few photos of random old school friends and funny videos people have shared. Not this bombshell. My stomach lurches. Even though Liza told me, being faced with the reality is hard.

I scrutinize the photo. She's blonde and pretty and looks at least ten years younger than me. Ethan is laughing and has his arm around her waist. He looks good. Like he's lost some weight.

FFS. What happened to the fat wet suit picture?

I feel crushed and utterly depressed. I am not going to parties and laughing with my arm around men's waists. I have not lost weight. I am eating chips and writing obituaries and going on soul-destroying online dates. I think about Nick and his Fitbit. Liza telling me it's my choice to move on.

Sod This. I log out of Facebook and into the dating app. I have a free month's subscription, and there's still over a week left. I can't give up after one date. I click on my inbox. Liza was wrong. It's not a choice; it's a question of bloody survival.

A Desperate Act

Inbox: You have a message from MrMountEverest

Hi, I saw your profile and thought you looked rather nice! I'm a genuine guy seeking a genuine girl and I like going out and staying in, watching movies, and taking selfies on Everest ☺ Perhaps you would like to meet for a coffee to get to know each other? I look forward to hearing from you. M x

Sent: Re: You have a message from MrMountEverest

Hi, what a coincidence, I like going out and staying in too!
I would love to meet you for a coffee and look at your Everest
selfies.
Nell x

The Photograph

Spring seems to bloom overnight. After months of wintery skies
and endless damp, gray days, I wake up to discover the sky is
blue, the sun is shining, and the street is lined with fluttery
pink-blossom trees. Sweet, warm air, like the scent of freshly
laundered clothes, wafts in as I push open the stiff sash window,
and when I reach into my wardrobe, I pull out a T-shirt—an
actual T-shirt.

Slipping my winter feet into flip-flops, I head briskly toward the
charity shop. I'm taking the last of Monty's clothes. I dropped most
of them off last week in the taxi, but one of the smaller suitcases
fell behind the back seat and was only discovered much later by the
driver. He brought it over the next day, but I've been busy so I'm
only taking it now.

The lady in the charity shop recognizes me as I enter.

"Back again!" She looks pleased to see me. It was quite evident
that Monty's clothes were of a higher quality than the contents of
most of the garbage bags left in the shop doorway overnight.

"Just one more." I gesture to the suitcase.

She smiles broadly. "Wonderful, thank you. We've sold so
many of the items you brought in last week. They've raised over a
thousand pounds already."

"I'll let his wife know. She'll be pleased."

"Such a difficult time." Her expression is sympathetic. "I hope she finds comfort in knowing she's supporting those in need."

"Yes, I'm sure." I nod, opening the case and taking out the rest of Monty's belongings. I know she's trying to be nice, offering up such platitudes, but having witnessed Cricket's heartbreak, there seems to be little comfort to be gained when someone you love dies. It's just a case of necessity. Of getting on with it. Of putting one foot in front of the other, and breathing in and out.

"Do you want to check through all the pockets, just in case?"

"That's not necessary, we did that already—"

"Well, if you're sure."

She takes them from me and begins shaking out his clothes and slipping them on hangers, ready for their new owners. I watch her pick up the raincoat Monty found in Paris and my chest tightens. I turn to leave.

"Oh, wait a minute, dear!" The lady calls me back. "This was in the inside pocket."

She's holding out an envelope. I go to take it from her.

"Oh, thank you. Good job you checked!"

"Well, it was here, look . . ." She starts showing me the raincoat. "It can appear just like a seam but it's actually a little secret compartment for tucking away your wallet, or passport, or anything important that you don't want to lose."

"Right, yes." I nod, slipping it into my bag. "Well, thanks again."

She smiles cheerfully as I say my goodbyes and leave the shop. Only when I'm outside do I take it out again for a closer look. It's addressed to Monty, and the edge of the envelope has been neatly slit by a letter opener. I was half expecting it to be postmarked Paris and contain some old love letter from sixty years ago, but it's more recent, by the looks of it, and the stamp says *España*.

As I turn it over, a black-and-white photograph slips out. Taken underneath a tree, it's of two men embracing.

My heart starts to beat a little faster. Is that—?

Written on the back is an inscription: *Monty, t'estimo per sempre, Pablo.*

I'm grateful for:
1. *Being the one who found the letter and the photograph, instead of Cricket.*
2. *Time to think. Because now it's up to me to decide whether to tell her or not.*
3. *Google Translate: it's Catalan for "I will love you forever."*

Mirror, Signal, Maneuver

I remember when I was learning to drive and I could never pass. My instructor used to try to coax me into putting my foot on the accelerator and going for it, cajoling me with cries of "it's all clear!" but I would stick resolutely to the slow lane, trundling along.

Which is basically a metaphor for my life right now. I'm firmly stuck in the slow lane. Actually, no, it's worse: I've pulled over onto the shoulder of the road, map splayed over the steering wheel, wondering where the hell I'm supposed to be going.

My living arrangements aren't exactly ideal, but they're tolerable. I'm dating—unsatisfactorily—but still. I've got regular work, though the money isn't great, but together with what's left of Dad's loan it's enough to cover my bills. I know I need to make some big changes and figure something else out, but for now everything is just sort of ticking along.

I spoke to Sadiq today, and he's really pleased with all my obituaries so far. He told me I've got "a knack for dead people," which I'm not quite sure how to interpret, so I'm going to take it as a compliment.

Thing is, I do actually quite enjoy writing them, because in a way it's like bringing the people that have died back to life again. Also, mostly, the people I write about are quite old, and I've found that when an old person dies, we tend to think "oh well, they're old" and sort of shrug it off, as though old people are different somehow. Especially when you don't know them.

But in doing my research I get to see they were young once, with thick hair and straight backs and high hopes; they fell in and out of love and they did brave and wonderful things, and they lived their lives, just like we're living ours. They're just ahead of us, that's all. We'll catch up eventually, and when we do I doubt any of us will think, "oh well, we're old" with a resigned shrug of our shoulders.

Cricket certainly doesn't feel like that, and I don't see her that way either. On Sunday we met for coffee and she turned up on her bike wearing her new bicycle helmet, which is bright plastic leopard print. We've become firm friends and she's invited me to see an exhibition with her next month at the Victoria and Albert Museum. I haven't yet mentioned the letter and photograph I found. I still don't know whether I should.

As for my friends, I haven't seen them since the baby shower last month, but I've exchanged a few texts with Holly and Michelle. Fiona, however, I've barely heard from. Usually we leave each other WhatsApp voice messages, but the last few times she hasn't listened to them, which is unlike her. Usually the ticks turn blue immediately. She must be busy with the children and David and her latest renovation. At the baby shower I overheard her mention something about Annabel helping her to redecorate the living room.

Which is fine, of course it is; I just miss our conversations. And I really miss her. All those silly references and jokes that only she would get. But the more time she spends with Annabel, the more I feel detached from her. In fact, the truth is a big part of me can't help feeling like I've lost her. That while I'm here, trying to figure it all out on the shoulder of the road, she's left me far behind and moved on in the fast lane.

I'm grateful for:
1. *Cricket's trip to Dublin to attend the funeral of an old theater friend, which means I have more time to decide whether or not to tell her about what I've found—we won't see each other now until the exhibition.*
2. *Shoulders, because we all need to pull over sometimes.*

It's Not You, It's Me

Online dating and I broke up. My free trial came to an end last week and I decided not renew it. I went on a couple more dates, but they were all pretty awful. There was nothing wrong with the men as such (though I do tend to prefer it when dates don't turn up already drunk or spend the whole evening bashing their "crazy ex-wife") so it was probably my fault; after all, I was the common denominator.

The thing is, I know it works for thousands of happy couples, but I'm just not cut out for it. The endless scrolling and emailing and trying to be cute and sexy when, to be honest, sitting in my robe eating chips, I felt like none of those things. I know some people love it. They're good at it. All that flirty cyber banter and going on first dates. I was rubbish. I failed badly at it. And, even worse, it made me miss Ethan more.

So I think I'm going to stick with the old-fashioned, crossing-of-paths, fate stuff. If love wants to find me, it will.

I'm grateful for:
1. *The deactivation button on this dating app.*

2. *Stopping scrolling, as I was in danger of getting carpal tunnel.*
3. *No more dick pics.*

The Last (Plastic) Straw

I haven't seen much of my landlord since my failed attempt at Murder by Essential Oils. Only joking. I wasn't *really* trying to kill him. Though I'm sorely tempted this morning, when I pad into the kitchen to make my coffee and catch him elbow-deep in the recycling.

"Morning."

Still half asleep in my robe and slippers, I ignore him and pat Arthur who comes to greet me, then reach for my coffeepot.

"You can't recycle Bubble Wrap." With his shirtsleeves rolled up, Edward plucks it out of the recycling and waves it at me.

"Why not? It's plastic."

"It doesn't have the symbol."

"So?" I stifle a yawn.

Edward almost chokes. "Please tell me you are actually looking at the symbols to check if it's recyclable or not."

"It's too confusing. If it's plastic I just chuck it in the recycling." Filling up my espresso pot with water, I take a spoon and begin ladling in coffee.

Edward looks like I've just told him I murdered our next-door neighbor. His eyes pop and his jaw clenches. "That's not how it works, Penelope. If just one non-recyclable item is included in the recycling, the whole recycling is contaminated."

I feel suitably told off.

"OK, I'm sorry, I'll check the symbols properly. But if it's plastic it should all be recyclable," I grumble, putting my coffeepot on the stovetop and turning on the front burner as he continues dragging things out of the recycling.

Ignoring my apology, he begins forming a little moat of glass jars and plastic bottles around him.

"And can you *please* wash them out properly!"

As he waves a can of baked beans at me accusingly, I can feel myself having one of those out-of-body experiences where you look at your life and think "*nowhere* was this in my vision of my future." I had such high hopes in my twenties. Imagine if I could go back and tell myself that no, I wouldn't be living in a nice house with color-coordinated scatter cushions, I would be standing in someone else's kitchen having empty baked bean cans waved at me by someone else's husband. And that's even before I've had my morning coffee.

"What's this?"

I suddenly realize he's inspecting a plastic container of creme bleach, which I use to do my moustache. I snatch it off him. "Is this really necessary?"

"Yes it is, Penelope," he says, looking pleased to finally have my full attention.

"Stop calling me Penelope," I snap.

"Why? It's your proper name."

"Because no one calls me that."

"Well, they should. People want to shorten everything these days."

"Well, it's a bit of a mouthful."

"It's four syllables."

"Exactly."

"If people cannot make the effort to say four syllables, then you shouldn't make the effort to answer."

"Is that why you insist on being called Edward, instead of Ed?" Folding my arms, I lean against the countertop and wait for my coffeepot to boil.

"My name's Edward. It's not a matter of insisting."

"Or Eddie?" I suggest. "Eddie's nice."

He frowns, and pushes back his hair from his forehead. "I don't feel like an Eddie."

I look at him. He could really do with a haircut. It's beginning to grow sideways as well as lengthways. But then who am I to talk? I haven't been to a hairdresser for ages, I'm so broke. I might have a go with Mum's old hairdressing scissors.

"No. I suppose not. You don't look like an Eddie."

He heaves a sigh. "What's this desire to shorten everyone's name? Do you think they called the Queen Liz?"

"Her Royal Highness Liz?" I laugh. "Maybe."

His serious expression softens. "I like the name Penelope. It suits you."

"I sound like a maiden aunt. Or a Thunderbird puppet."

"Lady Penelope." He raises an eyebrow and cocks his head, as if considering. "It's very elegant."

"I'm elegant?"

"Well, no, not as a rule. But you were the other night."

Unexpectedly, I feel myself blush.

"You brush up very well, Penelope."

"Why, thank you." I grin, and do a little twirl in my robe and slippers.

A smile flickers. "That's what my mum used to do."

"She did?"

"Yes. When I was a small boy, she and Dad were always going to parties. I was supposed to be in bed by the time they left, but I would sneak out and watch them through the banisters. Dad would go to bring the car around, and when he was gone she would always look up and pirouette for me. 'How do I look, Edward?' she would always say."

"And what would you say?"

It's the first time he's opened up to me, and I'm intrigued.

"Beautiful," he replies quietly, and for a moment it's as if he's no longer in the kitchen but back in his childhood, peering through those banisters. "You look beautiful, Mum."

"I bet she still is."

"She died when I was thirteen. I was away at boarding school."

"Oh, I'm sorry."

"It's fine," he says briskly. "It was a long time ago. Dad remarried. Sue's very nice. She's good for him. They live in France."

"Is that how you met your wife?"

"Yes." He nods.

I wait for Edward to offer more details, but none are forthcoming. Instead he changes the subject.

"So anyway, how was it? Your date."

"Pretty awful." I grimace.

"Oh. Sorry to hear that."

"Don't be. He was perfectly nice . . . for someone who wants fifty percent off a Fitbit."

"I'd like fifty percent off a Fitbit."

"Maybe you should have gone on the date."

That makes him laugh and I can't help feeling pleased with myself. Like I've got his approval somehow. Which I know sounds ridiculous, but Edward's a tough crowd. Just raising a smile out of him is quite an achievement.

The sound of my coffee percolating interrupts. He looks at his watch. "I need to go. I'm going to be late for the office."

We both look at the mess on the floor, and Arthur, who's sniffing it all curiously.

"Do you want me to clear that up?" I offer.

"Would you?" He looks slightly abashed now. "Thank you."

Rolling down his sleeves, he washes his hands in the sink, and then disappears into the hallway.

I pour my coffee. Finally. Peace.

I'm just taking a sip when his head reappears around the doorframe, wearing his bicycle helmet. "But will you please make sure to read the—"

"Edward," I warn. "Just shut up and go to work."

He looks surprised, as if he can't quite believe someone has spoken to him like that, and for a moment I regret being so blunt; after all, he is my landlord.

But then he grins and, for the first time, he actually does what I say.

Not Junk!

I wake up early on Thursday morning to finish my latest obituary. I need to file it by noon, only there's a bit of information I'm still missing and I'm waiting for someone to email me back. I check my inbox. Nothing. I wonder if it's gone into my junk folder instead.

I scroll through the folder and spot a message from the dating app:

> **You have a message from a member. To read it you need to reactivate your account.**

Ha, ha, as if. Talk about a blatant attempt to dangle the carrot at the lovelorn and tempt you to reactivate and sign up with your credit card. I don't think so.

Still, I click on the email. The message is blocked but they've provided a photo of the member. Hang on, is that—*Johnny!*

I zoom in. It's him. The Hot Dad . . . I mean, Fun Uncle!

Fuck. Where's my credit card?

I'm grateful for:
1. *His message, which I speed-read. It starts, "Hey, is that you, Nell? That's so wild we're both on this site," goes on to say that he noticed my account wasn't active which likely meant I'd been snapped up, but if not to message him back, and ends with, "P.S. You looked cute in the snow!"*

2. *Online dating, for taking me back after we broke up.*
3. *Being a bloody hypocrite, though this isn't strictly meeting someone online as Johnny and I have already met—randomly in a pub, then naked in an art class, then on the street in the snow.*
4. *Him saying I looked cute!*
5. *His quick reply to my response, asking for my number and calling me straightaway.*
6. *A miracle.**

---

* Otherwise known as a bloody, goddam, bona fide, with-the-only-man-I've-been-attracted-to-since-Ethan, DATE.

JUNE
#cuttothechase

Never Too Late

Recently I read an article about famous people who didn't achieve success until later in life. Apparently Laura Ingalls Wilder, the woman who wrote the Little House on the Prairie series of children's books, didn't have her first book published until she was sixty-five years old.

Sixty-five!

As soon as I read this, I felt immediately cheered up. Maybe I was going to be a late bloomer too. Comforted that it wasn't yet too late and I still had plenty of time to fulfil my dreams and aspirations, I felt reassured and inspired.

But it's catching. Now whenever I find myself reading an article about someone running a marathon, or starting a successful business, or changing their life and moving to Tuscany to renovate an old farmhouse, I'll quickly check their age.

Five years older than me? See! It's never too late! No need to panic!

Ten years younger? What have I been doing all this time? Depressed for days.

I'm grateful for:
1. *Yuichiro Miura of Japan, the oldest person to climb Mount Everest, who reached the summit in 2013 at the age of eighty.*
2. *Never wanting to climb Mount Everest.*

WhatsApp Chat with Fiona

Hi Nell, sorry I haven't got back to you, things have been a bit manic with all the redecorating (I'm doing the whole house now!) and school stuff. Speaking of, school sports day is next week and Izzy would love you to watch her race, would you come? Would love to see you too!

Hey, yes, of course, would be great to see you

Great! How are you btw?

I got a date with Johnny!

Who's Johnny???

You know, Hot Dad!

Fiona is typing

The naked guy from the art class!

What art class???

Except he's not Hot Dad, he's Fun Uncle.

Totally confused!
Tell me all about it next week. How exciting! XX

I'm grateful for:
1. *Being invited to the school sports day, as I've really missed Fiona and the children, and it will be lovely to see them.*
2. *Finally having a bit of exciting news to tell my friends when they ask me how I am.*
3. *Not getting upset when I realize Fiona doesn't know about Johnny because we've hardly seen one another, or feeling*

sad that we're not as close as we used to be. Because things
change and people change, and she and Annabel have much
more in common now.

4. *Gratitude being a daily practice, because I'm going to have to*
   do a lot of practicing the above.

The First Date

After a bit of a gloomy start to the month, London decides to
pull out all the stops for my first date with Johnny. A freshly
laundered sky. Bright sunshine. A balmy 75 degrees. It's one of
those perfect summer days that makes you fall back in love with
the city that held you hostage all winter and dicked you around
for most of spring.

In celebration of the weather, we choose to meet for a drink
at a local pub on the river. Everyone has had the same idea and
it's jammed with people. I look around me—at the crowds spilling
onto the terrace outside with their smiles and pints and Aperol
Spritz, and back to Johnny sitting opposite me at the wooden table.
The happiness is palpable.

"So, tell me, how can you be single?" he's asking now, as we
work our way through a bottle of wine and I officially decide there's
nowhere I'd rather be than here, with him, wearing a summer dress
and drinking rosé.

"Same reason as someone like you," I fire back.

"Because you haven't met the right person yet?" He raises an
eyebrow.

"Do you reckon everyone says that?"

"Well, it's a lot better than saying you cheated, or you're an
alcoholic, or your last partner dumped you because you have a
weird sex fetish."

"True." I laugh, before adding, "Why, do you have a weird sex fetish?"

He laughs. "Only sometimes."

"And what would that be?" I'm tipsy and flirting.

"I have this weird attraction to women who only wear one glove."

I groan. "I walked right into that one, didn't I?"

"I think you could say I led you," he replies, quick as a flash.

"But now I have a pair, remember? So you're cured."

The corners of his mouth turn up in a smile. "Oh, I don't know about that." He goes to fill up our glasses, but there's only a few drops left. "I think we need another bottle."

"I can't believe we've drunk all that already."

"Flirting's thirsty work," he quips.

Bloody hell.

As soon as he makes his excuses and disappears to the bar, I bolt for the ladies'. I'm dying to use the bathroom but, more importantly, I'm dying to call Liza. I can't quite believe it! Talk about chemistry. I couldn't have hoped for a better first date. As soon as I walked into the pub and Johnny greeted me with a smile, any fears or nervousness I might have felt disappeared. There was an instant ease between us. Well, I suppose seeing someone naked does break the ice.

We hit the ground running. I told him a bit about my childhood, growing up, working as an editor and moving to New York, and about my recent move back from the States. Admittedly I did give him the edited version, but doesn't everyone give a sort of "greatest hits" of their life when they first meet someone? Who needs to hear the crappy B-sides?

He described his childhood growing up in Surrey with his sister, how he used to be a professional tennis player—"nothing up to Wimbledon standards," but it paid for a deposit on his house and he got a few trophies "for my mum to polish." Now he works as a tennis coach at a private club, "when I'm not taking my clothes off," he said grinning, and has ambitions to open a vinyl-record store. He is funny and self-deprecating and attractive, and most definitely single after breaking up with his girlfriend of two years, who recently moved back to Canada.

"It seems too good to be true," I say, calling Liza from inside the stall.

"Stop being such a pessimist. Not all men are bastards. Just the ones I fall for."

"I'm just scared, that's all. Of getting hurt again . . ."

I finish peeing and flush the toilet.

"I think I like him."

"How much have you had to drink?"

"Two glasses of wine."

"Have another."

I wash my hands and peer at my reflection in the mirror. Luckily the wine has taken the edge off it and I feel all fuzzy and soft-focused. I put on a bit of lip gloss, fluff my hair, and go back into the pub. I spot Johnny sitting in the corner on one of those squashy button-back leather sofas.

"It was getting a little cool out there. I thought this might be a bit cozier."

He's already filled up my glass, and as I squeeze past the low table and sit down next to him, my bare leg presses against his.

"Thanks." I smile, accepting the glass from him and taking a large mouthful. He's bought Côtes de Provence. The palest kind; it goes down like water.

"This reminds me of when you and I met, when you were sitting in the corner at the pub—"

"Yes, I remember. It was my birthday."

"Really?"

For a split second I wish I hadn't mentioned that. I don't want to look like I have no friends. But the rosé is weaving its way through my veins and any filter I have is fast dissolving. "Yes, all my friends were busy so I ended up at the pub by myself with Arthur—to be honest, it wasn't a bad birthday in the end." I smile, remembering.

"Is that because you met me?" he teases.

I roll my eyes. "I think it was the fish and chips that did it."

He laughs. "I wish I'd known. It would have made chatting you up a lot easier. I could have just sung 'Happy Birthday' and been done with it, though my singing is pretty terrible."

I'm looking at him in astonishment. "You chatted me up?"

"Absolutely."

"I had no idea."

"How could you not notice? I even sent Oliver in as my envoy."

My eyes go wide. "That's child labor!"

"He got a packet of Haribo and an hour's extra screen time—he was pretty happy."

He's smiling now and gazing at me with those denim-blue eyes, and, as his words sink in, I can feel my disbelief turning to delight.

"I thought you were his dad. I thought you were married," I admit.

"Me? *Married?*"

"Well, don't look so shocked." I smile. "It's not beyond the realm of possibility . . ."

He laughs and takes a large mouthful of wine.

"Is it?"

"Are you asking me if I'm the marrying kind?" His eyes flash with amusement.

I feel suddenly flustered. "No, I wasn't meaning that . . . I was meaning . . ." Only now I've lost the thread of what exactly I was meaning, and I've had a bit too much wine and my attempts at flirting have gone awry—

"I'm only teasing."

I swat him.

"Sorry, I couldn't help it. Will you forgive me?"

"I'll have to think about that."

"Well, don't think about it too long."

"And why's that?"

Then, before I quite know what's happening, he pulls me toward him and he kisses me.

Afterward he holds my hand and walks me home. I can't remember much of what we talk about, but there's a lot of laughing and that flirty "banter" everyone mentions in their dating profile yet until now I haven't experienced.

"I take back everything about online dating. I'm a total convert," I say, as we pause for him to put his sweatshirt around my shoulders. It's soft and warm, and I relish the simple gesture. It's not just about the big stuff when you're single. It's often the little things you notice. When you're on your own, there's no one there to care if you're feeling the evening chill.

"Not a fan, huh?"

"I deactivated my account. I only signed up properly when I got the message from you."

"I should have asked you out that day in the snow, saved you the sixty quid membership fee."

"And the dates," I add ruefully.

"That bad?"

"I think the escape room one was the worst."

He laughs.

"Still, I take full responsibility."

"Oh, I don't believe that for a minute." He shoots me a sideways smile and, despite the sweatshirt, I feel a little shiver run up my spine.

"Well, I hope this one is making up for it."

"Hmm . . ." I pretend to think about it.

"Hey!"

"I'm only teasing," I say, mimicking him earlier, and he laughs. We both do.

But I don't say what I'm thinking: that this date is more than making up for it, that I feel happy and young and carefree, and that it's the first time since Ethan and I broke up that I've looked at another man and thought maybe this could be something.

I'm drunk, but I'm not that drunk.

"Is this you?"

Ten minutes later we reach my front door.

"Yes—" I begin to answer, when we're suddenly bathed in bright light as a security spotlight flicks on.

"Whoa, I'm being blinded." Johnny lets go of my hand.

"Sorry, it's a motion sensor," I explain hurriedly, shading my eyes. No woman of any age wants to have a bright spotlight on her at close to midnight after sharing two bottles of wine, with her date standing only inches away from her face.

But it gets worse. Arthur starts barking. And then—

"Who's that?"

I look up to where Johnny is pointing, to see the curtains twitching at the upstairs window and a bespectacled face squinting down at us.

Oh God.

"That's Edward, my landlord," I say, like it's the most normal thing in the world for someone in their forties to be renting a room and for their landlord to be peering down at them in their pajamas.

Well, OK, he's wearing what looks like a T-shirt, but seriously, it might as well be pajamas.

"Right, well then, I guess this is where I say goodnight . . ."

"Yes." I nod, looking away from the window. "I guess so."

But if I'm disappointed, it doesn't last long. Because then he kisses me again. Only longer this time, and as he wraps his arms around my bare shoulders, I feel like a teenager, kissing on my parents' doorstep, not caring who sees me, not noticing when eventually the light switches off, plunging us back into soft, streetlamp-lit darkness.

I don't know how long we stay like that.

I'm grateful for:
1. *That second bottle of wine.*
2. *Johnny being a really good kisser.*
3. *His text later, saying he had a great evening and inviting me out for dinner on Saturday.*
4. *Alka-Seltzer.*

School Sports Day

I wake up in a really good mood. Not just because of my date with Johnny, but because I'm looking forward to seeing Fiona and Izzy and Lucas. Plus, another gorgeous sunny day has dawned, perfect for a sports day.

But not so perfect for Fiona.

I'm just going out of the door when I get a frantic message from her, saying she's tripped putting out the recycling and rolled her ankle.

"It's nothing serious, but it's swollen up like a balloon. I've had frozen peas on it for the last thirty minutes."

"Ouch! That sounds painful! Will you still be able to make the sports day?"

"Yes, I can't miss it. Luckily the car's automatic and it's my left ankle, so I'm just going to strap it up. But it means I'm not going to be able to take part in the mums' fun run, and I know Izzy will be so disappointed."

"Oh no—"

"So I was wondering, would you take part instead?"

"Me?"

"It's only a short race—don't worry, it's not like one of Holly's marathons."

"Yes, of course!" I don't even have to think. "Anything for Izzy."

"Phew, thanks Nell, you're a total star!"

"It's just . . . well . . . I'm not a mum," I blurt, stating the obvious.

"You're Izzy's godmum—I'm sure it'll be fine." She bats away my concerns. "10 a.m. still OK?"

"Yes, fine—"

"OK, great! Oh, and don't forget to bring your sneakers!"

Izzy's school is impressively set in several acres of grounds and is a world away from my tatty comprehensive school days. The neighboring roads are lined with expensive cars belonging to parents attending the sports day, while the car park looks like a Range Rover dealership's parking lot.

I feel slightly intimidated as I get off at the bus stop and walk through the gates, where I'm greeted by some very glamorous mums milling around. There seems to be lots of competition, and not all of it reserved for the track. I feel like I'm back at school, only as a grown-up. I've heard Michelle complain about what it can be like at the school gates, but now I'm seeing it for real, it's actually all a bit scary.

Glancing around, there appear to be a few different gangs: the Glamorous Mums, the Popular Mums, the Goody-Two-Shoes Mums (they're the ones wearing the "helper" badges), and the Messing Around at the Back Mums.

I think I'd be one of those.

I spot Fiona hobbling toward me with Izzy and Lucas. We haven't met up since the baby shower when everything was so awkward, and I'm really glad to see her. I'm hoping that today we can get things back on track and return to normal.

Izzy breaks free of Fiona's hand and runs up to me, her red gingham dress billowing around her. Scooping her up, I give her a big hug.

"You're running the race instead of Mummy!" she chatters excitedly.

"Yes, I am." I smile happily.

"Nell, you superstar . . . thank you so much." Bringing up the rear with Lucas, Fiona limps over to me, rolling her eyes at her predicament. "What would I do without you?"

"Completely let down your daughter." I grin and she swats me, laughing.

"Are you going to win?" asks Izzy eagerly.

"I'll do my best," I say. "Are you going to cheer me on?"

She giggles and nods.

"But let's remember, it's not the winning but the taking part that counts."

A loud voice behind us makes me turn around, and I see a figure sprinting toward us, ponytail swinging, in head-to-toe Lycra.

Annabel. My heart sinks. She's like a gazelle in Lululemon.

"Isn't that right, girls?"

"Yes, Mummy!" cheers Clementine, nodding her head furiously as she runs alongside her. While Izzy looks unsure and clings on to me tighter.

"Annabel, you look amazing!" cries Fiona as they greet each other. "I'm rather glad I'm not racing now."

"Fiona, you poor darling, how *are* you?"

"I've been better." She smiles dolefully, showing her bandaged ankle.

"You know, I've got an *a-maz-ing* osteopath, he works miracles—he'll have you good as new in no time."

"Really? Oh, wow, thank you. That would be fantastic."

"Absolutely. I'm calling him right now." She reaches into her designer handbag for her phone.

"Luckily Nell stepped in to do the race for me."

"Oh, Nell, hi," she says, finally forced to acknowledge me. "Such a trooper. Always stepping into the breach."

"That's what friends are for." I smile.

Bitch.

"You left the baby shower early."

"Yes." I nod. I'm still holding Izzy, who's refusing to be put down.

"We haven't seen you for a while, have we, Fiona?" Flashing Fiona a smile, she adjusts her position slightly by taking a small step alongside her, then turns to face me. So now we're on opposite sides. Fiona and Annabel on one side. Me on the other.

I promise I'm not making this up.

"I've been helping Fiona with her house. It's looking amazing, isn't it?"

"Annabel has amazing taste." Fiona nods, smiling.

"Where's Clementine? Oh, there you are." She turns to her daughter, who's skirted around the back of my legs. "Clementine and Izzy, why don't you two go and play?"

Izzy finally allows me to put her down and they both go running off across the grass, toward where Lucas has found a gang of friends. I turn back toward Annabel and Fiona, who are now in conversation about light fixtures. The fun run has suddenly taken on huge significance. I'm not racing to cross the finish line first; I'm in a race for Fiona's friendship.

Annabel sees me looking and gives me the once-over, as if weighing up the competition. She seems smugly reassured.

"Are you going to run in flip-flops?" She raises an eyebrow at my footwear.

"No, I've brought my sneakers."

"Nell used to run track at uni," boasts Fiona.

"For one term." I laugh. "Before I discovered the bar on campus and could never make it out of bed before noon."

"What's your best time for the hundred meters?" challenges Annabel.

"Time? I thought it was a fun run?" I try to joke.

"I recently did it in fourteen seconds."

"Erm, well, it was a long time ago . . . I can't remember . . ."

"Look at you two! I had no idea you were both so competitive." Fiona laughs.

"Well, it's not me, I thought it was the taking part that counts—" I begin to protest, but we're already moving off and now my voice is lost in the cheering as the dads' race begins.

It's afterward, as Izzy and I walk over to the refreshment stand, that I bump unexpectedly into Johnny. He's with Oliver, chatting to some of the mums. I'm surprised to see him. A little crowd has formed around him, and they're listening to him attentively and laughing. I feel a tiny beat of pride, as well as pleasure.

"Oh, hi!"

He stops talking as he sees me and smiles. I feel myself blush a bit, remembering the kiss on the doorstep.

"Hey, fancy seeing you." I smile as he kisses me on the cheek. It's a bit different from last night, but I'm not expecting a repeat in public.

"What brings you here?" he asks, and I can feel the eyes of all the women upon me.

"This is Izzy, my goddaughter."

Izzy gives a little wave. "Auntie Nell's going to win the race," she informs him authoritatively.

I laugh. "Her mum's twisted her ankle, so I'm taking her place in the fun run."

"I'll have to make sure to watch that then." He grins.

"Hi, I'm Fiona."

Fiona reappears with several bottles of water and bobs her head at the group.

"This is Izzy's mum," I say, doing the introductions. "Fiona, this is Johnny."

"Nice to meet you." He smiles graciously, then turns to Oliver, who's tugging on his arm. "OK, I'm coming!" He laughs good-naturedly, then looks back up to us. "Well, lovely to meet you, Fiona and Izzy. Nell, I'll catch you later at the fun run." Giving me a wink, he disappears through the crowds.

"Phwoar! *Who* was that?"

Fiona looks at me agog.

"Johnny, the guy I had a date with!" I hiss, my face still flushed from seeing him.

"*That's him!* Oh my word, I want to know *all* the details—"

"Did I miss something?"

Annabel pops up. She's holding a bottle of coconut water and looking irritated that she missed out on the introductions. "I saw you talking to my tennis coach."

"Johnny's your tennis coach?" I feel a jolt of surprise.

"He's Nell's new boyfriend," says Fiona.

"He's not my new boyfriend," I protest, elbowing her as she giggles. Honestly, it's like we're eighteen again and back at university. "We've had one date," I explain, trying not to look as pleased as I feel.

"Remember when we were single," sighs Fiona, glancing at Annabel.

"I know." She smiles, then laughs lightly. "Can you imagine *still* being single?"

And reaching out, she gives my shoulder a little supportive rub.

Seriously. I could kill her.

Failing that, I have to win this race.

We're gathered at the starting line. I look around at the other mums and see they're mostly in various outfits of leggings and sneakers, though there are a few in dresses. I'm wearing my jeans, and a bra that's not supportive enough. Meanwhile, after a winter of muddy dog walks, my sneakers have lost their whiteness and are now the shade of chewing gum on the sidewalk.

Where's Annabel?

I look for her but can't see her. For a brief moment I wonder if she's changed her mind. Decided, perhaps, that a fun run is not up to her Olympic ability. But no, there she is, further along the starting line. She springs toward me until she's just a few mums away, before unzipping her hoodie to reveal a bra top that shows off her insane abs. I watch as every dad's head swivels toward her when she begins limbering up, while their wives shoot evil glances.

My heart is sinking into my muddy sneakers. I can barely touch my toes and the last time I sprinted was for the bus. I glance over at Fiona and the children, who are standing on the sidelines—they wave and smile cheerfully—then back at Annabel, who is doing hamstring and hip flexor stretches.

Most of the other mums are laughing and not taking it very seriously (though there is one in a pair of shorts who looks quite scary), but as Annabel meets my eye, there's no mistaking that look.

All I can say is, have you seen *Gladiator*?

The headmistress appears with a flag. "OK then everyone, if you're ready . . ."

There's an audible hum of anticipation.

"On your marks, get set—go!"

And we're off.

As we hurtle down the playing field, the *Chariots of Fire* theme tune begins playing in my head. Annabel is sprinting ahead, bounding along like a gold-medal winner, but I'm keeping pace. Chest heaving, heart hammering, I pump my arms as hard as they will go, filling my lungs as I race only a few inches behind her, my feet pounding on the grass.

Focus, Nell, focus.

I push harder. My mind is fixated on the finish line, but as I draw nearer it seems to disappear and all I can see is a montage of every moment of my friendship with Fiona: that first day at university when I saw her unloading her car and helped carry in her boxes of old vinyl records; the time she went to blow out the candles on her twenty-first birthday cake and her hair went up in flames and I put them out by throwing a pitcher of margaritas all over her; our trip to Paris when we were so broke we survived on just baguettes for a week and were so bloated we couldn't fasten our jeans; the

178

laughter and muddy tears at Glastonbury; her face when she told me she was marrying David; my face when I first held Izzy and she asked me to be her godmother . . .

And now I feel like Annabel is stealing all that away from me. And I can't let her. I have to catch up and overtake her. I can't let her win.

I dig deep. From somewhere I get an extra burst of energy. I feel myself gaining speed. The young girl that used to run track is coming back, and as I edge closer Annabel looks across at me, her eyes glinting with determination and disbelief and panic that we're neck and neck, and now I'm overtaking her—

I don't know what happens. Out of nowhere, I suddenly feel a sharp elbow in the ribs and I'm pushed sideways. I try desperately to keep my balance, but there's a huge collision and I trip and go flying, landing face down on the ground. While ahead of me Annabel races to victory, crossing the finishing line to a cheering crowd.

She's won.

I'm grateful for:
1. *Johnny, who got me some ice so my black eye isn't as bad as it could be.*
2. *Not feeling like a complete loser after faceplanting in front of everyone, as it was just an accident and not like Annabel deliberately tripped me up or anything.**
3. *Izzy, who gave me her own medal for winning the egg-and-spoon race and told me I was the best godmum ever.*
4. *ABBA's "The Winner Takes It All," which I play loudly through my headphones all the way home on the bus.*

---

* Of course she tripped me up, but this is a gratitude list and no place for murderous thoughts.

What Would Frida Do?

"It sounds hideous, but look on the bright side: it's better than a funeral, which is the only kind of event I get invited to these days."

It's a few days later and I've gone to meet Cricket at the V&A museum to see the Frida Kahlo exhibition, which has just opened. The collection of personal belongings is fascinating, but as she's just gotten back from Dublin we're multitasking and catching up as we move around the exhibits. Standing in front of a case of Frida's colorful Mexican clothing, I'm telling her all about what happened at sports day.

"I guess so." I smile ruefully. "So you didn't hear from Lionel and Margaret about the dinner party?"

"Of course not. I'd upset the table settings, being on my own. Plus, Margaret probably thinks I'll make a play for Lionel."

"*Lionel?*"

"As if I'd want someone else's husband, just because my own has died." She tuts. "And if I did, it certainly wouldn't be Lionel. Did you see the size of his ears? Monty always said he looked like a Toby jug—" She breaks off. "Just look at these amazing ruffled skirts."

"Gorgeous." I nod. "Look at the embroidery on this one."

"That Annabel woman sounds like a piece of work."

"That's one way to describe her."

Since the race I've had several messages from Fiona, saying how upset Annabel is about the whole incident and how she wants my address. "Between you and me, I think she wants to send you some flowers; she's really thoughtful like that. She's been letting me sit in her Jacuzzi with my ankle and even arranged for me to see this amazing osteopath, so it's feeling so much better."

"Brilliant," I messaged back, along with my address, though of course no flowers ever arrived. It was probably a hit man she was thinking of sending.

"Have you seen this hand-painted plaster corset?"

We move over to the glass case where it's illuminated.

"She must have suffered so much pain." I step closer to the glass to study it.

"How's your eye?"

Talk about going from the sublime to the ridiculous. "Still sore, but the bruising's gone down a bit." The last few days, I've hidden behind my sunglasses as it went from black to purple and now yellow. "Hopefully it will be nearly gone by Saturday, as I've got my second date with Johnny."

Cricket's face lights up at the mention of his name. I told her all about our first date earlier when we were standing in line for the cloakroom. "Where's he taking you?"

"Some fancy restaurant. He wants it to be a surprise."

"How exciting." She looks genuinely pleased for me. "Monty used to surprise me with dinner dates. He'd always say, 'Put on something marvelous, Cricket, we're going out.'" She smiles, then sighs. "I do miss him."

I think about the letter and the photograph in my bag. I still haven't mentioned it to her. Despite my reservations, I planned to give it to her today, but now doubts resurface. Why risk upsetting her and changing the narrative? What good will it do?

"You know, I've been thinking about downsizing," she says as we move into the next room.

"Moving?"

She nods. "I don't need such a big house anymore; it's just me rattling around in it. It seems silly. I've been thinking I should sell it and buy myself a nice little apartment."

"But you love that house."

"I do, yes, but it holds so many memories of Monty."

"Isn't that good?" I reason.

"In many ways, yes, it can be of great comfort . . ." She pauses, then gestures around her. "But life isn't a museum, Nell. I don't want to live in the past."

My protests fall silent.

"I don't want to spend whatever time I have left looking backward. I want to look forward. To new things. New places. New adventures. Otherwise I'm just living a life where a part of me is missing." She smiles bravely but her face crumples a little. "I feel his loss so keenly in that house. I miss the sound of his laughter filling the kitchen. The smell of his cigarettes . . . he was only supposed to smoke outside, so he would perch himself by the French windows and argue that technically he was."

Listening to Cricket, I can feel myself identifying with her. Our circumstances are so very different, but so many of the feelings are the same. Ethan might not have died, but our relationship did, and that was a huge part of the reason I moved back to London. I needed a fresh start, a life where I wouldn't be constantly reminded of him at every turn.

"I understand," I say, rubbing her arm supportively. "I think that sounds like a good idea."

She smiles gratefully, then: "Look at these amazing shawls!"

"It's wonderful they've kept all her possessions," I note.

"I'll have to get rid of so many of mine when I sell the house, and not just clothes. All our books alone would fill a library . . ."

I cast my mind back to Cricket's main hallway, lined with bookcases that reach up to the high ceiling, and remember my own, much smaller bookcase, in California. There must be hundreds of books in her house. Thousands, maybe.

"I suppose we could take them to the charity shop, though even they might not have room."

"My local charity shop in California wouldn't take my books," I say regretfully, "but luckily I heard about the free mini libraries."

"What's that?" She turns to me, curious.

"They're these little bookcases, filled with books that are free to take and read. People put them up on street corners or in front of their house. You could have one. The idea is you take a book and leave a book, but they always need restocking as people tend to borrow more books than they donate. But that wouldn't bother you, as you have so many books."

"But where would I put it?" Cricket looks fascinated.

"Well, we could do a small one in the front garden, where people walk past. Now with the local library closing, the neighborhood needs access to free books."

She's quiet as she absorbs the concept.

"Oh, I like that idea very much," she says finally. "Monty always said books weren't meant to be owned, but to be shared."

"I can come over one day and we can do it. It wouldn't take long."

We stop in front of an exhibit of Frida's prosthetic leg, complete with an embellished red boot.

"She never shied away from the truth, did she?" marvels Cricket. "I think that's what I find most inspirational about her."

My mind reflects on past events. It's true. They say the truth hurts, but these past few months have taught me that the human spirit is stronger than it looks. More often, it's the deception that destroys.

"Cricket?"

"Yes, my dear?" She turns to me.

"Let's go somewhere quiet for a drink. There's something I need to show you."

I'm grateful for:
1. *The truth, and having the courage to tell it.*
2. *Cricket's reaction when I gave her the envelope; she looked at the postmark, put it in her pocket, then simply thanked me and ordered another glass of wine.*
3. *That she didn't find the photograph until she was alone, because it wasn't my secret to tell; it was hers to find.*
4. *Museums, because unlike youth-obsessed society, they celebrate old things. Which is why I am going to start looking at parts of my body as if I am on a museum tour and viewing them as exhibits of interest, instead of shrieking at myself in the mirror.*
5. *Frida Kahlo, for being a true inspiration.*

The Second Date

"So how was the second date?"

It's the early hours of Sunday morning, and I've just got in from dinner with Johnny and am lying on my bed, still in full hair and makeup, FaceTiming with Liza. She's on the beach and I can see the ocean and palm trees behind her. Usually that would tug at something inside, but right now I'm too excited about my date to feel anything else.

"Better than the first!"

Pushing her sunglasses onto the top of her head, she makes goggle eyes into the camera. "Nell, that's awesome!"

After picking me up in a cab, he took me to his private members' club, full of achingly trendy people sitting on velvet sofas in darkly lit corners, and we drank cocktails with names like La Paloma and The Hemingway that were delicious and strong and went straight to my head, in that lovely way cocktails do. Followed by dinner reservations at a lovely French restaurant, where we ate incredible food and swirled red wine around in big glasses and flirted up a storm.

"And then, like the perfect gentleman, he called a cab and dropped me home."

Liza, who has been listening the whole time, her mouth agape, just says, "Wow."

"He was even really sweet about sports day and said I should've won."

"I'm so happy for you, Nell, this guy sounds amazing."

I didn't want to say it myself, for fear of jinxing it, but Johnny is pretty amazing. With my past history, I'm scared to let myself get excited, but there were moments during the evening when I found myself looking at him and thinking, "Could it be that I've actually MET someone?" That this was the reason things didn't work out with Ethan; that it had all been written in the stars after all?

Well, I had drunk two very strong cocktails.

"Oh, and get this, it turns out Annabel is one of his clients at the posh tennis club—"

"Like that's a surprise."

"No, but what is surprising is that she tried it on with him."

"What! When?"

There are many reasons I love Liza, but one of them is her ability to invest and be interested in people she has never met.

"I don't know, but he says that happens with a lot of his married female clients. It's a thing, apparently."

"So she's a cheater in more ways than one."

I laugh and as I do, I feel my eyes droop a little. Tiredness has suddenly hit. I try to stifle a yawn and fail.

"It's late. I should go to sleep, but first I want to hear all about *your* date. You said you'd tell me later, but you haven't mentioned it—"

"Oh, it was just someone I met at yoga," she says dismissively.

"I didn't think teachers were allowed to date their students." I smile.

"They're not, *technically* . . ." She shrugs. "It's all a bit complicated."

"Are you going to see them again?"

"I don't know . . . more importantly, when are you seeing Johnny again?"

"Not for a while. He's got to go away for nearly two weeks to coach. It's some pre-Wimbledon tennis thing."

"OK, well that gives you plenty of time."

"Time?"

"You know the third-date rule, right?"

"Is that a millennial thing?"

She laughs. "No, it's a now-you-get-to-sleep-with-him thing."

I'm grateful for:
1. *Thirteen whole days to panic about the thought of getting naked and having sex with someone new.*

MISSING!

LOST LIBIDO

**Have you seen Nell Stevens's
forty-something libido?**

**Large reward for any information
leading to its return.**

- Missing since her last relationship
  broke up and her heart was broken.
- Last seen about six months before she
  moved out.
- Urgently needs to be found before her
  third date with a new guy.
- Owner is worried sick.

IF YOU HAVE ANY HELP OR ADVICE PLEASE CONTACT:
hello@confessionsofafortysomethingfkup.com

IF FOUND PLEASE DON'T APPROACH.
IT COULD BE PERIMENOPAUSAL.

Plus-One

I'm deep asleep when the burbling of my phone startles me awake.

What the—?

My room's in pitch darkness and I fumble for it on my bedside table. I peer blearily at the name flashing up on the screen.

PARENTS.

Panic rushes in. Oh God, it's happening! That middle-of-the-night phone call you start to fear once they get past seventy. It's happening right now—

I snatch up my phone. "Is everything OK?" I gasp into the handset.

"Exciting, isn't it?"

"*Mum?*"

"Have you heard?"

My brain is doing a 180. "Huh, what? Why are you calling me in the middle of the night?"

"It's going on for half past seven. Surely you're not still in bed?"

I hold out the phone so I can squint at the time, whilst telling (deluding) myself that my eyes are only blurry because I've just woken up, and realize that while it might feel like the middle of the night because of my amazing blackout blinds, it's actually 7:28 a.m. Whoever saw the need to invent an alarm clock has never met my mother.

"No, of course not, why would I be in bed at half past seven on a Sunday morning?"

"Haven't you spoken to your brother?"

Mum, however, does not do sarcasm.

"No, why?"

"They've set the date for the wedding!" she excitedly announces. Mum's favorite thing in the world, next to Dad, is being the first one with the scoop. She was wasted as a mobile hairdresser; she should have been a newsreader breaking headline news.

And now, like a sprinter off the blocks, she's off, filling me in on all the details as I stumble into my robe and into the kitchen to make coffee.

"Oh . . . great . . . um . . . yes . . . fab . . . lovely . . ." I mumble through the list of flower arrangements, place settings, wedding venue details, and reception locations.

"I rather thought they might go for a registry office do in Manchester, but they're going to have it in Liverpool, where Nathalie's from . . ."

"Great," I reply, hearing the bubbling of my coffeepot on the stove and thinking there really is no nicer sound. I pour it into my cup, then turn to the fridge to get the milk, and notice the cleaning schedule on the door. It's been there since I moved in and I've religiously ignored it, but now there's a bright orange Post-it note stuck on top.

This is not a fridge magnet.

I break into a smile. Edward can be very funny sometimes.

Mum, meanwhile, hasn't drawn breath. ". . . they don't want a church wedding, so at least your father will be pleased, being an atheist. I had to drag him up the aisle . . ."

Arthur nuzzles my knees, wanting his breakfast, so I busy myself feeding him.

". . . it gives them a couple of months before the baby's born, so she'll be quite big by then, though of course it doesn't matter these days, not like in mine . . ."

It's warm outside, so I sit on the little balcony outside my bedroom and lift my face to the morning sun. Life is so surreal. Who would have thought a year ago I would be back in London, single and listening to plans for my brother and his pregnant fiancée's wedding, when it was going to be me getting married this summer?

Even more surreal is the realization I feel surprisingly fine about it.

"So, do you think you'll be bringing anyone?"

I zone back in. Mum is fishing again.

"Well, I haven't really thought about it," I begin, only for my mind to suddenly shoot ahead. Maybe I could take Johnny?

"Because at least now if you know the date, you can give *whomever* plenty of notice. It's only June, so they've got a couple of months' notice to make travel arrangements if, for example, they need to book flights or something—"

"Ethan won't be coming, Mum."

Boom. It's like dropping the mic.

For the first time since my phone rang, there's silence on the other end of the line. But I'm not racked by my usual guilt at letting everyone down. Now Rich is getting married, I feel I can finally be honest. After all, there's still going to be one wedding in the family.

"Well, it's not for a couple of months; people have a habit of changing their minds," says Mum after a moment.

"I won't change *my* mind."

"Oh, OK, well, it's just, you never said . . ."

My lack of guilt is short-lived. Mum sounds so disappointed. And now I feel awful for crushing her hope. She was so excited when I told her I was getting married; she showed all her friends the photo of my ring.

"Actually, I've met someone," I blurt. "It's early days, but we've been on a couple of dates."

I wasn't going to say anything. I mean, two dates hardly merits a relationship—there's still plenty of time for it to go wrong yet. But . . .

"Oh, that's lovely news, Nell." She sounds both surprised and delighted, and immediately cheers up. "Well, yes, maybe you can bring him as your plus-one—"

"Yes, maybe," I say, taking a gulp of coffee. It burns my mouth.

The Naked Forty-Something

In preparation for my third date, I go all out. No bristly area is left unwaxed. No dry skin is left unscrubbed and unmoisturized. No inch of cellulite is left un-body-brushed. (Is it toward the heart and clockwise, or away and counterclockwise? I can never remember. And if you do it the wrong way, does it make it worse?)

I do so many squats and lunges I can barely get off the sofa, and my knee gives out going up the stairs. I even attempt yoga in my kitchen, but decide if I want to be alive on my third date, it's probably best not to try and do a headstand against the fridge because those celebs make it look *very easy* and it's not. Plus, I share a house with my landlord and he happened to walk in when I was dismounting; I narrowly missed kicking him in the face.

I'm grateful for:
1. *Not passing out in the waxing salon.*
2. *All those workout videos, which I actually do instead of scrolling past them eating chips.*
3. *Mastercard. Whoever said sex was free should look at my credit card receipts.*
4. *Not breaking Edward's jaw.*
5. *Kegels.*

The Third Date

Drumroll, please.

It's Friday night and I'm fiddling with my hair before leaving to meet Johnny. We haven't seen each other for nearly two weeks and I'm *so* looking forward to seeing him, but I'm also really nervous. Not to put too fine a point on it: *ladies, it's been a while.* Plus, I'm older now than when I met Ethan. Back then I was on the right side of forty and trust me, I wasn't thinking about sleeves.

I don't know what's happened. When I was a lot younger sex was no big deal, but somewhere along the line I've lost my confidence a bit. Maybe it's having your heart smashed to bits. Or maybe it's looking in the mirror and seeing a few more wrinkles. Or maybe it's just getting older and feeling vulnerable, and knowing that when you like someone now it's actually a really big deal.

I'm planning on asking Johnny if he wants to stay over tonight. Edward is in the countryside so it's the perfect opportunity, as we'll have the place to ourselves. Which has got me thinking. I need to get my own place. It's six months now since I moved into Edward's apartment, but it was only ever meant to be temporary, just until I got myself back on my feet again. I need to start looking around for something a bit more permanent, something with privacy. I mean, seriously, I'm in my forties renting a room when all my friends are married and settled into nice houses. Kissing on the doorstep was fun the first time, but I don't want to make a habit of it.

That said, this arrangement has ended up working out great for both of us. Edward is hardly ever here, just a few nights during the week, and the reduced rent for looking after Arthur has been invaluable. And so has Arthur. What began as just an arrangement has turned into something so much more, and now he's my constant companion. I don't know how I would have got through the year without him.

As for Edward and me: for the most part we get along, though we have our ups and downs, like any other couple who live together.

But I won't lie. There are times when he drives me crazy. Like, for example, when he went on about the recycling, or turning off the lights, or me trying to kill him in the bathtub. And don't even get me *started* on the toilet paper argument, which from here on in shall be renamed The Toilet Paper Wars.

"There were two extra ones in the bathroom and now they've both gone."

It was last week, when I was in the kitchen. I was making a salad and trying to be healthy (with the added benefit of hopefully losing a few pounds before I had to get naked) when Edward appeared and fired the first shot.

I looked up from slicing cherry tomatoes. "I can't believe you're counting toilet paper rolls," I fired back.

"I can't believe you can go through a roll a week."

"Do you really expect me to explain?"

"Well, I'm just curious. What are you doing with all this toilet paper? There's an exorbitant amount going through the household each week. It's a complete mystery."

"It's basic biology," I said, incredulous, and then because he was still looking at me blankly, added, "You shake. We wipe."

But if I thought that was going to embarrass him into shutting up, I was mistaken.

"Are you grabbing handfuls? You only need to use one sheet each time you go."

"No, I am not *grabbing handfuls*." I waved my knife around a bit and wondered if I should kill him, or tell him about the practice of wrapping used tampons in toilet paper before putting them in the trash. Actually, *that* might kill him. He'd probably choke to death at the mention of, shock horror, *sanitary products*.

"Well, in that case, even if you go to the bathroom five times a day, that's only five sheets, and there's 240 sheets in each roll, so that's forty-eight days. I mean, it's simple math."

I looked at him in disbelief. Not just at him, but my situation. How had this happened? How did I miss the turn that led to successful adult lives with lovely homes and husbands and conversations about which fabulous summer holiday to go on, and instead take the one that led me here?

"Are you for real?" I cried. "I am not having this conversation with you. I am not having to account for my bathroom roll usage! Do you do this with your wife?"

At least he had the decency to blush at this point.

But it did trigger my thinking that I need to get another job that pays better, as I can't afford my own place on my obituary salary—but doing what? I have no idea. I keep reading about how we should all be "following our passions," but I can't exactly make a living out of looking online at property in the South of France . . .

But seriously—actually, I am being serious. I think about all my married friends. It's so much cheaper to be part of a couple. I remember when I lived with Ethan, our rent and bills were halved and he never mentioned toilet paper. Though he did other things. Worse things.

But that's all in the past now.

I look at my reflection in the mirror. After spending ages fussing around with my hair, I've decided to wear it up in a barrette. I pull a few tendrils down by my ears, then, grabbing my jacket and bag, close my bedroom door behind me and head into the hallway.

To hear a key in the latch and see Edward appear.

"I wasn't expecting you home tonight," I blurt, experiencing a crash of disappointment as he walks in the door with his folded-up bike. "It's Friday."

"I forgot something. I needed to come back and get it," he says, taking off his helmet. "I'm going to head back out soon, there's an eight thirty train from the station."

There is a god.

"Going out?" He takes in my outfit.

"Yes, I'm meeting Johnny."

"Oh good." He nods, but his expression is as unreadable as always. Well, unless he's talking about toilet paper or the environment.

As he goes into the kitchen and begins fussing around Arthur, I do a final check in the hallway mirror. I'm really not sure about my hair. I fiddle with it.

"It suits you better down."

In the mirror I catch Edward over my shoulder, watching me.

"Thanks." I smile, ignoring his suggestion. "But I like it better this way."

He looks self-conscious. "Oh, OK, well have a nice evening."

Giving Arthur a final tickle behind his ears, I say bye, then head out of the door. Only when I've gone five minutes down the sidewalk do I reach up and undo the barrette, letting my hair fall loose. Shaking it over my shoulders, I keep on walking.

Morning After the Night Before

So, last night was fun.

Standing over my coffeepot, I wait for it to start bubbling, my mind replaying the last twelve hours. I flirted. I drank. I cracked witty jokes. I felt sparks and butterflies and not even a *sniff* of companionship. Johnny had tickets to a local jazz club, a darkened, cozy space where we listened to Ella Fitzgerald and drank red wine.

On the way home we shared a bag of chips and a cigarette. A cigarette! I gave all that stupid smoking stuff up years ago when I got old and sensible and decided I didn't want to die of some horrible disease if I could help it, but last night it felt reckless and fabulous all at the same time.

So when Johnny told me how he'd wanted to sleep with me the first time he laid eyes on me and how it was now his turn to see me naked, I decided to do what it says in all those articles that tell us to live in the moment. Of course, the red wine helped. But I felt intoxicated in a different kind of way. I wasn't thinking about the past or worrying about the future, I was just totally absorbed in the moment.

Apparently psychologists call it "being in the zone." Personally, I call it finding myself naked with Johnny and not feeling invisible or nervous or laden with emotional baggage, but feeling like I was eighteen again. Admittedly I wasn't parading around the room with all the lights on, but that's what scented candles are for, right?

And he stayed.

I open the cupboard and take out two mugs. I've left him asleep in bed and come into the kitchen to make us both some coffee. While, of course, going via the bathroom to "freshen up." I rub the lip gloss in a bit more with my finger and smile to myself. Then catch Arthur studying me from his basket. He's used to me shuffling around in the morning, zombie-like, in a robe with bits of dried porridge on it. "I have a man waiting for me upstairs, how about that?" I whisper, bending down and tickling his ears.

I only stop when my coffee starts bubbling. Pouring it out, I add some milk and make my way back upstairs. Halfway up I hear my bedroom door and see Johnny in his boxer shorts.

"Hey, I thought you were asleep?"

"I just needed the bathroom."

I smile. "Well, you know where it is."

As I get to the landing, he reaches for the door handle. "I think there's someone in there—"

The words don't even have time to register before the door opens and Edward appears in his boxers. We all converge on the landing. Two men in boxer shorts and a woman in a T-shirt that's not long enough. It sounds like an entertaining rom-com.

It's not.

What it is, is *excruciating*.

"Edward! I didn't know you were here last night."

I'm standing frozen on the landing, still holding the two mugs of coffee, but my mind is scrambling. He was here? The whole time?

"There was an accident and the trains were severely delayed, so I decided to catch the early train down this morning instead."

Looks are flying backward and forward and I want the ground to swallow me up. This is SO awkward.

"Edward, this is Johnny . . ." Feeling the mugs burning my hands, I begin hastily doing the introductions. "Johnny, this is Edward, my roommate."

I can't say landlord. I just can't. Roommate sounds better. More normal. Oh fuck. None of this is normal.

"Hi, mate." Half naked in his boxers, Johnny is unfazed.

"Hi."

Half naked in his boxers, Edward holds out his hand to shake Johnny's. This is completely and utterly surreal. And mortifying.

"Edward's married and lives in the country with his wife and twin boys," I gabble, finally passing Johnny his coffee.

"Well, someone's gotta do it," quips Johnny.

"Excuse me?" Edward frowns.

"Live in the country." He laughs. "Only joking, I'm sure it's beautiful."

"Yes, it is." Edward's face doesn't flinch.

"I'm from the country," I pipe up, but no one's listening to me anymore.

"Well, Richmond is hardly the city," continues Edward, the muscle in his jaw beginning to twitch.

Oh shit.

"Johnny's a tennis coach. Edward used to coach tennis." Hurrah, I've found a bond.

Wrong. I've found a competition. They weigh each other up like rivals.

"Well, I must get on."

And then, just when I think they might actually come to blows, Edward goes back into the bathroom and shuts the door.

As the bolt slides into the lock, Johnny and I retreat into my bedroom and back into bed. But if I had been worried about what Johnny's reaction would be, I needn't have because he finds the whole thing hilarious.

"Did you see his face?" He laughs, pulling me down beneath the covers. "Someone needs to tell him to lighten up."

"Shhh," I whisper. "He's all right."

I feel disloyal talking about Edward behind his back, and oddly protective. It's OK for me to moan about him, but not for anyone else to. Like with family.

"Don't worry, I'll be quiet." Johnny grins, kissing me. Then he throws the duvet over our heads and—

Well, let's cut right there.

I'm grateful for:
1. *The mindfulness movement, though I'm not sure if deciding to sleep with your date is exactly what they mean by living in the moment.*
2. *Candlelight, which is very flattering.*
3. *The return of my missing libido.*

4. *Feeling like things are turning around for me and something is finally going right.*
5. *My 10.5 tog duvet, as it muffles quite a lot of noise.*

Group WhatsApp Message from Max

Our gorgeous son Tom was born this morning at 8:05 a.m., weighing 7lb 5oz. Mum and baby doing well. Dad is booked in for a vasectomy.

JULY
#throw~~back~~upthursday

Summer Holidays

Summer, it turns out, is up there with Christmas at reminding those of us who have fallen through the net of What Life Should Look Like. While all my married friends are getting ready to jet off somewhere hot and sunny or head to their coastal cottages with their families for their summer holidays, I have zero plans.

"We fly to Bordeaux next week, I can't wait," says Holly, after I drop Olivia off from Montessori on Monday afternoon. She rang me up earlier in a bit of a panic as her usual childcare arrangement had fallen through, and was there any chance I could do her a huge favor and go pick her up? Of course I could. If being freelance is good for one thing, it's being the fourth emergency service. So I dropped everything and tubed it halfway across London with my siren blasting.

"It's the first time Adam and I have gone away by ourselves since Olivia was born, and the Dordogne's supposed to be gorgeous—you can kayak past all these châteaux—"

"Sounds amazing."

"Adam wanted a beach holiday, but you know me, I'm not a sit-on-the-beach kind of person."

"I'll go sit on a beach with Adam," I quip. "It's supposed to rain all next week here."

She laughs. "What about you? Have you booked anywhere?"

"No . . ." I say, then add, "not yet."

I'm still buzzing from Johnny's sleepover and, well, you never know. Not wanting to get too ahead of myself, but if things carry on the way they're going, it's not beyond the realm of possibility that we might end up going somewhere together. For a few days. Maybe.

"Fiona mentioned something about you seeing someone?"

I'd seen Fiona on the weekend, when I'd offered to take Izzy to a party after completely screwing up my godmother duties at the school sports day. It was the first time we'd seen each other since then and, apart from Fiona asking how my eye was and me asking how her ankle was, nothing was mentioned. From the outside you'd think everything was perfectly normal, but from the inside it was obvious things were not.

Normal would be laughing until our sides ached about me faceplanting on the playing field, and gossiping about the celebrity dad who was spotted by the refreshment stand. Normal was not making strained conversation about her upcoming holiday to a rented villa in the Greek islands with Annabel and her family, while looking at new curtain fabric swatches she'd dropped over.

Still, afterward I got to spend the afternoon with Izzy, which is always one of my favorite things. I'm sure I'm biased, but she really is the best little girl in the world. She chattered away happily as we walked hand in hand to the party, though once we arrived she became strangely quiet. I think it was the clown, which, to be honest, even I found a bit scary.

Later, I got talking to him; it turned out his name was Chris and he was an actor. Chris was at great pains to tell me that he'd performed Shakespeare at the Old Vic and was just doing this temporarily until work picked up—I probably recognized him from his recent role as Car Crash Victim in a certain popular hospital TV drama? Alas, I didn't. Not even when he took off his curly red wig and nose in the kitchen and played dead, with his tongue lolling out.

"Well, it's early days," I reply cautiously to Holly. "I don't want to jinx it."

"That's great, Nell." She looks really pleased for me. "And you're not going to jinx it! Any man would be lucky to have you. Ethan was an idiot."

I know she's trying to be nice, but calling Ethan an idiot doesn't make me feel better, it just casts doubt on my judgment.

"Well, I should be going . . . I'm meeting Max and Michelle's new baby. Have a great holiday in the Dordogne."

"Oh, give them my love!" Holly pulls me into a hug. "Keep me posted on everything, and thank you so much again for today. You're a lifesaver."

Tom is tiny and perfect and I'm scared I might break him.

"Don't be silly," laughs Michelle. "If Max hasn't managed to break any of our four babies yet, I'm sure you'll be fine."

She tries to hand him to me, but I shy away and sit down in the chair opposite. "No, seriously, I'll drop him."

"I tried that excuse for changing the diapers," jokes Max, bringing through several mugs of tea and handing me one. "Didn't work."

"So how's everything?"

"Exhausting," they both say in unison, then look at each other and laugh.

"I'm going back to work this week, so Michelle's mum's coming to stay for a couple of weeks to help out."

"Oh, that's good."

"And then in August we're going to Cornwall," adds Michelle.

"You're going on holiday?" That didn't mean to come out sounding so accusatory, but even Max and Michelle with a newborn and three children under ten are managing to go away? I feel even more sorry for myself.

"Yes, we've rented a lovely house on the beach—the children are going to love it."

At which point the children make their entrance and come rushing into the living room, bombarding their new brother and me with various hugs, kisses, and glitter slime, and I make my escape. But not before offering to babysit, of course.

Truthfully, I've been too preoccupied by my fledgling relationship with Johnny to care too much that everyone is going away on holiday except me. After he left on Saturday, he texted to say how much fun he'd had last night and I texted back "me too." It's really quite amazing how young and alive a new romance can make you feel. It's like the world just opens up, and instead of seeing closed doors and dead ends, you see exciting journeys and possibilities.

Of course, even admitting that when I record this week's podcast, I feel a bit guilty. Like it's a betrayal of myself and I'm failing somehow. Even now I can hear the rallying cries in my head and from my (most likely nonexistent) listeners about not needing a man to complete me, and how I should be happy on my own. But the thing is, I'm in my forties. I've proved I can survive without a relationship. And no, I don't *need* a man. But I do have a fundamental need for love. I think we all do, don't we?

And while we're at it, I wouldn't mind a summer holiday either.

I'm grateful for:
1. *The mute button, so I don't have to see everyone's holiday photos of sunshine and endless blue skies while listening to the rain lashing at the window.*
2. *Chris the clown, for reminding me that things could always be worse in the job department.*
3. *Cricket, who isn't going on holiday either and texts to make plans to meet up this weekend.*
4. *The fourteen people who downloaded my podcast. FOUR-TEEN ACTUAL LISTENERS!*

Two Blue Ticks

The past week was spent working on a new obituary, recording a new episode of *Confessions*, and looking online at apartments to rent. And realizing that, unless renowned people start dropping

like flies and Sadiq begins commissioning an obituary a day instead of three a week, I can't afford my own place anytime soon.
Even poky studios are beyond my budget.

I try extending my search area, but moving to the suburbs when
you're married with a family is a bit different from doing it when
you're single. At least in London nobody stares and points and says,
"Mummy, look, a lady without a buggy or a four-wheel drive."

I'm joking. I'm not really single. I'm now *seeing* someone. Only,
the thing is, I haven't actually seen him this week. Or heard from
him. The last time Johnny and I WhatsApped was last weekend,
when he said he was going to be really busy for the next couple
of weeks, with it being Wimbledon. Apparently the tournament
inspires many of his clients to brush up on their serves, and he was
booked in to do a lot of coaching.

But surely, even if you're busy, a text only takes a minute to
send. An emoji even less. Two seconds, actually. I timed it when I
sent him one the other day. And I know he read it because of the
blue ticks. Remember in the old days when you could never be sure
if someone had got your text? Or when they could say they hadn't
read it? It's different now. Now I can be out walking with Arthur
and decide to send a quick text—nothing too heavy; I don't want
to appear too keen, but we have slept together, and there was lots
of back-and-forth WhatsApping before—and watch the ticks turn
blue and wait expectantly for a response. But nothing.

I hate those two fucking blue ticks.

Ghosted

"Excuse me?"

"I said, it sounds like you've been ghosted."

It's Sunday afternoon and I'm sitting on a bench with Cricket in Holland Park, enjoying the warm weather and admiring the flower beds, and telling her all about how I haven't heard from Johnny in over a week and how it's really weird.

"*Ghosted?*" I turn to look at her.

"Yes, it's when someone you're dating just disappears without any explanation or contact."

"Yes, I know what it is." I don't know whether to be more shocked that Cricket knows the term, or that it's only just dawned on me that Johnny's done exactly that.

"They were talking about it on some chat show the other day."

"I can't believe it."

"Well, I don't usually watch TV in the day—Monty would be appalled if he knew—but sometimes I just like a bit of background noise—"

"No, not that. About Johnny ghosting me."

"Oh, I didn't mean that he *had*, just that it *sounded* like that . . ." Cricket looks worried that she's spoken out of turn and upset me.

"No, you're right."

"*I am?*"

"Yes." I nod, my mind scrambling backward over the past week and realizing that this isn't about him being too busy with coaching to arrange another date, and it's not weird or odd that he's been reading my texts but hasn't got in touch; it's deliberate. I suddenly feel like a total fool.

"Well, what a complete shit!" Cricket explodes.

I snap back to the present.

"I'm sorry, excuse my language, but he is."

Feelings of shock, hurt, disappointment, and rejection are coming at me from all angles. My eyes prickle. I can't believe it. I'm such an idiot. Anger flares, but I still want to cry.

"You're right, he is." I nod, finally.

Then I laugh—not just because it's my default setting in times of crisis or because I still can't quite believe it, but because in life there are a few, rare people who can always make you laugh, even when it feels like you've got absolutely nothing to laugh about, and I'm lucky to be sitting right next to one of them.

And I *really* don't want to cry.

I'm grateful for:
1. *An eighty-something widow who swears like a trooper and never fails to surprise me.*
2. *Johnny's profile, which I never bothered to look at until now, where he says he's only looking to date women up to thirty-five. Thirty-five! He's five years older than me! No wonder he never came up in my search or as any of my matches. I feel annoyed and indignant and like a bit of an idiot, until I see his moody black-and-white headshot, which was taken about twenty years ago, look through his embarrassing bathroom-mirror selfies, and read the rest of his misspelled profile, which includes "your" instead of "you're" and "'there" instead of "their," and realize that actually, if anyone's the idiot, it's him.*
3. *It not being awkward between Cricket and me about the letter, which she didn't mention and so neither did I, as she obviously doesn't want to talk about it.*
4. *My stash of premixed gin and tonics (probably easier if I have this on my gratitude list as a default setting).*
5. *Still having fourteen podcast listeners, plus now there's another four! I can't believe it's gone up to eighteen!*

Guilty as Charged

A few days later, Edward and I had another one of our "domestics." This time it was the ice-cube tray.

"What's this?" he demanded, coming in from work on Wednesday evening and pointing dramatically at the ice-cube tray in the freezer drawer, like Hercule Poirot when he finds the murder weapon.

"An ice-cube tray," I replied.

"An *empty* ice-cube tray!"

Oh shit.

"Do you think it fills itself up?" he accused.

The thing is, no, of course I didn't. It'd just been a rough few days, and when I used the last ice cubes for my gin and tonic, filling up the ice-cube tray from the water-filter jug (which always seems to want filling and you have to wait what feels like forever while it filters through, drip by drip) and balancing it carefully in the freezer drawer, so it didn't spill when you tried to close it, was the last thing on my mind.

Of course, I told none of this to Edward. Edward is one of those people for whom filling up an ice-cube tray is a duty not to be shirked. He would never *dream* of being so slovenly as to shove an empty ice-cube tray back in the freezer, regardless of what else is going on. He does everything in the order that you're supposed to, whether it's the small stuff in life or the big stuff. He grew up, got married, bought a house, had children; he didn't miss any steps.

Which is why Edward has not found himself at forty-something with his life in a mess. He is not being ghosted and wondering where he went wrong, and drinking gin and tonics straight from the can because there are no ice cubes left, because some useless idiot didn't fill up the tray.

"You're right. I'm a terrible person."

"Well, thank you, but I wouldn't say you're a terrible person."

"I am. If I'd filled up the ice-cube tray, my life would not be in the mess that it is now."

Edward looked slightly alarmed by this sudden turn of events. One minute he was talking about the ice-cube tray and the next I was talking about emotions.

"Well, I'm not sure how you reason that . . ."

His body stiffened, as if bracing himself.

"That ice-cube tray is a metaphor for my life. What did I *think* was going to happen when I ran out of ice cubes? Huh? HUH?" I was upset about Johnny, and after bottling it up for the last couple of weeks, my emotions found an outlet and I suddenly burst into tears.

Poor Edward.

"Let me make you a drink. A proper gin and tonic, not like in those silly cans I keep finding in the recycling—"

"But we don't have any ice cubes," I wailed.

He smiled kindly. "They do at the pub."

So now we're here at the pub and it's a bit weird, being with my landlord. We've never been out of the house together, and it's strange to see him in a setting that doesn't include the microwave or the fridge. Like the time in California when I saw one of my favorite Hollywood actors in the pasta aisle at Whole Foods. It was so odd. I'd only ever seen him looking gorgeous on screen, and there he was in a dodgy tracksuit with a jar of organic marinara sauce.

"I wasn't sure what gin you like, so I got Hendrick's," he's saying now, coming back to the table with two drinks. "I hope it's OK."

"Thank you." I take a sip; it's very strong and I haven't eaten anything. I take another sip.

"I trust it's up to your usual standards."

It's an attempt at a joke, but for once I can't even manage a smile.

"Oh, I'm not fussy."

Edward shifts in his seat and I feel immediately guilty. I owe him an explanation at least.

"I've been ghosted," I blurt.

"What?"

I sigh into my drink. "Johnny. The guy I was seeing. He disappeared."

"As in, missing?" Edward looks concerned.

"As in I haven't heard from him in nearly two weeks and I'm not going to." I stab an ice cube with my straw. "I think you could say I've been dumped, Edward."

He looks sympathetic. "I'm sorry to hear that."

"And I keep wondering if I said the wrong thing, or appeared too keen, or slept with him too soon."

Sitting across from me, Edward's face is impassive, but now the muscle in his jaw twitches.

"I mean, what is it with me and relationships? You know, before I moved in with you I lived with my fiancé for five years, and look how that fell apart."

I'm on a roll now and I've already hoovered up my drink. Edward doesn't say anything but offers to buy me another one. I don't say no.

As he goes to the bar, I think about Ethan. I can't compare what happened between us with what happened with Johnny. I loved Ethan. I was completely *in* love with Ethan. We had a life together. I thought we had a future together. I was devastated when it ended. Johnny was a distraction from all that. He was handsome and charming and entertaining, but now I've had time to get some perspective I've realized we never had any proper conversations, never revealed our true selves. It was just banter and flirting and rosé and sex. And it was fun while it lasted.

Edward returns with another gin and tonic and several bags of chips. A man after my own heart. I dive into them hungrily.

"I just liked him, that's all, and I thought he liked me." I shrug, tearing open the cheese and onion.

"I'm sure he did. But men like Jonathan McCreary like themselves a lot more."

I stop mid-mouthful. "Jonathan McCreary? Hang on, is that . . . Johnny? *You know him?*"

Edward nods. "I know *of* him. We'd never been formally introduced until recently . . ."

As he alludes to that awkward moment on the landing, I feel myself cringe with embarrassment.

"But I've lived in the area long enough to learn of his reputation."

"*His reputation?*"

I look to Edward for an answer, but none is forthcoming.

"*What* reputation?"

"Let's just say he has an eye for the ladies."

"Why didn't you tell me before?"

"Well, it seemed a little late for that . . ."

We look at each other and this time I can't help but smile. It's so bad it's comical. Plus, the gin and tonics are really helping.

Edward opens the salt and vinegar and offers me one.

"At the end of the day, it's the rejection, really," I continue, taking one and in turn offering him the cheese and onion. "Have you ever been rejected? I bet you haven't."

"I've had my share of rejections."

"When?"

"Well, I didn't get into Oxford."

I roll my eyes. "I thought you were going to tell me about a girl!"

"Oh, it was much worse than any girl. Dad was horribly disappointed. He'd been at Christ Church and it was expected I'd do the same, and then follow him into banking and become a CEO or the chairman of a major financial institution."

"So what happened?"

"I went to Bristol and set up my software company."

"Well, that's good, isn't it?"

"Not for my father it's not. Three generations of Lewises have gone into banking."

I watch Edward pause to take a large drink of his gin and tonic. To anyone else he has a successful career, but not, apparently, to his own father.

"What about your mum?" I ask, remembering Cricket saying it was important not to be afraid of mentioning loved ones who have died. "What would she have wanted for you?"

"To be happy," he says, without missing a beat. "To do what I love. To follow my passion."

"So you did! Though I don't know how anyone can be passionate about software," I joke, pulling a face.

"Ah, now that's where the perception of software is so misconstrued," he replies good-naturedly. "My work is focused on the environment, and creating and developing software to deal with renewable energy solutions. Today's global challenges need new technologies and we're at the cutting edge of providing the software that will enable this, so it's really incredibly exciting."

He lost me at "renewable energy solutions." I'm two large gin and tonics in, and I honestly don't have much of a clue what he's talking about. But seeing how passionate he is about what he does, I realize I've been wrong about quite a few things concerning Edward.

And now I've finished another drink.

"Same again?" I stand up unsteadily. "This time it's my round."

"Same again." He smiles. "And more chips."

Funny how things have a habit of turning around, isn't it? I was so upset before, and now look at me—I'm really quite cheered up.

"More chips." I nod, doing a little mock salute before making my way to the bar.

Throwback~~back~~Up Thursday

I'm grateful for:
1. *The bucket next to my bed.*
2. *Being self-employed, so I only have to make it two feet from my bed to my desk.*
3. *My laptop, in case I can't even manage that.*
4. *Burnt toast and paracetamol.*
5. *Edward, who calls me later from the office to see if I'm OK and to tell me there's fresh orange juice and tomato soup in*

the fridge, that he was the one who put the bucket by my bed, not to worry about taking Arthur out as he's arranged for a dog walker, and to just get some rest.

6. *Knowing there are kind people in this world.*

Secrets and Lies

So I've decided: I'm going on a health kick. I swore I was going to turn things around this year, but it's already July and I'm still single, broke, and surviving on chips and alcohol. Er, hello, mind–body connection! How can I expect a fresh start and a new me when a smashed avocado on rye toast hasn't so much as passed my lips? I need to ditch the sugar, stay off alcohol, avoid carbs, and eat wholesome nutritious meals involving lots of ancient grains and fermented things.

No one said healthy eating had to be fun.

That said, it looks fun in all those celebrity cookbooks. In lovely white kitchens, with full hair and makeup. But I'm not sure I believe it. I lived with a chef who did amazing things with tofu, but no one was worse than Ethan when it came to junk food. He would fight you to the death for that last slice of pizza.

So anyway, I've spent the last week drinking green juices and eating salads. And I've never been as healthy, or as broke. Seriously, have you seen the price of a green juice in a glass bottle? Because, of course, I can't buy plastic. Otherwise, in looking after my health I'm destroying the health of everything in the ocean, which seems a bit at odds somehow.

"What can I get for you?"

Standing in line at a juice bar, I look up at the chalkboard.

"Can you tell me what's in a Green Detox, please?"

In keeping with my health kick, I made appointments this week to see my doctor and dentist for annual checkups, and I've just finished at the hygienist, which is around the corner from the health food store.

"Yes, it's kale, spinach, broccoli, celery, and apple," says the cheery bearded man.

"Great, I'll have one of those. But no apple, thanks."

They always try to sneak in apple, but I know that's because apples are cheap and it's a way of diluting all the good expensive green stuff. A little bit is fine, but if you're not careful you'll end up paying ten pounds for what's basically apple juice. So I always refuse all apple. Which means my juice always tastes absolutely revolting, but at least I know it's healthy.

"Here you go."

"Thanks." I take a sip through my paper straw and wince.

I leave the cafe and begin weaving my way back down the main street, looking in various designer shop windows and wondering what it must feel like to be able to afford all these expensive clothes. Imagine just walking in and not even having to look at the prices.

My bladder twinges, interrupting my daydream. It's all this green juice. It goes right through you.

Spotting a pub on the corner, I hurry inside and head straight for the ladies'. It's only on my way out that I spot a figure in the corner nursing a pint. Hang on, *is that—*

"Max?"

As he hears his name called, he looks up.

"It is you! I thought I recognized you."

"Oh . . . hi, Nell." He looks surprised to see me. "What are you doing here?"

"I could ask you the same." I grin, giving him a kiss on the cheek. "Aren't you supposed to be at work?"

"Lunchtime," he replies, as I slide into the seat opposite him.

I gesture to the clock on the wall showing it's three in the afternoon. "You have long lunches." I smile. "Is that part of your promotion?" Then I notice his eyes are a little bloodshot. I feel a pulse of concern. "Hey, is everything all right?" I lower my voice. "It's not Tom, is it?"

"No, I mean, yes, everything's fine. Tom's fine. He's great."

I relax, but only for a moment.

"It's my promotion."

So there *is* something wrong.

"What about your promotion?" I ask, and then, because he doesn't answer, I urge, "What is it? Too much pressure?"

"I didn't get it." He cuts me off.

"What?"

"I didn't get the promotion. It went to another colleague. He's fifteen years younger than me and hasn't anywhere near my experience, but . . ." He shrugs.

"But why? I don't understand. It was a reward for all your hard work the past year. You deserved that promotion!"

But Max doesn't answer. He doesn't even meet my eyes. He just tips the rest of his pint down his throat.

"Hang on—does Michelle know about this?"

He holds his empty glass and continues staring at it.

"Oh Max, you've got to tell her. So you didn't get the promotion—so what? It doesn't matter, you're being too hard on yourself." I reach out and rub his arm supportively.

"No, I'm not." Finally he brings his eyes up to mine and meets my gaze. "When I didn't get the promotion, there was some restructuring within the company . . ." He trails off, shaking his head. "My role wasn't needed anymore."

I'm looking at him, trying to make sense of what he's telling me.

"You mean—?"

"I've been 'let go.'"

Max looks so broken I don't know what to say.

"When did this happen?" I manage, trying to hide my shock.

"Weeks ago."

Abruptly I realize he's probably been in here all day. Every day. For weeks now.

"But they can't just do that—"

"They can, and they did." Wearily, Max rubs his face with the heels of his hands. "I'm self-employed. We were all on freelance contracts. They don't have to pay out redundancy. They don't have to do anything."

As the reality of the situation sinks in, anxieties begin mushrooming. Max has got four kids . . . he's the sole breadwinner . . . they've just had another baby . . .

"So Michelle doesn't know about any of this?" My voice is calm but my mind is racing. God knows how Max must be feeling. Getting up every day, putting on a suit, leaving the house as if everything is normal.

He shakes his head. "No, and you mustn't tell her either. I don't want her stressing out, not with the new baby."

"But you have to tell her."

"I know, but not yet. It will only worry her. I need to figure something out first."

"Have you tried looking for another job?" As soon as I say it, I wish I hadn't. Max looks at me as if I'm a complete moron. "Sorry, I didn't mean—"

"Just don't say anything, OK, Nell? Promise me."

I look at Max, fifty years old and a father of four. His dark brown eyes are all crinkled around the edges now, and he's got gray flecks in his hair, but he's still that gangly twenty-something who I caught the ferry with across to the Greek islands. Who lent me his sleeping bag because I was cold and he wanted us to sleep out on the top deck and watch the sunrise, and talk about the future and how great our lives were going to be.

My chest tightens as he meets my gaze. He's imploring me.

"I promise," I say quietly.

He was right about one thing. It was a beautiful sunrise.

Be Happy

Am I the only person in the world who's sick of being told to be happy?

This morning I woke up feeling a bit crap and looked at my phone . . .

Be Happy! Choose joy! Find your bliss!

And felt even more crap.

Can't we just be allowed to feel a bit *bleugh* sometimes without this constant pressure? Max certainly isn't happy right now. Cricket wasn't feeling joyful when she cleared out Monty's clothes. And bliss to me right now would be something to take away this awful PMS, and crawling back underneath my duvet. Sometimes life is crap, and wrapping it up in an inspirational quote isn't always going to make you feel better. On the contrary, sometimes it just makes everything feel worse.

Take the other day, for example. I was reading another article online about how important happiness is and all the different ways you can achieve it. But reading it just made me feel depressed. Which is a bit ironic when you think about it. I felt like there must be something wrong with me because, as hard as I tried, I *wasn't* feeling happy. Even worse, none of the author's suggestions helped either. So then I wasn't just abnormal, I was a failure too.

See, that's why I get annoyed. We're encouraged to be our true, authentic selves, but being told to feel happy when you're just not feeling it only encourages us to be the exact opposite. Life can be wonderful but it can also be scary and hard. We should be free to feel sad or gloomy or just downright bloody miserable, without feeling like there's something wrong with us.

Because sometimes happiness isn't a choice. Sometimes, no matter how hard you try, you can't find joy. Which is why I've decided to stop beating myself up by desperately seeking happiness and give myself the permission to feel exactly how I feel, when I feel it. In fact, maybe, it's not happiness we should be looking for after all—but acceptance.

I'm grateful for:
1. *Taking the pressure off myself.*
2. *Knowing there are going to be moments in life when you'll feel upset or scared or unhappy, just like there are times when you'll feel joyful and amazing and happy.*
3. *All those wonderful doctors and professionals and therapists, who are always there if it's not just about feeling a bit fed up for a while, but something much more than that.*
4. *Being happy today, and it had nothing to do with a motivational quote.**

The Doctor's Appointment

Monday morning finds me sitting in my doctor's waiting room, booked in for a Pap smear. Like I said, no one said this health business was supposed to be fun.

"Penelope Stevens?"

Hearing my name being called, I see the nurse appear holding a clipboard. As I stand up to follow her into her room, she gives me a warm smile that puts me immediately at ease. Nurses are just fab, aren't they?

So then we get down to business. She takes my details and asks me when my last period was.

"Um . . ." It suddenly strikes me that I can't remember. I've felt

---

* Though I confess there was a rather beautiful sunset involved.

a bit PMS-y for ages. In fact, hang on, now I'm thinking about it, wasn't it supposed to be last week?

"Don't worry, let me give you a calendar." She smiles, passing me one. "It's often easier this way."

I stare at the dates. "Well, actually, it was supposed to be the middle of the month . . ."

"Hmm. I see." She's still smiling. "Is there any reason you can think of why it might be late?"

"No."

"Have you been sexually active?"

Oh fuck. *Johnny.*

"Well, yes, but that's impossible," I say briskly, shutting down that thought as soon as it surfaces.

"Oh, you'd be surprised—one of my patients is forty-seven and pregnant with twins," she continues. Then, seeing my expression, she adds quickly, "But let's not get ahead of ourselves, shall we? If you'd like to pop behind the screen and get undressed from the waist down, then just hop on the bed . . ."

I do as I'm told. It's a bit uncomfortable. A speculum is both an instrument of torture and an instrument that saves life. I focus on the ceiling tiles as the nurse chats away, trying to put me at ease as she works efficiently. There's a bit of plastic that's broken around one of the spotlights. One of the bulbs is out.

"OK, all done." She smiles cheerfully, taking off her surgical gloves and handing me some paper towels.

"That was quick." I smile gratefully. "Thank you."

As she disappears behind the curtain, I quickly get dressed.

"Now, Penelope," she says as I reappear, "I'd just like you to do a urine sample for me." She holds out a little plastic bottle. "If you don't mind."

As I sit on the toilet, peeing into that little plastic bottle, a million different thoughts are going through my mind. Emotions are threatening to surface. It's hard to get a handle on them all, so

I don't even try. Don't go there, Nell. I screw on the plastic top tightly, give the bottle a quick rinse under the sink and dry it with a paper towel. The amber liquid feels warm in my hand. Whatever you do, just don't go there.

"You're not pregnant." The nurse is matter of fact. "So we can rule that out."

"Well, I didn't think for a minute—"

"But it does mean most likely you're going through the peri-menopause."

"Right, yes, I see."

In the space of a few minutes, the pendulum of youth has swung from Still Fertile and Possibly Pregnant to Old Crone with Rotten Eggs. Not that I wasn't already aware of my biological clock—what woman isn't?

From the moment I got my first period, everyone has had an opinion about my fertility. From the teacher at school who showed my class of thirteen-year-old girls our first sex education video and explained about contraception, warning against teenage pregnancy, to the nurse giving me a Pap smear at thirty-three who told me, in no uncertain terms, that if I wanted children I needed to "put a fire underneath it, honey."

So it comes as no surprise that for most of my life the thought of finding myself pregnant was the most terrifying thing in the world—until the poles unexpectedly switched, and suddenly more terrifying was the thought of leaving it too late.

"Which would explain your periods becoming erratic," the nurse is saying now. "You might find they get heavier, or lighter, and there can be other symptoms."

"Symptoms?"

"Hot flashes can be quite common, as can night sweats and mood swings, even depression . . . oh yes, and weight gain."

This Monday morning is just getting better and better.

"And how long does this usually last for?"

I'm hoping a few months, a year at the most for good behavior.

"Oh, it can be anything from a few years to about ten."

"Ten years?" Murderers get out in less.

"Yes." She smiles brightly. "But don't worry; usually by then you'll have reached the menopause."

I force a smile. "Well, at least that's something to look forward to."

I'm grateful for:
1. *All the money I'm going to save on tampons when the big M finally happens.*
2. *The family-size packet of cheese puffs and bottle of wine I bought on the way home, because if I'm going to be battling night sweats and depression, I need more than salads and green juice.*
3. *A bona fide reason for weight gain, and not just that I ate the entire packet of cheese puffs.*
4. *The beacon of hope that is the forty-seven-year-old pregnant lady with twins, not only for dialing down the panic by showing me that I have a few years left BITL, but for being a goddam superwoman.*
5. *Not actually being forty-seven and pregnant with twins; I feel exhausted just thinking about it.*

Panic and Potential

It's been a week now since I bumped into Max, and I can't stop thinking about him. I don't want to interfere—I promised—but I'm worried. Too many times I've read tragic stories in the news about what happens when the pressure becomes too much. Men just like Max. *He was the life and soul of the party. He'd just had a new baby, he seemed so happy. All his friends loved him. He was a brilliant husband and dad.*

I resolve to check in on him daily and bombard him with texts and voice messages. Basically it's the opposite of ghosting. It drives him crazy and he begs me to stop. I refuse. I'm like a kidnapper demanding a ransom: he speaks to Michelle and he'll get his life back, a life that doesn't include about twenty messages and several missed calls a day.

Meanwhile, I'm feeling a bit depressed after my doctor's visit. Being perimenopausal might not be as bad as losing your job (It's worse! I'm joking. Sort of.), but at least you can get another job, whereas I'm looking at a future of night sweats and hot flashes and elasticated trousers, because nothing else is going to fit me after I've gained all that weight.

Of course, I realize this is just a new stage of life, and one that—if all this midlife stuff is to be believed—I should be embracing. But what if you're not ready for this new stage? What if you haven't even reached the old stage yet? Even if you're not sure about having kids it's comforting to know you've got options. No one wants to be The Woman For Whom Time Ran Out. You want to be the one making the decisions. Sitting on the fence is one thing, but what happens when the fence is taken away from you? Do you jump off joyfully or fall crashing to the floor?

I don't know, but I'm sure someone has written an article about it. Because of course it's a free-for-all when it comes to women and the issue of children. I've lost count of the number of articles I've read about the perils of being a teenage/single/older mum (delete depending on what day it is). The warnings from "experts" against focusing on your career and leaving it too late, versus the shaming of teenage pregnancy. For young women today, to freeze or not to freeze, *that* is now the question. And let's not forget the endless debates about those who choose not to have children.

Everyone has an opinion about it. It's quite strange really, when you think about it, because we just accept it as normal. For years

I've been told that as a woman my thirty-fifth birthday was to be spent panicking as my fertility threw itself off a cliff. While if you believe everything you read, turning fifty appears to hold the joys of dealing with The Menopause.

I can't wait!

Meanwhile, men get to buy a sports car and a leather jacket.

Such is my excitement that I talk about this in my latest *Confessions* podcast. I also talk about Johnny. Being reminded of him at the doctor's is partly the reason for my slump. I'm still no closer to working out why he ghosted me, but I have a feeling it's going to be one of those unsolved crimes. "The Date That Vanished: A True-Life Mystery."

However, I have worked out that it's not really him I miss—after all, we only went on three dates—but all the promise that came with him. Being an anonymous podcaster, I refer to him as Mr. Potential because, if I'm honest with myself, that's what I was probably the most excited about.

It's a dangerous thing, potential.

I'm grateful for:
1. *"Feeling a bit depressed" and in a "slump" for being a world away from The Fear.*
2. *Having so many ways to contact (hassle) Max: email, text, WhatsApp, phone call (though he might not share my gratitude).*
3. *My podcast—I have thirty-two listeners!*
4. *The miracles of modern science for being able to help The Woman for Whom Time Ran Out become The Woman Who Has Options.*
5. *Not panicking.**

---

* Well, maybe sometimes, when I read one of those scary articles, but I think that's normal (and fully their intention).

Le Mieux Est l'Ennemi du Bien

At the weekend I go over to Cricket's as a local carpenter has finished making her little library bookcase. Shaped like a house, it's erected on stilts so that it sits over the railings, facing the sidewalk. Now we've just got to stock it with books.

"What about some Steinbeck?"

We're standing in the front garden surrounded by cardboard boxes, the contents of which have been taken from the bookcases indoors, trying to select what to put on the shelves. Cricket is in a really good mood. In fact, I'd say it's the most energized I've seen her. The project has given her a whole new lease on life.

"Ooh yes." I nod approvingly, as Cricket slots a couple next to some of Monty's well-thumbed John le Carré paperbacks and the collected works of Voltaire. "*The Grapes of Wrath* is one of my favorite books ever." I trace my finger down the raised gilt bands on the spine. "Hang on a minute . . ." I pick it up and flick open the first few pages, then stare at the imprint with disbelief. "This is a first edition!"

"Yes, I know," replies Cricket cheerfully. She continues rootling through the box. "How are we feeling about poetry?" She waves a volume of Keats at me.

"Cricket, this is really valuable! We can't put it out here." I can't believe I'm actually holding a first-edition Steinbeck. Somebody pinch me.

"Why not? I've read it. Let someone else read it now. As Monty always said, books are meant for sharing, not owning. No point in it just being stuck in my bookcase."

It's a good argument and a view I share—I'm always passing along books—but then mine are usually paperbacks that have been dropped in the bathtub. Not rare and extremely expensive classics.

"Let's just keep the first editions to one side for now," I suggest, not wanting to dampen her enthusiasm by telling her it will probably end up on someone else's bookcase, most likely a rich collector's.

"Whatever you think." She beams, holding out a stack of hardbacks. "So tell me, what did we decide about poetry?"

We carry on until late afternoon, sorting through books and selecting what to go on the three small shelves. In theory it should take twenty minutes. An hour tops, if you're really indecisive. But that wouldn't allow for chatting to all the different passersby who, interested in what we're doing, stop to ask questions.

Most people in the neighborhood have heard about the closure of the library and share our dismay; a free little library is exactly what the community needs, and their response is enthusiastic and encouraging. Several people offer up their used books, others ask questions about setting up their own library, while some just take the opportunity to stop and chat.

Every so often I catch myself looking across at Cricket, deep in conversation with someone, and can't help smiling. It's not just the little library that's coming alive, it's Cricket too. By giving something to the community, she's getting so much more back. People offer to drop by with books, numbers are swapped, introductions are made, hands are shaken and cheeks are kissed.

I listen to the stories of people who have lived here twenty, thirty, even forty years, telling me about how much the area has changed, how it used to be mostly antiques shops before it became gentrified and all the designer shops moved in, "pushing up prices and pushing people out." While on the flip side I meet a couple from New York who have recently moved to the area and are happily embracing the designer lifestyle, and chat to the mother of a little girl, who offers up some of her children's books while confessing to being sick of looking at her phone but not having time to read.

"Word by word, page by page," Cricket tells her cheerfully, "that's how a writer writes and how a reader should read. You'll get there in the end. Doesn't matter if it takes six months or a year or longer to finish it. That's what I always used to tell my husband."

She ends up borrowing *The Great Gatsby*.

"Well, that was fun," I say, as we finally say goodbye to the last person and make our way inside with our empty boxes. We already had to replenish the shelves during the afternoon, as so many people were eager to borrow books.

"Monty would have loved it," says Cricket, climbing the front steps and closing the door behind us. "Seeing everyone enjoying his books, it was like having him back again."

I follow her into the Bumblebee-yellow living room and we flop onto opposite ends of the sofa, sinking back into the worn velvet that's been warmed by the afternoon sun. For a few moments we both rest our heads and close our eyes, bathed in the shafts of light that stream in from the French windows. The room is quiet but for the tick of the clock on the mantelpiece.

"I read the letter, you know."

Still resting my head on the sofa, I turn sideways and look across at Cricket. Her eyes are still closed.

"It was a love letter to Monty from Pablo."

"I didn't read it," I say quickly. It's the first time we've spoken about it. "I just saw the photograph. I'm sorry, it just fell out of the envelope—"

"My dear girl, you've nothing to be sorry for." Opening her eyes, she turns to meet mine. "I'm not upset."

"You're not?"

"That my husband loved a man before he loved me?" A slow smile reaches her eyes. "No, I'm not."

We both look at each other, our cheeks still resting on the velvet.

"They met in Paris when they were in their early twenties," she continues quietly. "Pablo was a painter. Monty a struggling playwright. They became lovers. Monty never wanted me to know.

He was terribly ashamed of that part of himself. It's not like today. The younger generation are so fluid about sexuality, there's no shame . . . and why should there be? But it was different in those days. And I loved him, so I pretended I didn't know his secret."

"You knew?"

"All along," she replies, without missing a beat. "From our very first date, I knew Monty had a past. There were rumors. I suspected. I found a telegram, a few notes, a photograph . . . it didn't take much to piece it all together."

There's a pause as she casts her mind back.

"I knew Pablo had been his first love and theirs had been a brief but passionate affair. They reconnected later in life when Monty became ill. I saw a card that I wasn't supposed to see at the hospital. A missed call from a Spanish number on his phone. I never let him know."

Listening to Cricket, I wonder if I could be so accepting. "You're an amazing woman."

"Monty was an amazing man," she replies simply. "He wasn't perfect, but who is? What is? *Le mieux est l'ennemi du bien.*"

I frown, not understanding.

"Voltaire, the French philosopher, wrote 'the best is the enemy of the good,'" she explains. "Though I think a better translation would be 'don't let perfect be the enemy of good.'"

I absorb the words, twisting the phrase around in my mind.

"Would I choose that my husband loved a man before he loved me?" She turns her gaze to the ceiling, where the large ornate chandelier is catching the light. "No, and I struggled with it at first. Neither would I choose his shocking temper and his filthy habit of stubbing out cigarettes on his saucer. Or his fondness for finishing my *Times* crossword.

"But would I choose his generosity and his compassion? His brilliant mind and ability to quote Derek and Clive off by heart? Or how when I was in a room with him he made me feel like I wouldn't care if the rest of the world ceased to be?"

With our heads still resting upon the back of the sofa, we both watch the light display of rainbow prisms dancing around the walls. It's pretty obvious this isn't a question.

"Damn right I would. Every single time."

Text Exchange with Max

I told Michelle last night. You were right, I should have told her ages ago. Anyway, thanks for being such a good friend, Nell.

Oh good! I'm so glad. How's Michelle taken it?

She was great. Didn't chop off my balls.

No, she's leaving that to the surgeon ☺

Fuck off x

xx

AUGUST
#bikinibodiesandbabies

The Invisible Woman

When I was a child I used to wish I was invisible. Imagine how fantastic that would be? I could go anywhere, do anything, and I'd be completely unnoticed. Of course, it was only make-believe. But now, guess what? My childhood wish has finally come true. I'm invisible!

It's Thursday morning and I'm walking Arthur while keeping an eye out for Johnny. I haven't seen or heard from him for several weeks, and the last thing I want is to bump into him by accident. With this in mind I decide to take a different route up to the park, past the new complex of luxury apartments they're building, which is full of scaffolding and construction workers.

In my twenties, I dreaded walking past workmen. I used to cross the road to try and avoid them and hurry along with my head down, eyes glued to the sidewalk, for fear of being noticed. I hated it when they would wolf whistle and shout out. The feminist within would rage, "How dare they sexualize me!" I felt violated. Embarrassed. Totally self-conscious.

Fortunately times have changed. I think it's illegal now to shout things, though you can't stop them looking.

Well, actually you can. Turn forty-something.

Walking along in my jeans and T-shirt, I pause to let Arthur sniff a lamppost. It's not like you imagined as a child. It doesn't happen overnight—it's not as if one morning you wake up and you're invisible—but gradually you start to notice it. The barman looks right through you as you stand at the bar waiting to be served; the person in front of you lets the door swing in your face as if you're not even there; you can't get the attention of the waiter to even bring you some water, yet he's hovering attentively by the table with the pretty blonde.

And then one day you're striding past a construction site and—*poof*—you're invisible.

"Hey, watch out!" I cry.

A workman nearly hits me on the head with a scaffolding pole, as he's too busy staring at the girl in the crop top ahead of me to even look in my direction.

I have to duck for cover.

Seriously. WTF!

I'm grateful for:
1. *Crop tops, because my old ones make brilliant dishcloths.*
   #whoneedsyouthwhenyoucancleanthekitchen #joking #sortof

What's Your Superpower?

"He could have killed me!" I complain to Cricket the next day, when we meet up in a cafe near her house. I've come to help replenish her little library with books as it's almost emptied out, such has been its success, and we're having a coffee before we start work.

"Didn't he see you?"

"No, he was too busy staring at some young girl. It's like I was invisible."

"It's our superpower!" She beams. "A reward for getting older."

"I'm not sure it's much of a superpower," I grumble. "OK, yes, I admit it's a relief not to be on the receiving end of that kind of unwanted male attention anymore . . . I mean, seriously, who wants some idiot in a white van yelling at you out of his window?" I grimace at the memory. "But that's a lot different from being given a polite compliment, or being offered a seat on the tube—"

I break off as a waiter brings our coffees over to our table, then lower my voice. "Or being smiled at by the cute waiter who gives me my flat white." He puts down my cup without even looking in my direction and disappears. "See. He didn't even notice I existed." I pull a face. What's that saying about being careful what you wish for?

"Johnny noticed you."

"Apparently Johnny notices anything with a pulse." I rip open two sugar packets and stir them into my coffee in an act of rebellion. I don't quite know why I'm in such a bad mood.

Cricket studies me, her expression thoughtful. "I used to turn heads, you know. I would walk into a bar and men would crane their necks. I had legs up to here and I wasn't afraid to show them."

Thing is, it's impossible to remain in a bad mood when you're with Cricket.

I break into a smile. "I know, I've seen the photos. The one of you in that cocktail dress at the Savoy . . ." I raise my eyebrows and pretend to fan myself. "Seriously hot."

She laughs, her eyes dancing at the memory as she cradles her latte. "Back then I had a different kind of superpower." She takes a sip of coffee, then replaces her cup neatly in its saucer. "It's called youth."

Shrieks of laughter come from the corner and we both glance over to see a crowd of twenty-something girls, all on their phones, a tangle of long hair and long legs.

"You know, you never think you're going to get old. I still feel like that twenty-five-year-old girl inside." She stops watching them and turns back to me. "Sometimes I even forget until I look in the mirror."

"But you still look amazing," I protest, looking across at Cricket, who is wearing a large piece of costume jewelery as a choker and her trademark red lipstick.

"Oh Nell, you darling girl, you are sweet, but I don't look amazing. I don't *want* to look amazing. I just want to look good for my age." Her face creases into a smile. "You know, when I was an actress there was so much pressure on how I looked. Of course, talent is important, but as a director once told me, no one wants a wrinkled leading lady."

"What a bastard! I hope you gave him what for."

"I did more than that; I married him." She laughs delightedly at my expression.

"That was Monty?"

"It was indeed, and I made him eat his words for over thirty years. He ended up writing some very good parts for older women. 'But no one wants a wrinkled leading lady,' I would forever tease, and he would always reply, 'Oh, but I do, my darling, I do.'"

Abruptly her eyes fill with tears. She sniffs sharply, shaking her head. "Silly old goose," she mutters.

Reaching across the table, I place my hand on hers. "Silly old goose."

Our eyes meet. We share a smile.

"I'll let you into a secret, Nell." She leans in and motions for me to come closer. "It turns out being invisible is just how you imagined it was going to be when you were a child," she confides. "It's nothing to fear, just the opposite—it's wonderful. It gives you an incredible freedom to do what you want, wear what you want, say what you want—well, most of the time." Pulling a sheepish expression, she leans back in her seat. "And nobody gives a damn."

"Are you sure it's not you that doesn't give a damn?"

"Both." She laughs, taking another sip of coffee. "When I was much younger I used to be so concerned about how I looked, what people thought, how I was perceived. I used to worry all the time about trying to fit in." She shakes her head. "What a huge waste of time that was."

"But you met Monty, it's different. I'm still single."

She nods. "It's true, I was very lucky. And I understand we all want to be visible in some respects . . . to be seen . . . to be acknowledged. It doesn't matter what age you are . . . especially if you are looking to meet someone."

Putting down her cup, she fiddles with her wedding band thoughtfully.

"I don't have Monty now, and as a widow I felt very invisible. And then you knocked on my door."

We both smile at the memory.

"I'm not saying this to be trite or to make you feel better, but believe me when I say this: *the people who matter will see you, no matter what.*"

She looks at me and I know she sees me, just like I see her. Maybe that's our real superpower.

"Now then, I wanted to ask you something."

I sit back and drink my coffee. It's getting cold.

"It's about Monty."

"More books? Clothes?"

"It's his ashes, actually."

"Oh, Cricket—" I begin apologizing, but she quickly silences me, telling me not to be silly.

"I've decided where I want to scatter them and I wondered if you would join me. It's a place that was very special to him; he took me there soon after we first met."

A story Cricket once told me of Monty taking her to Hampstead Heath for a picnic comes flooding back.

"Of course. I'd be honored."

"I rather hoped you were going to say that." Reaching underneath the table, she pulls something out of her handbag. "So I took the initiative and booked two tickets."

"Tickets?" I look at her in surprise. "Aren't we going to Hampstead Heath?"

"Good Lord, no, whatever gave you that idea?" She hands me a British Airways ticket. "We're going to Spain."

I'm grateful for:
1. *The freedom that comes with being invisible.*
2. *Realizing that as superpowers go, youth is totally overrated because you never really know you have it until you lose it, which is a pretty crappy superpower if you ask me.*
3. *Being able to fly . . . TO BARCELONA!*

The Horrors of Overhead Lighting

But first things first: I need some new clothes.

A week later I find myself in a shopping mall, held hostage in a changing room, surrounded by clothes that seemed so full of promise but are not living up to their potential.

Which, now I come to think of it, could be a description of my love life, career, or indeed life in general.

But sod it, who cares? *I'm going on holiday!*

Guilt clears its throat loudly and taps me on the shoulder, reminding me of precisely why I'm going to Spain. It's not exactly a holiday. It's to accompany a widow on her journey to scatter her husband's ashes.

My phone beeps with a text. It's from Cricket:

Don't buy any suntan lotion. I've bought plenty!

Well, maybe it's OK to be a *bit* excited.

We're going away for a whole week. It was Cricket's idea. "I think we could both do with a nice break. Get some sunshine. Swim in the sea. It will do us a world of good." It sounds glorious. After recent events, I can think of nothing I would like more than to escape London for the Mediterranean. Plus, there's nothing to rush back for. I can work remotely on my laptop and, the rest of the time, pitch up on the beach with a book. I can't wait.

I just need a new bikini.

Just. It's such a misleading word, isn't it? It implies something quick and simple. A minor problem to be easily surmounted: just getting a coffee, just parking the car, just need to let the dog out for a pee. Nowhere in the word *just* do I see a carnage of bikinis around my ankles, the horror of my reflection in the overhead lighting (over which I shall draw a veil), and struggling to contort myself because the top and bottom are fixed together by those annoying plastic security tags, and in order to try them on at the same time, I'm having to bend myself double and twist, Quasimodo-style, to see myself in the mirror.

No, *just* doesn't do any of that justice.

Plus, I still haven't managed to find any summer outfits. They're all too short! Says a twenty-something never. The only ones I like are comfy but frumpy.

Feeling myself wilting, I FaceTime Liza. I need the advice of a millennial.

Thankfully with the time difference she's awake, and we quickly sift through a mountain of clothes.

"The blue dress is nice . . . not sure about the stripes . . . way too big . . . seen you in better . . . be nicer in white . . . LOVE the overalls!"

"Thanks, Liza, it's like having a personal shopper."

She grins. "I'm so excited for you. Spain is going to be awesome. You deserve a vacation."

"Well, it's not really a vacation." I tug on a floral playsuit.

"Yes, you said. The old lady sounds really sweet."

It feels strange to hear Liza call Cricket an old lady. At eighty-something I suppose she is, yet she feels anything but to me.

"Definitely no. That fabric makes you look like someone's curtains . . ."

I look at my reflection. It looked nice on the hanger, but in real life I look like I've been styled by Maria von Trapp. And now the zip's got stuck. Putting down my phone, I start trying to yank it over my head, but it gets wedged around my shoulders. Is it me or have they made the sizing smaller?

There's a ripping sound and I emerge red-faced, like a cork from a bottle, just as my phone chimes to signal a text.

"Hang on, I got a message, it might be Cricket about the trip." Relieved to have my arms free, I snatch up my phone and quickly switch screens.

> Hi Nell, how are you? Hope you are enjoying the sunshine.
> Johnny X

"What an asswipe!"

As I read it aloud, Liza reacts in the way you want your friend to react when the man who ghosted you a month ago just sent you a text message out of the blue. I've told her all about what happened and she feels guilty for encouraging me to online date. Not that it's her fault. I seem to have a habit of falling for the wrong men.

"I can't believe it." I stare at my screen in disbelief.

"Just ignore him," says Liza firmly.

And she's right. Of course she is. But my hurt pride won't let it go.

> Who is this?

Ha. That will show him.

> Johnny

Is he really that oblivious? I'm tempted to write back *Johnny who?* but I am a mature adult.

> Hi Johnny. I would be grateful if you don't contact me anymore.
> Thanks, Nell.

"No kiss," instructs Liza, "he's just fishing."

"Of course not." I press send. "Trust me, that will be the last I ever hear of him."

My phone chimes.

Just wondering why you disappeared on me?

"He's gaslighting you!" Liza gasps.

"I thought he was ghosting me?"

I'm so confused—so much has changed since I was last single—and now I have a headache. Probably from skipping lunch and being starved of oxygen in a floral playsuit.

Putting my phone on silent, I thank Liza for all her help and emerge from the changing room blinking into the daylight, where I'm reprimanded by the sales assistant for not putting everything back on the hangers properly, and end up buying the ripped floral playsuit out of guilt.

I still haven't found a bikini.

I'm grateful for:
1. *Being able to block people, so now Johnny can't ghost or gaslight me.**
2. *Keeping the little freebie sewing kit I got when I upgraded with air miles, so I'm able to fix the zip on the playsuit and give it to Max's daughter Lily, who wears it with a belt and the sleeves rolled up. Lily is seven.*
3. *70 percent off summer sales online.*

---

* Actually, he can still ghost me, but I won't know about it, so two negatives make a positive.

An Inspector Calls

Saturday night and I'm home alone with Arthur doing my laundry. I fly to Spain on Monday and I still haven't packed. I'm hopeless with packing. I never know what to take and always seem to pack the wrong things. With all the traveling I've done, you'd think I would have figured it out by now, but I'm forever reading those holiday articles about capsule wardrobes and rolling up a Breton top and a couple of scarves to make ten different outfits.

I did try it once when I went to Italy, but by midweek my Breton top was covered in pesto and my feet in blisters (who on earth can take just one pair of sandals?). And trust me, there is only so much you can do with scarves.

This time I'm adopting more of a "take as much as you can ram in your suitcase" approach and am washing my entire summer wardrobe, draping it all over the apartment to dry. Edward refuses to have a dryer—he says it's bad for the environment—so despite it being August, I've whacked on the heating full-blast and now the house is like a sauna. Poor Arthur is sweltering in his fur coat on my balcony.

I'm just taking out one load and shoving in another when the home phone rings. It'll be another one of those nuisance calls we keep getting.

"Sorry, we're not interested," I say, before they've had a chance to try to sell me something. I go to put the phone down.

"Is that Mrs. Lewis?"

"Excuse me?"

"This is Chief Inspector Grant from Brooksgate police station. I'd like to speak to a Mrs. Edward Lewis?"

"Oh . . . er, no . . . I'm his roommate . . . well, his tenant, actually. He's my landlord."

"And who would I be speaking to?"

"Nell Stevens . . . Penelope Stevens," I quickly correct myself. This calls for four syllables. "Is Edward all right?"

"Mr. Lewis was involved in an incident and is currently being held in custody for questioning—"

"*Edward?*" I'm in disbelief. "Is this a joke?"

"I'm a police officer, Miss. Stevens. I am not in the habit of making prank phone calls."

"Sorry, yes . . ." I step out into the hallway, away from the noise of the washing machine, to try and think straight. "Is he OK?"

"We need someone to come down to the station and bring a spare pair of his glasses."

"Why, what's wrong with the ones he's wearing?"

There's a pause, as if the inspector is considering how much information to give me. "Unfortunately Mr. Lewis's glasses were broken in the altercation leading up to his arrest."

Altercation! Arrest! Edward?

I'm still in shock an hour later as I reach central London and push open the doors to the police station. These are not words you associate with Edward. I half think they've got the wrong person, but it turns out the bedraggled figure with the black eye and bust lip is indeed Edward. Albeit he's almost unrecognizable.

"Holy shit!" As he's led out of the holding cell to greet me, I jump up from my plastic chair.

"Penelope?"

Abruptly, I realize he can't see me properly as he's not wearing his glasses.

"Yes, it's me, what on earth happened?"

As he comes closer I see the full extent of his injuries. He's really quite badly beaten up.

"A driver made an illegal turn and nearly knocked me off my bike, so I told him I was going to show the video from the GoPro on my helmet to the police as evidence . . ." As he talks, he winces and touches his swollen bottom lip. "And he got quite angry and knocked me to the ground and grabbed my helmet from me, most likely because he knew he was in the wrong—"

"But the police said you were the one to get arrested?"

"We ended up getting into a bit of a fight and my phone got smashed . . . along with my glasses and his windshield."

I listen, my mouth agape; I can't believe what I'm hearing. "*You were fighting?*"

"I was defending myself," he protests indignantly. "There's a difference. I was a victim of road rage! That's what I've been trying to tell the police—"

"WANKER!"

He's interrupted as a large, bald-headed man with a bashed-up face and a bandaged hand is led out of his cell. "You better watch out, next time I'll fucking 'ave you—" He's silenced by his wife, a tiny blonde woman, who grabs his elbow and hustles him away.

"He looks worse than you."

"Well, I did play rugby . . . Ouch."

Edward winces as he tries to smile. When he goes to touch his cheekbone, I notice his knuckles are cut.

"You were lucky, he could have had a knife," I say, feeling both angry and relieved that it's only a few cuts and bruises.

I glare at Edward and he looks suitably chastened.

"Anyway, I couldn't find your glasses, so I brought your contact lenses." As I take a pair out of my pocket, he squints at me through one eye. "Actually, maybe you just need one," I say, putting the other back.

"Mr. Lewis?"

We both turn to see a sergeant standing behind the desk. He's holding up a ziplock bag; inside there's a small leather wallet, some keys, and a smashed phone.

"If you'd like to sign here for the rest of your possessions."

Edward goes over to sign. "Thank you, officer."

"As the interviewing officer confirmed, you're going to be released on bail pending further inquiries, so please make sure you're available to come into the station for any questions during the next few days." The sergeant hands him the bag together with his bicycle helmet. "Now, how are you getting home?"

"Well, if you give me my bike back I can cycle."

The policeman raises an eyebrow. "I don't think that's a very good idea, do you?"

"I'm a very good cyclist."

"When you can see out of both eyes, perhaps," he says evenly. "And what about Miss Stevens? Is she meant to ride on the handlebars?"

The policeman shoots me a look and I stifle a smile. He's actually rather cute. I also notice he looks about fourteen. Is it just me or are policemen getting younger?

"C'mon, Edward, let's get the train," I say, looping my arm through his, and before he can argue I lead him out of the station.

"I can't believe they want to keep my bike as evidence."

We're sitting opposite each other on the South Western train from Waterloo, headed back home. In the bright lights of the carriage, the bruising around Edward's eye already seems to be turning all kinds of lurid colors.

"What are they going to do? Fingerprint it?"

"I don't know." I shake my head. He's still angry about what happened, but I'm not really listening. Something's been bugging me. "Edward, is there something you haven't told me?"

His expression changes and he looks suddenly shamefaced.

"Of course. I haven't even thanked you for coming all this way to get me, have I?" He rubs his forehead in agitation. "I'm so sorry, that's really terrible of me—"

"No, it's not that."

"It's not?" His brow furrows.

"Edward, what were you doing in town on a Saturday night? Why weren't you at home in Kent?"

My question seems to catch him out and he hesitates for a moment. "I was, but I came up on the train to meet a friend for a drink. He lives in the city."

I sit back in my seat and eye him doubtfully. "But you were

on your bike. You told me you leave it in the office at the week-end."

He looks at me. "Would you believe me if I said I had two bikes?"

"Not really."

"No, I wouldn't either." And, dropping his head, he stares at his feet for what feels like the longest time.

Then he tells me.

He tells me all about how he's been staying in a cheap hotel in town at the weekends for some months now, ever since he and his wife Sophie split up. And how he's been too embarrassed and ashamed to admit it to anyone. He tells me how they'd been growing apart for years, ever since the twins were small, and how the skiing trip in the New Year was a last-ditch attempt to try and save their marriage and bring them closer together. But how instead it only served to highlight how far apart they had become.

"And then at Easter she told me she wanted a divorce," he finishes, looking up at me.

"Oh, Edward, I'm sorry."

"Don't be. I'm not. It's true, at first I was against it. My family doesn't do divorce. I thought you just stayed in a marriage, whether you were miserable or not, because that's what married people do. I saw divorce as a failure. But Sophie had the courage I was lacking." Rubbing his temples, he sighs. "Our marriage was over a long time ago and staying in it wasn't going to fix anything, it was just going to waste the rest of our lives. I'm grateful to her for having the balls to do something about it."

"Have you told the boys?"

He nods. "They're teenagers and more interested in their friends and their phones than what their parents do anymore. They seemed pretty unfazed. They just asked us what took us so long. I guess we weren't as good as we thought at hiding it."

He raises a smile and I think back to my first impression of him when I went to look at his spare room. This happily married man with teenage boys and a gorgeous French wife, a successful career, and homes in London and the country, going off on family ski trips to Verbier. His life seemed so sorted compared to mine.

"Now it's a case of telling our family and friends. I'm sure my father will see it as just another way his son has disappointed him."

"But people get divorced all the time," I say supportively. "What's the statistic? One in three, or is it one in two?"

"Maybe." He shrugs. "But statistics don't stop you feeling like a failure."

I look at Edward and it's as if a wall has come down. There's a vulnerability I've never seen in him before. We're such different people, worlds apart really, but I guess in some ways we're not that different after all.

"You need to get some ice on your face." I gesture to his eye, which is now almost closed. "It'll help with the swelling."

"Christ." Catching sight of his reflection in the carriage window, he grimaces. "Is that really me?" Slowly turning his head from side to side, he studies himself. "You know, this isn't quite how I imagined my life was going to turn out . . ." He looks back to me. "Ever get that feeling?"

The train starts to slow as it approaches our station and, as I stand up, I can't help but smile.

"All the time."

Viva España

Note to self: When booking a flight, do not go for the cheapest one thinking, "Ooh, it's fifty quid cheaper! So what if it leaves at 4 a.m. and isn't from my closest airport? It will be fine!"

It will not be fine.

It will involve blearily stumbling around your bedroom and stubbing your toe in the pitch-dark at some godforsaken hour after having had only an hour's sleep, as you were worried the whole time about sleeping through your alarm (because who wakes up at 1:30 a.m., FFS?). Having to take two trains and a cab to get to the airport, which is miles away and will end up costing a fortune. And you will arrive broken and exhausted and realizing you have actually only saved a fiver.

With a big toe that has now doubled in size and is throbbing like a motherfucker.

Instead, take a leaf from Cricket's book and fly British Airways from Heathrow at a lovely, civilized hour, arriving refreshed and relaxed into Barcelona airport looking like the kind of traveler you've always wanted to be, rather than the bleary-eyed, crumpled one stumbling off a budget airline that you usually are.

We pick up our rental car. We're only staying here one night as tomorrow we're heading up the coast. I drive. After living in America I'm used to driving on the right, plus Cricket never got her license, despite confessing to "tootling around in the sixties" in a Mini which she later crashed into the back of a milk float.

"I keep meaning to take my test," she confesses as we head away from the airport. "It's on my list of things to do."

"You mean one of those bucket lists?" I pull down my sun visor and peer through the windscreen for signs to the city center and the motorway. Cricket's supposed to be in charge of directions, but I'm pretty sure her eyes are closed behind those sunglasses.

"Oh, I don't believe in those. My life's been memorable enough—I don't need to be jumping out of planes and swimming with dolphins."

"It doesn't need to be that, it can be anything."

But she shakes her head firmly. "I've always found that the best experiences in life are the ones you didn't plan, the ones you stumble across and they just happen . . . I remember Monty and I throwing this impromptu dinner party after the theater one night. Everyone came back to the house, and I fried up eggs with onions and potatoes because it was all we had— You missed the turning!"

"Damn!"

The story of my life. It's too late to turn and I sail right past, going in the opposite direction.

"Never mind, we can go a different way."

"We can?"

"Yes." She nods, looking at the map. "Take the next exit."

Indicating, I come off the roundabout.

"It's a bit of a detour, but it's not like we're in any rush, is it?" She shoots me a sideways smile. "It's the scenic route."

I turn down a smaller, winding road. "So, was it a good dinner party?"

"Probably the best one we ever had"—she nods—"and yet we had no wine and the house was such a mess. We ended up sitting on beanbags in the garden and polishing off the leftover port from Christmas . . ." She smiles at the memory. "You know, it never looks like you want it to, your hair's never perfect and it'll probably rain, but it doesn't matter. Those are your good old days. It's those times you always remember . . ."

Cricket trails off, lost in thought, and for a little while neither of us speaks. I keep driving, the buildings giving way to greenery as the road climbs higher and higher.

"Wow, look—" I gesture.

Ahead of us is the most spectacular view. A swathe of forest falls beneath us, leading to the city of Barcelona, which stretches its fingers into the sea, as if trying to reach the horizon beyond. I slow down and we marvel at the scene. Bathed in sunshine, it lies there, waiting for us.

I'm glad I missed the turning.

Barcelona

Normally the only thing that motivates me to get out of bed comes hand-roasted from Guatemala, but this morning I can hardly wait to jump up, draw back the curtains in my hotel room, and let the bright Spanish sunshine stream in.

Following a scenic detour through the stunning Serra de Collserola national park that sits above the city, it was midafternoon yesterday by the time we finally made it to the hotel and, after checking in, we both crashed out for a couple of hours. When I woke up I was keen to explore, but after getting no answer from Cricket's room, I left her sleeping and went off by myself.

I've been to Barcelona a couple of times, and each time I visit I love it more. On my wander yesterday I stayed away from Las Ramblas, the main tourist thoroughfare, and instead weaved my way through the myriad backstreets. I love a city you can walk around, and in my wanderings I lost all track of time. It was still pressure-cooker hot and minutes melted into hours as late afternoon gave way to evening. I arrived back at the hotel to discover it was almost 8 p.m., and found Cricket sitting in the bar.

"Sorry, I didn't mean to be gone for so long!" Apologizing, I slid into the seat next to her. "I didn't realize it was so late."

But she dismissed me. "This isn't late, this is Barcelona. The evening's just getting started. Now, what are you drinking?"

Rioja. Two Negronis. And a jug of sangria, as it turned out, thus throwing—nay, hurling—my attempts at a healthy regime out of the window, as I'm pretty sure that's well over the recommended number of units. But hey ho, *Viva España!* Which is basically the *Sod This* approach to life, but in a Spanish accent.

Much fun it was too, as it also involved staying up with Cricket into the early hours, eating lots of delicious tapas and watching street performers dance the flamenco, while plotting how I could move to Barcelona.

Before remembering fucking Brexit and needing more sangria.

And now, less than twelve hours later, we're all packed up again and setting off in the car to drive north. Cricket is in the passenger seat with Monty's ashes on her lap. We had a bit of a scare earlier when we couldn't find them and for a moment I thought our trip had turned into a bad rom-com. Visions of Monty in baggage claim going around and around on the conveyor belt, some poor unsuspecting soul taking a look inside, his final resting place ending up being Airport Lost Property . . .

Luckily we discovered the box in the trunk of the rental car, but from now on Cricket isn't taking any chances, and refuses to let him out of her sight.

"At least this way he gets to take in the view," I say brightly, as we leave the city behind us. She was so panicked earlier; it's my attempt to lighten the mood.

"I don't think he's seeing much, stuck in this cardboard box."

I suddenly realize how crass that sounded. "Sorry, I didn't mean—"

"No, I'm sorry," she cuts me off. "You're being nice and I'm being an arse."

"It's OK. You can be an arse."

"No, I can't." She shakes her head firmly. "My husband died. It happens. People die all the time. We can't all go around being arses to people."

I glance across at her and her eyes meet mine, then fall to her lap and the box resting there.

People talk about scattering ashes all the time. It's got these dreamy, almost romantic connotations. You imagine peaceful settings and exotic locations, a sprinkling of your soul and spirit. At least, that's always been my impression, but then I've never seen any ashes before now.

Instead, the reality is something resembling a shoebox filled with what looks like about seven pounds of gravel. It's anything but dreamy and romantic. It's bizarre and inconceivable and I'm struggling to get my head around it, so I can't even begin to imagine how Cricket must be feeling.

"But you're right, he is here," she says after a few moments, "but not in this cardboard box." She gazes out of the window as we speed along the motorway. "I was raised a Catholic but I never shared their belief in the afterlife. I can't believe in a heaven if I don't believe in a hell. But he's in my heart, my memories . . . the conversations I still have with him . . . and that's sort of an afterlife, isn't it?"

"Yes." I nod. "I think it is."

"Monty was a pair of bright black eyes, a sharp comeback and a roaring belly laugh that would shake his whole body." She looks down at the box on her lap. "Not these ashes. In fact, thinking about it, I've a good mind to throw them out of the window—"

"No!" Instinctively, my hand shoots out across the gearstick and grabs the box.

"What is it?" Cricket almost jumps out of her skin.

"You can't do that!"

"What?"

"Chuck Monty out of the car," I cry, before realizing what I've just said.

But Cricket's unruffled. "Oh, I wasn't going to really," she reassures me. "We've come all this way. And it wouldn't be very nice for the people behind us," she adds, as she glances in her wing mirror.

I check my rearview; almost touching my bumper is a canary yellow convertible being driven by an old man with a much younger woman sitting beside him. He's flashing his lights for me to move over.

Cricket and I both look at each other, but I don't remember which one of us bursts out laughing first. Only that we laugh until our eyes water and our sides hurt, and still we keep on laughing.

*

A few hours later we find ourselves elevated high above the sea, on a treacherous road that's twisting and dipping as it hugs the hillside. I grip the steering wheel, my nerves slightly fraught. Until, turning a corner, I see a horseshoe bay and catch my first glimpse of a whitewashed town below, set against the backdrop of glittering blue water. This is our destination for the week. It's breathtaking.

Spotting a parking area, I pull over.

"Is anything wrong?" Cricket turns to me.

I shake my head. "I just want to take a photo."

Opening the door, I climb out of the car. Cricket buzzes down her window to watch as I take out my phone to try and capture the magical view beyond. A gust of wind catches my hair, blowing strands across the lens, while the midday sun's shining right in my eyes; I can't see properly.

I take the photo anyway. Because this is my life and for the first time in a long, long time, it needs absolutely no filter.

I'm grateful for:
1. *Instagram, so I can post my blurry, silhouetted photo that I shot right into the sun, and show everyone that I do have a life, and it doesn't just consist of random funny things I see and my landlord's rescue dog.*
2. *My six likes—from Mum, Michelle, Holly, Liza, and Fiona, plus someone I went to school with and haven't seen for thirty years, who now has bunny ears and a garland of flowers around her head.*
3. *Being able to delete the comment from Mum asking me if I've scattered the ashes yet, thus ruining any attempt at pretending I'm on a romantic holiday with my lover in case Ethan looks.*

Bikinis and Babies

I'm lying on a sun lounger by the hotel pool, flicking through the magazines I bought at the airport. On the cover of one, a soap actress is showing off her new baby, while inside, following a whole column devoted to celebrity baby bumps, is an eight-page spread detailing the birth story in full hair and makeup: "It was touch and go!" "I've never known love like this!" and "Now I'm a mother I'm finally a woman."

So what does that make me? A nonwoman?

I reach for the next mag, only this time the celebrity on the cover is revealing her recent weight loss in a bikini: "Now my life can really start!" Exasperated, I get up from my sun lounger and head for a swim. Are we meant to believe a woman's life only has value by being a mother or looking hot in a bikini? (Or the pièce de résistance: giving birth and *bouncing back* into a bikini weeks later.) What about having a job you love or fighting for a cause or pursuing your passion?

Or how about just living your life and loving your body any way you damn well want, and not having to prove anything to anyone?

Is that it? Just two choices: a bikini body or a baby.

I jump into the pool feetfirst.

Which begs the question: What if you have neither?

I'm grateful for:
1. *The super fabulous Cricket:*
   a. *who doesn't have children, and is not only a woman but a frigging goddess.*
   b. *for pointing out, quite matter of factly, that if I want a bikini body, I just need to put a bikini on my body.*
   c. *for proving that abs are seriously overrated by rocking a one-piece.*

2. *The little shop near the hotel where I bought a lovely red-and-white-striped bikini.*
3. *The delicious Catalan meal of fresh gambas, grilled cuttlefish, patatas bravas, and tortilla that we ate down by the harbor, followed by two giant scoops of gelato, which gives a whole new meaning to "bump watch."*

Letting Go

It's day three of our holiday, and time has slipped and slowed into a gentle rhythm of morning coffees at the harbor, a delicious lunch at a little beach shack, followed by afternoons spent lazing by the pool.

We also manage to fit some exploring into our busy schedule. One time we drive up to a ruined church on a hill. Another time we discover a deserted beach, where Cricket goes snorkeling and I read a book, until we are joined by several hairy male cyclists who soon make us realize we've actually discovered a nudist beach.

"I'll never eat cuttlefish again," remarks Cricket.

Which is all you need to know about that.

But, hairy naked cyclists aside, it's so beautiful here. The Costa Brava has such a bad reputation for mass tourism, but this small fishing village feels like an undiscovered jewel.

Cricket tells me not much has changed since she first came here with Monty over thirty years ago. She's spent the last few days reminiscing, showing me their favorite spots and regaling me with anecdotes, relieved that any fears she may have had about returning here have been unfounded. At first she was worried the memories might make her sad, but if anything she's been revitalized by them.

"Spooks and shadows need to be swept away," she says. "Shine a light into them," she says. "Don't live in the past," she says.

She's also been busy making arrangements to scatter Monty's ashes, and has hired a small sailing boat with a skipper to take her out to sea tomorrow. So as a send-off we decide to drive up to the lighthouse this evening, to watch the sunset and toast Monty. It doesn't disappoint. Perched on a cliff edge, the view is incredible. There's a small bar and restaurant so we buy beers and go to sit outside, where we discover there's a band playing: a small group of musicians with Spanish guitars.

There are seats carved into the hillside and, finding two spots, we sip our beers and listen to the music, the warm evening breeze lapping our faces as the sunset forms a backdrop. It's one of those moments you stumble across and want to remember forever. To capture in a bottle and keep for when it's cold and dark at four o'clock, or life feels bleak or you're just having a rough day, and you can reach inside and pluck it back out and be reminded of how brilliant life can feel.

I want a whole cupboard of those bottles. Stuffed with all these random moments, like my grandma used to do with all her jams and pickles and preserves.

"I went to see him, you know . . . when we were in Barcelona."

Cricket looks across at me and I don't have to ask who. Ever since she said she was coming to Spain, at the back of my mind has been the letter from Pablo.

"How did you know where he lives? There was no address."

"Google," she replies, as if it's obvious, which I suppose it is, but somehow Cricket never fails to surprise me. "He's a painter, quite a famous one now, it would seem. I found the gallery where he's exhibited and went along there while you were sleeping—"

"*I* was sleeping?" So that explains why she didn't answer when I knocked. "So what happened?"

"He wasn't there. I left a note with my name and the number of the hotel, saying I was here to scatter Monty's ashes and inviting him to join me."

"You did?"

"Yes." She nods. "I'm not sure I did the right thing, but I felt I owed it to Monty." Her gaze flicks to the horizon and the sun that is slowly beginning to set. "Did Monty first bring me here all those years ago because Pablo brought him? Because he wanted to share with me something that was beautiful?"

She shrugs absently. "I don't know, but I do know love is love, at the end of the day. I wanted those who Monty loved and who loved him to have the chance to say goodbye . . . and I suppose, if I'm honest, I wanted to meet him."

She turns to me now. Her face is tanned from the last few days, and her eyes seem bluer.

"After all these years, I wanted to put a face to a name. To see who the other person was that Monty had loved, a part of Monty I never knew . . . It's always felt a little bit like unfinished business. I know he wanted to keep Pablo a secret from me, but I don't like secrets. You think you're keeping the secret, but really it's keeping you."

Listening to her talking about Monty and Pablo, of life experiences I know nothing of, her words resonate unexpectedly.

"Can I show you something?"

The words just come out. Impulsively, I reach into my purse and pull out my wallet. Tucked behind a photo of Mum and Dad, there's a small piece of paper I've kept hidden. Unfolding it, I pass it to Cricket.

"We called it Shrimp," I say quietly, as she gazes at the grainy black-and-white image on the ultrasound, "because it was too early to know if it was a girl or a boy, and Ethan said it looked like a little shrimp."

She looks at me, her eyes searching out the truth in mine, slowly understanding what I'm showing her.

"Nell, you don't have to—"

"No," I urge, pressing it into her hands. "I want to. You've shared all these things with me, you've always been so honest . . . about everything. Now it's my turn. I want to . . ."

I've kept this secret for so long. I've never told anyone what happened. I just locked it away, tried to pretend it didn't happen. She looks at me now and nods, knowing all too well that sometimes in life what you need is for someone to listen.

I start talking.

"On our first date, Ethan joked that he wanted enough children to make a soccer team." As my mind casts itself back, I find myself smiling. "He's from a large Italian family—babies are what the DeLucases do—but in the beginning we were both so consumed by falling in love we couldn't think of anything else but each other . . . Then we moved in together and started the business and we were just so busy . . . and as time went on I began to see lots of reasons for keeping it just the two of us—after all, we'd gotten this far and we were pretty happy, so why rock the boat?"

I've been gazing absently at the sun slowly sinking into the sea, but now I turn to look at Cricket. "Did you ever want children?"

"Not enough," she says simply. "I thought about it when I was younger—it was expected of you in those days—but there were so many other things I wanted more. I was relieved when I discovered Monty felt the same way. Of course, by that time I was much older anyway so it wasn't an issue. I was very lucky."

"Yes." I nod, my mind reaching further back. "I had doubts, but I pushed them aside . . . and so we rocked the boat." I take a sip of my beer. "I came off the pill and we waited for it to happen. But it didn't. It's funny, you spend your whole life trying not to get pregnant, you just assume that when you want it to happen it will . . . so we scraped together what savings we had left and tried IVF. But that didn't work either."

I stare out across the sea, gazing at the pink-tipped waves, at the sky turning a pale tangerine.

"At the time, I thought I coped pretty well with all the injections and hospital visits and the sympathetic looks from the nurses, but it took its toll. Ethan was so disappointed when it was unsuccessful and I felt like it was all my fault. The doctors said my body failed to respond to the drugs . . ."

I smile ruefully.

"We couldn't afford to try again but we were determined not to be sad. So we shifted our focus and threw ourselves into the business . . . and on the surface everything was fine. Summer came and went. The cafe was doing great . . . but looking back now, I'm not sure we were fine at all. Underneath I think we both buried a lot of stuff."

I pause, thinking back. I've buried it for so long, but talking about it now all the memories are coming flooding back afresh.

"In the New Year we went camping for a few days in Yosemite. Have you been? It's beautiful up there."

"No, never." Cricket shakes her head.

"I think that's when I must have got pregnant. When I found out it was such a shock. Neither of us could believe it. Not even when we went to the hospital and had a scan. I was only eight weeks, but there it was on the screen: our little shrimp."

I smile, but already I can feel my eyes welling up and I swallow hard.

"They said everything was healthy, but we decided to wait until twelve weeks to tell everyone, just to be sure. But instead of feeling happy, I was scared. I didn't want to get my hopes up. I didn't want to fail again . . ."

I pause. I know this story off by heart, but every time I tell it to myself, there's a part of me that hopes it has a different ending.

"A week later I started bleeding."

"My dear girl—" Cricket reaches an arm across my shoulder and pulls me toward her. I feel a sense of relief as I sink into her.

"I remember the nurse's face when she couldn't find a heartbeat. She was so sorry but I acted like everything was OK. Like it was my job to make everyone feel better." I roughly rub away a tear that's escaped down my cheek, remembering the stupid jokes I'd cracked. It's hard to believe now that my concern was for everyone else when I was the one whose heart was breaking.

"Afterward Ethan and I never really talked about it. We were both just too sad; we hid it from each other. I think we were trying to protect each other, but looking back all we did is shut each other out." More tears are falling, but now I let them. "Then a few months later we lost a big catering contract, and things started to fall apart. The business . . . us . . ."

The sky has turned a deep, vivid orange.

"When I found the text on his phone, Ethan didn't deny it. I'd gone to visit my friend Liza and while I was away he'd gone out, got drunk. He begged me to forgive him. He said it didn't mean anything . . . but it meant something to me . . ."

I watch as the sun finally disappears beneath the waves.

"I left a week later."

For a moment we're both quiet, neither of us speaking. I'm so grateful for Cricket's silence. Not asking questions; just listening as I've talked. I've needed this for so long.

"Sometimes I wonder if maybe it was for the best. I tried and I failed. Maybe deep down I didn't want it enough. Like you said, not everyone does."

"True." Eventually she says something. "But is that really you talking? Or is it your grief?"

"I don't know." I shake my head.

"And that's OK," she says quietly.

I raise my eyes to meet Cricket's.

"I'm eighty-one years old and I've learned if there's one gift you can give yourself in life, it's the freedom and courage to say 'I don't know.' Because I'll let you into a secret—you don't *have* to know. You don't have to know how you feel, or what you want, or if you're happy or if you're sad. Life is full of choices and decisions, and there is so much pressure on us to make all the right ones. But what if we don't? What if we have doubts and misgivings? What if we make mistakes and contradict ourselves?"

She looks at me, her eyes shining.

"What if we try our best and fail anyway?"

As her words stretch out before me, I think about myself, about everything that's happened.

"What then? Should we feel bad about ourselves? Why not just accept that we don't know? Because if you accept that, my dear girl, it will give you such immense freedom. It will allow you to change your mind, to take a different path, to grab opportunities that come your way that you might never have thought of . . . to be impulsive instead of being stuck, to stop feeling guilty."

Cricket looks at me, her face imploring.

"To stop feeling scared."

I don't know.

I sniff hard, wiping away the tears that are spilling down my cheeks, turning this new concept around in my head, looking at it. Embracing it.

How do I feel? What do I want?

I don't know, I don't know, I don't know.

Gently Cricket presses the piece of paper back into my hand and I gaze upon it. At what was once my imagined future. For so long I've been keeping this secret, but now I realize it's been keeping me. Keeping me stuck. Keeping me from changing my narrative from one of fear and failure.

I look out across the horizon, at this vast, wide open space, and I feel very small. In my hands I feel the paper fluttering in the breeze; all the sadness I've kept buried deep inside, all the ashes of my past waiting to be carried away on the wind.

And then I let go.

One Love

"I mustn't be late."

"You won't be late."

"I should never have worn heels. What was I thinking with these cobbles?"

"The boat won't leave without us."

"I just wanted to look nice. Monty liked me in a dress and heels. He was old-fashioned like that."

"You look lovely."

"I should have worn my tennis shoes."

"We're nearly here now."

"I wasn't sure about this dress."

"You look lovely."

I've never seen Cricket like this before. She's tense, almost nervous. We're making our way down to the harbor from the hotel. It's mid-morning and I've offered to accompany her on the boat today. I'd assumed she wanted to be alone, that it was a private moment, but she seemed grateful, relieved almost, and readily accepted my offer.

The small red fishing boat is waiting for us. Andreas, the somewhat gruff captain, is standing on the dock and greets us with a respectful dip of his head. He's decorated the wooden hull with bunches of fresh bougainvillea, bright cerise and blush pink, and their petals flutter and shine in the breeze like tiny butterflies. It's a thoughtful touch and makes Cricket relax and smile. I feel a blast of gratitude toward him.

He's taking Cricket's arm to help her board when we hear a voice.

"Catherine—"

Someone is calling her name. We both turn to see a figure waving as he hurries toward us. Smartly dressed, but for his espadrilles and straw hat. As he nears, I see his heavily lined face, darkly tanned other than his white beard and long hair, which he's tied into a ponytail. He needs no introduction. Sixty years must have passed, but he's instantly recognizable from the photograph.

Pablo.

He slows down as he reaches us, and for the briefest of moments I watch as they take each other in, before Cricket steps forward and together they embrace. It's my cue to leave.

A few minutes later I sit on a bench away from the harbor, watching as the boat sails toward the headland. The waves glitter and bounce and I watch it getting smaller and smaller, carrying its precious cargo: two people, one love. They have so much to talk about and share, reconciling their ghosts from the past and celebrating the man they both loved.

The sun shines brightly and a warm breeze blows. It's a beautiful day for it.

I'm grateful for:
1. *Pablo, who only that morning received the note, and drove as fast as he could to reach us just in time to scatter Monty's ashes.*
2. *All the questions to which Cricket finally got answers.*
3. *The peace that she found when Pablo told her, "Now I have met you I understand how he could leave me."*
4. *No more secrets.*

Notting Hill Carnival

It's the bank holiday weekend, and we arrive back from the airport in a cab to discover it's the carnival; we can't get anywhere near Cricket's house as all the roads are blocked.

How could I have forgotten it's Notting Hill Carnival? I ask myself, as we have to get out and wheel our suitcases through the crowds of revelers. I used to look forward to the carnival for weeks. It was the highlight of the year!

Because now you get claustrophobic in crowds and the music's too loud, replies my forty-something self as we reach the sanctuary of Cricket's house. And you're dying for a cup of tea.

It's been a long journey and, instructing Cricket to sit down, I put the kettle on. While I'm waiting for it to boil, I open the sash windows to let in some fresh air. The house is on the procession route and from here I get a great view of the floats going by in the street below, with their vibrant costumes and echo of steel drums. It's family day, and absently I let my gaze slide over the excited faces of the children and their parents as my thoughts drift back to Spain.

So much happened in that week; it feels like we were away for much longer. I left a lot of stuff behind there, and things feel different now I'm back. I feel lighter, freer. Almost, dare I say it, a little excited about the future . . . My eyes land upon a small girl across the street. Sitting on her dad's shoulders, she's holding a balloon and waving at the crowds. I'm suddenly reminded of that feeling on my birthday, when I was walking Arthur past all the houses and looking through the windows. Me on the outside, looking in on everyone on the inside.

"Here you go." I snap back to see Cricket passing me a glass with ice and lemon. "Screw tea, I thought we'd have gin and tonics." She smiles, clinking her glass against mine. "*Salud!*"

"*Salud!*" I smile.

If only I'd realized then how great the view from the outside can be.

SEPTEMBER

#jomo

YOUR INVITATION
to

NATHALIE'S BACHELORETTE PARTY!

Join us to celebrate the bride-to-be

September 8 & 9
at
A Luxury Spa Weekend!

It's going to cost an absolute fortune! The hotel doesn't do any single-room discounts and it's in Manchester, which is miles away! But the bride-to-be can't wait to see you and all her friends, who are at least a decade younger!

Lucky you will get to catch a delayed train from London and enjoy an array of expensive massages you can't afford, and rejuvenating facials where the team of beauty therapists will put lots of creams on your face and wipe lots of creams off your face, as you relax to piped music and your stomach rumbling, while wondering if your credit card is going to get rejected and there's anything to eat other than grapes.

Please RSVP when you've finished googling "100 ways to get out of a bachelorette party" and realized there isn't one.

The Dilemma

There are big, BIG problems in the world right now. I mean, HUGE. So in the grand scheme of things, an invitation to a bachelorette party spa weekend is not up there with, say, the destruction of our planet or the state of world politics. But in the World According to Nell, it's been the cause of a few sleepless nights.

When the invitation arrived a couple of weeks ago, I did that thing of shoving it on my desk and trying not to think about it. As if somehow this would make the problem go away, which, as we all know, doesn't work. Instead, it seems to have had the opposite effect and made the problem grow bigger.

As the days have crept by, it's sat there, nagging me to RSVP. Made worse by the other guests Replying All. I keep getting these emails pinging in morning, noon, and night from people I've never met telling me they "Can't wait!" and "It's going to be amazing!" and "Woo-hoo—bring on the party!"

I know I have to go; I can't not. This is my brother's wife-to-be, my future sister-in-law, the mother of my first niece or nephew. Not attending would be terrible! But I also know I can't afford it. Weddings aren't cheap, even when they're not your own, and I've already paid for a new outfit and a wedding gift, plus train tickets and two nights in a hotel in Liverpool for the wedding itself. My credit card is maxed out and my current account is almost running on empty. How am I going to afford to pay for a spa weekend as well?

Of course I've considered coming clean and telling Nathalie the truth, but I'm too embarrassed. And it was really sweet of her to invite me. That said, all her other friends are so much younger than me. Do I really want to show up like the Ghost of Bachelorette Parties Yet to Come? Single, childless, broke and forty-something, *and in sleeves*! I'm like a fearful warning of their future if they don't meet Mr. Right. My very presence will probably scare the living daylights out of them.

FFS, what a predicament. It's giving me a headache just thinking about it. In fact, I feel like I'm getting a bit of a sore throat
too . . . and is it just me or is it freezing in here? I might have to lie
down under the duvet. Boy, I'm exhausted. In fact, I think I'll just
close my eyes for a minute.

I'm grateful for:
1. *The flu.*
2. *Nathalie being so sweet about it all, and sending me a voicemail telling me not to worry about missing her spa weekend
   but to get better soon, and thanking me for her pregnancy
   massage.*
3. *My bed, which I don't get out of for a week.*
4. *Edward, for doing a great impression of Florence
   Nightingale.*
5. *No longer being scared of ghosts—past, future, or otherwise.*

Double Booked

On Thursday I get dressed for the first time in nearly a week. Which,
to be honest, when you work from home is not *that* unusual. But
no, really. I'm up and out of bed, and I've had a shower and washed
my hair and everything. I feel SO much better. Practically human
again. After a week of Theraflu I've even got my appetite back.

It's when I'm in the kitchen heating up a pan of tomato soup
that I get the text from Fiona inviting me to her birthday get-
together. It's next Saturday. The same day as Rich and Nathalie's
wedding. Apart from her liking my photo of Spain on Instagram,
we haven't been in touch since I dropped Izzy back from the party.
Things still feel weird.

I start drafting my reply to say I can't make it, but nothing sounds right, not even with a smiley face. Oh, sod it. I can't do this over text. Deleting it, I call Fiona's number instead. She never picks up, but at least it will sound better in a voicemail.

She picks up.

"Oh . . . er, hi Fiona!" Taken aback, I falter.

"Did you pocket dial me?"

Probably not the best start.

"No . . . of course not."

"Oh, OK, you just sound surprised."

"I was just about to leave a voicemail . . . about your birthday . . ." And now it feels all stilted and awkward. "I'm afraid I can't make it—"

"That's fine," she says before I can finish, in that way you know it's not fine. "It's all very last-minute."

"No, but I'd love to come. I've only ever missed your birthday when I was in the States, but it's Rich's wedding that weekend—"

"*Your brother's getting married?*"

"Yes, didn't I tell you?"

"No!"

Fiona has known Rich since our first year at university, when she came home to stay with me over the Easter break and became an object of desire for my spotty teenage brother. He stalked her for the entire week, lurking outside the bathroom door when she was showering for a glimpse of her in her towel. It was mortifying.

"Sorry, I meant to at Michelle's shower . . . it's just everyone was so busy, I didn't get a chance to speak to you properly . . ."

I trail off and there's silence at the other end of the line.

"Yes, it was all a bit manic," she says eventually, sounding a touch guilty.

"He's having a baby."

"Who? Little Rich?"

"Yes, Little Rich." I smile, feeling a sudden closeness to her as she uses our family nickname.

"I thought he always said he didn't want to settle down."

"He did, but then he met Nathalie."

"Wow. She must be quite some woman! I bet your mum's thrilled."

"That's putting it mildly." It strikes me how nice it is to finally be able to talk to Fiona about all this. If anyone understands my family dynamics, it's her. She's had years and years of it.

"We should have a drink when you get back, celebrate my infirmity," she's saying now.

"Sounds good," I reply, feeling that bond again that I was so worried we'd lost. "So what are you doing for your birthday? Is it down to O'Leary's as usual?"

O'Leary's is an age-old tradition of Fiona's. An Irish pub that serves Guinness and its famous fish stew and soda bread. Every year she invites the gang to celebrate her birthday. Something about her Irish ancestors, apparently. Though I have a feeling it's more to do with the soda bread.

"Actually, I thought I'd do something different this year; I've booked a table at a members' club in Soho."

"Ooh! Very posh! I didn't know you were a member of a private club."

"I'm not, Annabel is . . ."

Why did I not guess?

"But you always loved O'Leary's. It's your favorite."

"I know, but I thought it might be time for a change, something new."

"Who said that, you or Annabel?"

I can't help it. It just comes out.

"Nell—" warns Fiona.

"What?" I say innocently, but I know exactly what.

"Look, I know you don't like Annabel—" She sounds defensive.

"It's not that I don't *like* Annabel"—(OK, that's a fib)—"but I don't think she likes me."

"She's tried really hard with you, you just haven't been friendly to her."

"Me? Friendly to her?" I'm indignant.

"Look, I don't want to argue with you, Nell."

"We're not arguing," I protest, but I can feel our rediscovered closeness already slipping away. There's a heavy pause and I switch subjects before we lose it all. "Anyway, how are the children?"

"Really good, thanks . . ." She sounds relieved to be off the topic. "Well, actually, Izzy's been a bit quiet lately."

"Quiet?"

"Yes, did you notice anything different when you took her to the party a few weeks ago?"

"No, she was fine . . ." I think back. "Actually, now you mention it, she was her normal chatterbox self on the way there, but once we got inside she did go a bit quiet. I assumed it was because of the clown. To be honest, I find them scary too and I'm a lot older than five—"

"God, yes."

"Why? Do you think something's wrong?"

"Oh . . . no, I'm sure it's something and nothing . . . she's probably had another fight with her brother."

"I remember those." I smile. "Mum used to despair of my brother and me, and now look at us. I'm going to his wedding!"

"Well, have fun," she says, getting back on topic, "and send him my love."

"I will. And have a happy birthday."

I'm grateful for:
1. Our conversation; I'm glad I got to talk to Fiona, though things didn't really turn out the way I would have liked and I'm upset about missing her birthday.
2. The flip side, which is not having to spend an evening with Annabel.
3. Heinz tomato soup. Forget smashed avocado on toast; after the flu there is truly nothing finer.

Fab Female Friday

There's lots to hate about social media, but there's also lots to love. Like #throwbackthursday and #flashbackfriday, which is a wonderful opportunity to post old photos showing the world we were all younger and thinner once.

Maybe we should rename all the other days as well? Just think, you could swap them around depending on how you're feeling. For example, here's what this week looked like for me:

#motherfuckingmonday
Less #motivational and more #dyingofflu #selfemployed #still-needtowork.

#tellitlikeitistuesday
This week's podcast was recorded from my sickbed, surrounded by snotty tissues and not a hint of a sunset. Which got me thinking: there should be a movement to start telling it like it is one day a week. I propose Tuesday. Just imagine if every Tuesday we got to do a reality check. To throw off the pressure to present ourselves in a certain way and say we're sick of this bullshit. A day to embrace our messy, flawed, unfiltered lives. Our true, authentic selves.*

#gettingtherewednesday
As a child I used to love chemistry on a Wednesday afternoon, as I knew it meant I was halfway through the school week. This follows the same theme, but it's more about the feeling that you're finally getting a handle on all the stuff you needed to get done

---

* Trust me, this goes much, much further than a no-makeup selfie. Also, I'm using "we" in the royal sense of the word, as maybe it's just me with the messy, flawed, unfiltered life. And perhaps my twenty-seven listeners (it used to be thirty-two but I seem to have lost five).

this week—more "I've got this" than wishing it was the weekend already.

#wishIwasstillyoungandthinthursday
Basically how I felt after looking through all my old photo albums to find something to post on #throwbackthursday.

#fabfemalefriday
Because there are so many fabulous females out there who inspire and motivate. Incredible, empowering, trailblazing women, from Emmeline Pankhurst to Rosa Parks, from Malala Yousafzai to Jane Goodall, from Dolly Parton to Jane Austen. The list is endless.

And what about women like Cricket and my mum? Plus all the thousands of ordinary women who are quietly going about doing their thing, but are no less extraordinary. I want to be celebrating them every damn week, not just on International Women's Day. These amazing women give me more motivation than any yoga video ever could.

#stayinginagainsaturday
Hey ho.

#sodthissunday
The best day of all. When anything and all of it goes.

Cold Feet

A week later, I catch the train from Euston to Liverpool for the wedding. Sitting alongside me in the quiet coach is my plus-one: Cricket.

"I can't remember the last time I went to a wedding," she's saying excitedly. "I think it might even have been my own."

I look up from my book: a copy of Virginia Woolf's *Mrs. Dalloway* that I borrowed from the little library for the train journey. I first read it at school and it's even better than I remember.

"What was it like?" I ask, laying it down on the small flip-down tray table in front of me.

"Surprisingly wonderful, actually."

"Why is that surprising?"

"Because neither of us was ever particularly sold on the idea," she admits candidly. "It was only when we were faced with death and taxes, the two things you can't avoid, that we decided to make things official. When we were younger it didn't seem necessary, or realistic. Who can make that kind of promise when you truly have no idea what will happen in the next thirty or more years ahead?"

"Probably best not to share that view this weekend." I grin, and she lets out a hoot of laughter and claps her hand over her mouth.

The whole family is staying at the same hotel. My parents come down to reception to greet us, and Mum looks taken aback when she sees Cricket. Until last week she'd assumed I was bringing along a new boyfriend as my plus-one, after my foolish snap decision in the summer to tell her I was dating someone. There will have been high hopes to meet him. When I told her I was bringing along a girlfriend instead, she didn't say anything except, "Well, perhaps there'll be some nice single men for you both."

"It's lovely to meet you." I watch Cricket being as gracious as ever as she reaches for Mum's hand. "Nell has told me so much about you."

"All good, I hope!" Mum laughs self-consciously and I can imagine her desperately running through the seating plan in her head, wondering if it's too late to move Cricket from the singles table to the elderly relatives one.

I can also imagine Cricket hoping very much that it is.

Dad, meanwhile, looks relieved to see me. He's been forced into a smart shirt and a pair of trousers that look a bit tight.

"She's even made me wear a bleedin' tie," he bleats out of earshot.

"It suits you," I console.

"It's strangling me, more like."

"Where's Rich?"

"In his room. He's been there ever since he checked in. I think he's got a hangover. He was the color of that rug."

He gestures to the mustard carpet beneath our feet.

"Is Nathalie staying with her parents?"

"Apparently. Though it seems a bit of a daft tradition, considering she's already in the family way."

"She probably wants to enjoy her last night of freedom." I grin, which makes my dad laugh and tug at his tie.

"I swear, it's going to bloody choke me," he grumbles.

"Philip Gordon Stevens, that tie is not going to choke you." Mum appears at his elbow and hisses at him sharply. The use of his full name is reserved for special misdemeanors and her face is like thunder. "But if you don't stop showing me up with all that complaining, your wife will."

After we check in to our twin room, I leave Cricket to take a nap. "I prefer to call it a recharging of the batteries, if you don't mind," she says, as I go to find my brother.

Dad's right. He's the color of mustard.

"Have you got a hangover? You look awful," I say as he opens the door.

"I feel awful."

In case you haven't noticed, my brother and I don't do the usual hugs and greetings. We like to dive straight into the insults.

"How many beers did you drink?"

"I haven't been drinking."

"Don't tell me. A dodgy kebab."

"It's nothing like that . . . it's just . . . I'm not sure, Nell."

"Oh no, it's not flu, is it? I was knocked out the other week."

Having closed the door and followed him into his room, I look at him with alarm as he sits down on the edge of the bed and buries his head in his hands.

"No, it's the wedding." His voice is muffled through his fingers. "I don't know if I can go through with it."

Oh ha, ha. Very funny. Another one of my hilarious brother's jokes. I play along.

"Well, tough. Your face is on the dish towels."

"Huh?"

"Princess Di. Apparently that's what her sister said before her marriage to Prince Charles."

My brother looks up at me like I've gone mad.

"Nell, why are you talking about Princess Diana at a time like this?" He shoots me an anguished look, then buries his head further in his hands, scraping his fingernails across his scalp as if he's literally tearing his hair out.

Which is probably not a good idea, considering he's already thinning.

"Oh, c'mon Rich, stop fooling around." I'm tired now. I could do with recharging my batteries myself.

"I'm not joking! This is serious!" he explodes irritably. Jumping up from the bed, he begins pacing around the hotel room.

Oh shit. A jangle of my own nerves starts in the pit of my stomach. Surely he's not being *serious* serious?

"This is just nerves, that's all," I soothe. "You've got cold feet. It's normal."

"But what if it's not? What if I'm making a huge mistake?"

FFS. This cannot be happening.

"Getting married, having a baby . . . I'm just Little Rich, I'm not equipped. I can't do this."

I stare at him, momentarily dazed by this sudden new turn of events.

"Of course you can do this." My voice is sharp. He's not going to bail out at the last minute. He can't. I won't let him.

"But it's such a big commitment. It's for the rest of my life."

"So is supporting Carlisle soccer team, and I don't see you having a meltdown about that," I snap.

"Don't be angry with me, sis."

He suddenly looks like that ten-year-old who borrowed my Rollerblades and broke his ankle by trying to skate down the slag heap at the local slate mine. I feel my anger fade as quickly as it appeared.

"And if you don't marry Nathalie tomorrow, what will you do instead?"

"Is that before or after Nathalie's father has killed me?" Rich raises a smile.

"I'm being serious."

He props himself against the edge of the chest of drawers and shrugs. "I dunno. Maybe go traveling."

"What? And give up your start-up?"

He stalls as the reality is presented to him.

"You haven't thought this through, Rich."

"OK, but give me a break, will you?"

"No, I'm not here to give you a break," I reply, pulling rank as his big sister. "I'm here to make you think about what it is you'd be gaining that's worth throwing away everything you've already got."

"I love Nathalie, and the baby, it's just . . ." He shakes his head.

"You're scared."

He looks at me, then nods slowly. "Yeah, you're right. I'm scared."

"You know, when you were little you used to be scared of going to sleep, because of the monsters that lived underneath your bed. Every night I used to come in with my flashlight and check underneath for you. 'All clear,' I would say, and only then would you let me turn off the light."

He smiles. "Are you going to tell me not to be scared now that there aren't any monsters under the bed?"

"No." I shake my head. "Life *is* scary. But it will be a whole lot scarier if you lose the person you love."

Stream of Consciousness

At 2 a.m. I find myself wide awake: a combination of worrying about my brother and Cricket snoring. Unable to sleep, I finish reading *Mrs. Dalloway*. It's such a good book. I love how it all takes place on one day and is written in a stream of consciousness. It's totally inspired me.

OK, so I'll never be Virginia Woolf, but what better way for me to try and describe all my thoughts and emotions from the day ahead?

My Brother's Wedding

It rains. Brother is nervous. Bride looks beautiful. Mum cries. Dad fidgets in his suit. Look like an idiot in my fascinator. Wish it was me. Cricket squeezes my hand in vintage Dior. Feel teary. Spill canapés down my new dress. Try to get the stain out in the bathroom. Fail. Miss the best man's speech under the hand-dryer. Have a total blast with Dad on the dance floor. Feel happy. Regret wearing these shoes. Try to cover up my grease stain in the wedding photos by crossing my hands across my chest. Look like Tutankhamen. Eat too much cake. Drink too much craft beer. Miss Ethan. Feel confused. Best man tries to kiss me on the dance floor. Consider it. For a second. Cricket and Nathalie's great-uncle wow everyone with their fox-trot. Hug my brother. Do the Birdie Song. Know all the moves. Feel like I belong. Love my family. Love Cricket. Love the waiter. Get all soppy. Drink more beer. Smile a lot. Remember to drink lots of water. A perfect day.

A Separation

It's funny how things change. Back in January when I first moved into Edward's apartment, the thought of sharing a bathroom with him seven days a week would have been terrible. So terrible, in fact, I would have probably never moved in.

Truthfully, the bathroom situation is still not ideal, though there's currently a cease-fire in The Toilet Paper Wars. As for the Battle of the Thermostat, the days are still relatively long and warm so the heating's off. *For now.* Plus, there was almost a crisis when he discovered I'd thrown away a battery instead of recycling it in those special bins at the supermarket, but I blamed forgetfulness (rather than laziness) and it was swiftly averted.

But the dishwasher and the lights are still a constant source of disagreement. I liken it to politics. The two sides will never agree and you just have to live with it. Though now Edward's separation is official, I'm not sure for how much longer.

"So the divorce should be finalized before the end of the year," he's saying now, as we walk through the gate into the park.

It's Thursday and we're taking Arthur for his evening walk. Since I got back from the wedding we've started walking him together, and it's actually a nice change. Dog walking can be quite solitary, especially when you have a dog that prefers to chase squirrels and ducks, and not trot obediently by your side like practically every other dog I see.

"Wow, so soon."

"Yes and no." He nods. "It's long overdue. We should have done it years ago."

We begin to climb the crescent of the hill, toward the woods. Arthur bounds alongside us. After giving me the runaround for months, it's incredible to see the way he responds to Edward. With a few simple commands he sits, waits, and comes to heel with perfect recall.

"So, tell me, how was your brother's wedding?"

"Don't you think it's a bit odd to be talking about a wedding at the same time as a divorce?"

"Not at all. It's all part of life's rich tapestry." He offers a smile and stops to admire the view. The evening light is just lovely. Warm and golden, it lights up the trees and our faces. "So c'mon, tell me."

"It was a great wedding, they both looked really happy." I gaze up at one of my favorite trees, a large spreading oak that sits by the entrance to the woods. For the first time I notice its leaves are starting to turn amber. The seasons are changing. "Though I think the happiest was my mum."

Edward gives a sheepish laugh. "At least that's one thing to be grateful about now; Mum not seeing me get married means she doesn't have to see me get divorced."

"Sorry, I didn't think—" I feel suddenly insensitive.

"What? Oh—it's fine." He bats away my concern. "It was a long time ago."

Sticking his hands in his pockets, Edward turns and I follow suit. Together we continue walking toward the woods.

"So what happens now?" I ask, changing the subject.

He shrugs. "It's just a case of dividing up the finances really, selling off some assets. We've decided Sophie will keep the house. I don't want the boys to have any more disruption than is necessary."

"No."

"While they're still at school they'll stay living with her, but we've agreed they'll come and stay with me at weekends."

"Right, yes."

"So far, it's all been quite amicable."

I think about my question. So what happens now? Edward presumed I was asking him about the divorce and I was, but now I want to ask it again, only in relation to how it's going to affect our living arrangements. If the boys are going to be staying with him in his apartment in London, they'll need two spare bedrooms. And with me there, it only leaves one.

Furthermore, is he even going to keep the apartment? He hasn't mentioned selling it, but surely this is one of the assets he referred to. But I don't ask, and as we walk into the woods, I feel my stomach twist slightly. I don't like uncertainty. It makes me nervous.

Yet one thing is certain: at some point I'm going to have to move out.

The Package

At the weekend, I catch the bus to Notting Hill to visit Cricket. She left a message a few days ago saying she wanted to speak to me about something and inviting me for Sunday lunch. When I called her back she refused to tell me over the phone. "Much better to talk about it over moules frîtes," she explained, which of course led my overactive imagination and obsession with real estate websites to conclude she was moving to a farmhouse in the South of France.

"And do what? Rattle around with chickens and miss London?" she scoffs, when I mention it to her as she serves up lunch. Ladling out steaming hot mussels from the large pot on her kitchen stove, Cricket gives a little shudder.

"Mmm, this smells delicious." She passes me a bowl and I inhale the aroma of garlic, white wine, and shallots.

"Oh, I forgot the parsley." No sooner has she sat down than she promptly stands up again to coarsely chop a large bunch, before returning to the table and scattering a handful of leaves onto the shiny black shells.

"Oh, and the fries—"

"Sit down," I insist as she goes to get up again. "I'll get them."

"They're in the oven," she instructs. "If I can give you one bit of advice, it's never to make your own fries. Buy frozen. Life is too short to be peeling potatoes."

I smile and sit back down at the table with the tray of fries, which we both reach for even though they're too hot and burn our mouths. Cricket pours the bottle of wine I've brought and we say cheers, then break open the shells and scoop up the delicious garlicky broth.

"These are amazing."

"Aren't they." She nods, without false modesty. "I haven't had them for a while. There doesn't seem much point cooking them just for myself."

I nod, understanding. Since Ethan and I broke up, I've lost count of the number of ready-made meals I've consumed. Cooking has never been my strong point, but there seemed even less reason to make the effort when there was no one to share (or commiserate) with.

But recently, with Edward living at home full-time, we've cooked for each other on a few occasions. It makes more sense—especially for me, as he's actually a great cook, whereas I can only do two recipes, despite buying all the cookbooks: stir fry and an omelette. But still, it's a *really* good omelette.

"So, what did you want to tell me about?"

Twenty minutes later, all that's left is a pile of empty shells. I clear the bowls as Cricket refills our glasses.

She reaches over to the chair next to her, tucked under the table, and retrieves a large, brown A4 envelope. She pulls out its contents and places them in the middle of the table. It's a sheaf of papers, tied together with a piece of string.

"That looks like a manuscript. An old one," I observe, taking in its yellowing edges. "I've seen enough in my time as an editor."

"It is. An unfinished one."

I wait for her to explain.

"It came in the post this week. From Barcelona."

I frown. "Pablo?"

Cricket nods. "In his note he says he wanted to give it to me when we met in Spain, but there was no time to go back to his apartment and collect it. After getting my message, he came straight from the gallery . . ." Her eyes fall to the pages. "He's had it for years. It's a play Monty wrote when they were together."

I listen, what she's telling me sinking in.

"He worked on it for over a year, apparently, when he lived in Paris, but when he moved out of his studio he threw it away. Pablo discovered it later in the trash and rescued it."

"And Pablo never told Monty he'd kept it?"

"Once, years later when they got back in touch, but Monty just laughed and told him to make a fire with it. He was his own harshest critic."

"Have you read it?"

"Yes." She nods and there's a pause.

For a moment I forget to breathe.

"I think it's his best work."

A hush falls as we both gaze upon the typewritten pages sitting on the table. It feels monumental somehow. An undiscovered play by the award-winning playwright Monty Williamson. Since meeting Cricket I've read several of Monty's plays. No wonder he won so many awards. He was a skilled writer.

"May I?" I gesture toward it.

"Of course."

I carefully slide it over the polished wood toward me. Untying the string, I pick up the title page. I can see the indentations from the typewriter keys. I trace them with my fingertips, then lay the page down and pick up the next. "Act One." My eyes flick over the text, which is covered in pencil scribbles. I can see the wine stain where he's rested his glass: a smudge from where the ink wasn't dry. I imagine him in Paris as a young man, hunched over his typewriter, smoking Gauloises, drinking red wine, the clacking sound of the typewriter keys, his fervent imagination . . . I flick to the last page. The type stops and instead there are handwritten scribbles.

"I need someone to finish it."

Cricket's voice brings me back from the 1950s and the Parisian garret. I raise my eyes and see her studying me.

"Gosh, well, I haven't worked in publishing for a few years but I could try to find someone for you . . . I could get in touch with some old editor colleagues, ask for recommendations. I'm sure they know some good writers—"

"I already know a good writer."

All of a sudden it registers.

"Oh God, no!" I throw back my head and almost laugh at the ridiculousness of it. "You're not suggesting—"

"I'm not suggesting, I'm asking."

"No, that's just crazy." I'm leaning back in my chair and shaking my head in protest at the sheer preposterousness of such an idea. "I write obituaries. I'm not a real writer."

"Yes, you are—you wrote a wonderful piece about Monty."

Momentarily I fall silent, remembering. Her gaze meets mine. It doesn't flinch.

"Look, I'm really more of an editor."

"Well, that's fortunate, as it needs a good editor too—in fact it's mostly editing, apart from the ending, which needs a bit of work."

My chest tightens. I start chewing the inside of my lip. I want to protest, but deep down I can feel the faint tingle of something. A pulse beating.

"No one knows Monty as well as you do now."

"What about you?"

Now she's the one to laugh and throw back her head. "Monty would turn in his grave if I tried, considering how hopeless I was at editing him when he was alive. So to speak." She smiles. "And anyway, I'm too close to the narrative."

There's a pause as a battle rages inside me. Neither of us speaks.

"I'll pay you."

"No, you will not!"

"Of course I will. I'm not asking you out of the goodness of my heart, Nell. I'm asking you to do a job, because I think you're the best person *for* the job. Because there's no one I trust more with my husband's words than you." She looks at me, her jaw set firm, then sighs. "Will you just think about it?"

The excitement is palpable.

"Yes." I nod. "I'll think about it." But even as I'm saying that, both of us know I don't have to think about it. Because the answer, of course, is yes.

I'm grateful for:
1. *The double act that is moules and frites.*
2. *Cricket not moving to a farmhouse in the South of France anytime soon.**
3. *Someone believing in me.*

A Development

The week flies by. I can't believe it's Friday. Already!

After getting back from Notting Hill on Sunday evening, I

---

* She made a good point about the chickens.

stayed up into the early hours reading Monty's play. Cricket was right. It's brilliant. Of course, I immediately called her the next day and told her I couldn't possibly begin to try and step into his shoes to finish it. Even with his detailed notes, it needed a much better writer than me. There was no way I could do this.

She told me I was talking bollocks and my check was in the post.

So I began. Terrified *but excited*. More excited than I've been about anything for as long as I can remember. Sitting at my desk, my fingers hovering above my keyboard as if they were levitating, I felt almost giddy with anticipation at the task ahead. I think I stayed like that for about ten minutes, until finally I took the plunge and started typing.

Monty's pages are heavily annotated in parts. Pencil scribbles decorate the margins and dance between the lines of typewritten text: notes about plot and characters, words crossed out, new dialogue, ideas about themes . . . reading them, I can almost hear his rapid-fire thoughts jumping out at me. I begin a careful line edit, checking for typos and punctuation, before concentrating on crafting the rhythm and the pace, the development of character, the story arc.

The first and second acts are mostly written, but the third act . . . that could go so many different ways.

Just like my life.

How is this story going to end? It's a question I've asked myself a lot this past year. Often, when lying in bed at night, my restless mind has begun pacing up and down, trying to knock on the door of my future, demanding to know what's going to happen. How will *my* story end? How will my life play out? Before, I thought I knew. I had it all mapped out and then—*boom*. It's a scary thing, stepping into the void. It can overwhelm you: fill you with panic and fear.

But looking at these unfinished pages covered with scribbled ideas and suggested twists, I'm beginning to realize something more and more. Not knowing how the story ends can be fucking exciting too.

I'm deep in concentration when my phone starts ringing. I've been switching it off during the day as I've been working, but turned it on earlier to call my bank. After my conversation with Edward a couple of days ago, I signed up with a few local estate agents to look for an apartment, but instead of rentals, they put me through to Rupert in sales.

When I told him there'd been a mistake and I couldn't afford to buy, he asked me if I'd looked at shared ownership, as it was a lot more affordable. All I needed was a 5 percent deposit. My first reaction was to dismiss the idea as ludicrous. Me? Buy an apartment in London? Ha, ha, very funny. But then Cricket's rather substantial check arrived and it got me thinking: this could be my deposit.

And a tiny window of possibility opened, just wide enough for me to pick up the phone to my bank, even though I was certain they'd dismiss me too. But they didn't. In fact, the idea didn't seem ludicrous to them at all, and after taking down some personal details they said someone from the mortgage team would call me back.

It's probably them now.

"Hello, Penelope Stevens speaking." I try to sound like the kind of person you'd lend a large amount of other people's money to.

"Nell, is that you? It's David, Fiona's husband."

"Oh, David, hi." I feel mildly embarrassed by my telephone voice. I've known David for years, but I've always been slightly intimidated by him. He's very smart and very serious, and deals with multimillion-pound mergers and acquisitions. Years ago, I remember Max asking how he kept his nerve when so much money was at stake, and he simply replied, "You've got to have balls of steel," and I watched Max flinch and cross his legs.

"Listen, I can't get hold of Fiona. Her phone's turned off and Francisca—the nanny—has just called to tell me she's chucking up—"

"Ugh. I mean, oh dear—"

"Izzy needs picking up from school, and even if I cancel this next meeting, I'm on the other side of town. I can't get there in time."

"Don't worry, I'll go," I say immediately.

"Are you sure? I'd ask one of the other parents, but Fiona deals with that side of things, and she's got all the numbers—"

"It's fine, I'll leave right now."

"OK, thanks. I'll call the school and let them know."

To be honest, I love any excuse to see my goddaughter. Though it is a bit odd about Fiona. She often doesn't pick up, but never when it's about the children. As I jump on the bus I find myself wondering if everything's OK. Maybe she's got a doctor's appointment or something. Though she never mentioned it . . . but then she doesn't mention lots of stuff to me anymore. We used to message each other several times a day, about all kinds of random things, but now often a week goes by and I don't hear from her. Then again, I don't get in touch either.

As usual the school gates are a cluster of cars, engines running, and cars idling next to the yellow curb. As I rush past them, I spot a white Range Rover and recognize it as Annabel's. She's sitting in the driver's seat on her phone, her perfect manicure drumming the steering wheel.

I put my head down and hurry by. We haven't seen each other since the sports day, the memory of which still stings, and I want to avoid any awkwardness.

Izzy is waiting in the playground and looks thrilled to see me. Giving her a hug, I take her backpack and head toward the gates. The playground is filled with parents and nannies and, as Izzy scooters alongside me, chattering about her day, I don't see Annabel until it's too late.

"Nell?"

Engrossed in hearing a funny story about the class hamster,

I look up to find Annabel frowning at me. If she *could* frown, of course. As usual she's immaculately turned out, and as usual my outfit of the day is the same as yesterday's, only with egg on it.

"Oh, hi Annabel."

"Where's Fiona?"

"Busy." Well, I'm not admitting I don't know. "David asked me if I'd pick up Izzy."

"Oh, he should have called me!" She looks annoyed. "There's no need for you to come all this way. Izzy can come home with Clementine and me, and I'll drop her back later."

Clementine is playing with Mabel, their French bulldog, teasing it with a squeaky toy. I feel Izzy reach for my hand.

"They can play together in the pool."

"Can Mabel play in the pool too, Mummy?" giggles Clementine, as poor Mabel circles endlessly on her lead.

"Not today, darling, I think it should be just you girls." Annabel beams down at Izzy, who's gone quiet. "You can borrow one of Clementine's bathing suits."

I feel Izzy's grasp on my hand tighten.

"Thanks, but I think Izzy's tired. I'm going to take her home."

Annabel's smile sets. "I'm not sure Fiona would appreciate you denying her daughter some fun. The girls love swimming."

"I think I'll let Fiona be the judge of that," I reply cheerfully, and then before Mabel is strangled, I quickly say goodbye and we escape through the school gates.

It's only when we've made it to the bus stop that I realize Izzy has remained very quiet. Sitting on the red plastic seat to wait for the bus, I pull out some tangerines from my bag and begin peeling one.

"You didn't want to go swimming with Clementine, did you?" I ask, passing her half.

Studying each segment, she shakes her head but doesn't look at me. I'm surprised, but don't say anything. I watch as she carefully removes the tiny, pithy white strings, before, satisfied, she pops a segment in her mouth. She likes to suck them like boiled sweets.

"Would you be mad if someone called you poopy-pants?" she says finally, raising her eyes to mine.

"People have called me a lot worse." I smile. "Why, did someone call you poopy-pants?"

Izzy looks away and slowly selects another segment.

"It's just silly name-calling. Ignore them."

There's a pause, and then:

"Would you be mad if someone hit you?"

I feel myself stiffen. "Izzy, did someone hit you at school?"

She doesn't answer, but she doesn't meet my eyes either. Sliding off the seat, I squat down next to her so I can see her face. She's staring at the pieces of tangerine as if her life depends on it. "You know you can tell me anything, don't you?"

Her expression is serious. "They said I mustn't tell. If I tell I'm going to get into trouble." Her voice is almost a whisper against the rumbling of the traffic.

"Of course you're not—why would you get into trouble?"

"Mummy will be angry with me."

"Mummy loves you, she would never be angry with you. Why do you think that?"

Another pause. It seems to stretch out forever.

"Because we won't be able to go swimming at her house anymore."

And suddenly I realize what she's telling me.

"Because her mummy is my mummy's friend."

"I promise you won't get into trouble." I reach out my little finger. "Pinky promise."

Now her eyes meet mine and, linking her little finger with mine, she tells me who's been bullying her. But of course I already know.

Clementine.

The Next Day

All hell breaks loose.

OCTOBER
#peoplearestrange

A Week Later

They say a week is a long time in politics, but when it comes to bullying it's astonishing how quickly things can escalate, deteriorate, spiral, and transform in the space of seven days. (Can you even call it bullying at five years old? When it's done in a tutu and fairy wings?)

The moment Fiona arrived home and heard what had been going on, she promptly swung into action and called Annabel. I think her intention was to try and sort this out calmly and nip things in the bud, but bullying is a highly charged topic for everyone involved, and the result was similar to what happens in those awful videos you see of gasoline being thrown on a barbecue to try and fix it, and instead the whole thing explodes in a fireball.

Annabel was understandably shocked and upset but, at the same time, furious. Refusing to believe that Clementine could do such a thing, she strenuously defended her daughter and accused Izzy of lying. Accusations and emotions flew back and forth. Resulting in Fiona, who I don't think I've once heard raise her voice in all the years I've known her, doing a good impression of a mama bear defending her cub while threatening to call the headmistress, while Annabel did an equally good impression and threatened to call the police.

Thankfully, neither were called. In the week that followed, both Fiona and Annabel calmed down enough to meet with their daughters' teacher. The school has a zero-tolerance policy toward bullying and they took it all very seriously. They also knew how to deal with it correctly and calmly, resulting in the discovery that Izzy's claims were indeed true, and Clementine admitting to calling her names and hitting her on several occasions.

Which explained why Izzy had gone so quiet at the birthday party; it wasn't the clown she was scared of, it was Clementine. What it didn't explain was why Clementine was doing it.

"At which point Annabel broke down and confessed that she and Clive are getting divorced."

Sitting in the cafe, I look across the table at Fiona. She messaged this morning, asking if I'd meet her for a coffee after she'd dropped the kids off at school.

"Oh no, that's awful. I had no idea."

"Me neither." Fiona shakes her head. "Nobody did."

I think about all those photos and updates Annabel posts, showing off her perfect happy marriage. Maybe from now on, that should be a clue.

Fiona stirs her double-shot latte. She drove over to my neighborhood, and when she arrived I went to order her a herbal tea as usual, but she said fuck that—she needed something stronger after the week she just had.

"Poor Annabel."

I'm surprised by how much sympathy I feel for her. She might not be my favorite person, but I know how painful a breakup can be and I wouldn't wish it on my worst enemy. I feel a sudden solidarity with her.

"Apparently they've been arguing a lot. They tried to hide it from Clementine but . . ." Fiona trails off.

"Kids are smart," I note, and she nods.

"Which probably explains Clementine lashing out," she continues. "The counselor said that children often resort to bullying if there are problems at home; it's their way of expressing their anger at the situation."

"You saw a counselor?"

"They have one at the school. They've been very good, very supportive."

"So how's Izzy now?"

Fiona's body seems to relax. "She seems to have come out of this remarkably unscathed. Reports from the teacher say she and Clementine appear to have put it all behind them and are the best of friends again."

"Wow, that's good."

"I know." She smiles. "Ironically it's the adults that are struggling with their friendship." She takes a sip of her coffee. "Annabel and I are still not speaking."

It's funny, there was a time when that sentence would have given me great satisfaction, but now it's quite the opposite.

"I guess all that matters is that Izzy is OK and Clementine is too—I hope," I add, feeling my heart go out to her. Despite what happened, she's only a little girl, a little girl whose parents are splitting up and whose world, as she knows it, is about to change forever. The whole thing's just bloody sad.

"Yes, that's all that matters," agrees Fiona. Cradling her cup, she stares out of the window, before abruptly heaving a great sigh and sending it crashing into its saucer. "I just feel awful that Izzy didn't come to me first," she bursts out. "That she felt she couldn't tell me." Her eyes brim with tears. "I blame myself."

"Hey, now you're being crazy," I say firmly. "Of course it wasn't your fault."

"But if she'd told me, I could have done something about it earlier. Just the thought that I was with Annabel, thinking the girls were playing, when all the time . . ." She stops, sniffing hard.

"And I'm sure they were, most of the time," I reason. "Who knows how recently it all started happening? What's important is that she *did* tell someone, and it *has* been dealt with." Reaching over, I rub her shoulder supportively. "Stop beating yourself up."

She smiles sadly. "Isn't that part of the job description of being a mum?"

"I wouldn't know," I say. "I think it's just the job description of being a woman."

She looks at me then and for a moment we just sit there together, two old friends. I feel closer to her than I have done for a long time.

"I'm just glad she felt she could tell you," she says quietly.

"So am I." I nod.

"Look, about before—I'm sorry things got so weird between us."

"Yeah, me too."

"I don't know what happened."

"Annabel?" I quip, and she smiles wryly.

"No, it's not her fault." Fiona shakes her head. "It's mine. I shouldn't have let her take over Max's birthday or the baby shower . . . I thought she was just being nice, but looking back now I think she wanted to take control of everyone else's life because her own life was so out of control . . ."

"I think she was also being nice," I say generously, and Fiona nods.

"Annabel didn't do anything wrong; it was me. I got my priorities all wrong. I think when we met at the school and she wanted to be my friend, I was kind of honored. I was so in awe of her; she seemed to have it all sorted out." Now she laughs at how ridiculous it sounds. "Like here was this beautiful, successful, sophisticated woman with this amazing life, and she wants to be my friend."

"Unlike me." I grin, but Fiona doesn't laugh. Instead she just looks upset.

"No, but you're real, Nell. None of it was real, was it?"

"Well, the amazing house was," I point out.

"Yes, the house." She nods, and we both smile.

"Though seriously, imagine plumping all those cushions."

"Maybe she employs a cushion plumper."

"Is there such a job?"

"I dunno. Is there?"

And then we both start laughing, with our shared stupid sense of humor and a familiarity that's born of several decades of friendship.

"It's nice here." Fiona looks around at the cafe, seeming to notice it for the first time. "Do you like living here? I've never asked you, have I?"

"Yeah, I do," I realize. "It's taken a bit of getting used to, but yeah, I like it."

"You don't miss America?"

I have to think about it for a moment, and it strikes me that I haven't considered it for a while. My answer was always yes, but now—

"No, I don't." I shake my head. "Though I missed the Californian sunshine in February." I smile.

"And what about that guy you were seeing. Johnny? Gosh, I'm a terrible friend, I've never even asked you about him, how things are?"

"It was just a few dates." I shrug. "Over before it started, really."

"Oh, I'm sorry."

"Don't be. I'm not."

"We've got so much to catch up on."

"I know." I nod, smiling. "I've missed you."

"Yeah, you too." She smiles.

"By the way, I meant to ask, is everything else OK?"

With all this talk of Annabel's divorce, I'd forgotten to ask about David's phone call.

Fiona appears to stiffen. "Why do you ask?"

"It's just, when David said he couldn't get hold of you last week and I went to get Izzy . . ." I trail off, feeling a twist of anxiety.

"I was in a job interview."

It's the last thing I was expecting and relief is followed quickly by surprise. "I didn't know you wanted to go back to work."

"Neither did I," she admits, then smiles sheepishly, "until

I realized I was remodeling the kitchen for the third time in five years, and it wasn't because we needed new tiles—it was because I was so fucking bored and frustrated."

She rests her elbows on the table and puts her head in her hands.

"Nell, you have no idea how desperate I am to use my mind again," she sighs, looking up at me. "I spent three years studying archaeology. I've got a master's in Byzantine studies and Greek paleography. Before I had the children I was part of a team doing fieldwork on ancient sites in Europe; then I got my dream job as a museum curator and I was responsible for putting together exhibitions. And now—"

She breaks off, her frustration almost palpable.

"Now I look at curtain fabric and watch *Frozen* for the millionth time, and the only mental stimulation I get is trying to book the right time slot for the grocery delivery."

She laughs and I do too, but her laughter is that kind that's verging on hysterical.

"I miss my career. I want a job. I need to use my brain. I put some feelers out and sent a few emails and my old boss got in touch . . . He said they had something at the museum—it wasn't a senior position like I had before, but if I was interested . . . So I went in to see them—"

"And?"

"And I got it."

"That's fantastic!"

"Is it though?" She looks worried. "I haven't told David yet. When we had children we always agreed one of us would stay home and do the childcare, and of course it had to be me; David earned so much more. Then after I had Izzy I got awful postpartum depression, and we were lucky to find Francisca to help out part-time. I don't know what I would have done without her, but I still couldn't imagine leaving them—"

"You never told me you suffered postpartum depression," I say with concern.

"I didn't tell anyone." She shrugs. "I was too ashamed. I felt like there was something wrong with me. Like I was failing at being a mum."

As I look at my friend, I realize I'm not the only one to have kept things buried inside.

"But now they're older, they don't need me as much as they used to," she says, shrugging, "and we still have Francisca—she's part of the family now and the kids love her. It's just—"

"You feel guilty," I say, finishing her sentence.

She looks at me in surprise. "How did you know?"

"Because when we're not beating ourselves up we're feeling guilty about something," I quip, and she laughs.

"And now, especially after what's happened with Izzy, I'm worried about working full-time . . . how it might affect her. I could still do the drop-offs, so it wouldn't be much of a change really . . ."

"Well then?"

She shakes her head.

"Oh, I don't know, Nell. Am I being selfish? It's not like we need the money. We're lucky David does so well, but it means I can't even use that as a reason. This is purely for me."

I look at Fiona. I can see she's completely torn.

"Look, I'm no expert, but I say go for it. Surely it's better for Lucas and Izzy to have a mum who's happy and stimulated? And I'm sure David would think the same about it too. Talk to him, you might be surprised."

"Yes." She nods, her face brightening.

"And well done."

"Thank you." She smiles. "Now, what about you? Are you still writing the obituaries?"

"Yes." I nod. "But I'm working on a few other things as well . . ." Glancing at my watch, I notice the time. "I'll have to tell you all about it later."

"I'm glad we did this," says Fiona.

"Me too. Maybe next time we meet for coffee you should invite Annabel," I suggest.

"Extend the olive branch?"

"Yes." I smile. "Only make it a chai latte."

I'm grateful for:

1. *Making up with Fiona, because things aren't just back to normal; they're better.*
2. *David's reaction when she told him about the job; not only was he really thrilled for her, but he was also really thrilled for himself, as it means no more house renovations and having to look at curtain fabric swatches.*
3. *Izzy and Clementine being the best of friends again.*

The Weirdest Thing

So the weirdest thing happened today.

I was doing my latest podcast episode, yakking away into the microphone as I do every week, when midway through I absently wondered if the twenty-seven people who had downloaded it were still listening. Or if I'd lost those as well by now and was, quite literally, talking to myself.

(This would also mean that it's true what they say about turning into your mother; I grew up with her yelling, "Am I talking to myself?" on a daily basis. To which, of course, no one ever replied.)

It struck me that it was ages since I'd last looked at the analytics, a fancy word that basically tells you if anyone has downloaded your podcast or, in my case, accidentally stumbled across my ramblings and by some miracle thought they'd listen to them. My initial (obsessive) excitement at checking the figures and discovering I had fourteen listeners, and watching them creep up to eighteen and then thirty-two (thirty-two whole listeners!) waned a bit when I got stuck on thirty-two for weeks, then lost five. It felt a bit like I'd been dumped, only in anonymous podcast land.

So I stopped checking. It was all a bit disheartening. I mean, seriously, who needs the rejection? Plus, I started the podcast just for me; what did it matter if no one was listening? Then life took over and I completely forgot about it. Until today, when I remembered.

So I logged in while steeling myself to see that I had, in fact, lost all my listeners and it was true, I was actually the only person in the world who felt like a forty-something fuck up—

2,437.

The number on my screen stared out at me.

I looked at it, peered a bit closer, wondered if I was missing a decimal point somewhere, then suddenly it registered.

TWO THOUSAND FOUR HUNDRED AND THIRTY-SEVEN DOWNLOADS.

WTF?

For the latest episode of my podcast? No, that couldn't be right. There must have been some mistake.

Surely?

Surely?

I'm grateful for:
1. *This amazing, incredible, unbelievable news.*
2. *My wonderful listeners, who downloaded me and believed in me and make me feel part of an incredible tribe, and to all those who are out there and listening at home, thank you so much for making me feel like less of a fuck up. I am so SO grateful, I couldn't do this without you; this is for you.*
3. *Never winning an Oscar.*

Love Is All You Need

A few days later, I'm still trying to get my head around the amazing discovery that there are actual people out there who are listening to my podcast, when Liza FaceTimes me. It's been a while since we last caught up, what with going to Spain, my brother's wedding and Monty's play, and her being busy with her own life, and teaching yoga—and the not-so-small fact that we're on opposite sides of the Atlantic, with an eight-hour time difference that can be a real pain.

But then by some miracle our universes collide; a class gets canceled, she's got a break earlier in the day, my battery's charged, and here we are FaceTiming.

"It's been ages!"

"You were trying to find a bikini. Did you?"

"Yes, a lovely one, I'll show it to you—"

"And that asswipe texted."

"Johnny." I groan at his memory.

"Did you ever hear from him again?" Liza's asking now.

"No." I laugh (I actually laugh). "And I don't expect to."

"Good." She nods. "So c'mon, tell me all about your trip!"

"You first," I say firmly, "I want to hear all your news. How are you?"

"Really good." She smiles, and I know immediately. It's not one of those smiles that says you got a promotion at work, or you've lost five pounds or bought a new dress; it's the smile that says you've met someone.

"Who is it?" I demand.

Liza doesn't even attempt to deny it. Her face flushes. "How did you guess?"

I raise an eyebrow and she laughs.

"It's my yoga student, the one I told you about."

"That's great!" I smile. "So how did you manage to get around the whole ethics dilemma?"

"She stopped being my student."

Just like that it's dropped into the conversation. And just like that I pick it up.

"So c'mon, tell me all about her."

"You're not shocked?"

"Why?" I ask. "Because you've fallen in love with a woman?"

"Yes."

"Well, are *you*?"

For a moment she's quiet, then she shakes her head.

"That's the strangest thing. No, I'm not. I'm not shocked at all. I mean, I've never been attracted to a woman before. But then I met Tia and it was like I wasn't seeing her as a female, I was just seeing her as a person . . . and one I was really attracted to. It was weird, but it was also *not* weird at all, and that's what made it so weird—" She breaks off. "Am I making any sense?"

"Perfect sense." I nod.

"But initially, I admit I was freaked out by my feelings . . . I feel bad about how I pushed her away."

Her face stares at me from my screen, and I can't help thinking how so often we resist what our emotions are trying to tell us, because of some stupid belief that we shouldn't feel a certain way.

"But then, I just couldn't stop thinking about her."

"That's how you know."

"Yeah." She nods. "So after being totally miserable for a while, I thought, why am I doing this to myself? Why am I not being with the person I want to be with? So I called her up and I was lucky that she didn't tell me to fuck off and go away because, believe me, I'd been a total jerk." She grins. "But she didn't, and so we went out and she came back to mine, and, well, basically she hasn't left."

"So I'm not the only one who's been busy." I smile, and she laughs.

"Oh, Nell, I'm so happy, but I've been scared to tell people, because it's not how I thought it was going to look—me and a relationship, I mean. It's certainly not going to be how my parents thought it was going to look—" She breaks off again. "But I have to do what feels right for me, no matter what everyone else does and thinks . . ." She shrugs. "What the fuck, right?"

Silently cheering her on as I listen to her bravely pouring her heart out and following her own path, I raise an imaginary glass.

"What the fuck." I smile.

I'm grateful for:
1. *Liza finding the courage to give up what she thought would make her happy, so that she could fall in love with someone who makes her truly happy.*
2. *Living in a part of the world where we are free to follow our hearts, regardless of gender and race.*
3. *She's not with that fuckwit Brad.*

Independence Day

"Sorry, I must have mixed it up with mine."

I walk into the kitchen from a trip to the supermarket, to have a large envelope thrust in my face.

"Edward, can you just . . ." Exasperated, I wave my shopping bags around to show him I have no free hands.

"Right, yes, of course."

In normal households, comings and goings have a sort of grace period, a buffer where you get to enter, take off your coat, put your bags down and say hi, and perhaps exchange a few pleasantries; while leaving follows a similar routine of putting on your coat, calling out goodbye, and maybe having a little chat about what time you'll be back. It's a natural winding up and down of conversations.

Edward does not do buffers. Or grace periods. Or winding up and down of conversations. Whatever is on his mind is what you'll get as soon as you walk through the door. It's the same when you leave. His response to "bye, see you later" can often be a goodbye. But it is just as likely to be "I think we've got a rat underneath the decking" or "It's a bloody disgrace!" (With no reference to what exactly.)

I still haven't got to the bottom of whether it's because he's such a deep thinker and is always so focused on what's on his mind that he's not aware of his surroundings, or it's a deliberate attempt to drive me insane.

"Here, let me help you with those bags."

On the flip side, he can also be incredibly kind and helpful. And I'm being a total bitch after battling the aisles of the supermarket on a Friday afternoon, which is when fellow shoppers descend into a frenzy, as if there's about to be an apocalypse in southwest London and it's not merely the weekend.

"You know, you really shouldn't still be using plastic."

"It's a bag for life," I say defensively, as he spots the one plastic bag I have amongst all my eco-friendly ones.

"For the life of the planet, yes," he grumbles. "You know they're even worse than the single-use ones? You'd need to use them at least twelve times because of all the extra plastic used to make them."

"I was caught short at the checkout," I snap, but of course I know he's right, which is more maddening than ever. "What's your excuse for having that huge gas-guzzling four-by-four you drive in the countryside?"

Which is a bit below the belt, considering he's getting divorced and doesn't live in the countryside anymore, and it's not exactly fair to remind him. But that's how grumpy I am. Seriously, you didn't see the salad aisle.

"It's actually electric," he replies evenly.

"Of course it is!" Dumping my bags on the countertop, I snatch the envelope from him and tear it open.

It's a letter from the bank. Scanning my eyes quickly over it, I see a miracle has somehow happened. I stare at it in disbelief.

"Good news?"

"I've been approved for a mortgage in principle!"

"Oh . . . I see. Well, congratulations."

"I can't believe it!" I raise my eyes from the letter to look at Edward, who's standing on the other side of the counter. "Well, it looks like you won't have to suffer me and my bags for life much longer." I grin.

But obviously he doesn't think it's funny as he doesn't even crack a smile.

"That was a joke," I prompt.

But his expression remains deadpan. He really is angry about those bags, isn't he. And now I feel bad.

"I'm sorry. I didn't mean to snap . . . it's just, the supermarket was crazy and I was in a bad mood and—"

"No, I'm not cross about that, don't be silly," he interrupts before I can finish.

"Well, what then?"

"I had no idea you wanted to move out."

He looks genuinely hurt. I feel suddenly wrong-footed.

"You never mentioned anything," he continues.

"Well, I just assumed I'd have to . . . what with the divorce and everything . . ." My mind is scrambling. "I remember us having that conversation when we were walking Arthur, about having to sell your assets . . . needing rooms for the boys. There's only three bedrooms here."

Edward looks at me; his expression is unreadable.

"I'm presuming they're too old for bunk beds."

He finally smiles, and I feel a beat of relief.

"I'm sure we could work something out. You don't need to move out . . ."

"Thanks." I smile. "That's really kind of you."

"I'm not being kind, I like having you here."

"And I like being here," I agree, and for a brief second it strikes me how much things have changed. "But I need to get my own place," I say firmly. "Before I could never afford it, but now . . ." I wave the letter from the bank. "It's long overdue, really. I mean, look at me, I'm in my forties and I'm renting a room—"

"So? I'm in my forties and I'm getting divorced."

Then we both smile and I feel the tension between us evaporating. Just in time for Arthur to make his appearance in the kitchen, sniffing around the baseboards.

"What about Arthur?"

We both turn to look at him doing his impression of a hoover. I'm going to miss him more than I can imagine.

"What are my visitation rights?"

I look back at Edward and his eyes meet mine.

"How about shared custody?"

I'm grateful for:
1. *A friend like Edward.*
2. *Fiona, for getting me to email him about his room for rent, otherwise I would never have met him.*
3. *My bag for life, which I fully intend to use for my whole life, and not just the recommended twelve times.*
4. *Cricket, who makes me laugh by telling me that at eighty-something she feels a bag for life is a bit of a misnomer.*
5. *Someone in the bank thinking I'm responsible enough to lend all that money to.*
6. *Being able to look at apartments for sale—who would've thought it?*

Life Moves On

Cricket has accepted an offer on her house and is moving. But only around the corner. She's found a two-bedroom apartment that's on the first floor, with tall windows and a small roof terrace off the back that overlooks a church.

"So God can keep an eye on me."

"I thought you didn't believe in God."

"I don't, but I like to keep my bases covered," she replies. "At my age I'm getting closer to the call-up—"

"Cricket!" I admonish.

"What?" she protests. "Talking about the D word isn't going to make me die any quicker."

Walking back from viewing her apartment, we're wearing thick coats and boots. The weather has grown colder and the clocks have gone back. Leaves gather along the curbs. Big red jagged ones, and small frilly yellow ones the color of lemons. I look at them and think I must learn what trees they come from.

That's another thing about mid-life. When I was younger I'd never notice such things, but maybe learning to appreciate the wonders of nature is the payoff we get for aging. If you think about it like that, then a bit of a sleeve isn't much of a price to pay, is it?

"I do love it when they rake them into huge piles."

I look up to see Cricket gesturing to several large mounds of leaves ahead. Big heaps of them in the corners of the street.

"Reminds me of when I was a child. I used to love jumping in them, didn't you?"

"I wouldn't know." I shake my head. "My mum always used to say they'd be full of spiders, so I never did."

"Oh, I'm sure they are." She nods cheerfully. "But there are many worse things to be scared of than spiders." And, breaking free of my arm, she promptly jumps in a big pile of them, sending them scattering and twirling as she stomps and kicks. She looks like she's having so much fun.

"Oy!"

Until a street sweeper yells at her, and I wave apologetically and hurry Cricket away.

She's still smiling when we reach the house, where a teenage girl is putting a book on the shelf of the little library and exchanging it for another one.

"It's made me realize how much I missed reading," the girl confesses as we stop to say hello. She smiles warmly at Cricket. "It's such a great idea. I hope you keep it going."

"Well, actually I'm moving, but the new owners have promised to."

"I hope so," she says, but I see a flash of disappointment across her face.

"Do you think the new owner will?" I ask a few minutes later, as we shrug off our coats inside. I fill up the kettle while Cricket goes through to the living room to make a fire. I can't believe it's time for fires already.

"I hope so." Kneeling down, she begins stacking the pieces of kindling. "But who knows."

I stand in the doorway, watching her carefully building a tower of wood. I know not to offer to help. Cricket can be stubborn, but never more so than when it comes to making fires in her own certain way.

"I wish we could do more of them."

"Ah, well, that's something I was going to talk to you about . . ."

I watch her leaning over the grate, her back to me.

"I've been talking to a leading arts charity about starting a scheme to put up more little libraries across the borough, maybe even beyond. I thought now I'm selling my house I could use some of the money to fund it."

She lights a twist of paper and pushes it into the kindling.

"That would be amazing," I enthuse. "That's so generous of you."

She turns to me now, standing up and dusting off her hands on her skirt. She looks pleased.

"And it looks like they've agreed to help."

"Wow!"

"I'd like it to be in memory of Monty. It was his books that started all this, and you of course—"

"I just gave you the idea, that's all," I protest, but she shushes me.

"No, you gave me more than that; you gave me a reason to want to get up in the morning again. Building that free little library was the most invigorated I'd felt since Monty died. It was as though I came back to life."

Her eyes meet mine and she smiles.

"I'd been doing all the other things—the art classes, redecorating—but I was just going through the motions really . . . but then you suggested this and—"

She breaks off and sits down in an armchair.

"We all need a purpose in life, and before Monty died he was my purpose. It's probably a very old-fashioned thing to admit these days, but he was."

"What do I know about being fashionable." I shrug with a smile, gesturing to my dog-walking outfit, which I wore this morning and haven't yet changed out of.

"I still find it hard though," she confesses.

"Well, it hasn't been that long," I remind her.

"Yes, I know." She looks at the fire. The kindling has caught light, and the fire spits and crackles as the flames take hold. "But I'm finding it hard in a different way now. Not just because I miss Monty, but because my life is growing while his has ended." She turns to face me. "I mean, look at me, I'm having all these new experiences and new interests . . . new friends." She smiles at me. "And I feel guilty that I'm enjoying life again. That I should be grieving more."

Her smile drops. Her expression is troubled.

"What did you say to me once? That grief isn't linear?"

As I remind her, I see her face relax. "Thank you, Nell."

"The way I see it, you can grieve for someone and the past, but you've also got to live," I continue firmly.

Then I go to make the tea, and we sit by the fire and spend the evening talking about all the new plans she has. And it's only later, when I'm lying in bed, that I realize I wasn't just talking about Cricket and Monty; I was also talking about my own life.

I'm grateful for:

1. *Cricket asking me to be involved with her new scheme, and my promise that as much as I can, I will. Because, although I would never have imagined it a few months ago, I'm actually really busy these days with work, what with the obituaries and my podcast, and now the play. Maybe this is what happens when you get to this middle stage of life. You don't just have one job anymore; you have lots of different things. Some make money, some don't, but all together they make up a life fulfilled.*
2. *The street sweeper, for not arresting her.*
3. *The passerby who took the huge spider off me after I jumped in the leaves on my way home and nearly screamed the street down.**
4. *Finding a reason.*

A Haircut

"You look smart!"

The next evening I come downstairs to find Edward all dressed up. Not in his yoga gear or his work clothes. But in a really nice shirt and jacket—and is that a pair of designer jeans?

---

* I swear it was the size of a tarantula. Which proves that, of course, mums always know best.

At my compliment he looks very self-conscious and averts his eyes.

I narrow mine.

"Are you going on a date?"

"It's not a date. It's just dinner. With some friends," he adds quickly.

I have never known Edward to go for dinner with "some friends" the whole time I've lived here. There's been yoga. Drinks with people from his office after work. A couple of boozy Saturday afternoon soccer matches with someone called Pazza, who I've never met, but is apparently an old friend from Bristol who he's going to climb Kilimanjaro with, next year, for charity.

"Is one of these friends single and female?" I grin, unable to resist.

"OK, OK." He throws up his hands in surrender. "A colleague at work has been trying to set me up ever since I told him about Sophie and me, but I don't think you can call it a date when my divorce hasn't even come through yet."

"Oh, you can call it a date," I reply, remembering my own recent foray into the dating world. "I'm sure you'll have a great time."

He looks relieved that I approve.

"Though I'm not sure about that hair of yours."

His hand goes to his head.

"What's wrong with it?"

"Nothing, if you don't mind looking like you've had your finger in a socket." I laugh. "Let me give it a quick trim."

He looks at me like I've just told him I'm going to walk on the moon.

"You can cut hair?"

"Well, I wouldn't say I'm Trevor Sorbie, but my mum was a mobile hairdresser, so I've learned a few tips." I grab a dish towel before he can resist. "Here, take off your jacket and put this round your shoulders."

He takes it from me mutely as I pull out a stool, pushing it down until it's the right height.

"Now sit," I instruct.

He sits. I'm impressed. I've never known him to be so obedient.

"OK, so I just need some scissors . . ."

"Oh, I can reach those—"

He leans forward toward the kitchen scissors on the magnetic wall rack. The ones used for everything from cutting flower stems to trimming rind off bacon.

"No, not those!" I cry out.

He jumps back like he's been shot. "Why, what's wrong with them?"

I pull a face. I know there's little point explaining the difference between good scissors and bad scissors. Now, if it was the difference between paper and plastic . . .

"Hang on, I'll just go get mine. I've got a spare pair of Mum's somewhere."

A few minutes later I return with my scissors and the spray bottle we use for ironing, and start wetting his hair down and combing it. It's grown really long. He mustn't have had it trimmed all year.

"Put your head down," I instruct, tucking the dish towel over his collar.

He does as I say: I quite like this new feeling of authority. Up close, I realize his dark hair has gone quite gray, but it's still thick and wavy and I comb the curls over his collar, then begin carefully trimming the back, remembering everything Mum used to tell me when she would take me with her as a child, and I would sit transfixed in people's armchairs, watching her as she deftly cut and shaped.

Unexpectedly, I miss Mum. Since I broke off my engagement and moved back to the UK, we haven't really spoken much. Not properly.

"You're not giving me a crew cut, are you?"

"You mean you didn't want one?"

He laughs and I continue around the back, carefully combing onto the nape of his neck. He stays very still as I move around to the sides, using my fingers to pull his hair forward, snipping the edges with little feather strokes. I don't think I've ever been this close-up to Edward. He smells clean, like he's just got out of the shower. That will be the citrus shower gel I always see on the shelf. I notice a scattering of freckles on the sides of his nose that I've never seen before. See the pulse beating in his neck. A bit he's missed shaving.

"Ta-dah."

I finish cutting and, taking off the towel, give it a shake. Hair falls onto the floor.

"Don't worry, I'll sweep that up," I say as he stands up, rubbing his fingers through his hair, then disappears into the hallway to look in the mirror.

"Wow, you're actually very good."

He sounds surprised.

"I do have some talents, you know," I say, as he reappears in the kitchen. "Now you just need some product."

"Product?" He looks at me blankly.

"You might know a lot about saving the planet, but you don't know much about hair, do you?" I've brought some of my own out of my bedroom, and I squeeze a pea-size blob into my hand. "See, it textures and separates," I explain, reaching for his hair and rubbing a little in at the front where it's gone a bit fluffy.

Edward is looking at me as if I'm speaking another language.

"If you just tease some bits out, like this," I say, playing with his bangs and completely forgetting whose hair I'm touching.

Remembering, I spring back.

"Anyway, there you go," I finish awkwardly. I hadn't realized how intimate cutting someone's hair can be.

But Edward hasn't noticed. He's too busy looking at himself in the mirror again, turning this way and that as if he can't quite recognize his reflection.

I have to say, I did a pretty good job.

"I think it's the best haircut I've ever had," he announces finally.

"The tip jar's over there." I laugh, and he turns to me and smiles.

"Thank you so much."

"Anytime." I shrug, still smiling, as he puts on his jacket and waves goodbye.

Then the door slams and I see him from the window, walking down the street to go and meet his date with his new haircut. I watch him for a few moments, until he disappears out of view.

Anyway.

My hands are all sticky and, turning away, I reach for the dish towel.

Halloween

Halloween never really got to the Lake District in the 1970s. My brother and I grew up being told never to accept sweets from strangers, and our one attempt at trick-or-treating ended with us nearly getting shot by the local farmer for trespassing on his property. Plus, it was always raining. You try to keep a candle in a turnip alight in a ten-force gale while wearing an old bedsheet.

But things have changed. Fast-forward A LOT of years and we've embraced the American way of doing things; now it's costume parties and elaborately carved pumpkins and decorated neighborhoods filled with trick-or-treating children in amazing getups, collecting hauls of sweets.

This year I'm celebrating at Fiona's. She's decorated the outside of her Victorian semi to look like a House of Horrors and hired a dry-ice machine. My role is to hand out sweets and scare the children when they ring the doorbell (I decided not to ask why she thought I'd be good at that). Max and Michelle and Holly and Adam and all the kids are coming too.

And Annabel.

"She usually has this amazing party, but of course it's all changed this year with Clive moving out. She's bringing Clementine," said Fiona, when she called to invite me. "I thought it might be a good opportunity to bury the hatchet."

"Figuratively, I hope. It is Halloween," I replied.

Which made Fiona laugh and gave me an idea for my costume.

I found the axe in the garden shed. Halloween is supposed to be scary, and personally I can't think of anything scarier than Jack Nicholson in *The Shining*. Especially when he's trying to smash down the door with his axe (literally burying the hatchet in it). The charity shop had a checked shirt and I borrowed a jacket from Edward, who I did think about inviting but it turned out he was going on a second date (!). I was really pleased with my costume. Especially the fake door that I made out of cardboard and stuck my head through. When I did my impression in the mirror and waved my axe, I almost terrified myself.

I turn up to find Fiona in an amazing witch costume, Holly in her gym kit looking exactly the same as always, only with a skeleton mask she bought from a gas station on the way over, and Michelle apologizing profusely for her lack of costume, but telling us that after spending all afternoon with a glue gun making three costumes for the kids—while still breastfeeding—we're lucky she's even dressed.

Annabel, meanwhile, comes as a sexy nurse.

"How is that *even a costume*?" I hiss, as she arrives in a minuscule uniform and push-up bra, and promptly begins handing out sugar- and gluten-free sweets to the trick-or-treaters (note: it's the first time I've ever seen children put sweets *back*). At least she's had the good grace to add a bit of fake blood to her apron, but still. "Did she not get the memo? Halloween's supposed to be scary."

"Please tell me her boobs aren't real," whimpers Michelle.

The men, however, seem to like it. Max's eyes nearly come out on stalks (admittedly he's a zombie so they're supposed to look like that) and Adam, who's dressed as Dracula, is so fixated he trips over the polystyrene coffin and ends up in it. Meanwhile, werewolf David keeps having to clear his throat and starts going on about the state of the NHS.

"Olive branch, remember," hisses Fiona, before disappearing to the bathroom and leaving me alone . . . with Annabel heading toward me.

"Hi."

"Hello."

And now I'm cornered by the sub-zero fridge. We engage in a few awkward pleasantries, during which I mentally plot my escape, when—

"I owe you an apology."

I wasn't expecting that at all.

"Oh . . . no . . . don't be silly," I say, batting it away in the same embarrassed way I treat a compliment.

"I should never have elbowed you like that in the fun run."

All at once I feel vindicated. I *knew* it!

"Or tripped you up. I was totally in the wrong. I'm sorry."

Annabel looks at me, waiting for a reaction. Her eyes really are perfectly blue, with the brightest whites I've ever seen, and thick long lashes. I stand there marveling at her, with the fake cardboard door stuck over my head, and suddenly all my grievances fall away and all I can see is the funny side.

"I'm sorry too," I say, "but at least me faceplanting got a few laughs from the crowds."

Seeing me grinning, she smiles, then looks abashed. "I was jealous . . . of your friendship with Fiona. I felt threatened. I've never had a best friend like Fiona."

"I was jealous of you. Of you being so perfect," I admit.

"Well, yes." She nods, with a look of understanding. "I get that."

Oh.

"Friends?"

"Well, I wouldn't go that far," I joke, but I forget Annabel doesn't have a sense of humor and she stares at me blankly, her perfect smile appearing to set ever so slightly around the edges. "Sorry, yes, of course we are," I say quickly, returning her smile with an even wider one.

At which point she asks, "Nell, in that case would you mind putting down that axe?"

And I realize that, actually, maybe I'm wrong about the sense of humor.

By 7 p.m. the trick-or-treaters have all gone home, the doorbell has finally stopped ringing, and the men and women have separated into two camps:

In the living room, along with the children, who peaked earlier with an insane sugar rush and are now semicomatose in front of *Ghostbusters*, we have The Dads. Beers in hand, they appear to be "helping" the children eat all their treats and are more into the movie than the kids are.

In the kitchen we have The Mums and me, slumped and exhausted around the table, drinking wine and eating what's left of the Halloween candy. Scaring children is both a tiring and thirsty business. We're on to our second bottle. It's the first time we've all gotten together since the baby shower, and we're using the opportunity to catch up properly.

Music plays in the background. Max's iPhone is plugged into the stereo and his Halloween playlist is on a loop. As Fiona reaches for the remote to turn it off, Echo & the Bunnymen's cover of "People Are Strange" comes on.

"Oh, I used to love this," says Michelle, who's just finished breastfeeding Tom and is rocking him to sleep in his car seat. "It was from that film, what was it called? The one where they all turned into vampires—"

"*The Lost Boys.*"

"Only one of the best films ever," pipes up Holly. "I must have watched it a hundred times. I was in love with that actor, whatshisname—"

"Kiefer Sutherland?" suggests someone.

"No! But he was gorgeous too."

"Jason Patric?" I grab the name from the teenage depths of my memory.

"Yes, that's him!" Holly's face lights up. "I had a major crush on him. I used to dream I was going to grow up and marry him, and we were going to race around on a motorbike together . . ." She trails off wistfully. "And now I'm married to Adam and we get to drive around together in a Volvo."

"Life goals." I grin.

"I like Volvos," says Michelle, "I wish we had one instead of our old beater."

"I think I need a drink." Holly goes to get up but Fiona, ever the perfect hostess, is already on it.

"Still or sparkling?"

"No, I mean a proper drink."

"I thought you weren't drinking as you're in training," I say, turning to Holly who's been on water all evening, but Fiona's already raiding the fridge.

"We've got more wine, I'll open another bottle!"

She emerges, triumphant, a bottle of something from New Zealand held aloft like an Olympic torch.

"On a school night?"

A voice from the end of the table. It's Annabel. Met with a tableful of glares, she promptly falls silent.

"Fill her up!" Holly holds out her glass as Fiona begins to pour.

"Annabel?"

"Well, perhaps just a tiddly bit more . . ."

Fiona glugs the glass to the top, then fills her own and tops up mine.

"Are these really unhealthy?" asks Michelle, chewing on a red licorice twist.

"Not if you have it with avocado," I suggest.

Someone snorts with laughter.

"Fuck avocados," says Holly, playing catch-up and necking her wine.

"That should be printed on a T-shirt." Fiona laughs, waving the bottle around. I can tell by the flush on her cheeks that she's already quite drunk.

"I'll have another sparkling water," sighs Michelle, reaching for the bottle of San Pellegrino.

Sympathetic looks flash across the table.

"He's gorgeous. You must feel very blessed," says Annabel.

"Yes." She nods, taking a sip of water. "And exhausted."

"How *are* you feeling?" I ask, catching her eye. We've exchanged a few texts, but I haven't seen her since Tom was first born.

"Honestly?" Rocking Tom with one hand, she puts down her glass with the other to tuck a strand of hair back into her ponytail. "Overwhelmed. Old. Struggling to recognize my life anymore . . ."

There's a slew of supportive comments and she smiles ruefully.

"Don't get me wrong—I love Tom so much it hurts." She glances at him now, asleep in his car seat, his small fists curled up to his face, and her eyes light up. "But this isn't how I imagined it was going to be in my forties. I thought by now we'd be sorted out; the kids would all be at school, the mortgage would be almost paid off . . ."

She turns back to me, but she's got the attention of the whole table.

"I was looking forward to getting my life back, using my brain again. I'd even got the application forms to retrain as a counselor . . . Me getting pregnant again and Max losing his job was never part of the plan."

Tom gives a little whimper in his sleep and she strokes his head.

"Now we're back to diapers and sleepless nights, the house

isn't big enough, it's never tidy enough—I would kill for a kitchen like this with surfaces you can actually *see*"— she glances at Fiona, who looks suddenly guilty at having clean surfaces—"and we've had to remortgage so we'll probably be a hundred before it's paid off at this rate . . ."

Having begun at a normal volume, Michelle's voice is growing louder and increasingly more urgent, as if now she's started talking she can't stop.

"More than that, I feel like if I do one thing I'm failing at all the other things, because no way am I going to get through my to-do list . . . it's like I'm playing catch-up all the time, like somehow I'm back at square one whereas everyone else's lives are all sorted out."

Flinging her arm out, she gestures animatedly around the table. "I mean, look at all you lovely ladies! You're all so thin and gorgeous and in control of your lives . . . and look at me!"

Her eyes are brimming now.

"My husband's unemployed, my kids are feral, my house is a mess, I'm going to be sixty when Tom leaves school . . . and I can't even laugh about it all, rather than cry, because if I do I'll pee myself!"

Momentarily stunned after this outburst, we're all silent, and then—

"Are you sure you don't want that glass of wine?" asks Fiona.

Michelle's tears turn immediately to laughter. "You lot! Don't make me laugh," she shrieks, then pulls a horrified expression. "See! What did I tell you!"

"Come here, you." Leaning over, I give her a hug, while Annabel hands her a tissue and we all gather round her, offering words of support and back rubs.

"You've got to listen to this podcast," says Holly. "A girl in my office was going on about it—"

"Thanks," sniffs Michelle, blowing her nose, "but I really don't need anyone else making me feel bad by telling me how I should be feeling grateful and blessed and happy right now." Shaking her head, she pulls a face. "I read something the other day about how I should be full of bliss, and I thought right, yeah, you be full of bliss when you've got a screaming baby and a house that's a mess and you've had a massive row with your husband about the bloody dishwasher—"

She breaks off as she sees Fiona's concerned expression. "It's OK, we made up—he's promised to rinse first."

"No, but that's why you'll love it," insists Holly. "It's about all that."

We each turn to look at her.

"It's about how life just isn't how you imagined it was going to be, and how we're all struggling with the pressure of this perfect life that doesn't exist . . . I mean, we see it on social media, but it's not real." She shakes her head. "It's so funny and real, I've found myself laughing out loud at some parts. Seriously, it's SO my life."

Reaching into her bag, Holly pulls out her mobile.

"Actually, I think a couple of women at my Pilates class mentioned it," Fiona is saying now. "There was some reference to being in your forties and realizing it's time to start wearing a bit of a sleeve—"

"Now that *is* me," laughs Michelle, waggling an arm as if to prove it.

Watching this unfold from the end of the table, I feel myself freeze. No. Surely not. They can't be talking about my podcast. It must be a coincidence.

"Hang on, I downloaded it to listen to on the treadmill, but I only heard the first couple of minutes as my phone died . . ." Punching in her passcode, Holly presses play.

"*Hi and welcome to* Confessions of a Forty-Something F**k-Up, *the podcast for any woman who wonders how the hell she got here, and why life isn't* quite *how she imagined it was going to be.*"

Oh my God. I can't believe it. It *is* my podcast.

As Holly turns up the volume, I listen with disbelief and

embarrassment—do I really *sound* like that? I wish I didn't do that weird telephone accent. It's awful. It sounds nothing like me. I listen to my voice filling the kitchen and glance around at everyone's faces, waiting for them to realize it's me, but they're all focused on Holly's phone. This is completely surreal.

"*. . . ever looked around at their life and thought this was never part of The Plan. Who has ever felt like they dropped a ball, or missed a boat, and is still desperately trying to figure it all out while everyone around them is making gluten-free brownies—*"

"Oh yes, you're right. That *is* me," cries Michelle with delight.

"Gluten-free brownies!" snorts Fiona, clamping her hand over her mouth.

But it's not just listening to this that's surreal: it's the reaction of Holly, Fiona, and Michelle. They don't realize it's me talking, that it's my voice, and they're not just listening. They're identifying.

"*. . . struggling to recognize their messy life in a world of perfect Instagram ones and feeling like a bit of a fuck up. Even worse, a forty-something fuck up. Someone who reads a life-affirming quote and feels exhausted, not inspired. Who isn't trying to achieve new goals, or set more challenges, because life is enough of a challenge as it is. And who does not feel #blessed and #winningatlife but mostly #noideawhatthefuckIamdoing and #canIgoogleit?*"

"I googled how to find my house keys yesterday!"

"That's me! I have no idea what I'm fucking doing either."

"Don't we all feel like that?"

"Does that mean I'm a fuck up?"

"Nobody's a fuck up—if you listen that's the whole point of what she's saying," Holly is explaining loudly above the rowdiness. "It's just sometimes we can be made to feel like one."

"I'm a fuck up," says Annabel, taking a large glug of wine.

"*. . . about what happens when shit happens and still being able to laugh in the face of it all. It's about being honest and telling the truth. About friendship and love and disappointment. About* *asking the big questions and not getting any of the answers. About starting over, when you thought you would be finished already . . ."*

"Yep, that's me again." Michelle is nodding. "I thought I'd be done asking all the questions by now, but it's the opposite. Now I just lie in bed at night, unable to sleep, worrying about everything—"

"But does anyone really have the answers?" cries Fiona. "When I was a child I thought my parents knew all the answers; in my twenties I was adamant *I* knew all the answers; now the older I get, I realize *no one* knows the answers. Everyone's just faking it! No one seems to have a clue what they're doing. Just look at the politicians—"

"Fuck," groans Holly, "do we have to?"

". . . about feeling flawed and confused and lonely and scared, about finding hope and joy in the unlikeliest of places, and how no amount of celebrity cookbooks and smashed avocados are going to save you—"

"I'm serious, I think we should do that T-shirt!" enthuses Holly, topping up her wine glass.

"The exercise videos are worse than the avocados," groans Fiona. "They don't motivate me, they just make me feel guilty I'm not doing the plank every day."

"But you do Pilates!" cries Michelle.

"Only about once a week. I put on leggings every day with the *intention* of doing Pilates, but mostly I just go to the supermarket."

"Because feeling like a fuck up isn't about being *a failure, it's about* being made to feel like one. *It's the pressure and the panic to tick all the boxes and reach all the goals . . . and what happens when you don't. When you find yourself on the outside. Because on some level, in some aspect of your life, it's so easy to feel like you're failing when everyone around you appears to be succeeding."*

"The other mums at nursery terrify me!" cries Holly. "You know, one of them hand-painted all their Christmas cards last year *and* she's the CEO of some major company."

"But you're like Wonder Woman—"

"No, I'm not! I didn't even *send* Christmas cards last year."

"I'm a terrible daughter," confesses Michelle. "My sister is always going to see my parents, especially now Dad's got arthritis, but I haven't been for ages."

"I got invited to a reunion at my university," reveals Fiona, "but when I looked on Facebook everyone else in my year was heading up their own department, or doing these important research projects . . . one girl I knew had even published several bestselling books on Greek mythology!"

"So did you go?"

"No." Fiona shakes her head. "They were all so successful it was intimidating."

"That's how I feel when I look at all those celebrity mums with their bikini bodies, three weeks after giving birth," admits Michelle. "It doesn't inspire me; it does the total opposite."

"The no-makeup selfies are worse," groans Holly, "the ones where they've just woken up and are still lying in bed. I wish I looked like that when I've just woken up."

"*No one* looks like that when they've just woken up," says a loud voice from the other end of the table, and we all turn to see Annabel waving her wineglass. "Trust me, I should know. It's called 'filters,' ladies."

Through all this I've been listening, completely silent. I'm in a sort of daze. Until now it's never dawned on me that my friends might be feeling some of this too. Their lives aren't a mess, they haven't screwed up or taken a wrong turn, they have wonderful husbands and adorable children and gorgeous homes with underfloor heating (Fiona's kitchen really is something else). They can't be scared and confused and feeling like they're failing somehow, like life didn't turn out how they imagined and they have no idea what on earth they're doing half the time.

Can they?

"She sounds a lot like you, Nell."

I snap back to see Annabel staring at me. To be honest, I'm surprised it's taken this long.

"No, Nell has a much broader accent," disagrees Holly, shaking her head.

The podcast keeps playing, but my mouth has gone completely dry and my heart thumps hard in my chest. I suddenly feel absurdly nervous. I take a mouthful of wine and swallow hard.

"Well, actually . . ."

I look up and meet Fiona's eye. There's a pause and I clock the expression on her face as it registers.

"Oh my God, it is you!"

Holly frowns in drunken confusion. "Who? *Nell?*"

Everyone suddenly swivels to face me, glasses in their hands: Fiona, Michelle, Holly, Annabel—four pairs of eyes staring at me. Five, if you include Annabel's French bulldog, Mabel, who's also staring me down.

"Yes, it's me." I nod, and let out a nervous laugh.

There's a long pause, then—

"Oh my God! Nell! You've started a podcast? When? How? You clever girl! Why didn't you tell us? Can I be on it?"

Their reaction is one of astonishment and excitement and delight, and, like a dam bursting, their questions begin rushing at me thick and fast.

"It was a few months ago . . ." I trail off, my mind casting back to that moment in my old bedroom at my parents', and all the frustration and despair at my life. I felt so inadequate and so alone.

And yet, all this time I wasn't.

"I thought I was the only one who felt like this," I confess.

"*You?*" Michelle looks at me, incredulous. "But how can you feel like a fuck up? You're amazing, Nell! I look at you and see someone clever and talented and kind."

She smiles at me now and I almost feel like I'm going to cry.

"And you got to live in New York," she continues. "I always

wanted to live in New York! And you've traveled the world . . . I remember when I was stuck in the house breastfeeding Freddy and you were in Indonesia. I was so envious—"

"Yes, but I don't have what you have," I protest, looking at Tom, fast asleep.

"But you've got a pelvic floor," she fires back, and despite myself, I can't help laughing. "And freedom! Don't underestimate that. I'm looking at another four years of Peppa Pig, maybe three for good behavior."

"And you've never had to go to soft play." Holly grimaces.

"What's that?"

"You don't want to know." Fiona shudders. "It's like a human petri dish." But a look passes between us that makes me think I'm not the only one that's been guilty of making assumptions about others' lives.

"You even set up your own business!"

"And it failed," I remind them. "I lost all my money."

"So? Loads of businesses fail," says Michelle supportively.

"Money's not everything." Fiona shakes her head. "I know lots of rich people and trust me, a lot of them are miserable."

"And you haven't settled for the wrong man," cries Holly, waving her glass so the wine sloshes over the sides. "You've never compromised when it comes to relationships and ended up in an unhappy marriage where all you do is argue."

We all turn to look at Holly.

"Adam's the wrong man?" asks Michelle, as the table suddenly falls silent.

Seeming to realize she's spoken out loud, Holly hesitates, then—

"It's been pretty awful for a long time," she confesses. "I can't even remember the last time we had sex—"

"Oh God, who can?" says Fiona supportively. "By the time David rolls in from work he's always so knackered and I'm usually asleep."

"No, but it's more than that. I don't even think we *like* each other anymore." Holly's face seems to crumple. "The only reason I'm doing the triathlon is to try and get some control over my life . . . and so I don't have to sit at home in that horrible atmosphere."

"But you guys used to be so good together," says Michelle quietly.

"I know." She nods. "But things have changed, we got lost somewhere . . . Adam says he wants another baby so Olivia isn't an only child, but that just makes it harder to leave, doesn't it?"

She looks around at each of us in turn.

"And I know that makes me a horrible person, even thinking like that, and I know I'm denying my daughter a sibling—" She breaks off, shaking her head and draining the rest of her glass. "But I'm just so bloody scared and confused. I have no idea how I got into this mess and what I'm going to do . . ."

Reaching over, I squeeze her hand.

"You're not a horrible person, you're just normal."

Wiping away a tear that's rolling down her cheek, she smiles bravely and nods, but I know she's not convinced.

"Sometimes when I go with Clementine to feed the ducks, I look at them on the pond and think we're all just like them."

It's Annabel. The whole time she's been listening, not saying much, but now she starts talking.

"We're gliding along on the surface, but underneath our legs are paddling furiously, trying to keep afloat."

I don't need to look at my friends to know we're all identifying with the image. Seriously. I'm a bloody duck.

"Do you know how many photographs I had to take of myself in my swimsuit to get the one you saw online?" she continues. "Twenty-eight. I counted them. It was exhausting."

She twiddles the large diamond on her finger. It glitters like a disco ball.

"I wanted everything to be perfect. I thought if I could present this image to the outside world, it would be like that at home. I got to look at my life on social media and pretend it *was* my life." She shrugs her tiny shoulders.

"But it was all bullshit. All those happy family photographs to show how perfect everything was?" She snorts with contempt. "Clive was fucking his secretary. My daughter was so desperate for attention she was bullying. And me?" She shakes her head. "I'm on antidepressants and yet another diet. I swear, I think I've been hungry since 1998."

As Annabel makes this final admission, I realize it's been quite some evening. As revelations go, I didn't think anyone would be able to top Holly's, but it just goes to show. For all of us, it seems, life isn't always easy, and the lesson I've learned is that you're not fucking up if life hasn't worked out how you expected. Because *real* life is messy and complicated. Shit happens. One size doesn't fit all. Remove the filters and the hashtags and the motivational messages and we're all just as scared and confused as the next person. We're all just living our life, and it might not tick all the boxes or look Insta-perfect, but that's OK.

"And the quinoa cupcakes were disgusting, weren't they?"

Annabel is glancing around at us. We all look at each other, then nod slowly.

"Truly disgusting," admits Fiona, speaking for everyone.

"Here, you need one of these." Reaching into her bag, Michelle pulls out a box of her favorite chocolate teacakes. "I was keeping them for later, but you look like you need them more than me." Tearing open the packet, she passes them over.

Annabel looks at them uncertainly, then takes one. We watch as she peels off the silver foil and takes a bite, waiting as she chews the biscuit base and chocolate-covered marshmallow, before raising her eyes to meet ours and breaking into a huge smile.

She has chocolate all over her teeth.

"Take two," instructs Michelle.

I'm grateful for:
1. *Our forties and beyond; because this time in our lives is one of change and reinvention, of endings and beginnings that*

aren't all welcome or planned, but will end up taking us on new and different paths that will be as wonderful as they are scary.*

2. The realization we're all in this together.
3. Fiona, who later tells me I've got nice arms and I can still wear a spaghetti top—which is very sweet of her, but like I said, her eyesight's going.
4. Finding my tribe.

---

* At least, I bloody well hope so.

NOVEMBER

#aquestionoflifeanddeath

My Confessions

I've been bowled over by the reaction of my friends to my podcast. A few days have passed since they listened to the first episode at Fiona's kitchen table, and they've downloaded the rest and been sending me lots of texts and messages and laughing face emojis saying how much they're loving it, including some *very* funny "outfit of the day" photos.

It also turns out I'm not the only one with a superpower. Fiona's is "being a bloody mind reader," Michelle's is "being in two places at once," and Holly's is "being able to laugh in the face of it all," which, if you ask me, is the best superpower of all.

Added to this, I just checked the number of people who listened to my last episode and something incredible has happened—it's jumped up another twelve thousand! So now I've got nearly *fifteen thousand* listeners. Seriously. Pinch me.

But the best reaction of all has to be Cricket's.

"That's wonderful, Nell, I'm so proud of you."

I've gone over to help her pack for the move and we're in the living room, surrounded by Bubble Wrap.

"Thank you." Her praise means so much to me. "You know, it's all because of you. I was listening to that podcast you recommended, and that's how I got the idea to do my own."

"Well, it sounds marvelous!" she says cheerfully, wrapping a vase. "Can I be an eighty-something fuck up? Dead husband. No grandchildren. A social pariah at the bridge club."

"You can be an honorary member." I grin. "Why don't you let me interview you?"

"Fame at last!" She beams. "I think it's going to be one of those viruses."

"Viruses?"

"Yes, where it goes around the world."

I frown, wondering what on earth she's going on about, then smile. "Oh, you mean going viral."

She nods. "Yes, that too."

I'm grateful for:
1. *All my lovely new listeners, who make me realize more than ever that I'm not alone.*
2. *All the lovely feedback I'm getting.*
3. *Being in the top ten podcasts this week.*
4. *My interview with Cricket, which gets the most downloads ever, where she reveals her superpower is "being old and still getting excited about life," which she attributes to saying yes to everything—except joining the Blue Rinse Brigade.*

Bonfire Night

When it comes to November 5, Guy Fawkes has a lot to answer for. And no, I'm not talking about his plot to blow up the Houses of Parliament; I'm talking about sentencing every pet owner in the country to a night of hell. If there's one word that will strike fear into every pet and their owner, it's *fireworks*.

Don't get me wrong. I *love* fireworks as much as the next person. But where you see exploding rockets and cascading Catherine wheels, we pet owners see terrified animals trying to hide down the back of the sofa.

Or, in Arthur's case, squashed underneath my desk, covered in a beach towel.

Edward is out with "some friends" again, which I think is code for Date Three. Though I didn't ask. When he texted to ask me if I'd be home to look after Arthur, I couldn't exactly respond, "Yes, are you going to have sex?" To be honest, I'm not sure if I want to know.

So instead I turn off all the lights and watch the fireworks from the upstairs window. Gazing across the rooftops and beyond at the glittering bursts of color and shooting stars that leap and swirl across the inky sky, I feel like I'm witnessing a ballet. It really is magical. One of those things you want to share with someone.

Oh, FFS.

I grab my phone. At least I can share it on Instagram.

I spend the next few minutes taking lots of blurry photos of fireworks, before giving up and putting down my phone and just watching.

I'm not sure how long I stand there, alone in the darkness. But it feels like a really long time.

I'm grateful for:
1. *Everyone else's out-of-focus offerings, which teach me the valuable lesson that there is nothing more boring than looking at other people's photos of fireworks.**

The Phone Call

Tuesday night. My phone rings. I'm in bed and I've just turned out the light. It's probably Liza. Things are going great with Tia and she'll be wanting to chat. But I'm too tired. I'll call her back

---

* Though listening to other people's dreams might come a close second. Sorry, Edward.

tomorrow. I lean over to turn it on to silent—and see that the number flashing up on the screen isn't Liza's; it's Mum's mobile.

It's 11:04 p.m.

She never calls at this time. Worry flickers.

"Mum?"

"Nell—" Hearing my voice, she bursts into tears. She's hysterical.

"Mum, are you OK? What's happened?" Fear has me by the throat.

"It's your dad . . . there's been a terrible car accident—"

I can hear urgent voices in the background.

"Mum?"

"The police are here, he's been airlifted to the hospital—" Her voice is drowning under thick, heavy sobs. "They say it's really serious . . ."

More voices. A sense of panic.

"Mum, I can't hear you—"

"Nell, I've got to go . . . I'll call you from the hospital."

No Guarantees

Dad died in the air-ambulance on his way to hospital. He had a cardiac arrest, and his heart stopped for six minutes before they managed to shock him back to life. For six whole minutes, while I sat on my bed three hundred miles away, hugging my knees to my chest and desperately waiting for Mum to call back with more news, my dad was officially dead.

Thoughts don't come more sobering than that.

I get the first train out of London. Dad's been transferred to the city hospital for emergency lifesaving surgery. Scans have revealed a catalog of injuries: a fractured leg, broken ribs, a punctured lung, a ruptured spleen, internal bleeding, and a serious head injury.

I tell Mum I'll be there as soon as I can and that everything's going to be OK. I say it as much for my benefit as hers, but I can feel her clinging to my reassurances, like a frightened child to their mother. I call my brother, but his phone is switched off and my messages go to voicemail. I try Nathalie. It's the same. I keep trying them. The woman opposite me is giving me daggers. I realize I'm in the quiet carriage.

Vaguely I remember speaking to Edward, telling him what's happened. He asks me if he can do anything; I say no, and start crying. The woman who's been staring at me passes me a tissue and tries to console me. I notice people in the carriage are staring.

I don't care. Fear does that to you.

It feels like the longest train journey in the world. We pass through gray towns and bleak countryside, and I gaze absently upon trees that have lost their leaves, their skeleton arms reaching into the leaden skies. Rain splatters against the window. I see it all but take in nothing. My mind is elsewhere, flicking through a series of questions and fears, until it seems to freeze, like a computer when you're running too many programs.

Then finally I'm in a taxi from the station and I'm arriving at the hospital, rushing through the maze of corridors to find Mum. She's sitting in the waiting area, a small hunched figure in a winter coat, twisting her hands in her lap, her eyes all red and puffy from crying. She jumps up when she sees me.

"Oh, Nell" is all she says, over and over, as she clutches me tightly.

"It's going to be OK, Mum," I tell her firmly. "It's going to be OK."

I've never seen her this scared or helpless. She's always been so stoic, but now she crumples beneath me. I hold her tight. I haven't hugged Mum like this since I was a little girl, but now the roles are suddenly reversed and I know I've got to be the strong one. She needs me. I can't fall apart.

Dad had been driving back home from the rugby club when the accident happened. It had been a friend's birthday. "John, remember? He worked with him at the council." Mum was supposed to go but she had a bit of a cold. "I insisted he went without me. I told him to go," she explains through her sobs. "It's all my fault. If he hadn't gone, this would never have happened."

It had been raining heavily. According to the police report, visibility was poor. A truck on the highway lost control and veered into the divide, causing a multicar pileup. Dad was trapped in the Land Rover and had to be cut free by firefighters. An attending ambulance crew performed lifesaving surgery at the side of the road to stem the bleeding from his internal injuries. Without that he would have died at the scene. Not everyone was so fortunate. There were several fatalities. Dad was one of the lucky ones.

A nurse ushers us into a small office where we meet Dr. Reynolds, the trauma surgeon responsible for saving Dad's life. He informs us that Dad's just come out of surgery, that it went well, but he's still in a critical condition. Mum starts crying again. I don't know if it's relief or fear or both. The surgeon explains about Dad's injuries, showing us different scans and X-rays, informing us of what's happened.

The impact of the collision caused internal hemorrhaging. He's been given two blood transfusions and had surgery to repair his ruptured spleen and punctured lung. The Land Rover wasn't fitted with airbags, resulting in the head injury, which was caused by the blunt trauma of hitting the windshield. He's been put into an induced coma, to reduce the swelling and minimize potentially irreversible damage to the brain. The fracture to his right leg, most likely caused by slamming on the brake, has been stabilized until he can be transferred to orthopedics. He'll later need an operation to insert a metal plate and pins. That's if he makes it through the next few days.

It's an awful lot to take in. Dr. Reynolds is grave, but calm and assured. His language is matter of fact and littered with the kind of technical medical terms I'm used to hearing on TV, not in real life about my dad. He must have done this hundreds of times with hundreds of different frightened relatives who are pinning their whole worlds upon him. I listen and nod, feeling strangely detached as I struggle to absorb all this information. I think I'm still in shock.

Mum doesn't speak but looks at me for reassurance. She seems in a daze, her body shrunken beneath her coat. As the surgeon talks about risks and complications, I squeeze her hand and ask every possible question I can think of.

When he's finished, we all stand up and shake hands.

"When can we see him?" asks Mum, finally.

"Soon. He's being taken to ICU where he'll be made comfortable. If you take a seat in the waiting room, I'll get a nurse to attend to you."

As we leave his office, I tell Mum I'm just going to the restroom and I'll meet her in the waiting room. As soon as she's disappeared through the fire doors, I quickly double back.

Dr. Reynolds is still in his office when I knock on his door.

"I needed to speak to you alone," I say, closing the door behind me. I pause, wondering how to put it, then just blurt it out. "Is he going to be all right? You can level with me."

He's sitting at his desk. I notice the everyday details: the blind at the window behind him that's been pulled up unevenly; a potted plant (is it real or plastic? I can't tell); the silver-framed photograph of two young children on his desk. He's someone's dad too.

"Your father's condition is critical but stable. The next forty-eight hours are crucial—we'll know more then."

"Could he die?"

I say it out loud. The fear that's been circulating in my head ever since Mum called me last night.

There's a beat before he answers.

"We do everything we can for a patient." He meets my gaze and I silently will him to tell me the truth. "But with injuries this severe, there are no guarantees."

I'm grateful for:
1. *He's alive, he's alive, he's alive.*

Evie Rose

In the hospital, time slows right down. Outside normal life moves at a frantic pace, hands on a clock jumping whole hours since you last checked, but within these walls, time sags and stalls. What can feel like an hour is only five minutes. It's like in *The Matrix*, only not nearly as much fun.

Life as I once knew it ceases to exist. A million distractions shrink down to a waiting room lit with artificial light. It feels small and suffocating. A dismal cafeteria is my only reprieve from the agonizing wait.

We're taken to see Dad in ICU for a brief few minutes. I think I'm prepared, but nothing prepares you for seeing someone you love hooked up to machines and monitors, their body battered and bruised. Dad's always so larger than life, but he looks pale and still in his hospital gown. That strikes me the most. How still he is. How quiet. All we can hear is the rhythmical beeping and pumping of the various machines.

His body is attached to endless tubes and drains, and an oxygen mask covers his face. I look across at Mum. She's already sitting at his bedside, holding his hand. I do the same, but it's all taped up from the drip and he has clips on various fingers. I'm scared to touch him. To do something wrong. So instead I just sit beside him, watching his chest rising and falling, hearing Mum murmuring softly, swallowing down the lump that threatens in my throat.

Telling myself over and over that I've got to be strong, that he's going to survive, that this isn't really happening.

But it is.

Rich finally calls and we discover why he hasn't been answering his phone. Nathalie went into labor last night, but their careful plans for a home birth were abandoned and she ended up being taken to the hospital. Their daughter was finally born this afternoon, "eight pounds two ounces and just perfect," but in the hurry he'd left his phone at home.

He borrowed Nathalie's to call Mum and Dad at home to tell them the good news—they had a granddaughter! But there'd been no answer and he didn't know their mobile numbers by heart. He'd thought nothing of it. It was only when he'd gone home to take a shower and retrieve his phone that he'd got all our messages.

"I'll come straightaway," he's saying now, still in shock from the news of Dad's accident.

"No, you stay with Nathalie and the baby," says Mum firmly. "They need you."

"But I've got to be there—"

"There's nothing you can do, love."

I can't hear what my brother is saying, and after a moment Mum passes me the phone. "He wants to speak to you."

"Sis. Tell me. What's happening?" he says urgently.

I swallow hard. "His injuries are serious," I say, parroting the doctor. "They've put him in an induced coma. We've just got to wait."

Silence.

"Rich?" I step a few paces away from Mum. "Rich, are you OK?"

He sniffs hard, his voice breaking. "Is he going to make it, sis?"

Big sister. Looking after her little brother. Just like always. I hesitate. He can't be here. His priority is Nathalie and the new baby. He has to protect them, just like I've got to protect him. Just like I've always done.

"Yeah," I say, pushing down my fears. Then firmer this time. "Yes, he's going to make it."

I'm grateful for:
1. *Evie Rose Stevens, born November 7 at 5:10 p.m., 8lb 2oz.*
2. *Where there's life, there's hope.*

Dark Night of the Soul

It's late. Regular visiting hours finished ages ago but we've been allowed to stay for longer. "Special circumstances," I think that's what the nurse said. I can't remember now. Things are beginning to blur, yet at the same time they're intensified. Life has taken on a dreamlike quality.

We've been allowed into the patient recreational room. Mum is asleep in a chair but I'm wide awake. I look around at the dimly lit room, but it's empty apart from the two of us. There's a TV in the corner, but the volume is turned right down. It's some old film. A black-and-white I don't recognize. I lie back on the sofa and let my eyes rest on the screen. Anything to take my mind off the thoughts that are spiraling in my head.

Mum stirs. I look across at her, her face resting against her coat, which she's made into a makeshift pillow. She looks exhausted. After seeing Dad, she hasn't mentioned his injuries, choosing instead to fuss about missing the engineer who was due today to service the boiler, and a dentist appointment for Dad that she forgot to cancel.

I kept telling her it was fine, not to worry, it didn't matter, but then I realized she needed to worry about that stuff. It was her way of coping. It stopped her worrying about the real stuff.

The door opens and a female patient enters in a robe. I watch her softly padding toward me, wheeling a portable oxygen tank. She looks like a ghoul, with her pale face and sunken eyes. Even in her robe, I can see she's so very, very thin.

I smile warmly. "Hi."

She looks at me hesitantly, then smiles back. "I haven't seen you here before." Her voice is raspy; she's wearing a breathing tube.

"No." I shake my head. "It's my dad. He was in a car accident. He was admitted this morning."

"Oh dear." She sits down next to me. Up close I can see the jutting of her cheekbones and the yellow of her eyes. "People drive too fast nowadays . . . not that I'm saying—" she adds.

"No." I shake my head again and there's a pause. "Have you been here long?" It's a weird kind of small talk. We're two strangers, but the situation is so intimate.

She nods. "Six weeks. It's my lungs."

"I'm sorry."

"It's all right, love." She smiles to reassure me, and I'm struck by how she's trying to protect my feelings. "I've been admitted before, but this time . . ." She shrugs her bony shoulders, then glances up at the TV screen. "Oh, I used to love these Busby Berkeley films!" Her face lights up girlishly as she gestures to the dancing showgirls. "I used to watch them with my nan."

We both gaze at the screen, watching them forming kaleidoscope patterns. Their legs kicking in perfect symmetry. Arms waving. Faces smiling. And for a while time seems to stand still, our thoughts taken away from the painful reality and absorbed by the magic of Hollywood.

"Well, I'll be going, love," she says eventually, getting up from the sofa. "I hope your dad's all right."

"You too." I manage a smile.

Wrapping the robe's belt around her tiny waist, she gives me a haunted look; we both know she's not going to be.

*

Afterward I go to the bathroom. Washing my hands, I splash water on my face and stare at myself in the mirror. I've aged a hundred years. I dig out my phone. I haven't looked at it all day. Gallows humor flickers. Having someone you love in intensive care is one way to limit your screen time.

There are a couple of missed calls from Edward, but he hasn't left a voicemail. I look at my watch. It's too late to call him back; he'll be asleep.

I have a sudden urge to speak to someone. I can't talk to Mum. I couldn't talk to Rich. Everyone's leaning on me, but who can I lean on? I just want someone to put their arms around me. Someone to tell me it's going to be all right.

Oh God, I miss Ethan.

It's like a wave rushing over me. I've not thought about him for months, deliberately at first, and now when he enters my mind it's fleeting. But I'm suddenly desperate to hear his voice.

I dial his number before my rational mind can stop me. I know it off by heart.

I hear it ringing. My heart pounds. I'm about to hang up.

"Nell?"

His voice, so familiar, sounds in the darkness.

"Yeah, it's me."

Its effect is immediate. I close my eyes, pressing the lids tightly shut, but tears are already leaking down my cheeks.

"Hey . . ." There's a pause. "What's wrong?"

"It's Dad. He's been in a terrible car accident. I'm at the hospital." It's like opening a release valve. "Oh Ethan, I'm so scared of what's going to happen—"

"It's going to be OK," he reassures me immediately.

"But how do you know?" I've been holding my body so rigid, trying to stave off the shock, but now I realize it's shaking uncontrollably.

"Because whatever happens, it will be OK. You'll be OK."

My teeth begin to chatter. But it's not from cold; it's with fear.

"I can't do this." I clench my jaw hard to try and stop it.

"Is your brother there?" Ethan tries to deflect my rising panic.

"No—" I break off. I don't want to tell him about the baby. Not now. "I'm sorry . . . I should never have called."

"I'm glad you did."

"I just—" But I can't finish the sentence. I have no idea what I'm even thinking.

"He's going to pull through, you know. Your dad's a fighter. Remember how he was when we first met? I was so scared."

Through the panic a memory flickers. Mum and Dad flew over to visit and we all went out for dinner. Dad must have asked Ethan a hundred questions. It was more an interrogation than a meal at a sushi restaurant.

"And he's got you by his side, that's quite something."

I listen silently, pressing the phone to my ear, willing him to tell me something good.

"I've thought about you, you know . . . I've missed you . . ."

I wipe away a tear that's running down my cheek. I think about what happened between us, about the girl Liza saw him with. It seemed so important before, but now it all seems so trivial.

"I moved to San Francisco when you left. I'm head chef at a new restaurant. I get to plan the whole menu—I do my puttanesca with olives and capers and parsley that you love."

And I'm right back there again. Just Ethan and me.

"That's great . . ."

"But anyway—" He breaks off. "I didn't mean to talk about my stuff. How's your mum holding up?"

For a few brief moments I was somewhere else, away from all this.

"She's OK . . ."

There's so much I want to say; I have no idea where to start.

"Ethan, I—"

"Nell, sorry, hang on a minute." On the other end of the line I hear muffled voices. "That was a delivery. I'm at the restaurant.

It's early but we've got a big lunch party coming in . . . What were you saying?"

But the moment's gone. Whatever it was I was going to say has slipped through my fingers before I could catch it.

"Oh, nothing . . ."

"Look, I'm really sorry, I'm gonna have to go—"

"Yeah, me too. Mum will be worried."

"Please send her my love, tell her I'm thinking about her . . . and your dad . . ."

"I will." And now I'm back on autopilot.

"You stay strong. I'll call you tomorrow."

I know he won't, but it doesn't matter.

"Bye, Ethan."

"Bye, Nell."

I hang up.

Afterward I go back outside into the corridor. I need to head back to the patients' lounge—Mum might be awake, she'll be wondering where I am—but first I need a few minutes by myself. I don't know what I was hoping for, ringing Ethan, but it's left me feeling more alone than ever.

I start walking, pushing through fire doors, no direction in mind, when I see a sign for the hospital chapel. The door is open and I pause there. For once in my life I wish I was religious. That I could drop to my knees and pray to God and seek some kind of comfort. Somewhere, deep in the recesses of my mind, I can still remember the Lord's Prayer from school assembly. Just as I can remember my dad's reaction when he discovered I was having to recite the Lord's Prayer. "She can decide what she wants to believe when she grows up," he'd gruffly told the headmaster. "You're not deciding for her."

Sniffing back tears, I smile at the memory. Mum was horrified; what would they say at parents' evening? But Dad trusted me to think for myself. He believed in me. He's always believed in me, even when I haven't believed in myself.

Turning away from the doorway, I rest wearily against the wall. I think about Dad. How since the day I was born, he's been the one man in my life who's always been there for me, never letting me down, loving me unconditionally, even during those teenage years of rows and shouting and slamming of doors.

Boyfriends have come and gone. Fiancés too. But not Dad. He's always been protecting me, even from afar. Nothing bad could ever happen to me while he was alive, because he's the net into which I can always fall. A world without him is unfathomable.

I slump to my haunches and bury my head in my hands. A howl, like an injured animal, echoes down the silent corridor, and I become aware of someone wailing with grief.

Then I realize it's me.

The Next Morning

We finally left the hospital in the early hours. Mum had been there for over twenty-four hours and the doctors advised me to take her home in a cab to get some rest. It was hard leaving Dad behind, but even harder returning to an empty house. It felt weird without him being there, like a part of the house was missing. *This is what it will be like if he doesn't come home*, I thought as we both went straight to bed, exhausted.

It's not even light when we set off back to the hospital again. They've just called saying Dad's taken a turn for the worse in the night. We need to be there. This time I'm driving Mum's car and we sit in silence. The doctors have told us we need to be prepared. But how can you ever prepare yourself for something like this?

Mum sits next to me in the passenger seat, hands in her lap, twisting her wedding ring. Fear has my chest in a vise as we pull into the car park. Because it's so early, it's almost empty as I head toward the entrance. I'm trying to be strong, but the truth is I've never been so scared. All I want to do is run away. But I can't. I've got to get out of this car and walk into that hospital and face up to whatever it is that's waiting for us.

I tighten my grip on the steering wheel as I swing into the parking spot. For once the spaces are wide open. Except for one other car.

"Well, we're here," I say to Mum, straightening up and switching off the engine.

So this is it. Heart thumping, I reach for the car door and push it open. A sharp gust of wind blows in.

"Nell!"

Someone calls my name and I whip around. And that's when I see him, walking toward me.

"Edward?"

I peer at him in the dawn light, in disbelief.

"What are you doing here?"

He looks disheveled, as if he's slept in his car.

"I got here as soon as I could."

I almost weep with relief. I have never been so grateful to see anyone in my whole life.

"But . . . how?"

"I drove through the night. I was worried, I didn't hear from you."

My mind is grappling. "But how did you know where to find us?"

"You told me the name of the hospital on the train, remember."

Except I don't. I don't remember anything about that train ride.

"And you just came?"

"Yes." He nods. "I just came."

And in that moment, I know I will love him forever for doing that. Not love in the romantic sense, but love in the true, deep sense of the word. Without even being asked, he's driven through the night to be here for me. So I can lean on him when I need to lean on someone the most in my life. In the most desperate of times. When I thought I was alone. He was here. Waiting for me.

And if that's not real love, I don't know what is.

Inside the hospital we're met by Dr. Reynolds, who tells us an undetected tear has caused more internal bleeding and Dad needs urgent surgery. Mum signs the consent form and we spend the next three hours pacing corridors and drinking bad coffee. But this time it's different. Edward is here and he's the support against which both Mum and I lean. He doesn't say much; he doesn't need to. Just being here is enough.

After surgery, Dad is taken back to ICU. Dr. Reynolds is grave but "cautiously optimistic." I feel a tiny chink of light find its way into the darkness that has engulfed us for the past two days. We're allowed to see him. Edward waits outside while Mum strokes Dad's hair and I tell him he's going to get better.

I don't know if he can hear me, but just in case I tell him his favorite joke too, the one about the man at the bar and the talking peanuts. Dad loves that joke. Every time I see him he makes me tell it, even though he's heard it a million times. But this time, when I deliver the punch line, there's no laughter, just the sound of machines beeping in the silence. For a moment I gaze upon him, blinking back the tears that are threatening to fall, before, leaning closer, I whisper in his ear.

"You've got to get better, Dad. Who else is going to laugh at my jokes?"

Tea and Biscuits

"Here we go."

We're back at home and I'm sitting in the living room with Edward as Mum appears with the tray of tea and biscuits. Earlier, when I introduced her to Edward, she was confused—my landlord? Driving all this way to see me? I think she was worried I was behind with the rent or something. But after I explained he was my friend and he'd come to lend his support, she was insistent he come back to the house.

Not that Edward would have put up much of a fight anyway. Unshaven, with heavy bags underneath his eyes, he looks in desperate need of my mum's sofa.

"So, are you staying for the weekend?" she's asking now, handing him a cup of tea. I notice she's brought out the proper cups and saucers, and not the mugs with the funny slogans we usually drink out of.

"I'm sure he'll need to get back—" I cut in quickly.

"Actually, I don't," he says, thanking Mum, who's now offering him a chocolate biscuit. KitKats, no less. "I dropped Arthur off with Sophie and the boys when I went to pick up the car . . . Sophie's my ex-wife," he adds, for Mum's benefit. "Well, soon to be."

Mum looks across at me and I shift in the armchair. Subtlety is not one of her qualities. Edward notices but pretends not to. Now I know how Lizzy Bennet must have felt.

"What about her allergies?" I ask.

"I think she can handle a few sneezes for the weekend," he says, then turns to Mum. "To be honest, I think it's more me she's allergic to."

Mum laughs at his joke. It's the first time I've seen her smiling in days.

"Well, you're very welcome to stay. I can make up Richard's room. They're not arriving till Monday . . ."

My brother called earlier to say he was driving up with Nathalie and the new baby after the weekend. I'd been keeping him informed of what was going on, and he was as relieved as we were with the latest news about Dad.

"Well, it is a long drive from London and I've never been to the Lake District before," Edward is saying now, looking at me.

I take another chocolate biscuit. "Well, that's decided then."

I'm grateful for:
1. *So many things right now, but if there's one thing life-and-death moments teach you, it's not to give a fuck about how many KitKats you eat.**

The Weekend

It's funny being a tourist in your own town. I take Edward on a tour of the area and show him all the famous bits. Wordsworth's cottage, Beatrix Potter's house, Grasmere's famous gingerbread shop.

"Whoa, this stuff's delicious," he declares as he finishes off the last square. Having scoffed at me for raving about the best gingerbread in the world, he's now sold. "Who knew?" he says, going back into the shop for more.

Who knew indeed.

Who knew that I'd be coming downstairs in the morning to make coffee, to find Edward on a kitchen stool, clean-shaven after using one of my disposables, eating toast and chatting comfortably to "Carol," my mother, like he's known her all his life.

Who knew that Dad's rain gear would fit him, and we'd hike

---

* If you're wondering, I had four.

Scafell Pike in the freezing horizontal rain and share a flask of hot tea at the summit, and I'd wonder why I never realized getting drenched could be so much fun.

Who knew that where I grew up and longed to escape from would feel so different now, and when Edward marveled at how lucky I was to grow up in a place this beautiful, I'd nod my head proudly and agree.

Who knew so many things could change in the course of just a few days.

When it's time to go back to the hospital, Edward insists on driving. The feminist within me tries to put up a fight, but Mum seems to take comfort in having Edward at the wheel, so I give in. Plus, to be honest, Edward's car is much nicer than Mum's ancient Ford Fiesta. Especially when I discover it has heated seats—which, frankly, when it's 35 degrees outside, I'm totally happy to give up my feminist principles for.

On our second visit we're called into Dr. Reynolds's office and told they've successfully brought Dad out of his induced coma, and all the signs are looking good. He's been transferred to a general ward. Would we like to see him?

I let Mum go first. They might be my parents, but they were a couple of teenage sweethearts first, and they need some time alone. When I join them she's stroking his hand, her face flushed with the kind of joy you don't see often. It comes from the very real fear of thinking you might lose the most precious thing in the whole world. Of having peered into the abyss and being safe again.

I wouldn't recommend it, but boy does it get your priorities straight.

"Hello, Dad." I go to give him a kiss on his forehead. He's surrounded by "Get Well" cards, plus a large fruit basket that Ethan's sent.

"Nell, love." His eyes well up when he sees me, and that immediately sets me off.

"How are you feeling?"

"Like I've just done ten rounds." He manages a groggy smile. "I was just telling your mother, I can't remember anything about the accident—"

"Just as well. You gave us all quite a shock."

Dad groans. "You haven't all been worrying, have you?"

"Just a bit." I smile, and squeeze his hand. I've never felt so grateful to feel him squeeze mine back. "At least it makes a change from you worrying about me."

His eyes meet mine and a look passes between us. It's one I don't think I'm ever going to forget.

"What about you, Carol?"

He glances at Mum.

"Oh, I'm fine," she reassures him quickly. "Nell's been taking care of me." She looks at me across the hospital bed. "I couldn't have done it without her."

"We make a good team." I smile, and in that moment I realize that whatever barrier I've been putting up has long since fallen away.

Dad couldn't look more pleased.

"My two girls . . ."

"Three now," corrects Mum.

"So when am I going to meet my granddaughter?" he asks. Mum must have already told him all about Evie.

"They're coming on Monday, after Edward's left."

"Edward?"

I'm actually surprised it's taken Mum this long to mention him. But instead of feeling annoyed with her, I can't help smiling.

"My roommate," I explain to Dad.

"He drove us here. He's got a lovely car, Philip. Heated seats and everything."

"Well, where is he now?"

"Waiting outside."

Dad looks appalled. "The poor man's driven all the way from London and you're keeping him waiting outside? Invite him in!"

"Are you sure? The doctor did say we mustn't tire you out—" But even as I'm protesting, I know resistance is futile.

I find Edward on a plastic chair reading a leaflet on strokes.

"Dad's asking to meet you . . . do you mind? You don't have to be long, just say hello . . . I think he's just curious . . ."

It's funny seeing Edward and my dad meet. And in such circumstances. Edward is well mannered and gracious in the way that seems to come so easily to the privately educated middle classes, and Dad is jokey and gruff and rough around the edges, and tells an awful joke about heated seats that is frankly unrepeatable. But to my surprise, they really get along.

Later, when we're driving home, I give Mum the passenger seat while I sit in the back, gazing out of the window. Thinking about it now, I don't know why I was surprised. On the outside Edward and my dad might seem very different, but they're actually very similar. When I've needed them the most, neither of them have let me down.

Now Dad is on the mend, I feel slightly embarrassed about my reaction to Edward's arrival that morning in the car park. In the way you do when you're vulnerable and reveal too much of yourself.

"Sorry if I was a bit overemotional," I say to him on Sunday afternoon.

He's leaving in a couple of hours to drive back to London and we're in my brother's room, stripping the bed. I've told him I'll do it after he's gone, but he's insisted on doing it himself.

"Don't be silly." He frowns, tugging off a pillowcase as I perch on the edge of my brother's old desk. "It's good you're emotional."

"It is?"

He turns his attention to the duvet cover and begins trying to wrangle it free from the duvet. "Instead of being a deeply repressed public schoolboy like myself, yes," he says, then smiles when I catch his eye and realize he's joking.

Well, sort of.

"I've repressed some things," I say quietly.

He looks at me curiously, as if not quite believing this could possibly be true, then nods slowly. "Maybe from now on we should always say what's on our minds. It doesn't matter what it is."

"Even if it's my murderous thoughts over the thermostat?"

"Even if it's your murderous thoughts over the thermostat." He nods.

"OK, you're on."

"Good." Elbow-deep in flowery cotton fabric, he meets my eyes and we both smile. "Now, are you going to just sit there watching or give me a hand with this duvet cover, or what?"

Auntie Nell

So I got to meet my niece today. I'll be honest, beforehand I was really nervous about how I would feel. I was happy for Rich and Nathalie, but I was worried I might be sad for me. So when Nathalie handed me this tiny little bundle, I was prepared for all kinds of emotions.

Only when she gazed up at me unblinkingly, I realized there was one I hadn't prepared myself for.

"How does it feel to hold your new niece?" my brother asked.

I couldn't take my eyes off her.

"Love," I replied. "It feels like love."

Breathing Space

It's over three weeks since the accident and Dad keeps improving every day. As soon as he was strong enough to leave ICU, he had the operation to pin together his fractured fibula and tibia. Today he's coming out of the hospital. It's a miracle really. When I cast my mind back to those first seventy-two hours, it's a day I never thought I'd see.

Mum's sister, Auntie Verity, has come to stay. She used to be a practice nurse before she retired and moved to Spain, but she's flown over to help look after Dad.

"And drive me bloody crackers," he grumbles, when we go to pick him up from hospital.

"Verity's going to be a great help," says Mum firmly, as I push his wheelchair out into the car park. "She knows how to change dressings and everything."

"She's not changing my dressings—"

"Philip—" Mum's voice is sharp.

We've been warned by the doctors that patients can often suffer depression and low mood after a head injury, and that it could take some time for Dad to feel like himself again.

"Now, Dad, if you take these crutches I can help you into the car," I interrupt.

"She's so bloody bossy—you've said it yourself," continues Dad, shifting himself into the front passenger seat where he can stretch out his leg, which is encased in a cast. "A week of your sister and I'll be wishing I was back in a coma."

Climbing into the back seat, Mum lets out a gasp.

"Philip! Don't you dare joke about that! It's no laughing matter!"

She slams the car door and I begin reversing the car out of the space. But as I look in my rearview I hear Dad chuckling and catch her smiling. I don't think we need to worry too much about things getting back to normal.

*

With everything that's been happening with Dad, I've lost track of the days, but I surface to find myself at the end of November. Less than four weeks to Christmas. Or, as I'm constantly reminded, "Only twenty-five shopping days left!"

Even worse, yesterday when I went into town to run errands for Mum, I noticed all the stores have their decorations up already. Then, as I was driving back, I turned on the car radio to hear Mariah Carey blasting out at me, and I started yelling "Too soon! Too soon!" and quickly switched it off.

I like Christmas and I actually love that song, but come on, people: can we please wait until the first of December?

(Of course, the answer to that is a very festive "fuck off, no we can't.")

But maybe it's just me and I'm not ready yet. London has already officially turned on all its Christmas lights, so I'll be seeing them tomorrow as I've booked my ticket back. It feels like the right time. Friends have sent lots of texts and messages of support, but I've missed them and I'm ready to return. It feels like I've been gone forever.

The one good thing about being out in the wilds of Cumbria is the time and space it's given me to focus on finishing Monty's play. There's not much else to do in freezing cold November when it gets dark at three o'clock—and trust me, Auntie Verity hasn't just been driving Dad mental. It's been a good excuse to lock myself away in my room and get a lot of editing done.

Cricket is excited to read it. She's been sending me lots of lovely messages while I've been away and keeps telling me she can't wait for me to return—"Not just because I can't wait to read the new play and give you an update on the little library plans, but so you can see what I've done with my new apartment."

I also heard from Ethan. A few days after that telephone conversation in the hospital, I got an email from him asking how Dad was. It was short but friendly, the kind of email you write when you don't want the person reading it to infer any extra meaning. A few lines that take about twenty careful minutes to write. But I appreciated him getting in touch, so I wrote back—the same kind of email, short and friendly, telling him Dad was on the mend and thanking him for the fruit basket.

A brief blip of a connection that came and went. I haven't heard from him since.

But that's OK. This month has taken me to the edge and back. We nearly lost Dad. I fell in love with my niece. After everything that's happened, I want things to get back on an even keel. No more life-and-death moments. No more shocks. No more drama.

I'm grateful for:
1. *The NHS, and all the amazing doctors and nurses who saved Dad's life, and with him a whole family.*
2. *Mum, who when I finally told her what happened with Ethan, simply said she had never been more proud of me, and that the best was yet to come.*
3. *The funny cat videos Liza keeps sending, of the big fat ginger tom she and Tia have adopted from their local shelter.*
4. *My noise-canceling headphones, because it's true what Dad says: Auntie Verity's voice really is louder than a foghorn.*
5. *Being stronger than I ever thought I was.*
6. *Boredom. I think it's seriously underrated.*

To: Penelope Stevens
Subject: Your Dad

Hey Nell,
    I'm so glad to hear your dad is out of the hospital. That's amazing! You must be so relieved. I told you he was a fighter!

So I have some news—it looks like I'm coming to London next week. The owners of my restaurant are opening a sister restaurant over there, and I'm being sent to oversee the kitchen and menu. They're putting me up in a hotel in Soho for a few days. Do you want to meet? It would be good to see you.

Ethan.

DECEMBER

#thingsgettangledanditsnot justthechristmastreelights

A Christmas Drink

Beep beep beep beep . . .

Covent Garden tube station is packed. As the doors of the elevators slide open I'm greeted by crowds of people. Tourists, office workers, theatergoers, revelers . . . it's as if the whole world has descended here.

I spill out amongst them and am propelled along by the throngs behind me, through the turnstiles and out into the freezing cold night air. A steel band is playing "Jingle Bells," giving the festive atmosphere a Caribbean feel, and I'm tempted to pause awhile to listen. I check my watch and change my mind. Better not, I don't want to be late.

I turn and make my way across the cobblestones, weaving through the mime artists and drunken partygoers. I look again at the address I've punched into Google Maps. If I take the next left it should be just down on the right . . .

My breath makes little clouds as I navigate the sidewalk. I like to walk quickly, but tonight I've worn heels, and I'm not good in heels. Fiona can run the hundred meters in five-inch stilettos. Not me. I totter and sway, ankles *always* on the verge of rolling. Still, it's a small price to pay to look taller and slimmer, and tonight it's very important that I look taller and slimmer.

Shame heels don't also make me look younger, but hey, two out of three ain't bad.

I see the hotel ahead of me and, reaching the entrance,

I pause to check my reflection in the large glass doors, smoothing down my hair, taking off my winter coat, fiddling with my blouse, adding a bit of lip gloss then wiping it off again.

I've come to meet Ethan.

I'm not sure why I agreed. I told Fiona it was because I'm curious. Liza, because I wanted closure. Cricket, because it's only a drink.

What I didn't tell anyone is that I also want to see if I still love him.

Oh, Nell.

Yup. I know.

He's already sitting at the bar. I see him before he sees me and, for a split second, I get to observe him. His dark hair is cut short and he's wearing a white shirt. He looks unusually smart; at home he was always in T-shirts. He also looks ridiculously tanned and healthy compared with the rest of us pasty Londoners. Nursing a beer, he's looking at his phone and rubbing his chin with his thumb in that way he always does when he's concentrating.

It's so weird to see him again. I was going to spend the rest of my life with this man. He's so familiar. Yet it's like looking at a stranger.

"Hey." He looks up as I near him and smiles. It reaches his eyes. Dark, almost black, I used to think I could look into them forever.

My stomach twists. "Hi." I smile back.

"I'm glad you came."

"Well, I couldn't not . . . when you're in the same city."

"You look well."

"Thanks, you too. Very smart." I gesture to his shirt.

"Oh, I've come straight from a meeting—here, sit down."

He pulls out the barstool next to him and I slide onto it.

"How's all that going?"

"Yeah, good."

Oh, the joys of well-mannered small talk with an ex, when the last time you saw them you were puffy-eyed and snotty-nosed and your heart was breaking. It's like we're performing a respectful dance around the jagged edges of our breakup, for fear we might slip and pierce ourselves on one of the shards and bleed to death.

"You?"

"Great . . . thanks."

But this is what we do when we're grown-ups, isn't it? We side-step and skirt around and keep our feelings in check. We're not hormonal teenagers at the mercy of our emotions (though, in my case, the hormones are still doing a number on me). We're old enough now to know how to conduct ourselves, not to say everything we're thinking, and that no good will come of that third martini.

Of course, knowing and doing are separate things entirely.

"Same again?"

"Why not."

It's an hour later and we've moved to a booth. I've told him all about Dad and his accident, he's told me all about his new job, we've asked after the health of each other's families, and caught up with the goings-on of our respective friends. By rights the quick drink should be over and I should be standing up, putting on my coat, and saying bye. I'd be home by nine thirty.

"Remember those lychee martinis we used to drink at Gillespie's?"

"Oh God yes, best martinis ever!"

But instead of heading to the tube, we're heading down Memory Lane. And I'm two drinks in. I ask for a glass of water.

"I went there a couple of weeks ago when I was back in town. Billy the owner was asking after you."

"What did you tell him?"

"That you left me."

I raise my eyes to meet his.

"That I screwed up. That I lost the best thing that ever happened to me . . ."

I let his words hang there.

"I think 'she's good' might have sufficed," I say finally.

Ethan looks at me and we both start to grin. *This*. This is what we had. This is what made me call him after we first met at that bar.

"I'm sorry, Nell."

"Me too."

And just like that, all the rage I felt toward him, all the loss and hurt and conflict that surrounded us like barbed wire, seems to disappear, and all that's left is the two of us.

His eyes never leave mine, and when he asks, it feels inevitable.

"Come home, Nell."

Going Viral

Something quite bonkers has happened: my podcast has gone viral. Or, as Cricket would say, I've become one of those viruses.

Actually, being December, it's both. I go viral *and* I get a nasty cold virus that turns me into a seething mass of germs and snot.

Reaching for another tissue, I blow my nose, trying not to ruin my makeup.

"It's been almost a week now, so I shouldn't be contagious," I apologize to the makeup girl, who's aiming a can of hair spray at me.

I'm being featured in a magazine. Me! In a magazine! I know, I can hardly believe it either. But here I am in a studio in the East End, having a photo shoot done to accompany my interview. Full hair and makeup, the works. Music is playing. There's a photographer. There's even a stylist who brought in a rack of clothes, and we went through them all, trying them on.

Outfit of the day: a very expensive designer dress, provided by the stylist of the glossy magazine I am being featured in.

I mean, come on, are you kidding me?

Actually no one is kidding me, it's happening, and I should probably act a bit cooler and not keep grinning excitedly at everyone, but sod it, I'm not going to.

"So how did you get the idea?" the twenty-something features writer cheerfully asked me earlier.

"I think it was the moment I found myself broke, single, and forty-something, and sleeping in my old bedroom back at my parents'," I replied, and watched as her face visibly paled.

Because that's the thing: I think that's still a frightening prospect for most people. Or versions of it. But actually, I'm here to tell you it's not really. Because it's not the end. On the contrary, it might just be the beginning.

After Dad's near-fatal crash, I emerged blinking in the daylight to find a bulging inbox. When I finally got down to reading all my emails, I discovered that, as well as ones from estate agents and LinkedIn, there were several requests from magazines and other publications wanting to interview me. At first I thought it was some kind of weird spam. Until I checked the analytics of my podcast and discovered tens of thousands of new downloads.

It's been surreal. People have been tweeting about it. It's been mentioned on blogs. I've been given my own hashtag. Even my mother has listened to it! (For the record, she says she likes it, though can we have less of the swearing.) Once I started replying to all the emails everything snowballed, and since getting back to London I've done a couple of interviews, been asked to go on the radio, and even been approached by a big-name beauty brand offering sponsorship (apparently they can help improve my Crinkle and Sag).

Personally I'm not convinced anything can help on that score, and I'm not about to go into paid partnership with something I don't believe in. Now, if it was a coffee company, that would be different. There are many days when coffee is my morning motivation. Or, even better, what about the makers of those little cans of G&T? After all, there was a time earlier in the year when frankly I think I owed my life to those little cans. Yes, I can totally believe in gin and tonic.

But I'm getting carried away. Still, it would be amazing if one day I could get paid for doing something that I love. Because I do love doing my podcast, and I love all my listeners and I'd love to keep doing it, only bigger and better. Because if what started out as me just trying to be truthful and tell it like it is has struck a chord with other people feeling just as flawed and confused as I do—and if in some small way it's helped by showing them they're not alone; that I'm here and I hear them—then that's the biggest bonus of all.

The mirror is surrounded by light bulbs, like those ones you always see in Hollywood, and I look at my reflection. It's so funny, I hardly recognize myself with all this makeup and my hair blow-dried. It's true what they say about smoke and mirrors. I hardly recognize my life right now either. I used to think it was supposed to look a certain way; I had no idea all this could be waiting for me instead. I keep thinking that any minute now someone is going to say there's been a mistake, they've got the wrong person.

"OK, all done." The makeup artist smiles.

"Thank you so much!"

But that hasn't happened yet, so I'm going along for the ride.

"Just one last blast."

I hold my breath as she starts squirting. That's if I don't suffocate in a cloud of hair spray first.

I'm grateful for:
1. *All the forty-something fuck ups (or thirty-somethings, or fifty-somethings, or whatever-you-want-to-be-somethings)*

who keep downloading and listening and blogging and tweet-ing and posting.

2. *The good news we got from Dad's recent checkup at the hospital.*
3. *Sadiq's offer of my own column about feeling like a forty-something fuck up.*
4. *This life, which looks nothing like I expected.*
5. *All of it.*

New Beginnings

"So what do you think?"

"It's very different."

"You don't like it."

"No, I do like it, it's just . . ." I search around for the right word, but none of them seem to do it justice. "It's kind of . . . *outrageous*."

It's as if I just paid her the highest compliment. Cricket's face lights up like her Christmas tree. "Why thank you, Nell, that's so very kind of you to say."

It's Wednesday evening and we're standing in the doorway of her living room, surveying the newly painted walls of her new apartment. A dark inky shade covers the far wall and chimney breast, highlighting the white marble fireplace and crimson velvet sofa, while the ceiling is painted a burnished copper.

It's not how you'd expect an eighty-something to redecorate her apartment, but then Cricket isn't exactly your typical eighty-something.

"I wanted something completely different to the old house."

"Well, it's certainly that."

"Top up?"

"Yes, please."

She reaches for the bottle of champagne I brought over as a housewarming present, and refills our glasses. I did think about prosecco; even with the extra money from the play I can't really afford champagne, but there are certain times in your life when only champagne will do, and this is one of them. I'm so proud of my friend and the courage she's shown in navigating this new chapter of her life, and it needs to be celebrated properly with Veuve Clicquot.

"I think Monty would've approved," she says, as we make ourselves comfortable on the sofa.

"Of the paint or the champagne?"

"Both." She smiles, taking a sip of the ice-cold bubbles. "Oh, did I tell you Christopher is wildly excited about staging his new play?"

"Only about half a dozen times." I grin, and she laughs.

Christopher is a revered theater director and was one of Monty's oldest friends and colleagues. Cricket sent him my finished script a few days ago, and within hours he was on the phone to her, "begging" to cast it. I think "begging" is a bit of an exaggeration on Cricket's part, but still, it's very exciting news. Not to mention a huge relief on my part.

Ever since Cricket asked me to edit Monty's play, I've been so worried that I wasn't up to the job. With most of the third act just a mass of scribbled notes, I've had visions of this being a complete disaster. Letting Cricket down would have been one thing, especially when she's put so much faith in me, but I certainly didn't want to damage Monty's reputation as a playwright by not doing this play justice. Not to mention making a complete fool of myself.

But apart from a few suggested edits from Christopher, he's been thrilled with the result. And it's made me realize that I underestimate myself. I think so many of us do. When Dad nearly died, it made me realize I'm a lot stronger than I ever thought I was. It's just a shame it's taken me this long to find out.

"He wants to secure funding so he can start casting in the New Year."

"Wow, that's fantastic!"

"Isn't it?" Her face is animated, and then her mind goes somewhere else and her smile slips. "Oh, I do wish Monty were here to see all of this."

It comes out, loosened no doubt by the champagne, but I know she thinks this a dozen times a day. Mostly it just goes by unspoken. I knew it before, but since we came so close to losing Dad, her loss has an added resonance.

"You know, I was worried how I was going to feel, leaving the old house," she admits, looking across at me now. "When the removal van left, I walked around all the empty rooms remembering how Monty and I had walked around those empty rooms together when we first moved in . . . and it didn't feel like thirty or more years had passed . . . it felt like the blink of an eye . . ."

I see her fingers tighten on the stem of her glass, the light catching the bubbles that are fizzing to the surface.

"The estate agent was waiting outside, and I gave him the keys and got in a cab . . . and as I drove away, I actually felt fine. And I kept feeling fine. Even when I spent my first night alone here in the apartment. I kept expecting this wave of grief to hijack me, but . . . no . . . nothing." She gives a small shrug of her shoulders. "I put it down to being so busy, what with my meetings with the council for the new little library scheme, and Monty's play. I didn't have time to feel sad—"

For a moment her words seem to hang there as she contemplates them.

"Then a few days later I went to get a Christmas tree. I wasn't going to bother. After all, it's only me and it seemed a terrible fuss . . . but Monty loved Christmas, especially getting the tree."

She smiles now. It's one of those vague smiles of affection when you remember something amusing from the past.

"He'd spend an entire evening carefully positioning the baubles and lights, standing back each time to check and admire his work . . ."

"You didn't help?"

Cricket gives a look of mock horror. "Goodness no, I was never allowed to touch it. Once I made the fatal mistake of adding a bit of tinsel . . ."

I laugh as she mimes Monty having a fit of panic.

"So anyway, like I said, I got a tree."

We both look across at the six-foot Christmas tree, heavily decorated and sparkling with lights.

"It's a very nice tree," I enthuse.

Cricket tilts her head to one side as if weighing it up. "I was determined I was going to make this the perfect tree. I wanted to make Monty proud . . ." She pauses, and I notice that her eyes are glistening.

"So I started with the lights, just like he showed me, but they were all tangled . . . and the harder I tried, the more knotted they got . . . and I couldn't unravel them"—and now her voice is breaking—"and I raged against him for leaving me with these bloody tangled Christmas tree lights . . ."

A tear escapes and rolls down her cheek.

"And then I started crying in frustration, and once I started I couldn't stop . . . not because of those stupid lights but because he's gone and I'm still here, and this isn't how it was supposed to be, this isn't what we planned."

She sniffs hard, rubbing her cheek, and it's so difficult not to try and offer up some well-meaning words of comfort, but I don't want to offend her by trying. Because nothing is going to give her comfort and nothing is going to make it better, and I'm not going to insult her by pretending otherwise.

"It fucking sucks," I say.

Because that's the truth. Because she needs her grief to be acknowledged. And because as a friend that's all I can hope to do.

"It fucking sucks." She nods.

I might not have lost my husband, but I know about loss and having to start over.

"It's going to be a year in January."

Cricket is talking about Monty's death, but at the mention of the date I'm reminded of its significance in my own life. Has it really been nearly a whole year since I moved into Edward's apartment? Since I sat on my bed, surrounded by suitcases, and swore to myself that by this time next year I'd turn my whole life around?

"It's true what they say: life does go on and joy does return, and often it's in the most unexpected of places," she continues, "but you never *get over* losing someone; you just get better at coping with it."

I gesture toward the tree. "You untangled them in the end," I say, thinking how symbolic this is.

"Like hell I did." She snorts, and flashes me a smile. "I threw the bloody things away and bought new ones."

I'm grateful for:
1. *Christopher's reaction to the finished play and the unbelievably exciting news, just in, that he's secured funding for it to go into production, with a famous actor reading for the lead.*
2. *The unexpected joy that my friendship with Cricket adds to my life.*
3. *She didn't ask me about my drink with Ethan.*

Things I've Learned from Cricket

- Don't let perfect be the enemy of good.
- Take risks.
- Forty-something is very young when you're eighty-something.
- These are your good old days.

- Most people are good; it's just that it's the bad people who make the news.
- If those shoes aren't comfy in the store they're never going to be comfy.
- When it comes to money, only think six months ahead: any more and you'll panic; any less and you'll buy that dress you'll never wear.
- How someone deals with a parking ticket, stepping in dog shit, a delayed train, and a dying bee says a lot about them. The same goes for what they do with their supermarket cart.
- Be anything, but always be outrageous.
- Find your tribe.
- Never join the Blue Rinse Brigade.
- Some things can't always be untangled.
- Don't worry too much about people liking you; liking yourself is far more important.
- You can never have too many hats.
- Drink that bottle of red.
- Friendship is family.
- Rubber gloves and determination can solve anything.*
- You will regret those heavy earrings.
- You never really know what you're doing, so do it anyway.
- The best anti-aging secret is to stop looking in mirrors.
- Take videos of those you love.
- No one ever died of cellulite or wrinkles.
- You never own a book; you just get to look after it until you pass it on to the next person.
- The same story is different for everyone.
- Say yes to everything, unless it involves stand-up comedy.
- Aging is not for sissies.
- Acknowledge everyone, from the person at the checkout to the driver of the bus to the barista who serves you your coffee.

---

* Failing that, tequila.

- What doesn't kill you makes you stronger.
- The view is great from the outside.
- Take an extra five minutes (especially when it comes to putting away Christmas tree lights).
- Always buy the bigger size.
- There are many ways to live a life.
- None of those creams work (much better to buy a hat).
- There is no age limit on adventure.
- You're not too old, it's not too late, and yes you can.

Christmas Cards

I left America and moved back to the UK because my relationship fell apart. Because I needed a fresh start. Because my visa ran out and my business failed. Because I was broke and brokenhearted. Because I was sick of the blue skies and sunshine when all I felt was gray inside. Because I missed my family and friends. Because I couldn't bear to stay and be reminded of everything I'd lost.

And because I didn't know what else to do, and tea tastes better here.

All of the above is true. But I should have added one more. *Because of the Christmas cards.*

Christmas isn't easy at the best times, especially if you find yourself single. Worse still, *forty-something and single.* We're forever being told that Christmas is all about family, so if you haven't managed to bag one of your own and a lovely home to put them in (along with a gorgeously decorated Christmas tree), there's a chance you might feel like a bit of a fuck up.

But just to make sure, your friends will send you Christmas cards to prove it.

Unlike the Brits and their packs of generic charity Christmas cards, Americans have a tradition of sending personalized cards with smiling family portraits on the front. A bit like our royal family do, only with much better teeth.

And these photographs are lovely, truly they are, whether they're professionally shot in black and white or taken with a phone on a beach wearing Santa hats. And the kids always look cute and your friends always look happy, and when you read the update inside telling you everything they've been up to that year, how the kids are doing at school and news of any accomplishments, you think how proud they must be of their family and everything they've achieved.

And then you put them on your mantelpiece and go to pour yourself another gin.

No, but seriously.

Actually, I am being serious.

Because when everything fell apart last December, it was all too painful. As soon as the first one arrived, I knew I couldn't sit around to open the rest, and went to stay with Liza. I loved seeing my friends happy in their lives but their family portraits only emphasized what I didn't have. I looked at those cards and saw the ghosts of a future that I once thought was mine but now I'd lost.

So, anyway, being back in the UK this year, I don't have to worry. It's all glittery reindeers and jokey cartoons about snowmen and carrots. Picking several off the doormat, I wander through to the kitchen, tearing them open. That one must be from Holly and Adam; it's just his sense of humor. I look inside. It's Holly's handwriting but she's signed it from Adam as well. Apparently they've started counseling. I got a text from her just last week saying it was the first time they'd really talked in years. I hope they make it.

I stick it on the shelf, next to Mum and Dad's snowy woodland scene; it's one of their usuals from the National Trust. Some things never change. This year I've never been more grateful.

But it looks like it's going to take more than a transatlantic flight to shake off one particular Christmas card. I look at the envelope and recognize the handwriting. It's from some friends in Houston. To be honest, they were Ethan's friends really. He went to college with the husband and I met them once at a Thanksgiving dinner, but they always sent cards with family-photo montages and these mammoth updates on their children.

A few months ago, the wife had emailed to ask me for my new address so she could send a card. I tried to gently put her off, telling her it was fine, not to worry and save the postage. But she insisted. I tried again, saying I wasn't sure if I was going to be spending Christmas with my parents or in London, but instead she'd asked for both addresses. "I'm sure it will find you eventually," she'd replied cheerfully.

I DON'T WANT YOUR BLOODY CHRISTMAS CARD TO FIND ME! is what I'd wanted to type back, all in caps, and equally as cheerfully, but that would make me not a very nice person. She was only trying to be kind by chasing me down with her glad tidings. After all, it's Christmas. Goodwill to all men and all that.

So of course I emailed her both my addresses and said I couldn't wait to receive her card, and Happy Holidays!

On the front is a photo of them all in matching Christmas sweaters. Even the dog. And is that a rabbit too? I smile, then stick it behind the large vase that used to belong to Edward's great-aunt.

"Anything for me?"

I hear the front door go, and Edward appears in the kitchen wearing a scarf and beanie. He's holding a take-out flask and a yoga mat, and looking like people only look when they've been up since 6 a.m. doing a Bikram class.

No, not smug. Healthy.

"Christmas cards. Here, there's one addressed to you." I hand him an envelope.

"Thanks."

I turn my attention to my coffeepot.

"Well, I've had better cards."

"It can't be worse than the matching Christmas sweater one." I laugh, grinding my coffee beans.

"Hmm . . . well, it's less Merry Christmas and more Happy Divorce."

"Huh?"

I turn around to see him holding a piece of paper instead of a card.

"It's my decree absolute."

"Oh shit . . . I mean, wow."

I have no idea what you say to someone when they get their final divorce papers through.

"Better than the matching Christmas sweaters then."

But I'm pretty sure that's not it.

"Yes." He nods, but his expression is unfathomable.

"Are you OK? That's good—isn't it?"

"Well, I'm not sure you'd ever describe a divorce as good, not when there're children involved."

"Sorry, I didn't mean—" I feel tactless. Told off. Stupid.

"No, you're right," he says quickly, seeing my expression. "It's the right thing. I'm glad for both of us." He smiles, but I'm not sure for whose benefit. "We're free to start our new lives now. Move on properly."

"Yes." I nod, and I wonder if he's referring to the woman he's been seeing. I want to ask but something stops me.

"So what are your plans for Christmas?"

And now we've changed subjects.

"My parents—"

"Of course." He nods.

"My brother and his wife are coming with the baby; it's going to be quite a full house. I'm going to invite my friend Cricket too."

"I must meet this Cricket friend of yours one day," he says, emptying organic porridge into a pan and adding oat milk.

Edward really should be on Instagram.

"Yes." I smile. "You must." And now I'm wondering if I should invite Edward too. I don't want him to be on his own at Christmas.

"I'm taking the boys skiing."

"Oh, that will be fun," I enthuse, "and it's good you get to spend time with the boys."

"Yes, and their iPhones." He grins.

Lucky I didn't invite him. That would have been embarrassing—asking him if he wants to kip on my parents' sofa when he's probably going to be staying in some fancy five-star resort.

"Sophie's going away with her boyfriend."

"Wow, that's quick."

"It's not really, though. We've been broken up for a long time." He's not looking at me as he stirs the pan. "Both of us have wasted too much time. Life is short."

Edward glances up at me now and a look passes between us. Since getting back to London, neither of us has spoken about what happened at the hospital. I've hardly seen him. I've been so busy and he's been out at a slew of Christmas work things. But looking at him now, we don't need to say anything. *He was there.* It's like having an indelible marker scored across some hidden part of me that nobody else can see but him.

I think about Ethan. I think about that time in my brother's old bedroom, when Edward said from now on we should always say what's on our minds. I look at him next to me, only inches away, and think about all the stuff I want to talk to him about. Stuff I need to say.

"Your coffee's boiling—"

"Oh, yes . . . thanks."

But I don't say any of it.

I'm grateful for:
1. *The print shop on the corner, where I make my own Christmas cards with a selfie of Cricket and me on the front; the one taken on the beach in Spain this summer, where we're both several Negronis in and I'm grinning like a loon in a bikini. Inside there's a little bit about what I've been up to this*

year, including news about my podcast, the play, and being disqualified from the school fun run, plus some nice photos of Arthur and a message wishing everyone a very Merry Christmas and a wonderfully messy and gloriously unfiltered New Year.

2. *The news from friends in Houston saying everyone is happy and healthy, including the rabbit. Though I'm not sure an update on little Jimmy's potty training was needed, it's still good to hear he finally got there. Go Jimmy, and Happy Holidays!*

3. *Edward.*

Frankenstein and Myrrh

If you don't have children at Christmas it's easy to feel like you're missing out, so I'm really pleased when Fiona invites me to watch Izzy perform in her school nativity play. Apparently the new headmistress has introduced a gender-neutral policy and the nativity is to reflect that. Hence Izzy is one of the wise men and Lucas is one of the angels.

Which makes a change from my politically incorrect seventies school days, when only blonde, blue-eyed girls could be angels, so my best friend Sameena and I were relegated to being "travelers." Little of which I remember, except that the costumes were very itchy and Mum said I picked my nose the whole time. Unlike Rich, of course, who in later years took the starring role as Joseph and positively nailed it.

Actually, thinking about it in context, that's probably the wrong choice of words.

But anyway, I was really looking forward to the nativity, and when I walk into the large assembly hall it couldn't feel more

Christmassy. It's all been decorated by the children: colorful paper garlands are strung across the vaulted ceiling, there are displays of Christmas artwork, and a huge tree covered in tinsel and paper stars takes pride of place by the piano.

"You look fab, I love that dress!"

Fiona clocks me and races over, arms flung wide.

"EBay, only ten pounds. You look great too!"

Seriously, Fiona looks amazing. But it's more than that . . . invigorated, that's the right word.

"I look like a woman who hasn't slept for weeks since starting her new job because it's all I can think about."

"Oh, wow, how's it all going?"

She can't stop grinning.

"Bloody brilliant. I should've done it years ago."

"That's so great, I'm so pleased."

"I know, right? I was so worried about it all, but it couldn't have worked out better. And it's not just me—David has cut back on his hours now I'm working, so he gets to come home while the kids are still up and spend more time with them."

"See," I say, "I knew it would all work out."

"No you didn't." She laughs. "But I appreciate you telling me to go for it."

"Anytime," I grin.

We go to find our seats and run into Annabel.

"Hi." She smiles, looking perfect as always in a white trouser suit.

Only Annabel could wear that: if it was me, it would be covered in coffee dribbles and dog hair in two minutes.

"Hey." I smile, as we do the double-cheek kiss and Fiona chats away about school stuff; the decision to ban plastic in the cafeteria, the use of a drone to do some of the overhead nativity shots, Clementine's part as Mary (or "the lead role," as Annabel keeps calling it). There's also mention of Clive: he's moved out and is renting close by, he's giving her the house, he's got a new girlfriend already. But instead of being upset, Annabel seems mostly relieved and unscathed by it all. It's business as usual.

That said, while her hair is blow-dried poker straight and her lips and nails are both painted a matching festive red, it's as if the gloss has worn off a little.

"You know, I listened to your podcast," she says to me, as Fiona nips to the restrooms before the performance starts.

I brace myself.

"Motherfucking Monday."

"Excuse me?"

"You were talking about Throwback Thursday and Flashback Friday, and I wanted to tell you I'm totally embracing Motherfucking Monday."

I smile. "I like that."

"Me too." She grins, before turning and finding her seat on the front row.

Of course.

As for the nativity play, it was everything it should be. Baby Jesus's head fell off and rolled off the stage. One of the angels wet himself. Clementine did a wonderful Mary, no doubt one that will be talked about for many years to come, but she did fall foul to my nativity faux pas by deciding to pick her nose all the way through it. While the finale saw the drone crashing into the velvet curtains and having to be rescued by one of the dads who, it turns out, is divorced and made the headmistress blush bright red when they got tangled up together in the aforementioned curtains.

And as the immensely proud godmother, I can state that Izzy and Lucas were both wonderful. Of course. I particularly loved that Izzy mispronounced frankincense and ended up giving a gift of Frankenstein to Baby Jesus instead.

And I cried a bit at "Silent Night." Of course.

I'm grateful for:

1. *My gorgeous goddaughter Izzy, who made me smile and laugh and swell with pride and fear my heart would burst when she sang her solo.*

2. *My recent haircut, highlights, and very flattering dress when I bumped into Johnny, who was at the nativity to watch his nephew Oliver.*

3. *My extremely witty comeback when he told me I looked great and asked me how I was doing.*†*

4. *My ability to redo conversations in my head and make them better the second time round.*

5. *Annabel, who later mentioned at the mulled wine stall that it was in fact Johnny who had made a move on her, not the other way around, thus adding proof that he did me a huge favor by ghosting me. #luckyescape #noproofisneeded*

The Nightmare Before Christmas

Otherwise known as Christmas shopping.

In an attempt to support local businesses, I decide not to do it online and instead brave the main street. It's mayhem. Stores are awash with sequins and frazzled shoppers and heated to about a hundred degrees, so I'm forever taking my coat on and off as I dive in and out of different stores trying to tick *anything* off my list.

Still, there are pluses. You don't get all that festive buzz if you're at home ordering online, do you? Though truth be told,

---

* Because of course I did not think of an extremely witty comeback. In fact I thought of no comeback at all, witty or otherwise, but instead exchanged polite pleasantries before excusing myself to the restroom. Where of course I thought of loads of brilliant things I should have said, but by then it was too late.

† But who cares. Because more important is that when I saw him I felt nothing. Except perhaps a mild irritation. And the realization that he was wearing mom jeans.

I'm not encountering much festive buzz in the aisles of our local department store. Though I do encounter quite a few worried-looking men as they hear a salesperson breaking it to them in hushed tones that they've sold out of scented candles.

I'm sympathetic. I'm not having it easy either, but husbands and boyfriends seem to have it much harder when it comes to knowing what to buy at Christmas. Upstairs I spot someone's husband looking at a set of pans and know there is going to be an extremely disappointed wife out there somewhere. No woman, however practical they might be, wants to wake up to a gift-wrapped frying pan on Christmas morning. I think it was Liza who always used to say that presents should come in small packages.

I sidle over and guide him toward the Le Creuset. Well, if it's going to be pans, it might as well be expensive ones.

Every year I try to be imaginative with my Christmas presents. Unlike Rich, who always does gift cards and always seems to get away with it. Maybe it's just me, but I can't help thinking gift cards are a last resort. Last year I got the whole family those DNA tests, which I thought was really cool, until I read an article about all these people discovering more than they bargained for. Less "10 percent Iberian Peninsula" and more "my mother had an affair with the postman and he's my real dad."

I had a bit of a wobble. "Are you serious?" My brother laughed, pointing to our noses when I mentioned it to him. "Sis, I don't think we have to worry about DNA." There's no denying we have both inherited what is known in the family as "The Stevens Nose," and he argued that we didn't need a test to prove it.

Though it did, of course. Together with the fact my mother is 1 percent Neanderthal, which my father has never let her live down.

However, this year is proving a bit more difficult. Mum and Dad buy everything they want as soon as they want it, and I've racked my brain for what to get Freddy, my godson. What on earth do ten-year-old boys like these days? Other than terrorizing babysitters, and I'm not sure you can find that in a size small. Plus, I can't find all the other stuff on my list.

I wonder if they sell gift cards?

I'm grateful for:
1. *Amazon Prime.*
2. *Being single; at least there's one less gift to buy.*

Christmas Eve

I rent a car and drive up to my parents' with Cricket in the passenger seat and Arthur in the back. It seemed easier (and cheaper) than catching the train. We sing along to Christmas songs on the radio, encounter traffic jams, and eat too many things wrapped in plastic from service stations. Edward would kill me.

We finally turn off the motorway and begin our drive through some of my favorite bits of the Lake District as dusk falls. Just in time to catch the light off Lake Windermere and the colors of the fells as we weave our way through a patchwork of bracken and moss. Snow is forecast, but for now it's just damp and cold, with spires of smoke rising up from the slate chimneys.

Christmas never felt like Christmas in California. At first I loved the novelty of it all. Spending Christmas Eve on the beach, sunbathing on stripy towels, and Christmas Day eating sushi. But the novelty quickly wore off and I was soon spending a fortune to fly home for the holidays.

Ethan came with me the first time. He said he wanted us to be together and it would be fun. Mum made a big fuss. Dad took him to the pub. Rich got him a spare ticket to the match. He seemed to love it, when he wasn't shivering or struggling to get 4G (it's the middle of the countryside; frankly you're lucky if you get a phone signal) or trying to find a soy chai latte.

It wasn't his fault. We might speak the same language (though he found it quite hard to understand a word any of the locals said), but you only have to try and explain our very peculiar British tradition of panto to a bemused American and you'll see how different we really are. I think quaint wore off quite quickly.

Oh no it didn't!

Anyway, it was a first and last time. Ethan never came again; from then on we spent Christmas separately, him with his family in California and me here. Except for last year, which I spent alone in the apartment packing up the last of my things. But this year we're both on this side of the Atlantic for New Year's Eve. The London restaurant has a big event planned and he's helping with preparations. He's flying back over in a few days' time—

"Oh, isn't this charming?" Cricket exclaims as I turn down the drive. The house is decorated in twinkling lights and Mum's already at the window waving. I give a little toot of my horn as we pull up, and Arthur starts barking. Dad appears on his crutches and opens a window, and I hear the TV blasting and Mum yelling not to let the cold air in.

It's Christmas! We're home.

I'm grateful for:
1. *Mum's mince pies.*
2. *Baileys.*
3. *Calories don't count at Christmas.*

Christmas Day

Christmas Day is spent in a haze of Baileys and Stilton. As usual, Mum refuses to sit down and spends most of the day in the kitchen, conducting an orchestra of bubbling pans, while the rest of us pop in and out, offering to help while helping ourselves to more Baileys. Dad, on the other hand, spends most of the time sitting down on the sofa, with his leg stretched out on the coffee table. Raising it up and down like Tower Bridge when anyone wants to get past.

Evie, of course, is the star of the show. Still only a few weeks old, she has the complete attention of six adults. I never knew it would be impossible to tire of gazing at her tiny fingers or marveling at all those funny facial expressions—which cause us all to stop whatever we're doing and gather round to look and exclaim—or talking about whose ears she has or where her red hair has come from.

"It must be Nathalie's side," Rich says with conviction, until Mum produces a photo of our grandmother as a teenager with long auburn hair.

"But I always remember her with curly blonde hair," he says, shocked.

"Oh, that was a wig," interrupts Dad. "She said she always fancied herself a blonde."

"Go, Grandma." Nathalie grins, giving Evie a kiss as she finishes feeding her, before passing her to Rich to have her diaper changed.

I've never seen him look more delighted than he is to be changing a dirty diaper. As he dutifully takes her, she spits up on his shoulder, all over his new shirt. He just laughs. I like this new brother of mine.

As is the tradition at our house, we exchange gifts in the morning, gorge ourselves on all the liqueur chocolates by noon, then sit down to Christmas dinner. This year it's a tight squeeze around the table, even with the extending leaves. Auntie Verity has flown back to Spain, but we have two extra people: Cricket and Nathalie. And baby Evie, of course. Plus Arthur, who gets in the way of everyone's feet underneath the table, but refuses to come out in case a rogue piece of turkey should find itself there.

Mum finally agrees to sit down, while Dad carves. Rich makes a toast to families old and new, and I watch Cricket mentally disappear somewhere, then raise a toast to Monty too. We're not into big emotional speeches in our family, but we're all aware of Cricket's loss. Mum passes her the roast potatoes and Cricket smiles gratefully. What can you do for someone who is spending their first Christmas without the love of their life but offer them roasted potatoes?

Later, after dinner, we break open the chocolates and I Face-Time Liza. She's spending Christmas with her family in Austin, Texas, and Tia has gone with her too. I know Liza was nervous about introducing them to her new girlfriend, but any fears she had were unfounded.

"I can't get her and Mom out of the kitchen." She beams. "And Uncle Frank is just totally in love with her . . . not that I blame him."

It's great to see my friend so relaxed and happy. Ever since we've known each other, her relationships have always been fraught with problems and misunderstandings. But with Tia all that's changed. "There's nothing to tell, it's just easy," she'll say whenever we WhatsApp. "We're really boring." And then she'll laugh and I know she's not being serious, but seriously, I think that's where so many of us go wrong. To make the mistake of thinking a relationship that's easy *is* boring. That the ones with drama are exciting. When in fact, it's the other way around.

Mum nods off in the armchair. I stack the dishwasher. Rinsing the dishes, I'm struck by the realization that there's no Edward to tell me where to put the knives. I'm free to stack any way I want. Except the funny thing is, I find myself wanting to do it his way after all and it dawns on me that he's rubbed off on me, in more ways than one.

Then Dad cries, "Look outside!" because it's started to snow. Big, fluffy snowflakes that whirl and dance around the lampposts, out across the chimney pots and the valley below.

"Look, Evie, it's your first snow," whispers Rich.

And as we all gather around the window, I think these are the real moments in life. The small, unscripted moments that don't need any photographs or likes; these are the moments that matter.

I'm grateful for:
1. *Socks, says a young person never, but I have now reached an age where they are not a boring present at all; which proves, if any proof was needed, that there's always a bright side to getting older. And you can never have too many socks.*
2. *Mum, because frankly she IS Christmas.*
3. *Evie, who we all take turns passing around and proves to be a big hit with Cricket, who later confides that although she never wanted children, she would have rather liked being a grandmother, "because you can give them back."*
4. *My Christmas present from Fiona, who gave Michelle, Holly, and me T-shirts with "Forty-Something F**k Up" emblazoned across the chest.*
5. *Great minds thinking alike, and the photo Fiona sent me of her wearing my Christmas present: a T-shirt with "F**k Avocados" written across her very large chest.*
6. *Family, which should be redefined as simply "those you love."*
7. *There are 365 shopping days till Christmas.*

Boxing Day

Pretty much the same as yesterday, but with more Stilton.

The Days In Between

On the 28th, I drive back to London with Cricket and Arthur. After the snowy magic of the Lake District, London looks a bit gray and wet and business as usual. But that's OK, I've got a lot to do.

Edward is still away skiing, so I take the opportunity to have a good clear-out. It's amazing how much stuff you can amass in a year. I moved into his apartment with just a couple of suitcases and a few books, but at this rate I'm going to be moving out with a removal truck's worth of stuff.

I find a bunch of old photographs. Actual, physical ones of Ethan and me when we first met. His flight lands tomorrow. We've arranged to have dinner.

My mind flicks forward, but I drag it back again. Like I said, there's a lot to get done here. New Year, fresh start and all that.

To: Ethan DeLuca
Subject: Us

Dear Ethan,

You told me to take some time to think about it, so I've thought about it. To be honest, I've thought of little else since we saw each other a few weeks ago. When you told me you still loved me and wanted us to try again, I thought at first my answer would be obvious. For so long, you and me and our future together was all I ever wanted. And I've missed you so much this past year, there were times when it's all I wanted to hear you say.

But things have changed. I've changed and I can't change back. I'm not the person I used to be anymore and I don't want to be. I'm glad we finally got to talk about everything—we should have done it ages ago—but if we're both honest, things weren't right between us before we lost the baby. That was just the catalyst.

I took some time to write because I wanted to be sure I was making the right decision. But the truth is there was only ever one decision. I'm not coming back, Ethan. It's not my home anymore. My life is here. But never doubt that I loved you very much, and I will never forget the good times or your puttanesca ☺

I'm sorry to let you down about dinner, but there didn't seem much point. I think we've both said everything there is to say.

I wish you only good things. Take care of yourself.

Nell.

Then, for the first time in my life, I don't reread what I've written before I press send.

To: Penelope Stevens
Re: Offer on Apartment 2, Princeton Avenue

Dear Ms. Stevens,

I am delighted to inform you that your offer on Apartment 2, Princeton Avenue has been accepted! The owners are currently away until the New Year, but wanted to extend their delight and assurances that they are eager to proceed quickly with the sale. The office is now closed until January 2, but I wanted to give you the good news before sending out the official Memorandum of Sale, upon which your solicitor can begin the relevant searches.

Kind regards and a very happy New Year!

Marcus Brampton,

Sales Manager, Brampton & Proctor estate agents

New Year's Eve

I can't believe it. How are we here already?

It's New Year's Eve, and while being forty-something has its challenges, today is one of its pluses. When I was younger, I always felt so much pressure to go out and find the best party and have the most fun. It was FOMO times a hundred. But now those days are long gone. Now I've got JOMO and I'm just as happy staying in with a good movie and a bottle of wine. Thrilled, actually.

But no, this year I have an invitation to a party!

"Well, it's not really a party as such," I explain to Cricket, as we peruse the cheese counter of her local deli. "It's just my friends Max and Michelle cooking a curry and having everyone over."

"Sounds like the perfect New Year's Eve." She pauses to focus on a ripe Brie. "Do you think I could try a sliver?" she asks the sales assistant.

"It's a triple-cream from the Loire Valley." He passes her a piece.

Cricket looks to be in raptures. "Marvelous. One of those, please."

"So who's this woman that's invited you tonight?"

On the way over to the deli, Cricket has been telling me about a New Year's Eve dinner party she's been invited to, and how "everyone always takes something sweet, but I think a good ripe cheese says a lot about a person."

"She's my upstairs neighbor. A widow like me."

"Wow, that's great—well, you know what I mean," I add quickly, but she laughs.

"It seems there are a lot of us about." She nods. "Oh, and can I have some of that delicious quince jelly?" she says to the assistant.

"Who else is going?"

"I'm not sure. I think she has quite a lot of friends. She's a bit younger than me." She hands over her credit card. "She did mention she was inviting a man who lost his wife last year. She thinks we'll have a lot in common. He used to be an actor."

A look passes between us.

"I'm not interested. I'm happy being single."

"You never know."

She pulls a face. "I don't want to see some old man in his underpants."

The assistant hands her a bag with her purchases and a receipt.

"Wonderful, thank you."

"Monty was an old man in his underpants," I point out, as we leave the deli.

"True." She nods, then smiles. "But he was my old man."

I've invited Edward tonight. He just got back from skiing this afternoon and hadn't had anything planned. "I was just going to stay in with a curry," he said, with no mention of the girl he's been seeing.

"Perfect, that's exactly what we're doing," I replied, and so he got in the shower.

We take Arthur along too. We can't leave him at home because of the fireworks, plus it wouldn't be the same celebrating without him. Michelle has promised to lock the cat in the bedroom.

"It'll be fun," she says cheerfully. "And it means we all finally get to meet this mysterious landlord of yours."

"No pressure then," says Edward, as we knock on their door. He's made his special stuffed olives and looks unusually self-conscious.

"None at all." I grin, as it's opened by Max wearing a chef's hat and an apron.

"Hello! Come in, come in, don't want you freezing to death." He wafts us inside. "Not like some, eh?" He laughs, winking at Edward while I deeply regret telling him about the Battle of the Thermostat.

The rest of the gang have already arrived. Fiona and David have left their children with the nanny while Holly and Adam have found a babysitter. "It's a date night," she informs me, as I give her a hug. "The counselor says it's important to remember what we liked about each other in the beginning."

"And is it working?"

She looks across at Adam. He's with Freddy, who's showing him something on his phone.

"I think so." She watches him, her expression one of fondness. "I don't think I want to kill him anymore."

"Great news, Nell!"

We're interrupted by Max, who charges over to top up our glasses before returning to the stove, where two vats of something delicious are bubbling. "About the apartment—Michelle told me. Well done."

"Oh, thanks." I smile.

"So how's it going to feel losing your lodger?" asks David, looking across at Edward, who's been deep in conversation with Michelle about some new environmentally friendly diapers.

I'd told him earlier about my offer being accepted; he couldn't have been more pleased for me.

"Well, I'm not going to miss the heating bills." He grins at me now, and I smile.

"Can all the men live together, please," suggests Fiona, appearing from the restroom. "Honestly, he's the same as David. Let them all shiver together."

"Just because you're having hot flashes, darling, doesn't mean we all have to," says David, and Fiona bats him affectionately.

"Bet you're going to miss her," she says loyally.

"Yes." He nods. "Arthur will too."

"The apartment's only a bus ride away," I say quickly. "We can still go for walks and I can look after him while you're at work."

"I think Adam and I need to get some tips from you." Holly grins and Adam looks up.

"Oh, I don't know, we're not doing so badly, are we?"

I watch as a smile passes between them.

"Well, I think it's brilliant," says Michelle. "You'd better do a big housewarming and invite us all."

"I don't think you'll all squash in."

"It's amazing what you can do. Who would think six of us could fit in this tiny house?"

"Small house, big life," cries Max, waving a dhal-covered wooden spoon. "Though if I get this new job I'm interviewing for, we could have a slightly *less* small house."

"How many interviews so far?" asks David.

"Six. Just one more to go."

"I got engaged after fewer dates," says Edward, then frowns. "Though actually, maybe that's not a good comparison, considering I'm now divorced."

"So, are you seeing anyone?" asks Fiona, spotting an opportunity to sweep in.

Uh-oh. I glance at her, but she's steadfastly refusing to look at me. When Edward and I first walked in together she gave me A Look, and when she got me on my own demanded why I hadn't mentioned how handsome he is.

"No." He shakes his head.

I feel a jolt of surprise. *No?* Fiona glances across at me. She does her Big Eyes, the ones that she always thinks are subtle and no one else can notice, and of course everyone always notices.

"I thought Nell mentioned you had a date . . . or something."

I suddenly get very busy helping Max with the rice.

"Oh, I had dinner with some friends." He smiles. "They tried to set me up . . ."

I can tell he's trying to tail off, but Fiona is having none of it.

"So, what happened?"

Bowls. We need bowls.

"She was perfectly lovely but not for me . . . or me for her, I imagine."

So that's it. There is no other girl.

"Oh, I don't know, you seem quite a catch—"

"Food's ready," I interrupt loudly, "who wants poppadums?"

The Indian food is amazing. Max is quite the chef; we have chana masala and a delicious spicy dhal, and there's a chicken tikka masala for the meat eaters. Plus all those delicious chutneys and lime pickles and raita that you scoop up with the leftover poppadum, even though you feel like you can't possibly eat another thing.

Afterward, we clear away the tables and Max puts on his New Year's Eve playlist, and we dance around to Prince and wonder for the millionth time how someone as talented as him can be gone. We say this about David Bowie and Tom Petty and George Michael, and the children ask us who we are talking about and look at us as if we are silly old people. Because I suppose we are. Silly old people.

Then we cram ourselves into the living room, where we turn on the TV to watch Jools Holland's *Hootenanny* and wait for the firework display over the Houses of Parliament, and now we're counting down to the New Year: twenty, nineteen, eighteen—

But Adam's started the countdown at the wrong time and it's actually: three, two, one.

And now we're all kissing and hugging and wishing each other Happy New Year, and the fireworks are exploding over Big Ben on the TV screen, and Adam has his arms wrapped around Holly, and Fiona is collapsing with David onto the sofa and spilling her drink, and Max is disappearing into the kitchen to get a cloth and warm up a bottle while Michelle is helping herself to another tequila.

And Edward is kissing me and I'm wondering why it took us so long.

New Year's Day

The early hours

I'm not sure what time we end up leaving, but we don't even try to get a cab. Instead we walk back along the river with Arthur, still drunk and giddy, until after a while we fall silent and Edward reaches for my hand. I take his. Like it's the most natural thing in the world, and we continue hand in hand, with just the noise of our boots on the towpath and the water lapping against the riverbank.

It's a rare thing to find a comfortable silence with someone, and it makes me think about Dad. I called him earlier to wish him and Mum a Happy New Year. There was a moment when I feared I might never be able to do that again. That night when I broke down outside the hospital chapel, I thought I was going to lose him. I'll never forget it. I was in such a dark place, but it was as if the lights finally came on. And they shone so brightly on what was important in life. Real, true love, where you'd do anything for that person. Where you never, ever want to let them go.

That's it. None of the other stuff matters.

When I saw Edward in the parking lot the next morning, it was like the flicking of a switch. Something had changed.

Or was it me that had changed?

Because instead of seeing Edward I saw this kind, wonderful, selfless, gorgeous man, and I knew I didn't ever want to be without him. And I realized that just when you think you've finally got it all figured out, you haven't even started.

So much has happened these past twelve months. I've learned so much, not least that it's OK not to know the answer. I've found friendship and joy in the unlikeliest of places. I've discovered a strength I never knew I had, and a sense of humor that I know will never fail me. I've realized that I'm not alone, I still don't have a clue what I'm doing, and guess what? Nobody else does either.

And I've fallen in love.

But it wasn't just in that parking lot—it's with my life. Not the one I had imagined or planned, but the one that was always there waiting for me when I was brave enough to embrace it. My messy, flawed, perfectly imperfect life.

"Edward, remember when we said we should always be honest with each other . . ."

I stop walking and let go of his hand. We turn to face each other.

"I knew it. You hated my stuffed olives."

"No—" I start to protest, then start laughing. "Well, they were pretty awful. I mean, I love olives, but with *peanut butter*?"

"They're a speciality."

"Whose?" I ask, and he starts laughing too.

"So c'mon, if it's not about the olives . . . ?"

He raises an eyebrow, and I don't know if it's the cold night air or what I'm about to say but I feel myself suddenly sober up. Digging my fingernails into the palms of my hands, my chest feels as if it's going to burst with everything I've been keeping inside these past few weeks.

"I think I love you."

There. I've said it. Because what I've come to realize is that real, true love is the most romantic kind of love you can think of.

Edward looks at me, his expression unreadable. I wait for his reaction. Oh God, whose stupid idea was this truth stuff?

"Well, that's lucky, because I think I've loved you since the moment you walked into my kitchen."

Shock. Relief. Delight. Then outrage.

"What happened to being honest?" I cry indignantly.

"Well, it would have looked a bit weird, don't you think? I'm not sure you'd have wanted to rent a room if I'd told you."

"True." I break into a smile.

"So—"

"So—"

A look passes between us.

"What happens now?" he asks quietly.

People always talk about happy endings, but I think it should be happy beginnings. Who wants to talk about endings when ahead is a brand-new year, stretching out before you. One filled with infinite possibilities and wonderful new opportunities and decisions to be made and doubts to be had and a whole lot of love to be explored.

And a forty-something who's still making this up as she goes along.

"I don't know," I admit, and he smiles and pulls me toward him. Then he kisses me again, properly this time.

This Year's Gratitude List (Revised)

I'm grateful for:

1. ~~My loving husband, who tells me every day how much he loves me with fresh flowers and mind-blowing sex.~~
   My loving friends, being able to buy myself flowers, and great sex with Edward when we're not too knackered and the thermostat is set to 68.

2. ~~Snuggles with our own little miracle, who showed her proud grandparents that Mummy was not a forty-something fuck up for whom time finally ran out.~~
   Snuggles with my niece, who showed her proud Auntie Nell that loss is all part of life, that love is infinite, and that nobody knows what's going to happen in the future but whatever it is she'll be just fine.

3. ~~A successful, high-flying career that provides both satisfaction and a six-figure salary, which I will spend on lovely clothes I see in magazines, and not spend hours trying to find a cheaper version on eBay.~~
   All the lovely listeners of my podcast, Monty's play, which is opening in the West End in the summer, my role in the Monty's Mini Libraries scheme that Cricket is rolling out, and my new newspaper column. It isn't how I used to define a high-flying career, but it's pieces of different things that I love and give me fulfilment, and together pay my mortgage and allow me to still look for things on eBay, because seriously, who pays those crazy designer prices?

4. ~~A Pinterest-worthy home in which to host lots of lovely grown-up dinner parties for all my friends, who are amazed~~

by my flair for interior design and conjuring up delicious, nutritious meals, and teasingly call me the Domestic Goddess.
My little apartment, in which I intend to squash all my
friends for a housewarming when I finally get the keys, where
they will exclaim over my clever mix of junk-shop finds and
IKEA while eating takeout off their knees, because I will
never be a domestic goddess and that's why God made delivery apps.

5. This feeling of strength and calm that comes from doing
yoga in my new Lululemon outfits, and knowing I am finally
where I want to be and am not going to die alone in newspaper shoes.
This feeling of strength and calm that comes from realizing
you're never really going to know what the hell you're doing
but it's never too late to start over. Because it's only when
you are ready to surrender the life you thought you were going to live that you finally get the life you were always meant
to live.*†

---

* And it doesn't involve yoga.
† But does involve Edward, who told me to stop worrying about newspaper shoes, as
I can always borrow his wellies.

Obituary of a Forty-Something F**k Up

Nell Stevens, who fought a long and brave battle against feeling like a forty-something fuck up, has died. Never one to mince words, Stevens, a lover of gin and tonics and cheese puffs, was a woman who never really knew what the hell she was doing or how on earth she'd gotten here.

As a young girl, life seemed so full of potential. After graduating from Manchester University with a BA Honors degree in English literature, Stevens found a job at a renowned publishing company, where she was quickly promoted to senior commissioning editor in the children's books department, a role that saw her move to the bright lights of New York City.

Yet while her professional life was a success, love seemed to elude her, until a chance meeting with successful chef Ethan DeLuca, as she was hurtling panic-stricken through her late thirties, resulted in an engagement and a subsequent move to California. A happy ending seemed guaranteed; alas, a failed business, huge overdraft, and broken engage-

ment made a mess of that and saw Stevens return to the UK, where her inability to get a mortgage, do any yoga poses, or find any joy in clearing up the mess that was her life saw her renting a room, wearing a bit of a sleeve, and weeping into her iPhone.

Once she was quoted as saying her life could be summed up in just three words: Eat. Scroll. Weep.

Never married, with no children, and without the sense to have bought property in the nineties, for a large part Nell Stevens seemed to stumble through life. Unlike all her married-with-children friends, she went through a variety of relationships and a series of terrible online dates, which provided grist to the mill for her podcast, but resulted in what she perceived as failure.

However, this forty-something had both determination and an ability to laugh in the face of it all, and in the last year of her life she made new friends and found new paths that led to unexpected joy. Her feelings of things not working out as she'd planned, time running out, and having a life that didn't resemble that of any of her friends (or those portrayed on social media) and a body that no longer resembled that of her twenties saw her begin a podcast of the same name which went on to become a huge success.

More so, the recent production of Monty Williamson's award-winning play, which she edited, and the successful Monty's Mini Libraries project, of which she was a cofounder, saw this forty-something fuck up appearing not to be a fuck up at all. In fact, as she enjoyed the delights of becoming a homeowner and choosing scatter cushions for her lovely new apartment, she also found what had eluded her for so long: real true love, with Edward Lewis, owner of a successful environmental software company, who described Nell as "a shining light—literally, as she leaves all the lights on."

Yet despite her yearlong battle to turn things around, the cause of death for this forty-something fuck up was not failure, but falling in love with her life. A life that, on her deathbed, she explained she only discovered when she was brave enough to embrace it.

Moreover, while this new life may have appeared in her many recent magazine interviews to be a success, it was still messy and flawed and complicated. In her most recent podcast episodes, Stevens let it be known that there would no doubt be plenty more times when she would feel like she was fucking up and failing, when she would turn a corner and run into The Fear, when she would look in the mirror and think FFS; as this is just life.

As her dear friend Cricket, who visited her before she took her last breath, declared:

The Forty-Something Fuck Up is dead. Long live the Forty-Something Fuck Up.

Nell Stevens is survived by her proud parents Carol and Philip, annoying little brother Richard, gorgeous niece Evie, and her sense of irony at this crazy thing called life.*

---

* Correction: Since going to print it has been confirmed that this fuck up is in fact not dead as first reported, but living her best forty-something fuck up life. Sincerest apologies to all concerned.

Acknowledgments

A huge thank you to my truly fabulous and talented editor Trisha Jackson, and the incredible team at Pan Macmillan. From the very beginning they *got* Nell and her story and I am so very grateful for everyone's enthusiasm and hard work. I am over the moon that my book has found such a wonderful home.

It takes a village to publish a book and I'd like to say a special thank you to Sara Lloyd, Stuart Dwyer, Hannah Corbett, Leanne Williams, Sarah Arratoon, and Natalie Young; and on the Rights team, Jon Mitchell, Anna Alexander, and Emma Winter. A big thank you also to Jayne Osborne for all her invaluable help and Mel Four for creating such a brilliant cover.

Special thanks to my American publishers and the amazing team at Harper Paperbacks. I am so very lucky that my novel has found such a wonderful home across the Atlantic and I would like to say a huge thank you to my wonderful editor Amy Baker for all her talent and enthusiasm. Also thanks to Sophia Kaufman, Megan Looney, Heather Drucker, Dori Carlson, Alison Throckmorton, Robin Bilardello, Joanne O'Neill, and everyone else who has worked so hard to get this book into your hands.

As always, a big, big thank you to my agent Stephanie Cabot. I can't believe it's been twenty years since I first walked into her office and am forever thankful for her loyalty, encouragement, and wisdom.

Special thanks to my friend and fellow author Chris Manby for her tireless encouragement when I needed it the most.

Thank you also to Elizabeth Gilbert for giving me permission to use her wonderful words as the epigraph to this novel.

It's a strange job being a writer, creating characters and stories from your imagination and daring to hope that other people might enjoy them too. To all my readers, all over the world, I'd like to thank every single one of you. It's because of you I get to do the job I always dreamed of. You have no idea how happy it makes me to receive all your lovely messages.

Finally, to my beloved AC for his continued love and support and always believing in me; my mum and sister who encourage and inspire me every single day; my dad whose photograph sits on my desk cheering me on; and the rest of my tribe: thank you from the bottom of my heart. I couldn't do any of this without you.

I'm also grateful for:

- *My wood-burning stove and whiskey, for getting me through a winter spent hunkered down, writing.*
- *Elton, for no longer chewing the cushions and being the best canine companion an author could have.*
- *All of it.*

About the Author

Yorkshire born and raised, Alexandra Potter lives in South West London with Mr. California and their Bosnian rescue dog. When she's not writing or traveling, Alexandra is getting out into nature, trying not to look at her phone, and navigating this thing called mid-life.